Alison Kervin is an award-winning freelance writer and journalist who has previously worked as the Chief Sports Feature Writer of *The Times*, and the Chief Sports Interviewer of *The Daily Telegraph*. She has written eight highly-acclaimed books, including two previous novels, *The Wag's Diary* and *A Wag Abroad*.

D1586108

Acknowledgements

Many thanks to everyone at Ebury for all their hard work and enthusiasm, particularly Gillian Green, my editor, who's been such an enormous help, but also to Louise and Hannah and everyone in the sales and marketing team whose unseen work is hugely appreciated.

Thanks, as always, to Sheila Crowley; my agent, friend and ally and the only one I can really rely on to come drinking with me when everyone else has hung up their glass long ago!

Thanks to Detective Inspector Martyn Barnes of West Mercia Police for his help with the police related aspects of the book and for explaining in such clear and gory detail how murder investigations work. Any mistakes in this section of the book are mine, not his.

Thanks to Richmond Theatre for their help, and to The Sun Inn in Richmond for their wine. The only reason I went there night after night was to research, you understand.

To everyone at the Hampton Court Palace Rose Garden – thanks for telling me all about the roses.

Thanks to the Gower family and all my relatives in Wales – Ken, Marie, Keith, Yvonne, Andrew, Mark, Anne, Anthony, Geraint, Vincent and Jocelyn, and all their families, for a fantastic weekend of cows, sheep, food and great company.

Thanks to George for laughing at the jokes and suggesting names for the characters (Yoda didn't make it, but I'm grateful for the suggestion).

Finally thanks to Jayne Kearney, Charlie Bronks and Lee Marr for reading the book and coming back with such fantastic help and advice – it was much appreciated. I hope you enjoy the finished product . . .

CELEBRITY BRIDE

Alison Kervin

EBURY
PRESS

1 3 5 7 9 10 8 6 4 2

Published in 2009 by Ebury Press, an imprint of Ebury Publishing
A Random House Group Company

The Random House Group Limited Reg. No. 954009

Addresses for companies within the Random House Group can be found at
www.randomhouse.co.uk

A CIP catalogue record for this book is available from the British Library

The Random House Group Limited supports The Forest Stewardship
Council (FSC), the leading international forest certification organisation. All
our titles that are printed on Greenpeace approved FSC certified paper carry
the FSC logo. Our paper procurement policy can be found at
www.rbooks.co.uk/environment

Typeset in Adobe Caslon by Palimpsest Book Production Limited,
Grangemouth, Stirlingshire

Printed in the UK by
CPI Cox & Wyman, Reading, RG1 8EX

ISBN 9780091932114

To buy books by your favourite authors and register for offers visit
www.rbooks.co.uk

For George Kervin-Evans.
And for Mum & Dad, with thanks.

Chapter 1

'You'll be famous!' squeals Mandy, clenching her hands into the tightest of fists and shaking them at me in a rather terrifying fashion. Her deep blue eyes are alight with delight and her cheeks fairly quiver with excitement. She couldn't look more impressed if I'd announced that I'd just won the Nobel Peace prize. 'Perhaps you'll be in *Heat* magazine!'

'Wooooah . . .' says Sophie, and all three of us gasp at the very thought. Mandy plonks herself down onto our rust-coloured, worn and tatty sofa, quite giddy with disbelief at the whole thing. She's shocked herself so much that her legs have entirely given way beneath her and now she just sits and looks from me to the torn and well-thumbed copy of the world's greatest magazine, poking up out of Sophie's fake Marc Jacobs bag. Sophie drops her gaze too, so we're all staring at *Heat* as if it's about to get up and break-dance across the room.

'I don't think so,' I say, still staring. 'I bet nothing will change really; I'll be living there instead of here – that's all. I won't be famous.'

Except that I know that's not true; from the tips of my killer heels to the ends of my wavy auburn hair, I realise that my whole life is going to be flung up into the air like the pieces of an intricate jigsaw. I don't know what sort of picture they're going to create when they land. All I know is that it'll be different from the picture of my life right now.

You see . . . this is the situation – today is 28 October and I live on £15k a year from my work as an administrator at *Richmond Fringe Theatre*. I struggle to stay below my overdraft limit. I drink cheap white wine, which tastes as if it's been made from bleach instead of grapes, and – when I can afford them – I indulge in Domino's pizzas that are so full of fat that I can feel my arteries filling with every bite I take. When I'm feeling super-rich, I blow twenty quid in Primark; if I time my visits well enough sale-wise (and I'm an expert at knowing when the Primark sales are, to be fair), I can emerge with a top-to-toe outfit and still have enough left for chips on the bus home.

The thing is though, from tomorrow, things will be different because I'm moving out of the flat that I've shared with the girls for the last year and a half, and I'm moving in with a guy called Rufus George. We've been together for six months (exactly six months tomorrow) and it's been fantastic . . . amazing . . . totally brilliant . . . and all the other superlatives you can think of – all rolled up together. Just super-awesome. He's lovely, sweet, kind and generous . . . Oh yes – he's also the most famous actor on the planet. He gets paid about £20 million for every film he stars in and most of the single women in Hollywood would die to be with him. Yep, I'm dating *the* Rufus George, and I have a feeling that my days of catching the bus to Primark and getting chips on the way back are about to be left behind. All this is great, of course, because it means I'm going to be with the man I love; the man of my dreams;

the man who makes me shiver inside whenever I think about him. But it's kind of sad at the same time, in a strange way; I'll miss running to catch the bus with my hands full of grease. Na! What am I talking about? I can't wait to throw myself head first into my new life with Rufus. I just adore everything about him.

And, you know, through this enormous adoration, I've ended up developing a bit of a habit; not a crack cocaine or marijuana habit or anything like that . . . no, no, that's not me at all. I don't even smoke, let alone indulge in illegal substances. No, I have a different, though equally addictive habit – it's a glossy mag habit. I'm totally obsessed with reading them because Rufus is in every one. He's certainly been in every copy of *Heat* magazine that's been published since we met; I know this because I've taken to cutting out articles about him and keeping them. The sad news for my flatmates is that there's nothing left of the magazines by the time I've finished with them. It's been driving poor Mandy and Sophie up the wall. They're halfway through a feature about Britney Spears' latest tremendous weight loss and, just as she's about to explain how she lost eight stone in two and a half hours, they turn the page and there's a Rufus-shaped hole cut out of it. 'Kellll . . .' I hear them cry, but there's nothing I can do to stop myself. I have to collect all the pictures I can of him; it's the only way in which I feel I have any sort of control over events. Like a teenage girl tracing the activities of her boy through the pages of Facebook, I find myself scanning every colourful, glossy sheet of the weekly magazines in the hope of catching a glimpse of him, entering into his world a little and, most importantly, checking there aren't any beautiful girls wriggling their nubile flesh too close to him.

There are pictures of my man striding across a sunbaked golf course with Tiger Woods, slapping Brad Pitt on the back in a manly fashion as they head out to dinner, and chatting companionably with Kofi Annan. He's pictured in designer clothing in sumptuous palaces, and looking mean and moody in camouflage gear as he meets the troops in Afghanistan. He is so way out of my league that he's in a league on a different planet altogether. And yet, somehow, he's fallen in love with me. Mandy and Sophie are the only people in the world who know about our relationship. I'm almost scared to tell anyone else; it's as if speaking the words 'I'm dating Rufus George' will break the spell and he'll look up, say 'Who the hell are you in cheap shoes, fake jewellery and with no Hollywood film deals? Get out of my life now, and send in Scarlett Johansson.' Things like this don't happen to normal girls like me.

'Will you be OK finding a new flatmate?' I ask Sophie. She's said hardly a word to me since I told them I was going to be moving in with my secret lover. I have to say that I'm worried about leaving the two of them in the lurch. Not worried enough to turn down Rufus's offer of co-habitation, you understand, but worried all the same. We've been best friends for years and have been through some great times together. These past eighteen months have been the best fun ever. We've gone out and got drunk together and stayed in and got drunk together; usually while watching terrible late night 'real crime' programmes and all the reality TV we can find. We've got a bit of a thing about this frightening woman called Zadine who's going out with Joe Collins, the footballer. She's the world's most awful person . . . fact!! She has massively inflated lips, enormous boobs and the level of intellect you'd expect from a footballer's girlfriend. She's on every reality TV show and we all give a loud cheer and vote for her whenever we see her on anything; just because she's so utterly rubbish and awful that it seems a laugh to keep her in the jungle or in the *Big Brother* house for as long as possible.

Whenever we're in together, we flock to the sitting room. I'd never think of sitting in my bedroom on my own. There'd be no point; you can't get any peace and quiet anyway. Our flat is tiny and you can hear everything that goes on through the badly decorated, paper-thin walls. It means there's nothing I don't know about either of my two lovely flatmates. I know things about them that I really shouldn't know. I've heard Sophie having sex on the counter in our horrible avocado-coloured kitchen that looks if it was painted by a blind man clutching a handful of moss and river weed. I've heard Mandy taking a bath with a man old enough to be her father. We heard him wheezing and coughing at one stage and Sophie and I sat on my bed choking with laughter about what on earth we'd do if he collapsed in there.

'We'd have to drag him out before the ambulance came,' Sophie said wisely. 'We couldn't have the paramedics going into the bathroom; it's horrible in there. We'd never live it down.' The prospect of the bathroom décor being revealed to strangers seemed so much worse to us than the prospect of them seeing the age of Mandy's aqua lover. And this is why . . .

Our bathroom's a kind of mucky caramel colour with very ornate brown swirly tiles which are immediately reminiscent of an Indian restaurant. The bath itself is all scratched and full of those nasty white watermarks that make it look as if it needs a good clean. Mandy did well to get him in there in the first place to be honest. There aren't many people who'd volunteer to bathe in there. Perhaps his eyesight wasn't what it used to be.

My bedroom was the worst decorated of all the rooms though when we moved in. My God, what were the previous occupants thinking? It was done out in a nasty shade of orange that reminded me of Oompa-Loompas. It had a kind of fluorescent quality to it which made your skin buckle when you looked at it. It wasn't wise to put the main light on unless you were wearing sunglasses, and even then it wasn't to be advised. A bit like looking directly at the midday sun, but with none of the vitamin D and tanning advantages. Even after two coats of cream emulsion the walls still glow a kind of carrot colour when the sun rises in the morning. I put up some rather tasteful and arty posters to distract from the worst of it – they are great; I nicked them from the theatre and they are huge, glossy, gleaming pictures of Hollywood greats. Audrey Hepburn peers down at me sheepishly with those wide-awake chocolate-coloured eyes, while Marilyn Monroe oozes so much sex appeal I fear it may all come gushing out of the picture in great waves and engulf me.

By common consensus, I made something of a triumph out of my tangerine-coloured abode. Which I was very glad about when I met Rufus. I'd have hated taking him in there when it was that vivid satsuma colour. The first time he came to the flat I spent the day on my hands and knees scrubbing the place to ensure that it was worthy of him. I washed the walls. (I know. How ridiculous is that? I mean – who washes walls? Girls inviting film stars home – that's who!) I Hoovered and polished and rearranged the furniture; when it was spotless, and looking as good as our flat ever does, I nipped out to see Katy (she's one of the girls at work) to borrow their cushions for the evening (we have a kind of time-share approach to soft furnishings). I got back clutching the tasteful, plump and homely cushions, to discover Sophie and Mandy lying on the sitting-room floor, both so drunk they couldn't speak, and accompanied by two of the bouncers from our local nightclub. They'd been drinking all afternoon. The girls both have Thursday afternoons off and go in an hour early in the morning to make up the time and so spend most Thursday afternoons in the pub.

The flat stank of beer, blokes and pizza when I walked in. Rufus was due in twenty minutes. Fuck. I stood there, open-mouthed, while the girls grabbed the cushions off me and promptly rested a large Pepperoni Feast on the top of them. 'Want some?' they asked.

'No. And you have to go!' I shouted. 'Don't you remember? Rufus is coming.'

The girls giggled and smiled and looked like they didn't even remember their own names, let alone who was due to visit. When the bell rang I thought my heart would stop.

I opened the door slowly and tried to convince Rufus that we should go to a local pub instead. 'Come on, let me in. I wanna meet your roomies,' he said.

'OK. But don't say I didn't warn you.'

In the end, everything was fine. As it tends to be with him. He's so easy-going and fun that he was soon down on the floor, eating their pizza and phoning up to order more. We all got hammered. Rufus thought the flat was 'a pretty cute apartment'. He even said the sitting room was 'quaint and characterful' which is plain lying. The sitting room is one ugly-looking place. There's the old-fashioned fire that looks as if it belongs in an episode of *Coronation Street* circa 1970, and the jumble of mismatched sofas and scatter cushions plonked indiscriminately around the room as if they just dropped there from a great height, with no regard for artistry; a sea of oddly placed foam furniture vying for attention on a nasty-stained cream carpet.

'So, will you be OK?' I repeat.

'Of course we'll be OK,' says Sophie, pushing her short, light-brown hair behind her ears. There's the slightest hint of bitterness in her voice. 'Don't worry. We'll be absolutely fine. Just you concentrate on your new, exciting life without us.'

She winks as she speaks and gives me a smile, so I know she doesn't mean any nastiness, but I can tell she's worried about me. She thinks I'm about to enter a world I'm unprepared for. 'It's like sending a child to war,' she said rather dramatically, when I declared my intention to move to Richmond Hill. She's right; I couldn't be less prepared for a world of mega-stars and flash cars, but what do I do? I'm just going to have to rely on Rufus to guide me gently around the obstacles thrown up by life in the spotlight. He has done so far. Our dates have been a series of long and increasingly complex lessons in social etiquette on the road to refinement. I've gone from cherry-flavoured lip salve to cherry-coloured lipstick, and the comfy round neck jumpers and zip-up fleeces have been replaced by gently plunging necklines and wrap-around dresses

'I'll obviously pay rent until you find someone else,' I offer.

The girls are just staring at me now. Sophie's heavily kohled eyes reflect her misgivings on the subject while Mandy's eyes just gleam with the thrill of it all. They'll get used to the idea. I know they will. We'll be friends for ever and ever and I'll introduce them to some fabulous men on Richmond Hill, and they'll come and live there too. That's what best friends do, and friends don't come any bester than these two.

'Cup of tea?' asks Mandy. 'Then I'll help you pack if you like.'

To be honest, tea's the last thing I fancy. Christ, it's my last day in the house. Soph doesn't say anything either, giving a clear hint as to what's really required on an occasion like this.

'Wine?' Mandy tries, looking ever so guilty about suggesting such a thing at 4 pm in the afternoon. There are enthusiastic nods all round, much to Mandy's delight, and she heaves herself out of the soggy sofa cushions and wanders off in the direction of the kitchen; she's clapping, skipping and singing a little song about the glory and beauty of wine. I haven't seen her this excited since that guy Andy asked her out. God, you should have seen that guy – man was he ugly, with his wide boxer's nose and fleshy face. His eyes were like the smallest of slits and his skin was the colour of chalk; I don't think he ever went outside in daylight. He was also permanently chaffed, like he had some terrible eczema condition or had been rubbing his face and hands with sandpaper or something. No one could understand what Mandy saw in him. I mean, I know finding the perfect man is a little like trying to nail jelly to the wall but still, the man was like something out of a horror film. But Mandy has the most peculiar taste in men. 'I like 'em big and ugly,' she's always saying, and, boy, has she stayed true to that declaration. I think Mike Tyson would be judged too small, pretty and delicate for her.

She fancied Andy from afar for ages – giggling like a drunk whenever he walked past her, she'd smile up at him in awe and wonder, as if she were meeting the pope for the first time or something. Then when he finally asked her out . . . my God! I thought she was going to explode with excitement. She got so bloody flustered while getting ready that she put ear drops into her eyes and almost blinded herself. Her eyes were still watering so badly by the time of the date that she couldn't see properly so we had to walk up the road with her, to meet him, or she'd have wandered into the traffic or knocked herself out on a lamppost or something. She had to pretend to Andy that her dog had just died, and that's why her eyes were watering constantly. He was a horror though. She ended up dumping him after about six dates because he once spiked all our drinks. It was terrible. I was driving and not drinking, so he told me to have this fruit punch he'd made. I should have known straight away that something was up. I mean, you didn't have to know him too well to realise that he really wasn't a fruit punch making sort of guy. The drink had quite a kick to it but he muttered something about ginseng and ginger and I fell for it. I drove home, got stopped and was done for drink driving. It was horrific. I kept swearing I'd had nothing but fruit punch, and yet the officers said my car was swerving down the road and I was well over the alcohol limit. She dumped him straight away after that but it didn't save me from the humility of having mugshots, DNA taken and losing my licence for a year. I've been paranoid ever since. I don't even have a car now the whole incident worried me so much. Imagine if someone had been hurt? The thought terrifies me. I could have hit someone. I could have killed someone: a child or something. Urghhhh . . . it's just too awful to contemplate.

'We've only got the nasty stuff that Dave brought – the wine he said he brought from Greece,' Mandy says, standing in the kitchen doorway, holding a dusty bottle containing ginger-coloured liquid, and grimacing at it.

'Don't worry; it's fine,' I say, because this drink is not about the quality of the wine at all; this is all about toasting and celebrating the quality of the friendship we've shared and will continue to share for years to come. It doesn't matter that the wine will taste like it's got furniture polish in it, and has arrived in our kitchen courtesy of dodgy Dave – the good-looking bloke who had a complete crush on me then, when I rejected him, went for Sophie. He told her he adored her and worshipped every last breath she took. He was such a drama queen; he even tore the phone line out and threatened to strangle himself with the cord one time when Sophie couldn't see him. The damned phone has never worked properly since. He went straight back to his wife the minute Sophie fell in love with him though. Nope, it's not about the wine, or the dopey blokes that scuttle through the door every now and then, then scuttle out again much faster a few weeks later because the word 'commitment' has allegedly raised its little head; nope, this is all about me and my two best mates.

'Cheers,' we all say, raising our glasses and surveying the colour and clarity of the liquid in considerable dismay; it has nothing in common with the colour you expect of wine. It's not like cheap wine has to do too much, but it does have to sit there looking roughly the right colour. This stuff looks like Tizer and it tastes like paint stripper. 'To us,' I say, as we all link arms and wince as the abhorrent taste and unlikely consistency hits our tongues. It was worse than any of us could have predicted.

'Where the fuck do you think he got this from?' asks Sophie, gagging and twisting her jaw in horror.

'Best not to think too hard about that,' I suggest, while coughing and choking back the lingering effects of it. 'Best not to think about where Dave got anything from. He said it was from that boys' holiday he went on in Athens but who knows.'

We've all brought some rough blokes back to the flat in our time, but Dave brought the concept of roughness down to a whole new level. He made Andy look suave. The thing with Dave was that he was very, very goodlooking, but seemed hell-bent on doing everything within his power to look as ropey as possible. He looked like he'd just escaped from the Foreign Legion or something; the tattooed head and permanently stubbly face. Those dirty, nicotine-stained fingers and nails chewed down so far that they were always blood encrusted. I've never liked that big stubbly face, bald head thing. There's something altogether wrong about a human being with more hair on his face than his head. It's like the women who have more fat in their lips than they have in the cheeks of their bottoms. It's all wrong.

Dave would come rushing up to the door when he came to collect Sophie, looking around shiftily as he piled in, as if he were being pursued by the police. If he ever brought presents, they were invariably crap, and they looked as if they'd been nicked from the garage forecourt (literally). He'd undo the zip of his scruffy bomber jacket and out would tumble an in-car air-freshener, a Pot Noodle, an *A–Z* or something else from the list of 'Worst Things a Girl Can Receive from her Boyfriend'. I remember Sophie asking for the receipt so she could change a bottle of screen wash he'd bought her one time (Sophie wasn't being ungrateful, it's just that she doesn't drive).

'Receipt?' he said, with incredulity spreading from one pierced ear to the other. 'Receipt?' Then he laughed like I've never heard a man laugh before.

You will understand that, in this context, a bottle of wine, however undrinkable, was a real treat. 'There's no way he could have nicked this,' said Sophie in delight the next morning, as she showed off the bottle. 'They keep the wine in the shop; he must have paid for it!'

An improvement, certainly, but it's not exactly Shake-speare, is it? Not exactly what every little girl grows up dreaming of. And, as mentioned, Dave was soon off –

back to the wife whom he'd left just weeks before. A wife, I should add, that none of us knew existed.

I don't know what I'd have done without the girls over the last couple of months. They've been fabulous throughout my whirlwind romance. I told them everything about Rufus from the start. They were there for my initial panic when a new artistic director called Sebastian Kemp-Cooper joined the theatre and we all thought we'd lose our jobs. I thought I'd lose mine because Geoff, the director of the theatre group, and the man who brought Sebastian in, had asked me out a few times and I'd turned him down; I was sure I'd be first for the chop. It was funny; I've never been all that much into my 'career' but the minute I thought I might lose my job, I realised how much I enjoyed it. The theatre's a wonderful place to work – there's a real buzz as we approach an opening night, and the excitement of the actors arriving, the costumes and set designers. There's an unmatchable excitement about the place, and I love that it's such a creative atmosphere, with all these arty types drifting in and out. So much better than working in a bank or somewhere like that.

When we were chatting at home about whether I'd lose my job or not, the girls were brilliant. They told me not to worry, and assured me that they'd cover my share of the rent . . . somehow. There's a solidarity between us that has been tested over the months and years and has never been found wanting.

Worry turned to delight, though, when it turned out that Sebastian was completely lovely. He strutted into the office – tall and proud with a mop of sandy-blond hair that was so dishevelled it looked as if he'd got it on backwards. His confidence fairly bounced off the walls, and his enthusiasm filled the theatre from floor to ceiling. We loved him from the moment he walked in – all bubbly and excitable like a puppy but with this incredibly loud voice that you could hear from the next room. 'Lovely to meet you all,' he said, smiling from ear to ear like he genuinely meant it. He was wearing a ridiculous ensemble; it looked as if he'd borrowed clothes from a friend who was a completely different shape and size to him. He wore fawn-coloured cords that sat just above his grubby white socks, so that when he sat down and crossed his legs we were treated to the sight of four inches of pale freckled shin covered in strawberry-blond hairs. On top he wore a creased white shirt (too big) and a mustard-coloured jacket (too small). He wasn't wearing a tie on that first day, but whenever he did wear one after that occasion, it invariably gave you a clear view of exactly what he'd had for breakfast.

Despite all that, though, there was something charming and erudite about our cuddly new boss; he was bursting with ideas for adaptations and alterations, and ways in which we could make improvements that would secure the theatre's future.

The best thing about Sebastian was that he kept us all on, and started bringing in loads of new funding. Suddenly the future was looking very bright. I was promoted to head administrator and given much more responsibility. No more money, of course; we lowly theatre administrators do it for love, not financial remuneration! The promotion was great though, because it took me a little nearer to where I wanted to be – in the marketing department.

I still wasn't allowed to work on marketing plans, or even go anywhere near the marketing leaflets, but I was put in charge of internal communications which was a real step forward.

Every day at work was filled with optimism as we looked forward to a future which looked brighter than we ever thought possible.

There are three of us sharing an office at the theatre: me, Katy and Jenny.

Katy's a real laugh; the sort of girl who's the centre of attention and always cheering people up. I can't think of anyone more fun to work with – she just beams all day and makes sure everyone is happy and enjoying life. She's always taking the mickey out of me, and saying that all the men fancy me, and she hates going out in public with me because of it. The truth is that Katy is very attractive, though she clearly doesn't realise. She's good-looking in a very grown-up sort of way; you'd almost call her 'handsome' rather than 'pretty'. She looks like the teacher at school who all the boys secretly fancied.

Jenny's quite a different character; she's less outgoing than Kate, and more formal in some ways. She's very intelligent and always reads the newspapers while Katy and I are scouring *Heat* magazine. Jenny's not what you would call attractive, but she has an incredible figure. She's very tall and incredibly slim. She holds herself well, too, and as she walks around the office, with her head held high, her shoulders back, and her arms swinging elegantly by her side, she looks like a ballerina or something. The thing is – she's just not interested in how she looks, and doesn't make much effort at all. She has grey speckled through her auburn, bobbed hair, even though she's only thirty-two, and wears these really unflattering glasses. I don't think I've ever seen her wearing jewellery or make-up of any kind. I always think that if Gok Wan or one of those other makeover people was to get hold of her, they'd make her look absolutely stunning in no time.

The three of us get on brilliantly and have such a laugh, which makes work great fun every day.

One bright, sunny morning, Katy and I had been busy comparing suntans when Sebastian called us in and announced that a Hollywood heart-throb would be joining the cast of *Only Men* – a new play set to start with us at our little theatre and move on to the West End.

'Who?' we all asked, imagining Orlando Bloom setting himself up at the desk next to us.

'You'll have to wait and see,' said Seb enigmatically as he swept dramatically out of the office, leaving us to speculate wildly.

'That's it then,' said Jenny with a weary shrug. 'It's going to be someone old and distinguished who we've never heard of.'

There were nods all round. It was bound to be some dull Shakespearean actor with very little hair and a collection of brightly coloured cravats.

The next day, as we were guessing which octogenarian would appear before us, Seb disclosed that the actor was Rufus George, the sexiest man ever to walk the earth (and that's official – he's come top of the *Cosmo* list for the past two years, beating Brad Pitt and George Clooney). The prospect of the world's biggest film star treading the boards in Richmond shook the very foundations of small

London theatres. Artistic directors everywhere started reaching for the stars.

Within the theatre we almost died of excitement; we Googled the mega-star until our fingers ached. Within hours, there was nothing we didn't know about him. He was 8lbs 8oz when he was born. His mother was an interior designer with high cheekbones, large earrings and a wardrobe which appeared to consist entirely of expensive beige separates. From the photos she seemed like one of those women who always looks like she's just walked out of the hairdresser's. You know the type? Basically, a real stuck-up cow, or that's how she seemed to us.

Rufus's career started because of his mother. She wanted to be an actress herself, so when she left Rufus's father (breaking the poor man's heart, by all accounts; he died the next year), she took her six-year-old son to live in LA so she could pursue her dreams of making it big in Hollywood. Rufus was dragged along to auditions and screen tests and forced to go to drama classes while his mother fought to be taken seriously as an up-and-coming actress. Ironically, though, it was Rufus who ended making it 'big in Hollywood' when he was picked out of his drama academy and given a role as a young boy who had to be rescued by Michael Douglas after he was cast adrift on a fishing boat. His mother never made it beyond a couple of walk-on parts in minor films, and when the ageing process robbed her of any chance of being the starlet she'd so yearned to be, she turned to interior design and worked with some of the biggest names in Hollywood, taking millions from them to deck out their homes.

While his mother cut a dash in the world of soft

furnishings, Rufus's career grew. He played an angst-ridden teenage boy in *Tease Me*, a highly acclaimed film which was loved by critics but largely ignored by audiences, and played a pirate in a *Pirates of the Caribbean*-type epic. Then, when twenty-one, he took the lead role in a remake of *Tarzan* and became a huge household name and world-wide pin-up. It was the biggest grossing film of the year. There can't have been a young girl in the land who didn't fall helplessly in love with the tall, dark, handsome young man swinging through the trees wearing little more than a tea towel.

'God, do you remember that film?' says Jenny, waving her legs from side to side and nearly booting Katy in the shin.

'Gorgeous,' whispers Katy, while I just stare at the apparition on the screen. We were all too young to fully appreciate the film when it came out seventeen years ago but boy can we appreciate it now.

After *Tarzan* came *Tarzan II*, unsurprisingly, in which Rufus looked even better: more manly, less 'cute'. The boyish good looks had been replaced by a rugged hand-someness that left Jules, Kath and I struggling to stay upright.

'Jeez, he's perfect,' said Katy.

'Mmmm . . .' Jenny and I responded, both of us having lost the power of speech by this stage. Rufus starred in a collection of top box office films after *Tarzan*, including *Dead of Night* and *Justice for James* before playing a psychotic killer in *The Jewelled Dagger*, two years ago – a role that earned him an Oscar.

There wasn't much to be found on his private life. He'd

been linked to a couple of actresses, but no one for very long. Most of the references to him away from films featured his charity work.

'He's too fucking good to be true,' said Katy excitedly. 'I mean – looking like that and having no girlfriend.'

'He's probably been concentrating too much on work,' I suggested. 'Or he's gay.'

'No,' said Jenny, decisively. 'He's been saving himself for me!'

'Yeah,' Katy and I chorused, but let's be honest, it seemed unlikely.

When Rufus finally blessed us with his presence in a one-off visit to meet the staff, I don't think I'd ever seen such a handsome man; he was gorgeous. He walked into our scruffy little office with its peeling walls and old wooden desks, and we all started swooning. We'd been in the final rounds of the World Malteser Throwing Championships when he arrived, so we didn't take too much notice of the door opening initially. I was first receiver and had eight Maltesers buried in my cheeks when they walked in. I was standing, feet shoulder-width apart, ready for Katy to hurl a Malteser from behind the pile of coats.

'Ready?' asked Jenny (she'd been appointed chief official for the occasion because she's more sensible than the rest of us – she's in charge of theatre accounts).

'Yesh,' I replied, jiggling the eight Maltesers that I'd already caught in my mouth as I spoke. One of the rules of the game is that you're not allowed to swallow until you've finished catching. Your turn ends when you miss a Malteser. Eight was the most we'd ever done; this Malteser was crucial.

'Five, four, three, two, one,' she said.

Katy tossed the small chocolate ball towards me with a degree of accuracy born of long hours training (most of our salaries go in buying Maltesers). If she'd put that amount of work into the accounts, she'd be running the theatre by now. I caught the chocolate in my mouth, fair and square, thus setting a new theatre record ... yeeeesssssss ... but when I looked up – hands aloft, chocolate dribbling down my chin and cheeks full to bursting – expecting there to be cheering and congratulations echoing round the office, there was nothing. Jenny was just staring at the door like a mad woman, and Katy had collapsed down onto the desk. I followed Jenny's gaze. Fuck, fuck, fuck.

Sebastian was standing in the doorway, surveying us all quizzically and, next to him, was Rufus George. Oh-my-God. He was beautiful. He was flawless. He oozed sex appeal. There was something so solid and purposeful about him – not just physically, but in his presence. It was like he'd been carved out of granite. He was even more gorgeous than he looked in his pictures, and let's be very clear about this – he looked bloody gorgeous in his pictures.

'Nice to meet you,' he said, looking directly into my eyes. I returned the gaze because, with a man who looks like Rufus, that's what you do. I was well aware, though, of the chocolate-drenched spittle escaping from the corner of my mouth, and I was painfully conscious of the fact that I would have to crunch these Maltesers before I could return the greeting. I did that – masticating madly before swallowing the sticky mess and feeling it claw its way down my throat so slowly that I was forced into making vigorous gulps to help it on its way. What with the almost choking, mad swallowing and chocolate everywhere, it wasn't the ideal position in which to meet a Hollywood heart-throb. I looked up at him again, hoping I looked adorable now I no longer had hamster cheeks, but I was all too aware that the smile playing on his lips probably had more to do with the fact that my teeth, lips and tongue were now all brown, than any warmth he may be feeling towards me.

Then, out of the blue, the most amazing thing happened.

'Let's have a go,' he said, walking behind me, and gently touching my waist as he did so. I felt my hips burst into flames. No, really, I did; I had to look down to check my tight black skirt hadn't caught fire. He took up his position in front of the coats and nodded towards Katy.

'Come on!' yelled Sebastian. 'You can do it. It's boys against girls.'

Jenny continued in her role as chief adjudicator as Katy and I battled for the fairer sex, while Sebastian and Rufus did their best for mankind. We won.

'I think I need some lessons,' said Rufus, looking straight at me afterwards. 'Perhaps you could teach me your technique.'

And that's how it happened. That's how I ended up going for a coffee with a thirty-eight-year-old, completely gorgeous millionaire. He said that the combination of a tight black skirt and top, large breasts, big brown eyes and a vibrant personality did it for him. He also admitted that the fact that I would taste of chocolate was appealing. Coffee turned into a drink, turned into dinner, turned into snogging madly like teenagers. He was captivating, delightful and beautiful. He was just perfect and lovely. I'd never met anyone even remotely like him before, and I knew I never would again. The bizarre thing was that it all felt so natural, relaxed and, well, nice. But this was a mega movie star. How could this be happening? I'd spent the previous six months madly in lust with Paul, the set designer at the theatre, who thought himself too sophisticated for me. He was probably right; sophisticated is something you could never accuse me of being, so why would Rufus George like me?

What surprised me about Rufus was that he was terribly sophisticated and I wasn't, but that didn't bother him. Rather than look me up and down in a sneering way like Paul did, he'd say things like 'we should celebrate our differences' as I walked into small walls and always turned the wrong way when coming out of shops and restaurants. So it took me twenty minutes to find my car in the multi-storey. Suddenly I wasn't 'a dope' (Paul), I was 'sweet and adorable' (Rufus).

'If it's too much trouble to find the car, just take the driver,' he'd say, and he wasn't being patronising either. He genuinely seemed to like the fact that I differed from the ever so sophisticated Hollywood types that he was used to meeting and dating. Imagine that?

'I've told Brad and Carl about you,' he said, soon after our first date.

'Brad Pitt?' I asked, somewhat astonished, but delighted, obviously, to be the subject of conversation between Hollywood hunks. Perhaps 'Carl' was a codename for Angelina Jolie? Was I the centre of all conversations taking place in the Pitt household?

'No, Brad Court,' he said, with a laugh. 'That must be the one and only time that old Courty's been mixed up with Pitt. Courty and Carl Deevers, known as Deeves – they're my best buddies from home. We go back years.'

'Oh,' I said, surprised, for some reason, that someone like Rufus would have 'best buddies' in his life. 'But cool,' I added because I guess it was really. It was nice to see that he had proper friends with whom he went a long way back. It made him seem more grounded, and more real.

'We mainly drink beer and watch films,' he added. 'Deeves is a baseball nut. Yankees. He gets plenty of abuse.'

'Are they both living in America?'

'Amerecaar,' he responded, mimicking my English accent playfully. 'Yes, they're both in the US. In New York these days, hence the Yankees connection, but when I met them we were at school in LA. We were all complete sports nuts: basketball, baseball, football . . . proper football, not your kicking it around rubbish. We were obsessed. Brad's a teacher now, and Deeves runs a sportswear shop in Brooklyn. I still get abusive texts off them every day.'

'Just like me, Mandy and Sophie,' I suggested.

'Just like that,' he said warmly. 'Now come here. You are soooo beautiful.'

What's lovely about Rufus is that everything he says is reflected in his face. His lovely green eyes have always said the same thing as his words; every time he tells me he loves me he says it with every part of his face. Since day one he's been like that, and I genuinely think he found me attractive from the moment he saw me. I mean – I'm not being silly – men have found me attractive before.

People are always saying that I have a pretty face. A few have even suggested I could model. (Though admittedly the latter's usually followed by 'If you lost a stone.') But I'm not what you would call Hollywood attractive. I'm really curvy for a start, not skinny like all the women he's used to seeing. I bet they've all got ribcages that double as toast racks and I'm sure they never eat solids. I think my breasts alone weigh more than they do. I'm so curvy it's a bloody nightmare sometimes. I end up with jeans that are about two sizes too big on the waist just so that I can get them over my hips and bum, and dresses that swamp my narrow shoulders so that they're big enough to cover my 34Es. These Hollywood types don't have such problems. Any large breasts they have were put there, not by Mother Nature, but by leading cosmetic surgeons.

I bet they're all beautifully groomed too, with perfect nails and hair, and shoes that don't need mending and clothes that always look immaculate. I'd gamble big money on the fact that they don't wrap Sellotape around their stiletto heels when the plastic peels off, and I'd wager they don't own any earrings that are so cheap they leave horrid greeny-black marks on their ears. They all get their eyebrows done professionally, I bet, so they don't have a lopsided face with one brow ever so slightly longer and bushier than the other because they slipped with the razor one time when they'd left it too late to pluck. They're all perfect and I'm not . . . and yet, he's in love with me and I'm moving in there. Yeeeahhhhhhh . . .

Chapter 2

'What are we going to do tonight, on your last night?' asks Mandy, fiddling with her baby-fine, long blonde hair. She's got lovely hair, has Mandy, but it doesn't suit her face. We're always trying to persuade her to get it cut shorter because it hangs down by the side of her ears, looking limp and lifeless. She's got a really round face (very pretty, but completely circular; the guys all call her 'moon face'). The style of her hair does nothing to compensate for this. I think she'd look great if she got it cut into a soft bob or something sexy, but she clings on to every last inch, refusing to go near the hairdresser's because Andy – that terrible grotty joke of a boyfriend – once told her it was her only nice feature.

'Well?????' she says. 'What do you fancy doing? It's your last night. It has to be special.'

I'm not sure about all this talk of my 'last night'. It sounds as if I've got the death penalty or something. 'I don't mind what we do,' I say, because I don't.

'You know what I think we should do,' says Sophie, and there's something about the tone of her voice that makes it clear to all of us exactly what she's thinking.

'Suga Daddys!'

'It would be rude not to,' she continues. 'We certainly can't sit in here drinking this crap all evening; we'll be ill.'

'Suga Daddys?' Mandy queries, alarm ringing through her high-pitched voice. 'But it's so tacky there.'

'Er, yeees,' Sophie and I chorus. 'And?'

You see the whole point of Suga Daddys is that it's tacky. That's the appeal of it. It's a nightclub cum naked dancing type place right next to our flat and it's a bloody disaster zone – a magnet for the area's low life . . . mainly men, so there's always lots of fighting, which is the worst part of it. The thing with us is that because we're a) girls and b) neighbours, we get well looked after. Jimmy Lapdance (his real name's Jimmy Lavance so, obviously, we've changed it to Jimmy Lapdance) is the guy who runs the place, and he's after an extension to his licence so he can sell food. (He came up with the surreal idea of offering 'free chicken wings' to women in order to attract them into the club. He's always trying to think of ways of getting more women into the place. I think maybe less fighting and fewer strippers would help, but he's convinced that chicken is the answer. Makes you wonder what sort of women he meets. Anyway, when he offered the free chicken, the council came down on him like a ton of bricks after complaints from neighbours, and he was told in no uncertain terms that he did not have the sort of licence that allowed him to cook chicken on the premises. We did laugh – he can have semi-naked girls cavorting around, and fights every night but chicken wings – no, no, no, no, no.) So, he needs the neighbours on his side when he goes for his licence extension, so whenever we go in there it's free drinks and a bouncer assigned to us for the entire night lest anyone steps out of line and offends us.

Jimmy's a great local character and is the most incredible caricature of a nightclub owner that you could ever wish to meet. When I first moved into the flat, my dad painted the front door for us. He was busy wielding his paint brush when Jimmy went swaggering up to him and said, 'Cooor . . . your girlfriend's a bit of all right, isn't she?'

'She's my daughter,' said Dad assertively.

I think Dad wanted me to move out of the flat right there and then.

Jimmy's club is like something out of the 1950s because, bizarrely, it's both depraved and desperately innocent all at the same time. Its innocence comes from the fact that it's a shambles in there – Jimmy Lapdance would like to think that he's running Stringfellows, but the reality is that he presides over the most unerotic titty bar in the western world. He had a pole in there at one stage but his bikini-clad lovelies were heftier than one might expect from pole dancers and the whole thing came tumbling down one night. There were no injuries, but a girl called Chelsey tried to sue, claiming she was mentally scarred and unable to pole dance any more. Jimmy never put the pole back up and decided, instead, that the barmaids would be topless and dancing from 11 pm (although dancing is a generous description of what they do after 11 pm; as far as I can see, all they ever do is jig around a lot).

We were first alerted to the presence of the club when we found ourselves looking out of the window of the flat at 7.30 pm one night, soon after we moved in, hoping to catch a glimpse of the gorgeous guy from the estate agents'. I should emphasise that this was all way before I met Rufus. The guy from the estate agents' tended to lock up at 7.30 pm on the dot. Locking up involved him bending right over to do the locks on the bottom of the door. Not that we were stalking him or anything, but the window of our flat did afford us the most astonishing view of his trousers tightening over his firm buttocks as he did this. We craned and strained to see the estate agent through a small pair of cheap binoculars that Mandy bought for this very reason (OK, I admit, this is probably sounding a little bit stalkerish now, but it was all very innocent really . . . and I'm sure he knew we were doing it; he'd taken to bending over ever so slowly and staying down there much longer than was strictly necessary). One night, Mandy, who was still looking through the binoculars, said, 'Oooooh, what's this then?'

It was 8 pm We knew that estate agent man had been and gone. What was Mandy referring to? Another handsome man bending over in the street? Surely life couldn't be that kind to us.

No, it was a ridiculous pink, open-top Mercedes backfiring as it made its way down the road with smoke billowing out of the exhaust pipe. It spluttered and banged like a bloody clown's car before screeching to a halt just next to our flat. These girls climbed out of its leopard-skin patterned interior, wearing hideous seven-inch Perspex-heeled shoes and clad in dresses that looked like cobwebs. They had long scraggy hair, orange skin and shrieky voices. It wasn't pretty, but it was very, very amusing. From then on, estate agent man was second favourite viewing to the daily 'arrival of the strippers'. It came to occupy an important place in our timetable.

'They're here, they're here,' one of us would call through the flat, like children spotting the arrival of an ice-cream van; we'd race to the window and practically hang out of it in order to get the best view possible.

Jimmy would come sauntering out of his bar when the car arrived, his small shoulders bouncing from side to side inside his heavily shoulder-padded jacket – like a gangsta rapper from LA, not the middle-aged short-arse from Twickenham that he was. His signet rings and many neck chains glinted along with his gold tooth. If he wore his big cufflinks, I feared we'd end up scorched from the glare.

'Hello, doll-face,' he'd greet each and every one of them as they clambered out, in such an ungainly fashion that you feared for their ability to dance behind the bar later that night. As we got to know Jimmy, we realised the full strength and scope of his delusions of grandeur. He really fancied himself as a big-time criminal, but there was no way he was. He claimed to have been mates with the Krays, and to have modelled himself on them, but he looked more like Del Boy, with his little, tubby body, short legs, astonishingly hairy chest and large gold medallion. He was simply too nice, too kind and too thoughtful to be truly bad. He'd speak of a childhood shaped by the gutter, and by parents who didn't care. Sadly, he was let down by the full force of reality when his parents popped in to visit him one night – two sweet, kind and loving parents eager to check their son was OK. I'm sure he'd have looked less embarrassed if his mum had offered to take her clothes off and dance naked behind the bar for the evening.

One day, the doors to the strippers' Mercedes wouldn't open, and all the girls had to climb out through the open-top roof. I thought that me, Mandy and Sophie might actually die laughing. None of the strippers had knickers on, and two of them had no pubic hair. Now, just in the interests of absolute clarity, this is not the sort of information that I wish to have in my head. I bet the Hollywood starlets don't know about the downstairs hair arrangements of poorly paid lap dancers from Twickenham. I bet their focus is on things on an altogether superior intellectual level. That's what I mean about me and these Hollywood types – we're so different it's like we're different species altogether.

'Come on, let's get ready,' said Sophie. It was 6 pm.

'Get ready?' said Mandy, astonished. Mand doesn't really like getting dressed up, so the concept of spending three hours working out which eyeliner goes with which top, or whether boots or high heels would be best for a night in a topless bar is rather lost on her. She just hates the whole process of dressing up, and always has. She wears the same simple clothes every time we go out, and always with flat shoes. She insists that she's 'too hefty for heels', so slips little ballet shoes on while Soph and I go tripping down the street in the highest shoes we can find. Mandy never wears anything tight either, because she's paranoid about her huge chest and what she describes as her 'ample thighs'. One of her rules about dating men is that they should always have bigger thighs than she has. That's one of the reasons why she always goes out with such humongously large men. Mandy's always to be found in long, flowing, loose and feminine dresses, which cover up every inch of her. Nothing we say or do will change her views on dressing. She's such a sweetie though, is

Mandy, that there's nothing about her any sane person would want to change anyway. She's just this gorgeous, sweet old-fashioned girl who always stops and tells tramps that she won't give them money in case they spend it on alcohol, but she will buy them a cup of tea if they want (they never do). She picks up litter, smiles and stops to talk to old people. Christ, she doesn't even have a mobile phone – that's how old-fashioned she is!

'Shouldn't we help Kelly to pack first, before we get dressed?' says Mandy.

'Shit. I'd forgotten about that,' said Sophie. 'I guess we should, but let's get a move on – we want to make the most of our last night together.'

Clutching our glasses, we wander into my bedroom, which is stuffed with things that I rarely use. Rufus's place is immaculate and desperately stylish and all those things I yearn for mine to be, but can't quite manage because I like shopping and hate throwing things away. He has seven bedrooms in the main house and a west wing containing his office, sitting room and dressing room. I've never even asked what's in the east wing. I have just the one room and it's packed with stuff and I mean *packed*. You move one thing and twenty-seven others tumble down after it.

We tip the contents of my drawers onto the bed and look at one another in dismay.

'You're going to have to throw some of this crap away,' says Sophie. 'Honestly, mate, it needs to go.'

'No, take it. If he loves you, he'll love your stuff,' says Mandy. She's the exact opposite to Sophie; she's the glass spilling over type. Mandy's desperately optimistic about everything and Sophie's the living, breathing embodiment of pessimism. For example . . . Sophie hates her body and says that I don't know how lucky I am to have an hour-glass figure. She hates her face and says that I don't know how lucky I am to have my looks. She hates her short, fine hair and says I'm so lucky to have my long, thick hair . . . and on, and on . . . . Mandy just says that everyone's beautiful in their own way and that it's not good to be jealous. We should all just be grateful for what we have and what we've been given. Christ but that woman's a martyr. Give her a few years and she'll be marching around the place with a sandwich board about her neck, singing the praises of the Lord. When it comes to Rufus, Mandy's just thrilled for me and thinks good things happen to good people. If that's true then Mandy will end up married to God.

'You know, I always knew you'd end up marrying someone rich and famous,' says Sophie. The edge to her voice has subsided a little, but it still rings with concern.

'I'm not marrying him,' I say defensively.

'No, but you will,' she says. 'I remember when you went on that first date you said, "It won't amount to anything; I'm only teaching him how to catch Maltesers in his mouth." Now look at you!'

I remember that first date as if it happened yesterday. It was 29 April. I mention the precise date because, for some reason, the 29th has become an important number in our courtship; it's the day of the month when things of significance seem to happen to us. Back then, in April, I'd never been more nervous in my life. I went out and bought a lovely new outfit from New Look in an emerald-green colour. It nipped in at the waist and made my breasts look massive and my legs look long and shapely. I wanted him to think me elegant and demure so I vowed not to drink and certainly not to go back to his. As far as I was concerned, we'd just be playing Malteser throwing ... except I guess I knew that there was more to it than that. Sophie and Mandy both told me not to do my bikini line and certainly not to shave my legs then I'd not sleep with him. It's a good policy and, to be honest, it's served me well several times in the past. However drunk you get, it's funny how you don't sleep with a man if you know your legs aren't shaven. Something inside you kicks in and stops you going too far, no matter how much white wine and lemonade you've hurled down your throat. Well, that had always been my experience ... until Rufus. Perhaps that was when I knew he was 'the one'; because I couldn't resist his manly charms even though my legs looked like they belonged to a small mountain gorilla.

I was mortified in the morning of course. I woke up bathed in light, as the spring sun flickered through the slats in the blinds and cast dancing shadows across us as we slept. He's got thick cream curtains that he draws across in the winter but, when I first met him, it was just thin slats of expensive wood between us and the morning sunshine.

I got up and tried to sneak away but it was hopeless. The house is too big to go rushing off anywhere. I tiptoed into the long corridor outside Rufus's massive master bedroom and had no idea how to get out. Eventually I headed off towards the enormous sweeping staircase, taking stealthy little steps, hoping I wouldn't be heard. But then, suddenly, I saw this girl standing in front of me who looked exactly like me.

'Ahhh ...' I screamed, running down the stairs, taking

them three at a time. As I did so, all the alarms burst into life. I mean all of them; you'd think a prisoner had just escaped from Broadmoor with the noise they made. I stopped dead in my tracks in case there were snipers hidden somewhere and turned to face the girl at the top of the stairs but she was gone.

Rufus jumped out of bed and came running after me. 'Where are you going?' he asked, running his hands absently through his hair and leaving it all mussed up and looking incredibly super-sexy.

'I thought I'd head off home. I have to get to work.'

I glanced up to the top of the stairs and that's when I noticed the enormous, antique floor-to-ceiling mirror. Great, so I screamed and ran down the stairs when I saw my reflection. Marvellous!

Rufus persuaded me to come back to bed for a while (to be honest, he didn't have to beg too much), then he insisted on organising for Henry, his driver, close friend and general good guy, to take me home. I was sneaked out through the staff doors that run off one of the kitchens (I know, I know, two kitchens: what's all that about?). A girl called Julie, who works in the kitchen, and must be about the same age as me, smiled at me and told me not to worry, the press couldn't get to the back of the house. I smiled back, feeling incredibly grateful for the fleeting moment of warmth and friendship in this big, beautiful, strange house.

I was hidden between two huge bouncers and chauffeured off in a massive black car. Relief flooded through me as the car moved out of Richmond, across the bridge and towards Twickenham. I'm just not the sort of girl to have a one-night stand and the idea of being caught doing so by the world's press filled me with horror. In the end, of course, it turned out not to be a one-night stand, but the beginning of a glorious relationship. If only I'd known that at the time!

To my unending amazement, Rufus waited fewer than twenty-four hours to contact me. He rang early the next morning and said that he'd like to see me again . . . very soon.

The thing is, and this is why the story is odd, Rufus really liked the fact that I was natural and down to earth. I was fighting to be as sophisticated and demure as possible, but he liked the real me. I tried to diet like mad to get down to a size zero but the reality was that he couldn't get enough of my body – saying that he adored my curves and was obsessed with the softness of my breasts (he hadn't touched real ones for twenty years). He loved the fact that I didn't take hours to get ready, and he thought that it was fabulous that I wasn't a diva. It seemed to be that the more I was 'myself' around him, the happier he was. Being myself comes easy to me, of course, so we both ended up being very happy.

'You're going to live with Rufus George. He's the hottest film star on the planet,' says Mandy all of a sudden, more to herself than to either of us. Perhaps she needs to keep saying it out loud to herself in order to believe it's true. I know how she feels. I've pinched myself so much over the last six months that I'm quite sore. I'm going to be living on Richmond Hill. Me! On The Hill . . . the one that's full of – this is the important bit – huge celebrities. It's beyond mad.

'Can I tell people about it now you're moving in

together?' Mandy has been beseeching me about this for the past month.

'No!'

I forced the two of them to take a vow of silence on the subject of my relationship with Ruf because I wanted to get to know the man without it being all over the bloody newspapers. I went to extraordinary lengths to hide the fact that I was dating the most eligible man on the planet: crawling under garden hedges, buying a false wig, pretending to be from a cleaning company and turning up there in a little pink uniform clutching a mop and a basket of cleaning utensils in order to get past the paparazzi at his gated mansion (he liked that one, actually, and we did have quite a bit of fun with the sponge and the feather duster). The last thing I need right now is for Mum, Dad and Great-Aunty Maude, who thinks the war's still going on, to be interviewed by a bloke in a suit from the tabloids. 'I'm really keen for people not to find out yet, Mand,' I say. 'Please don't tell anyone.'

The three of us are staring at the huge jumble sale that used to be my bedroom; I know we're all thinking the same thing.

'Your stuff is never going to be packed up in time,' says Sophie, eventually. 'And how will you get it over to Rufus's place?'

'I'll throw it all in a cab,' I say, but the reality is that I have an entire £30 to my name and we've just agreed to go out tonight. I must remember to put a couple of quid aside for bus fare to Richmond. One of the funny things about dating someone so incredibly rich is that he doesn't think about money. Rufus looks after me astonishingly well but he wouldn't realise that for me to find £10 for a taxi to Richmond is quite a big deal. He buys me fabulous coats worth hundreds of pounds and I end up wearing them in our flat because it's freezing cold and we can't afford to put the heating on. I'm definitely going to be arriving in my glamorous new world with a bus ticket in my pocket which is odd, really, considering he has a driver, four cars and a hundred million dollars in his bank account.

Money's been the hardest thing to handle since I started seeing Rufus. I felt I had to save every penny to make sure I had enough to get my nails done, my hair blow-dried properly and clothes which looked vaguely OK. Rufus has bought me loads of beautiful clothes and jewellery, but they're terribly impractical – which is great. I love the designer (fake) fur stoles and diamond earrings, but a jumper would be nice. He insists on paying for everything when we're out, thank God, or I'd have been bankrupt. It was the make-up, clothing and hairdressing costs in advance of the dates that were crippling for me. I knew it simply wouldn't do to turn up with badly chewed fingernails, so I had nail extensions. Do you know how much it costs to maintain those things? I could have had two girls' nights out and a takeaway curry for the cost of pointy nails. Every time I was with Rufus I'd flash them at him to make sure he was aware of them, so I hadn't wasted my money. I'd tap them on the table seductively, increasing the racket I was making in response to his lack of interest in them.

'Are you bored?' he asked me once when I was bashing along with quite some vigour.

'No,' I replied quickly, and I stopped the nail drumming right there and then.

The girls have sat down on the bed. They've tipped the contents of the drawers onto the floor. There's stuff everywhere and I haven't even told them how much is nestling under the bed.

'It might be a silly thing to have done, seeing how much crap you've got, but we've bought you a present,' says Sophie, her brown eyes looking suddenly very sad. 'It's for you to wear at fancy parties.'

She leaves the room and reappears clutching a white carrier bag. Primark! Oh my God!

'Ahhhhhh . . . I love you, I love you,' I declare as I pull out the fabulous fitted grey dress that I've been lusting after for simply ages. It's gorgeous, perfect, ideal . . . Thank you so much,' I say, really meaning it. I've been in love with this dress for weeks. Every time we walked past the Primark window, we'd stop and I'd peer in longingly. Rufus has bought me so many things since we've been seeing each other – expensive perfume, jewellery and this gorgeous velvet coat that is unbelievable. He's taught me about designer labels and introduced me to the sort of restaurants I'd only ever read about before, but there's nothing quite as lovely as having spotted something in a shop, lusted after it, and had it bought for you by your best mates. Especially when you know how difficult it would have been for them to afford it.

'Thanks,' I say, hugging them closely. That's when the tears start falling – tumbling from my eyes as we hug each other tightly in this room littered with clothes, shoes, jewellery and a lifetime's 'stuff'.

'I'll miss you two,' I say between giant sobs. 'You have no idea how much I'll miss you both.'

Chapter 3

**HOLLYWOOD STAR SETTLES DOWN
WITH HIS BRITISH STUNNER. EXCLUSIVE**
By Katie Joseph
Daily Post Showbiz Correspondent

Handsome film star Rufus George, the world's most eligible bachelor, is in love. I can exclusively reveal that the heart-throb star of *The Jewelled Dagger* and *Love in the Summer* is dating Kelly Monsoon a 28-year-old theatre assistant from Twickenham. Last week the pretty brunette moved into George's £5 million house on Richmond Hill and friends of the actor say he's in love for the first time. She has given up her job and the two are practically inseparable.

It's a real Cinderella story for curvaceous Kelly who met George when he starred in *Only Men* at Richmond Fringe Theatre. The couple continued to date when George moved with the production to the West End.

They have fought hard to keep their love a secret. Even Kelly's family knew nothing of the relationship when approached by the *Daily Post* yesterday, at their family home in Hastings.

Maude Monsoon, Kelly's great-aunt, reacted with alarm at the news that her attractive great niece was living with a Hollywood star. 'She's gone to fight in the war,' she said, with a wave of her ration book when we approached her at her nursing home in central London. Shortly afterwards she was restrained behind the net curtains by a kindly care assistant.

There is no question that the world which Kelly now inhabits – among the richest and most glamorous people in the country – is a far cry from the one into which she was born.

Do you know Kelly Monsoon? If you do, call the Showbiz desk now on 020 7765 0064, or email showbiz@daily-post.com.

Noooooo . . . I'm lying on the world's largest bed, under a duvet as soft as bunny rabbits' tails, thinking that nothing in the world can ever go wrong for me again, when Rufus drops the *Daily Post* onto the end of the bed and I'm greeted by the news that I am, in fact, the news. I've been here a week and I've been rumbled already. Where's all this come from? And what's all the 'Kelly has given up her job' crap? Just because I take a week off, they think I've left.

'There are photographers all around the house,' says Rufus. 'I was in the kitchen just now and could see them on the CCTV cameras.'

Shit, shit, shit, fuck, shit. Was it Sophie who spoke to the journalists? I don't understand. It can't have been. Me, Mand and Sophie stood there in Suga Daddys a week ago, on that last night together, drinking, and our shoes sticking to the alcohol-drenched carpet, while we batted away the manly advances of nine hairy builders stinking of beer and fags. I told the men we were lesbians, then Mand, Soph and I swore that we'd look after each other for ever.

We joked when Mandy took a picture of me and you could see the topless dancers in the background. 'We'll be able to sell that once people find out that you're going out with Rufus George,' whispered Sophie.

'Oh no,' I cried in mock horror as we hugged each other tightly, much to the delight of the leering builders. The girls swore on their lives that they'd never talk to the press under any circumstances. I promised that I'd never lose touch with them. 'I'll be there for Mand's birthday party on the twelfth. No question.'

'And lunch on the Saturday,' said Mandy. 'Don't forget that.'

'Of course I won't,' I said. 'I'm looking forward to it already.'

It had been such a brilliant evening; me in my beautiful new grey dress, looking a million dollars and attracting loads of attention – all of which was unwanted, of course; since I met Rufus I've been a one-man woman. I wouldn't even let Jimmy buy me a Malibu and pineapple. (That was nothing to with being a one-man woman, though, that was because Malibu and pineapple is truly the worst drink ever created and Jimmy always serves it in a long glass with glacé cherries, tinsel, cocktail sticks and about three umbrellas. He thinks he's working in the bar in *Only Fools and Horses*.)

'We're the Three Musketeers,' Sophie had said, raising her glass rather suddenly and dramatically, causing her to splash us all with Purple Nasty. (Yes – Purple Nasty – you heard me correctly – that's snakebite with blackcurrant in it. She's started drinking it since hearing that Charlotte

Church and Girls Aloud knock it back at celebrity parties.)
'We will never be parted.'

'Never,' said Mandy.

'Never,' I agreed.

Then we did that thing where you entwine your arms
and drink through the arms of the person next to you and
we all ended up covered in more Purple Nasty. It was a
great night though, and I guess what I'm saying is, I can't
imagine either of them letting me down after they promised that they wouldn't.

'Sorry,' I say to Rufus, despite my conviction that the
article is nothing to do with my mates. I feel the need to
apologise because the quotes in the piece relate exclusively
to me. I hope Mum's OK. And Great-Aunt Maude. She'll
wet herself if she sees the article. No, she will, really. She
wets herself a lot.

Mum's a complete star with Maude; she really looks after
her. She's the only one in the family who does. She's always
going to visit her even though Maude's own children don't
have anything to do with her. I don't know how Mum does
it. Especially coping with all the nonsense about the war.
You walk out of the sitting room to go and make tea and
Maude bursts into tears, thinking you're off to fight them
on the beaches or something. 'I'm only going to the kitchen;
I'll be back in a minute,' I say, but Maude's never convinced.

'They all say that but most of them never come back,'
she mumbles, sobbing into a lace hankie.

'The press in this country are a nightmare, but we'll
survive, sweetheart,' says Rufus, seeing the worried look
on my face as I stare down at the article. He smiles at me
endearingly and heads off to find David and request more

coffee. Rufus has one of those posh coffee-makers in the drawing room that I love; it radiates a smell like a Parisian café. You press the button on the side and suddenly it's so French you can almost hear the sound of accordions and feel the presence of the Eiffel Tower. The whole place pulsates with the aroma of roasted coffee beans. It's a bit different from the old flat where the mink-lined kettle chugged into action very reluctantly, making more noise than a small factory as it nudged its way to boiling point. When you poured the water out it was full of limescale – like out-of-date almond flakes scattered throughout the water, filling your mouth and lodging themselves in your throat and under your tongue.

David appears at the bedroom door (all these staff wandering around the place are taking a lot of getting used to), and hands a tray to Rufus who puts my cup of coffee onto the lovely cream bedside table, which was imported from France at great cost. Every time I look round this amazing house it strikes me that there are pieces of furniture in here that are worth more than my parents' home.

When I arrived last week, struggling along with my suitcases and carrier bags brimming with clothes, the staff came out to greet me at the main gate and took me through to the elegant brown leather and wood filled sitting room. There's a sitting room and drawing room at the front of the house, then a library, backed with those really old books you see in stately homes, and a games room with a cinema screen in it as you go back through the house. There's also a high-tech gym and a lovely, cosy snug with a breakfast table in it. At the back, there's a terribly elegant dining room, with modern-looking kitchens at either end. The staff who live in (four of them, including David) are based in the outhouses on the land at the back. And this is Rufus's casual London place. His main house is in Los Angeles, then there's the ski lodge he owns in Aspen and the flat in New York, not to mention the villa nestling in the Tuscan hills. He took me there early in our courtship and I've never seen anywhere so stunning.

I did used to worry about the disparity in wealth between Rufus and me – I don't have anything of value while he is surrounded by things of value – but what difference does it make? Actually, that's not true anyway; I do have something of value: a gorgeous little jewellery pot that has been passed down through the generations of my family. It's porcelain (I think) and tiny and I adore it. On its lid there are three simple diamonds in a row. I keep my grandmother's wedding ring in there, and it means more to me than any other possession. I haven't even had it valued because that seems disrespectful somehow. Why do I care what it costs?

I was given the jewellery pot by my grandmother; 'pot' is such an inelegant and insufficient word to describe my beautiful nineteenth-century porcelain jewellery box, but that's what it's always been called. Granny Edith said that the round porcelain box with its azure blue, enamel-tiled interior and beautiful tiny diamonds on the top would be mine. It's been in the family for generations, and we're really not the sort of family that has heirlooms or anything like that 'handed down' through the family. We're a make-do-and-mend sort of family – full of people who remember the war with great affection because it was a time when people looked after each other. My family's origins are in the East End of London.

They moved out of the area when I was ten years old. I think they realised that if they were going to make the move, they'd better do it before I went to senior school and got settled in. We moved down to Hastings where Dad was working. I remember it being just as rough as where we'd come from but somehow so much nicer with a blast of sea air drifting through it. It's amazing how nothing's quite as bad when the beach is round the corner.

The newspaper's still spread across the bed in front of me. I see Rufus looking over at it as he sips his coffee.

'And what's all this about me quitting my job?' I rant. 'I haven't given up my job! I've taken a few days off.'

'You could you know . . .' he says with a lazy smile.

'Give up work and do what?'

'Anything you want. You don't need to work. You could be around here, help me out.'

'What? Turn into a housewife?'

I may not have pictured myself as a madly focused career woman but I'd certainly never seen myself as a housewife at the age of twenty-eight. Sophie would beat me to a pulp if I left the theatre and turned into a domestic goddess.

Rufus just shrugs.

'We need to take stock of things,' I say, looking up at him sternly as he places his cup next to mine. I want him to know that I'm taking all this seriously, and that there won't be any leaks.

'Mmmm . . .' He lies down on the bed next to me, leans in close and stares at me with eyes the colour of palest moss. He has the most amazing thick, jet-black eyelashes, fluttering out from around these astonishing eyes. The fact that everything about Rufus is dark except for his eyes seems to highlight their lightness even more. His skin always looks tanned, his hair is thick and dark and glossy, but those eyes – they lift out of his face, full of laughter, joy and this alluring intensity. God, he's gorgeous. He pulls me towards him. 'That's enough taking stock. Stock all taken,' he says as he pulls the duvet off me and I feel his eyes travel the length of my body before resting on my breasts. 'Come here,' he growls, throwing the duvet over us.

I can feel his erection digging into my leg. 'Mmmmm,' I murmur back as he begins to kiss me and all my worries about Great-Aunt Maude and shadowy figures on the CCTV screens drift quickly from my mind.

We're sitting at the breakfast table in the snug enjoying a range of berries and some fruits I've never heard of before, like goji berries. *Goji berries?* We only had apples and bananas at home. And, maybe, strawberries if we were feeling flush. Now it's all star fruits, lychees, pomegranates and goji berries (which, for the record, are foul; I don't care if they're a superfood, hand picked by Tibetan monks and consumed by the world's skinniest actresses and super-models). I munch through the fruit plate, which has been prepared by Pamela – one of the housekeepers. She's my favourite one, actually; she looks like every great house-keeper ought to, with her large barrel-shaped body and her light-grey hair fashioned into the tightest of curls on her head. She always wears an immaculate white apron over her long grey skirt. She and Julie have been so lovely to me. Ever since I started coming to the house regularly, all those months ago, they've looked out for me, and make an effort to come and say 'hi'. I'd count them as friends, to be honest. I often pop in to have a chat with Pamela about her husband who works too hard and her son who can't get a job. I feel as if I know her family well. I tell Pamela all about my family too, and I often talk to Julie about Mandy and Sophie and what great mates they are. I'm going to take Julie for a night out with the girls soon; as soon as I get myself organised.

I have a notebook in front of me on which I've drafted out an important list of things to do. First thing on the list is 'call the girls'. This is proving harder to do than I'd predicted because there's only one way of getting hold of them and that's through Sophie's mobile. Mandy doesn't have a bloody phone and the one in the flat never worked properly after Dodgy Dave tried to strangle himself with it. One of my main tasks over the coming weeks is to get someone to mend that phone in their flat so that the three of us can actually talk to each other in the evenings. I guess I never realised how important it would be to be able to call them regularly; I had these ideas of popping round there in the evenings, but since it turns out that the press are permanently outside, I can't leave the flat unless it's under armed guard, and with three decoy cars ahead of me, so 'popping' is not really an option.

'Why would you write "call the girls" on a list?' asks Rufus in his simple male way, nuzzling his stubbly chin into the back of my neck. 'Why not just call them?'

'I've tried a million times,' I exaggerate. 'I've put it on the list to remind myself to keep trying. They're very hard to get hold of. Neither of them has a PA! Imagine that?'

'Funny lady,' he says. 'I'll have you know that I know people without PAs too.'

'Yeah right,' I respond sarcastically. 'Your milkman probably has a PA.'

He grabs me from behind as if to strangle me. 'You'll be sorry,' he growls. 'I'll teach you to take the mickey out of me.' Just as I start to fear that he might actually start to wrestle with me, he tickles me playfully and wraps his arms around me.

'I hope you don't really think I'm like that,' he says. 'You do know that my two best friends hang out at baseball games trying to get autographs. Deeves spent the whole of last summer selling hot dogs at the Yankees games so he could watch 'em all without paying.'

'Did he?' I ask. 'Why didn't you just buy him a season ticket?'

'Because the man has pride,' Rufus says, shaking his head. 'What can you do? Have to say I love him for it though. I reckon he must have been sneaking himself some free hot dogs somewhere along the line to make it all worthwhile.'

'You are friends with a sausage thief?' I suggest in mock horror.

'I fear so,' he retorts, sounding as British as he can. 'Now, I have an idea . . . an idea about how we might pass the time.'

'Yeah, I know what your idea of us passing the time involves, and it seems to necessitate me being naked and in bed!' I say light-heartedly.

'Not necessarily in bed,' he says, rubbing his chin thoughtfully. 'But definitely naked.'

'Mmmm . . . thought as much,' I say, rubbing my cheek affectionately against his.

'But I had another notion today,' he says. 'Oh yes, believe it or not I do have thoughts about you that don't involve you taking all your clothes off.'

'My God!' I feign concern and look deep into his eyes. 'Are you unwell?'

'Nope.' He pulls me in close to him. I love the way he does that: squeezes me so tightly that I can barely breathe and end up sucking in light raspy breaths – it makes me feel all wrapped up and protected. When he hugs me like that I feel that no harm can come to me.

'I think we should go shopping,' he suggests. 'I'd like to go and buy you the necklace to match it.'

'Match what?'

'Oh, didn't I mention?' he says mischievously. 'I've bought you a bangle.'

'A bangle? Oooooooo.'

There are times when living with Rufus is a bit like starring alongside Rufus in one of his films. And, I tell you, I know all about Rufus's films. From the rom coms to the epics, the war films to the horror films – he's been in so many different types of films; that's what makes him so special as an actor (and the fact that he's drop dead gorgeous). In the early days of our courtship, I seemed to spend all the time I wasn't getting ready to see him, watching his films. I could quote most of the lines from *Tarzan II* by the time our third date came along.

'If you come with me, I will love you for ever.' (Him).

'I will, Tarzan. I will.' (Some dumb blonde actress playing Jane).

'Then come, now. I take you away.' (Him again).

When he's not running around in a loincloth or winning

an Oscar for his portrayal of a killer, he's playing the dashing hero with whom everyone falls in love. The charm that lights up the screen and sends millions of teenager girls into swoons and sighs is as evident off the screen as it is on it.

He pulls out a bag and hands it to me. Inside there's a Tiffany's box. Oh my God. 'Thank you,' I say, smiling up at him as I pull the turquoise ribbon off and watch it fall softly and gracefully to the floor. Even the disposable packaging is stylish on this gift. I lift the lid and stand back in sheer delight and amazement. The bangle has three diamonds on it – in a row . . . exactly like my beautiful, favourite jewellery pot. 'It's exactly the same!!' I say, genuinely awe-struck by the beauty of the piece of jewellery. 'I can't believe it.'

'Neither could I when I saw it,' says Rufus, grinning from ear to ear. 'I'm glad you like it.'

'I do, I do,' I say, trying to fix it around my wrist as he pulls me into his arms again.

'They have matching necklaces,' he says, squeezing me close to him. 'I ordered one and it's in the store. I was going to ask Christine to collect it, but why don't we go?'

'Can we do that?' I'm aware that going anywhere with Rufus demands an operation of military-style proportions and precision or the shop will be full of fans. 'Will we have to parachute in under the cover of darkness?'

'We can do it,' he says cautiously. 'And, if we get it right, probably without parachutes. Henry can drive us and we'll go in by the back door.'

I sit back and watch as Rufus briefs Christine in that gentle way of his, making her feel like the only girl in the world as he asks her to call ahead to the manager and request that the shop be shut when we arrive.

'Thank you,' I say. 'You're very thoughtful.'

'It's my pleasure,' says Rufus, taking my face in his hands. 'I love you.'

'I love you too.'

I wish I could reciprocate in some way; I wish I could buy Rufus something that he would adore, and would make him go as mushy and adoring as I go when he buys things for me. But how? What could I buy that he couldn't afford to get himself two million of? When it comes to purchasing power, our relationship feels so unbalanced that I find it very difficult. He's only got to say in an interview, at a party, or anywhere else, that he quite likes the look of the new Burberry suits, and the entire winter menswear collection will turn up in seconds. What's the point of me saving up to buy him a tiepin when the manufacturers will give him every tiepin ever made?

'Ready?' We've arrived at the back door of Tiffany's in Bond Street. Rufus pulls his cap down and his collar up and looks around shiftily, as if he's off to hold up a bank or something. We go darting through the doors that swing open to greet us. Now this is something I've really noticed about Rufus's world: doors are being opened for me constantly. I can't remember the last time I deigned to do my own door opening. In fact, it's been so long I'm not sure I can remember what to do. Everywhere I go there's someone expecting me and swinging the door as I arrive in greeting. Like magic!

Rufus places the necklace around my neck and it hangs, sparkling wildly but elegantly, against my skin. I can't speak. I just stand, looking into the mirror, while the sales assistants coo and say 'gorgeous' while clearly looking at my boyfriend. I notice how he doesn't return their admiring glances though – ha! He keeps on looking at me, like he's absorbing me with his eyes, like there's no one else in the room. He may be the world's most adored film star, and – yes – I know there are women queuing up to be with him, but at times like this I just know, *know*, that he would never cheat on me.

If I'm honest, I knew by the second date with Rufus that I was falling in love. What I never expected was that he would fall in love with me. I wasn't alone in this view. My friends, Sophie in particular, warned me strongly against getting too close to the world's most sought-after man. They never said it, but what they were thinking was – it can't last . . . just think about how many beautiful women are throwing themselves at him. It can't possibly last. 'By all means go out with him,' they said. 'Have fun, have a good time, but don't fall in love with him.' But how could I not? Christ, there are teenage girls who've never met him who are head over heels in love with him. What choice did I have when he was wining and dining me and taking me dancing under the stars?

'Don't fall in love,' screamed Sophie, when I set out on our second date together, and I went out there and fell completely and hopelessly in love with him.

For our second date, we planned to go out for the day, and he wanted to take me somewhere very English.

'Leave it to me,' he said in his strong American accent.

'It'll be the Changing of the bloody Guard,' said Sophie. 'You know what Americans are like.'

'Or Kensington Palace because he'll want to show you where Princess Diana lived, because the Americans adore her, don't they?'

The 'guess where the American's going to take you on an English date' game became quite serious. When Rufus appeared at ten am that warm late summer morning, I'd been reliably assured by Soph and Mand that we were going to Buckingham Palace, Kensington Palace, Harrods, tea at the Ritz or to play croquet and watch cricket. I was quite excited by the time he arrived at the door.

Not knowing where we were going would normally have produced sartorial terror of cataclysmic proportions in me. If you don't know where you're going, how do you know what to wear? But with Rufus I'd kind of got used to the fact that nothing in my wardrobe was ever going to be appropriate for anything we ever did anyway, so it didn't really matter that I didn't know what we were doing – if you know what I mean. Just gave me an excuse for being wrongly dressed!

I jumped into the back of the car next to Rufus and he introduced me to Henry, his driver, who'd come over with him from America.

'He's been driving me for fifteen years,' said Rufus.

'And he's been driving me insane for just as long,' said Henry.

The two men joshed and took the mickey out of each other as the car wound through the streets of Twickenham, heading out of town. Out of town? What about tea at the

Ritz? Did he not know where the Changing of the Guard took place?

'You have to tell me where we're going,' I said, as the car eased towards a beautiful bridge with boats and canoes sweeping along below. Henry pulled over and Rufus jumped out. He ran round to the back of the car and swung my door open for me. 'Welcome to Hampton Court,' he said.

I have to admit, I was amazed. The place is about twenty minutes from my flat and I'd never been there before. Rufus, on the other hand, seemed to know the place intimately. We walked through the old Tudor kitchens and down into the giant greenhouses housing the world's largest vine. 'How do they know?' he whispered at every new historical fact. 'Have they measured every vine in the world? I bet they just make this stuff up.'

'Spoken like a true American,' I retorted as we escaped through a small wooden door and out into the palace court-yard with a beautiful fountain in the middle.

'Make a wish,' said Rufus, digging into his pockets for coins. He handed me enough money to keep a family of six fed for a week and urged me to throw them. I tossed the coins into the air and watched them fall and splash into the sparkling water; pennies from heaven. 'OK, my turn.' He threw his money into the fountain and made a wish that nothing would change between us.

'I want us to stay like this for ever,' he said, wrapping his arms around me.

'Me too,' I said, smiling like I'd never smiled before.

'I want us to get to know each other and for us to get closer and closer, but most of all I want the special bond between us to stay like this.'

'Yes,' I replied, almost breathless with joy. 'I want to know everything about you too.'

'Me first,' he said with a big smile. 'Tell me ... what is the naughtiest thing you've ever done? Go on; tell me something about yourself that I don't know.'

Oh shit.

'Go on. It can't be that bad,' he said, sensing my reluctance. 'Can it?'

'I got banned from driving for twelve months,' I said sheepishly.

'How fast were you going?' he asked.

'No, drink-driving. But I hadn't been drinking. Well, I had, but I didn't know I had. I mean, my drinks were spiked by this guy that Mandy was going out with. He didn't like the fact that I wasn't drinking and put loads of alcohol into this fruit punch and fed it to me all night. I drove home, was stopped by police and ended up getting banned. Luckily no one got hurt ...'

Rufus was silent for a moment and then gave me a hug and a wry smile. 'Wow. I'm dating a convict,' he said. 'Did you have mugshots done and fingerprints taken and everything?'

'Oh yes. The whole works.'

'Poor thing. Right, come on. I know what'll cheer you up ... I've saved the best till last. Come with me,' he said, taking my hand and whisking me away from the courtyard, past the maze, and out to a gorgeous rose garden. The smell as we approached was unbelievable, hanging in the air as the flowers smiled and basked in the afternoon sunshine.

The sun was shining. I was surrounded by beautiful

roses. That's when I fell in love. Later I would call my friends and family and try to enthuse them about a rose garden in a palace on the banks of the river. I'd try to explain about the magical pull of the scents and the immediate sense of relaxation we'd both felt. I'd tell them about the smiling gardener called Frank who came over and said hello, resting wearily on his hoe as he admired his roses and grinned engagingly, telling Rufus it was so nice to see him again. 'It was paradise,' I'd sigh. There's no question that they all thought I'd gone mad.

Rufus led me past the benches dedicated by one devoted spouse to another to a bench with no dedication on it at all. 'This is my favourite bench,' he said, and I almost squealed out loud. A man with his favourite bench! Who'd have thought? 'I call it the bench with no name.' We sat holding hands in companionable silence for a few moments.

'So do you bring all your girls here?' I teased, fairly sure of the answer but I had to ask.

'You're the first and only.' He smiled back at me. 'You know I've always felt this was a very special place. But now it will be our special place. A place that only the two of us know about.'

We have a special place! Our place! All our own. And it's in a palace and it's full of roses! I looked up and saw butterflies playing beside us; fluttering their wings as if in courtship. The sentiments of the moment seemed to be reflected in the nature all around us.

'It's amazing! I love it. I love—' I broke off, scared of what I was in danger of revealing but Rufus kissed me again, giving me the courage to try. 'I mean . . . I think you should know I'm falling in love with you . . .'

'Good, because I feel exactly the same way.' He smiled. 'Only you should know what your getting yourself into, Kelly. My life is crazy. The press follow me most places. I have to guard my privacy where I can. I want to protect you from that craziness but once the press know we're together . . .' He paused. 'Once the press know we're together, life is going to get very difficult. Until you live through it, you have no idea how hard it is to cope with the constant intrusion.'

Rufus looked so serious all of a sudden, I was overcome with the need to lift him out of his solemn thoughtfulness.

'Whenever they upset us we'll come here,' I suggested, looking at the picture of beauty and solitude painted in the brightest colours all around us. 'We'll escape to the Rose Garden and hide in the bushes like squirrels and no one will find us.'

'That's a lovely thought,' Rufus said, flashing me that incredible smile of his and speaking with such love and warmth. 'From now on, this is *our* rose garden, our refuge. The place we first declared our love to one another and somewhere we'll always come when things get tough.'

I breathed deeply. 'We'll never, ever tell anyone about our rose garden, Rufus; it's just for us . . . our special place. I'll never breathe a word to anyone about it, then no one will know.'

I smiled then, feeling lost and dizzy in the thrill of the moment.

Chapter 4

EXCLUSIVE: FILM STAR SET TO MARRY AS GIRLFRIEND HAS MASSIVE BOOB JOB
By Katie Joseph
Daily Post Showbiz Correspondent

Wedding bells will soon be ringing for Rufus George, as the steamy love affair between the hunky film star and his knockout English girlfriend, Kelly Monsoon, grows stronger by the day. As George plans the wedding of the decade, his stunning girlfriend is rumoured to have undergone a huge breast enlargement operation to please her man on their big day. According to sources close to the star, the loved-up couple have not been seen in public since they were spotted at a jewellery shop on Bond Street last weekend.

'We can't say what they purchased, but we can confirm that it was specially ordered and has three diamonds,' said a shop assistant.

The news indicates clearly that Hollywood's biggest star is preparing to propose to the drop-dead gorgeous Richmond theatre administrator who has captured his heart. Family and friends are expecting an announcement at tonight's dinner party, being hosted by Rufus at his mansion on Richmond Hill to honour his new girlfriend.

Meanwhile Kelly has been making sure that she looks as good as possible for the wedding of the year. The already busty lovely was seen entering London Valley Hospital, where many celebrities undergo breast implant operations. It's all an exciting new development in an exciting new world for Kelly. Don't forget to read our exclusive interview with Kelly's former boyfriend Greg Clarke in this Sunday's paper. 'She went like a train,' said Clarke. 'I've never had sex like it.' Lucky Rufus! Read more EXCLUSIVELY on Sunday.

Do you know Kelly Monsoon? If you do, call the Showbiz desk now on 020 7765 0064, or email showbiz@daily-post.com. We will pay for information and your identity can be kept secret.

'Whaaaaaaaat? Rufus, have you seen this?'

I can hardly believe my eyes. There, in a national newspaper read by millions of people (including my friends and family – I know this because they've been texting me a load of bloody insults all morning), is a chicane of complete lies about me. I went like a train? I hardly know Greg. He's just a barman who I went out for a drink with once. I never even kissed him, let alone slept with him, so I don't know how he knows that I 'go' like a train. Bloody hell. I'm no virgin but I definitely never slept with him!

And boob job? I mean – hello – of all the people in the world, I really don't need a boob job. I'm 34E for crying out loud, what would I inflate them to? I'd look like I had two footballs stuffed down the front of my shirt.

Rufus glances at the page I'm reading and raises his thick, black eyebrows. He looks like a man who's seen this sort of thing time and time again; which, to be fair, is exactly what he is.

'I've got people looking at them,' he says rather enigmatically.

'Looking at what? My boobs – the ones that I've apparently had inflated?'

'No, silly. I've got my lawyer looking at the allegations in the piece. Don't worry. There's nothing we can do now; the lawyers will act if there's anything to act on, if not, we'll put in measures to limit the chances of this sort of thing happening again. We'll try and stop them from printing the interview with your ex-boyfriend on Sunday.'

'He's not my ex.'

'Well, whoever he is . . . train man . . . we'll stop him talking about having sex with you.'

'I didn't have sex with him. Can we get this really clear, Rufus: he's not my ex-boyfriend and I didn't have sex with him.'

This is the thing with me and Rufus; he's polished, professional, never flustered, always calm and in control whereas I feel like squealing and running out and buying every single copy of the paper to make sure that no one else can see the lies they've written about us.

'I just don't believe it,' I say, largely to myself, but Rufus hears and ruffles my hair affectionately.

'Don't you?' he says. 'Did you think we'd be left alone to develop our relationship in peace? I'm afraid I've had a working lifetime of this. They don't let up; they're always after stories, always wanting to hear more gossip. That's why we have to be careful who we trust.'

'I just didn't think it would be like this,' I say. And that's what I mean. I'm not stupid; I knew the journalists would want to write stories but it didn't occur to me that the newspapers would be this interested in the minutiae of our relationship until we appeared in public. I imagined that once we started going to events and parties together, the journalists would spy us and want to write about us but I just didn't expect this . . . I didn't imagine for a minute that if they couldn't find a story, they'd make one up!

I guess I thought I could control things; I thought that by not going out and not doing anything wrong, I'd be OK. I always realised that if I was caught falling out of a nightclub, taking drugs, or working in the slave trade, the story would hold extra interest because of my link to a film star, but I didn't think that by doing nothing, I'd still end up in the papers. As it is, I seem to be even more of a target for the media by not doing anything. *Heat* magazine announced that I was 'oops . . . too fat by far' this week, after they got a picture of me clambering out of the car. I nearly cried and realised, perhaps for the first time, that when you're looking at these pictures as a non-celebrity they seem harmless and fun. But when you're the target of the pictures, they feel like a real attack and very difficult to take. It's all so personal. I've never realised before how undermining and cruel so many of the jibes are in magazines.

As Rufus and I sit in the sitting room, looking at the latest missive from bloody Katie, my phone bleeps again.

'I no that's not true,' reads the text from Sophie. 'You've got the massive-ist knockers in the world.'

There's another bleep minutes later. It's Mandy texting on Sophie's mobile. She hates texting and, on the rare occasions when she does it, using someone else's phone, her messages are always spelt out in full and grammatically perfect. 'Are you OK? Call me if you want to talk. Love Mandy.'

'I guess I was naive,' I tell Rufus, and I guess I was. After all, I've been cutting pictures and articles about Rufus out of magazines since the day I met him. I, above everyone, should be well aware of how much publicity he gets.

'I went to the hospital to visit Great-Aunt Maude,' I tell Rufus. 'That's when they must have seen me and thought I was going for a boob job.'

'Listen. I don't want you to worry,' says Rufus in that calm way of his. It's OK for him; he's become immune to it over the years and he knows that his friends and family will know it's all made up. My mum read it and asked me whether my cup size had changed dramatically because she was planning on buying me a nightie for Christmas. 'Noooooo,' I said. 'It's all made up.'

'Are you sure?' she asked, as if this was something I might have had done and then forgotten about.'

'Yes, I'm sure. It's not true,' I said defiantly, but she wasn't having any of it.

'It must be true; it says so – in the paper. Go and buy it. It's there in black and white.'

Rufus can see I'm miles away; I'm mentally scanning through all the people who might have read the paper and establishing to what sort of conclusion they may have come. I'm forced out of my dreamlike state by the sound of Rufus's mobile.

'Courty!' he shouts into the phone. 'How ya doing, buddy?' There's a pause during which Rufus smiles from ear to ear as he listens to his friend recounting a story of some kind.

'Ha, ha, ha,' Rufus says in reply, his voice rising with every laugh. 'And you had it coming to you,' he adds, pointing abstractly at the wall as he does so. 'You had it coming, bud. Now, hold on, let me put you on loudspeaker so you can talk to Kelly . . . Can you still hear me?'

'Sure can, buddy.'

'Kelly, say hi to Mr Brad Court, one of my oldest friends.'

'Hey, less of the "old", Tarzan,' says 'Courty', adding: 'Kelly, are you there?'

'Hello,' I say nervously. 'Nice to talk to you.'

'Hey, it's great to talk to you too,' he says. 'How's it going with old misery chops?'

'Hey,' Rufus shouts, over my shoulder. 'Watch it.'

'It's going OK actually,' I say. 'He hasn't introduced me to the world of baseball yet though; I understand you're a real fan.'

'God, I love your accent,' he swoons. 'It's soooo sexy.'

'Enough,' shouts Rufus over my shoulder, taking the phone. 'I need time alone with the accent now, so you, my friend, are history. Talk soon, buddy.'

'Sure thing,' says Courty. 'Nice to talk to you, Kelly. If you're as hot as your accent then Rufus must be one hell of a —'

Gone. Rufus cuts his friend off in his prime and tucks the phone back into his trouser pocket, looking over at me.

'Courty's a really nice guy. He's a proper, decent, honest guy; he's like your friends Mandy and Sophie. People like that don't worry about what's in the paper. They know the real person behind the headlines and they take no notice. Don't worry too much about what the likes of Katie Joseph write. She's really not worth worrying about. Just concentrate on having a lovely time today, getting ready for the party tonight,' he says. 'Remember Elody's coming over to meet you at 3 pm. I'll be at a lunch, but she's eager to meet you before tonight.'

'A lunch? Oh . . .' I hear myself saying. I've spent the past week nailed to my boyfriend's side; it feels odd that he's going out without me.

'Yep. I have to; a work thing,' he says, before standing up and walking towards the door. 'It's about a new role and to firm up details for a promo tour. All very dull . . . but I have to go, sweets. Anyway, you'll have tons to do before the party tonight, won't you? I know what you girls are like.'

Tonight – ah yes, the party I've been dreading since I arrived here a week ago. I secretly hoped that Rufus might want to cancel the party after the article in the paper this morning. 'We can't do the party now, dear, can we?' I say, before urging with childlike unreasonableness for him to abandon all plans for the event that a team of eight has worked for a week to organise.

'It'll be fine, don't you worry,' he says whenever I object or admit to my fears of being judged by his rich and famous friends. 'They'll love you like I do.'

The party is where I get to meet some of the neighbours on the Hill. Rufus has chosen some of those whom he thinks I'll get on best with, just to give me a gentle introduction to his friends. Before arriving here I was desperate to see them, mingle with them and join this exclusive set, but now I just want to stay inside with Rufus and not meet anyone. Ever.

Three couples are coming tonight, along with Elody – the brilliant, brilliant Parisian stylist. She's the one who used to set all the trends around the world by dressing the most glamorous and influential of people. You know – the one who was half of the madly famous 'Jelody' fashion couple with Jon Boycott, the fashion designer. He created beautiful clothes and she dressed the world's biggest stars in them. They had the perfect relationship; they were both incredibly attractive – he with his skinny, weathered but incredibly sexy look, and she with her immaculate eye for detail and her innate flamboyancy. They made millions. I remember reading about them when I was a teenager and thinking that they had the perfect life. They dominated the fashion world until he died, suddenly, a few years ago from a drugs overdose. His death turned him into a legend, but it turned Elody into a shadow of her former self and, if what I read is true, she's never got over losing him. It's made her a little 'brittle' (Rufus's word) and she is quite a sad, lonely figure these days. She doesn't work much any more, not that she needs to financially, and has few friends whom she trusts.

'She needs people around her who care,' said Rufus. 'I don't know her too well but she's a doll,' he insists.

All I know about her is that she oozes sophistication.

She is a byword for cool, urban chic (see, I've been Googling her, too, I know all the lingo).

She wants to see me before the party to check I've got something appropriate to wear. Not quite sure what 'appropriate' is but I'm sure she'll tell me! Rufus says she'll offer to lend me something, go shopping with me, and style me – whatever it takes to make sure I feel happy and comfortable tonight. He did warn me time and again that she has a rather brusque manner, and can be a little intimidating. He assures me though that she'll be my biggest ally, and that her bark is much, much worse than her bite. 'She's been through a lot,' he said. 'I genuinely think her heart's in the right place, you just have to cut her a little slack because she's still damaged from Jon's death. She was devastated when he died, absolutely devastated. I met her and Jon on the set of *The Jewelled Dagger*; the two of them were in charge of wardrobe and Jon designed half the set too. Elody looked me up when I moved over here. I think you two could be great friends.'

I find myself hoping, madly, that she wants to be my friend. Luckily I've got the beautiful grey dress that the girls bought me as a leaving present, so I should impress her when it comes to talking party wear, and I now have the world's most outstanding necklace and bangle to wear too. She'll be really bloody impressed when she sees me.

'I'm looking forward to meeting her,' I tell Rufus, loving the way he smiles at me, with such love and warmth.

One of the interesting lessons I've learnt this week about the rich, famous and beautiful residents of Richmond Hill is that they're a rather petty clique. I know the party planners have found it hellishly difficult to arrange tonight's little soirée because of the various in-fights going on in this exclusive set. You simply can't sit so-and-so next to so-and-so because of the incident with the futon at Rodney's bash in Hollywood and you can't put Lady what's-her-name next to the hellraiser – she'll run a mile. Most of the problems, though, appear to be caused by two women on the scene who seem to have upset everyone and hate each other so can't be seated anywhere. One of them may end up in the garden and the other in one of the outhouses.

The first of these women is the aforementioned inimitable Elody Elloissie – a fashion legend. I'm acutely aware of her work through the pages of *Heat*. She's a sultry French version of Rachel Zoe, with glossy black hair, razor-sharp cheekbones and an even more razor-sharp tongue. The other woman whom everyone's worried about is Isabella, a doctor who spends her time injecting collagen, Botox and other toxic substances into the faces of the rich and famous. Isabella fell out with Elody when she told *Marie Claire* magazine that she had treated the world-famous stylist. Elody responded by telling *Vogue* that Isabella had no style and that her world-renowned parties and charity galas were clichéd and boring. Isabella's husband is Edward, the plastic surgeon to the stars. Isabella and Edward are, apparently, single-handedly responsible for the faces, breasts, stomachs and thighs of everyone coming to the party tonight.

They avoid Elody, and Elody avoids them. Rufus won't tolerate such nonsense though –he's invited them all. What fun! Not . . . I wish Mandy and Sophie were coming, or even the girls from work. I'd have much more fun if Katy and Jenny were there chucking Maltesers at each other and putting up charts to show who's the reigning Malteser champion (me, last time I looked, unless they've had a small triumph while I've been off this week).

It's 3 pm and I'm wearing my dress for the evening to show Elody. I have that air of confidence that only comes from wearing something new and flattering. I've sponged off the worst of the Purple Nasty from our night at Suga Daddys, and there's hardly a mark on it. I've also painted my fingernails this gorgeous shimmering colour that makes them look healthy and lovely and shows off my tan. I'm hoping she'll take one quick look at me and declare that I'm perfect, so we can have a glass of wine and become mates.

More than anything, I'm hoping I'll be as easily accepted into Rufus's world as he was into mine. I took him back to my parents' house on our fifth date. We drove down to Hastings one gentle day ... It was a lazy, timeless morning in early summer. One of those days when morning fades into afternoon then merges softly and seamlessly into evening. A beautiful warm day that glowed from within and hinted at hot summer months ahead.

I'd told Mum and Dad that I'd met a man. I'd even started telling them that the man was called Rufus and that he was a world-famous actor, but if you knew my family, you'd know that explaining to them that you're going out with a Hollywood sex god is a little like explaining nuclear physics to a terrapin.

'Tarzan?' said Mum, when I started to tell her about the films he's been in. 'You mean Johnny Weissmuller? I thought he was dead. Is he dead?'

Christ, it shows how long it's been since she went to the cinema.

I heard Mum yelling through the house. 'Tony, Tony, come quickly. Is Johnny Weissmuller dead?'

'I don't know, dear,' I heard Dad's frustrated voice in the background. 'How on earth would I know something like that?'

'Your father doesn't know whether he's alive or dead,' said Mum as if she'd added something that was in any way worthwhile to the conversation.

'Mum, it doesn't matter whether he's dead or alive; I'm not going out with him. I'm going out with Rufus George.'

'Oh, Tony, have a word with her, would you,' she said. 'She doesn't care whether Johnny Weissmuller's alive or dead.'

Oh God. Why's it so hard?

We arrived at Mum and Dad's house in something of a state, with Rufus having nearly killed us en route. He didn't mention that he was yet to drive on the left, having designated all previous driving to Henry. Rufus said he was eager not to have Henry drive us on this occasion for fear that it looked too 'flash'. It seemed slightly ridiculous given that Rufus is an international film star and one of the best-looking guys on the planet. He'd look 'flash' lying in rags in the gutter, begging for food. Rufus is the very personification of 'flash'. He could no more avoid being flash than I could avoid being female – that's just what he is. Still, I appreciated the gesture. I was glad he was worried about how he might be perceived by my parents. I loved that he cared. Just a shame that he had to demonstrate it by risking both our lives.

'Mum and Dad, this is Rufus,' I said when we arrived at the front door.

'Oooo, hello,' said Mum, patting her hair and fussing over her flowery apron. She might not know her Rufuses from her Johnnys, but she knows a pretty face when she sees one.

'Nice to meet you, son,' said Dad, patting him on the back in a manly fashion. 'Do you want to shove that car of yours up onto the drive so it doesn't get bashed into? The cars come round at a hell of a pace.'

Mum and Dad live on a crescent, and most of Dad's life is spent fixating on what's going to become of the cars parked outside.

Rufus thanked Dad and headed off to 'shove' his Maserati onto the drive while Dad stood there in his brown cardigan, directing him into the tiniest space, with all the skill of a drunk. It was a scene which had disaster written all over it.

'Come inside, dear,' said Mum. 'We'll leave the men to it.'

I looked over at Dad waving his arms wildly as if to indicate acres of space, while Rufus manoeuvred the car slowly and cautiously into the three inches available. The very last thing I wanted to do was to 'leave the men to it'. It seemed to me that 'the men' were far from capable of being left to it.

Still, I followed Mum into our small, cluttered family home. The smell of cooking leaked out from the kitchen. Even though it was a beautiful hot day, Mum was preparing a large Sunday roast for my new boyfriend. I walked into the kitchen to find eight of our neighbours, all crammed up against the window and peering through it as my boyfriend and father bonded over car manoeuvring.

'Oooo, Betty, he's better looking in the flesh isn't he?' said Margaret, the lady who runs the coffee shop at our local church.

'He is,' said Betty with a leeriness to her voice. 'Oh yes, he definitely is.'

'Hi,' I said, and watched as the ageing ladies jumped back and pretended to be admiring the petunias on the shelf by the window.

'Lovely shade of purple, Jayne,' said Betty. 'Oh, Kelly, how nice to see you.'

The others mumbled their greetings, commented on how well I looked and how gorgeous my dress was. 'Must have cost a fortune!' declared Doreen. 'But I guess you can afford it.'

I walked into the sitting room and pushed the cats off the sofa so I could sit down. Mum ran in behind me.

'Sorry, love, I couldn't stop them!' she said. 'Once I told them about Rupert they all wanted to come and see him.'

'Rufus, Mum. His name's Rufus,' I said.

'Rufus. Yes. Funny name. He seems nice though. I'll throw this lot out when he comes in, and I can get to know him a bit better. Pretty dress. It must have cost a fortune.'

I often think that Mum and Dad's generation are obsessed with how much things cost. They mention the price of things all the time, and whether things seem cheap, expensive or reasonably priced.

'Rufus bought it for me,' I replied.

As we sat side by side in the warm sitting room, enjoying the sunlight streaming through the patio windows at the back of the house, it sounded as if a small commotion was developing in the hallway. We rushed out to see what was going on to find that Rufus had come into the house and Mum's friends had all gone diving out of the kitchen to say hello, with the result that he couldn't get in. The problem was further complicated by the fact that local boys had seen the Maserati and were gathering outside to see who it belonged to. One sight of Rufus and the crowd got bigger. Rufus needed to get in to escape the throng outside, but was prevented from doing so by the throng in the hallway. It would be safe to say that nothing like this had ever happened in Leemarr Crescent before.

Mum pushed past me and moved herself onto the stairs that run just off the hallway, next to the sitting-room door. She clapped her hands loudly and everyone fell silent. 'You can all meet Rufus later,' she said. 'But right now I'd like him to be able to get into our home, so would you mind leaving. There'll be plenty of time for auto-graphs later.'

There was mumbling and moaning from inside the house, and grunting and groaning from outside but, to be fair to the old dears, they did depart, and the youngsters outside retreated to pore over the car.

'Thanks,' said Rufus to Mum, causing her to blush hysterically and giggle like a ten-year-old.

Before long Mum and Dad were chatting away to Rufus as if they'd known him all their lives. We sat in the kitchen to eat 'because it's more cosy', and Mum had drawn the blinds, just in case there were a few people still hanging around outside. 'Now it's really cosy!' she exclaimed as we sat in half-darkness while the sun shone gaily outside.

'More lamb?' she asked Rufus.

'No, I'm full. Thank you very much.'

'Not dieting are you?' she enquired. Mum doesn't think that men should be on diets. She thinks it's 'unmanly'.

'No, just very full now,' he said.

'Leave the boy alone,' Dad interjected, protectively. I loved the way Dad talked about Rufus; treating the multi-millionaire film icon as if he were a snotty-nosed teenager. He called him 'boy' constantly and talked about the financial instability of Rufus's 'line of work'.

'Must be tough for you,' he said, on more than one occasion. Happily Rufus had the good grace to nod and smile in the semi-darkness, and failed to mention that he earned enough to buy the country.

'Why don't we pull the blinds up, Jayne, there'll be no one there now,' said Dad, as Mum laid huge bowls of apple pie and custard down before us. 'It would be nice to enjoy the sunshine at the end of the day.'

'Good idea,' she said, pulling the cord. We all looked up, and there, in front of us, stood around 500 people, packed onto the lawns, peering right through the window and cheering madly at the rising blind as if at a rock concert.

'Rufus, Rufus, Rufus!' they chanted. 'We want Rufus.' Camera flashes exploded and people came running towards Mum's little kitchen from all directions.

'Jayne, let's not have the blind up after all,' said Dad, quickly and calmly. 'It's quite nice to eat without the sun bothering us.'

Elody sweeps into view at 4 pm – a whole hour late. (One thing I've noticed about Rufus's world already is that everyone is late . . . all the time. I don't understand why. Can't they just leave a little earlier and get places on time?) By the time she appears, I've worked myself into quite a panic about whether she'll like me or not. What if she doesn't? Will Rufus think less of me? Is this a test of my suitability as a girlfriend? I could fail it. Oh God, no.

I got myself into such a state worrying about the whole thing that I went down to talk to Julie in the kitchen. She's great Julie is, really down-to-earth and honest. I get the impression she's a good judge of character. She's roughly the same age as me and the sort of girl who has views on the world and is very happy, no, delighted, to share them with you!

She looked up from a pile of sea creatures when I walked in and grinned at me, while tearing their limbs off, cracking a claw and throwing it into a large pot. There were crabs, lobsters, prawns and some unidentifiable gruesome animals that look as if they'd kill you without a second's thought.

'Dangerous work,' I said.

'I'm hoping there's no such thing as an afterlife,' she laughed. 'Because I'm sure these poor bastards will come and find me and tear me limb from limb as revenge.'

'Talking of being torn limb from limb . . .' I said. 'I'm about to meet Elody Elloissie for the first time, and I hear she can be a bit of a nightmare.'

Julie's lip curled and she laid down the big, clumpy axe thing in her hand. 'Uuuummmm,' she said. 'How do I say this?'

'So she's a nightmare. I get it.'

Julie's twisted and contorted face at the mention of Elody's name told me everything I needed to know.

'Well, she's not easy,' Julie conceded. 'But she's been through a lot. I hear that if you get to know her, she's OK. I'd warn you to be careful though, love. I mean, I'm sure she's fine, but keep your wits about you.'

Elody slides out of her car and walks as if on water; there's no clumpiness or heavy footfall, just a gentle glide from the car as if she's on ice. She's dressed all in black and is painfully skinny. One interesting accessory is a water bottle, which she grips like a marathon runner as she floats effortlessly towards the house. Despite the water bottle though, she's clearly never run a step. You know how you can look at someone and just know that the most athletic thing they've ever done in their life is to open a bottle of wine? Well, I know that about her.

I don't like what she's wearing at all – a kind of black cape thing that flies out behind her. Underneath it, a corset-style top clings to her tiny frame; she's Batman with tit-tape. She has skin the colour of freshly fallen snow and tomato-red lips. In fact, no, not tomato – the lips are blood coloured. The whole bizarre costume screams 'transvestite vampire woman'. I guess it cost her half a million quid to look like that, so I'm not saying it's not fashionable or desirable or anything, it's just not, well ... pretty. Is it old-fashioned of me to say something like that? She looks like a vampire bat instead of a woman and, where I come from, that's not a good thing.

She kisses me on the cheek when we meet and I feel myself hoping she's not going to bite my neck.

'I think we're going to be the best of friends,' she says confidently, and with a surprising amount of warmth.

'I hope so,' I reply with a smile.

'Pretty face. Now go and get yourself dressed in your party gear and make yourself utterly fabulous and I'll see if I can help make you look even more gorgeous,' she says to me after looking me up and down with an unnecessary scowl on her face.

'I am dressed in my party gear,' I say, feeling about three inches tall. I thought my look screamed Marilyn Monroe (but without the suicidal tendencies obviously), but no, apparently not. It screams something different entirely. Something that Elody is struggling to come to terms with as she moves from one searingly expensively shod foot to the other.

'You're dressed?' she enquires. 'Dressed for the party? You can't be serious.'

Shit. 'Yes, I'm dressed for the party,' I say, trying to sound confident but feeling utterly deflated.

'OK,' says Elody quite kindly when she sees how offended I am. 'Look. There's no problem; my challenge today is to convince you that the glamorous clothes I have with me will be better suited to the party than the ones you have. Trust me, and don't look scared. I'm here to help. You'll look more lovely than ever by the time I've finished with you.'

'Oh thank you,' I say, and I feel myself cheer up instantly. Indeed there are times, as Elody talks, when I feel real warmth coming from her, despite the deathly appearance. She seems to genuinely want to help me to fit into this new lifestyle that I've come stumbling into.

'Now, let's have a look at you,' she says, standing back and letting those scary catlike eyes travel up and down my body. She's stroking her chin and I feel like a piece of meat being sized up by a butcher. 'Lovely décolletage,' she says. 'Good bone structure too.'

Then, there are times when she talks when I feel so stunned by her rudeness that I can barely stay upright.

'You obviously like eating chips.' She scowls.

Whaaat? I mean, really. Is there any need for that? The truth is that of course I like chips – who doesn't, for God's sake? But I'm not fat. I'm a size 12. Is that fat? According to Elody it is.

'I'm sorry. I don't mean to be rude,' she says, and I feel like saying, 'Well, lady, you just have been . . . whether meaning to be or not.' But I don't, of course, I just stand there feeling like the fattest person in the world.

'Everyone I deal with professionally is incredibly slim. You are more . . . um . . . generous in the flesh department. But – no worries. I'm a professional; I can handle this, and I can help you lose lots of weight if you want to . . . trust me – I have a very easy way of doing it.'

I look at her with raised eyebrows, eager to hear her weight loss tips, but she's moved on.

'Now then.' She takes one of my hands in hers and looks at my nails in amazement.

'Goodness gracious, was this for a joke?' she says, grimacing at the sight of the pale-orange colour on them.

'Don't you like this shade?' I thought I was on pretty firm ground with the pale-peach fingernails.

'Mmmm . . . beautiful colour on a fruit like an apricot,' she says. 'But, interestingly, absolutely horrible as a nail polish colour.'

OK, that'll be 'no' then!

I totally understand now when Rufus said that Elody's

bark is worse than her bite, and why Julie grimaced into the crab claws at the mention of her name. The woman has this quite breathtaking habit of seizing upon every opportunity to criticise without quite realising that she's doing it. As soon as she realises that she's caused offence, she backtracks by saying it's not a problem and she's here to help, but the offence has been done by then. I guess it's because of all she's been through. I accept that the woman is deeply injured, and I keep trying to remember what Rufus said – that Elody has been through a lot, and I need to cut her some slack – but it still doesn't make the abuse any easier to take.

Many of her criticisms arrive silently, like a knife in the ribs. Some of them come thundering towards me with all the subtlety of a herd of charging rhinoceroses.

'It must be odd to be so busty,' she says. 'I mean, don't you feel a bit cumbersome? Like a lactating cow?'

'No,' I say, alarmed at the suggestion. 'I've never felt cumbersome. In fact, not until this very minute.'

'Oh sorry,' says Elody, presumably sensing the resentment she's caused. 'No offence meant; I guess I was just thinking out loud, because I know I'd hate to have big lumps of lard stuck on the front of my chest. Now, what have we here?' She reaches over and pulls swirls of taffeta and sheets of silk from her bag; they ripple to the floor, a great wave of blues, greens and azures shimmering in the light. 'You'll look gorgeous when I've finished with you,' she says, scooping the dresses into her arms and leading off towards the bedroom. 'Just you wait and see.'

How does she know where the bedroom is?

It takes just ten minutes for Elody to convince me that

she really knows what she's doing when it comes to fashion styling, and that she genuinely wants to help me in any way she can. I'm like putty in her hands. She makes me feel gorgeous; she might be the best friend I ever had. In fact, by the time she's layered the chiffon dresses over one another, pulled the whole lot in with a chain loosely slung round my waist, and added earrings, I've quite forgotten my concern about how on earth she knew exactly where the bedroom was. The truth is that I look amazing! Sorry, I don't mean that to sound arrogant or anything, what I mean is that I look more like one of the girls you see in magazines than I've ever looked before. I look stylish; that's the right word. I look as if I understand clothes, as if I have a great apartment and a super job. I don't just look attractive, I look like I'm bursting with attitude and sophistication, something that I've never really grasped before.

For the first time this week I find myself actually looking forward to the party; looking forward to meeting the host of celebrities who will become my new friends.

'Happy?' asks Elody.

'Yes,' I say, beaming. This lady's not so bad after all; I reckon me and Elody could become quite matey. Give me a couple of nights with her and she'll be Malteser catching like a demon.

'I'm glad you're happy,' she says. 'You deserve to be. You seem nice. Now, don't worry about jewellery, we'll sort that out later. I think you need a great statement piece. Do you know what I mean? If you're going to wear a necklace, you should always make sure it says something exciting, like mine.' Around her neck is a platinum chain with two small diamond-covered stars on it. 'Stars are very much of the moment; everybody is reaching for the stars; everyone wants to be a star. Stars say something worth listening to. Jon was a star.' Then she stops and bursts into tears. 'It's from Jon,' she says. 'Jon bought it for me.'

I don't know what the hell to say or do. It's awful. I hardly know her and she's crying like I've never heard a woman cry in my life before: howling, shrieking and mumbling into her hands as she falls to the floor.

Holy fuck.

Chapter 5

Oh God, he is. I'm not just imagining it. Shit. He's playing footsie with me. Fuck, fuck, fuck. I pick up my spoon (probably completely the wrong one but, to be honest, cutlery etiquette is the last thing on my mind right now), and begin to tackle the seafood consommé in front of me. Jesus, he's doing it again. Fuck. I don't know what to do.

Rufus is at the opposite end of the long, long table; he smiles lovingly at me, and I wish more than anything that I could be sitting next to him. I had hardly any time to talk to him after his lunch. He sauntered home much later than I expected, wearing a large grin and followed by a rather large entourage of men in suits. They trailed in after him as if he were the Pied Piper, taking up residence in the sitting room where their deep voices carried through the house. Their debates ranged from issues like contracts and intellectual property rights to whether Rufus should be willing to do nudity.

'Ass double,' shouted a voice that I recognised as belonging to Rufus's rotund, cigar-smoking agent. 'Tell 'em Rufus doesn't do his own ass work. Not ever.'

'And we own your face,' the agent added. 'Make a note of that too. That's a given.'

It seemed inappropriate to interrupt when their high-level talks had strayed into areas as surreal as ownership of my boyfriend's face and discussions about his 'ass' so I retreated to the bedroom instead and pondered the issue of what you have to do in life to own someone's face. Do we not just all own our own faces, or am I being naïve?

If I'm honest, I had hoped that Rufus would sense that I wanted to spend some time with him before the party, and join me in the bedroom so we could chat while we got changed. What I was forgetting was that getting changed doesn't mean sticking on a dress while dancing around to Pink and drinking cider any more. It means having a vast army of experts descend on your body and dress it as if it were an abstract concept and not really part of you at all. Being in Rufus's world is almost like going back into the Victorian times when maids would rush in and attend to your every need. I get told off for so much as pushing my hair out of my eyes. 'Stop, stop, stop,' they say. 'Hairdresser, tend to the fringe please.'

So, for the party preparations, a host of people descended and swarmed towards me like a rather terrifying mob of angry wasps. They spoke to each other more than to me, talking about my body and the unique challenge it represented to them as if I weren't there at all. The truth is that my view wasn't relevant: they were the experts, they would do the job. I saw Rufus for about a second, when we passed on the huge landing area. My team and I were heading to the massive floor-to-ceiling mirror at the top of the staircase. That mirror still makes me giggle every time I walk past it because of that first night with Rufus when I became convinced that a woman just like me was standing there! While we were mirror-bound, Rufus and

David were going to his dressing room on the far side of the house.

'Hey, how did lunch go?' I asked. 'I haven't had time to talk to you properly.'

'It was excellent, sweetheart,' he said. 'Sorry we haven't had time for a chat but I'll tell you everything later. I'll be going to LA though – that much is definite. This is going to be an era-defining movie.'

There were murmurs of excitement from the women gathered around me clutching clothing, shoes and all manner of beauty implements, but I must admit that my heart fell. It wasn't the concept of him staring in an 'era-defining movie' that gave me the shivers, but the 'I'll be going to LA' bit. When? With whom? For how long? Sadly, there was no time for further debate as I was dragged off by a rather gay-looking hairdresser, who was clutching straightening irons and all manner of lotions and potions. 'Come on, sweetie, if we don't let the dressers do their thing, there'll be no time for hair and make-up.'

Rufus smiled and winked. The gay hairdresser giggled helplessly. Then Rufus and David, his loyal man servant, wandered off towards 'his' wing of the house.

Rufus is now smiling at me from his end of the table. He even blows me a kiss which cheers me up, but I still can't help thinking LA? When are you going to LA? I smile and blow a kiss back but I'm distracted beyond belief. It's not just the LA trip that's causing me anguish but the actions currently taking place beneath the table.

I mean – tell me – what the hell am I supposed to do about Lord James Simpkins, octogenarian and the single most important person in the world of British theatre, who is right at this minute rubbing his expensively shod foot up and down my exquisitely stockinged leg while his wife, Lady Simpkins, sits directly opposite her husband, chattering away to me in her unimaginably cut-glass voice, entirely unaware of all sub-table activity.

Lady Simpkins is an odd character. She hoots like an owl whenever something remotely funny happens. Actually, I take that back; she hoots like an owl – full stop. Random hoots escape from her pale, spongy face at irregular intervals regardless of what's being said or who's saying it. She has something of the woodland creature about her; she wiggles her mouth around like an inquisitive ferret, and extends her neck upwards like a stoat. Add into that the hooting and it's like spending an evening in the forest. Except that these are not small woodland creatures gathered on the seat next to me – Lady Helen Simpkins is a huge woman. She's not just seal plump, she's warthog fat. Not so much well-upholstered as over-stuffed. Her face looks like it's been moulded out of uncooked dough. Her eyes are small and beady in the middle of the mad shapeless face and her mouth is so thin and coated with badly applied brown lipstick, it looks as if a child has drawn it on with a chocolate finger.

The lady's thick, wiry hair is contained by vast quantities of hair lacquer and is fashioned into a style not unlike that sported by Princess Anne. I bet that hair hasn't moved for thirty years. When I look at her husband to see what he's making of it all, he rubs harder against my leg and is almost salivating with glee. Oh God.

'It was divine, wasn't it, Edward?' Lady Helen is saying to the distinguished-looking doctor sitting next to her.

I know that his name is Edward and that he and his wife, Isabella, sitting opposite him, are the foremost anti-ageing doctors in the western world. Apparently, if you spend enough time with these two, you just won't get old. They'll iron out wrinkles, remove bags and fill out crevices until it's impossible for you to look as if you've passed your fortieth birthday (referred to here as your thirty-tenth birthday). I look older than some of the guys round the table tonight, yet I must be a good twenty years younger.

Who'd have thought age would be such an abstract concept. You'd think you just got older and looked older, but no. It's clear that no one is quite what they seem, age wise, or indeed in any way. As if to remind me of this, my balding companion with the tufts of hair shooting out of his nose shifts his foot a little higher and is now rubbing with a fury verging on the painful against a spot somewhere just below my knee. I knock his foot away sharply and attempt to pull my legs round to the other side, but he's not a man who gives up easily, and soon the foot is back there, pushing against mine.

This is clearly one of the downsides of looking better than you've ever looked in your life before and, I have to confess, it was something I hadn't predicted. Not at any stage in the hour that Elody spent, working her magic on me earlier today, did I think, 'Better watch out – there'll be a randy pensioner at the party who'll take a real shine to you.'

Elody turned me from frumpy to fabulous by squeezing my wobbly bits (the bits that Rufus likes but that the skinny stylist can't stand) into 'shape wear' (these rather hideous, really tight, really big knickers in an unflattering pale flesh colour). She then draped and layered, pulled in, flared out and floated dresses over my newly squeezed-in form until I looked like a goddess of the sea.

'It's Cindy Crawford meets Jane Russell,' she squealed as a team of make-up artists appeared out of nowhere (I have a feeling she keeps them in that huge bag that she carries around with her). They painted gunk onto my face in quantities that would cover a wall in the average sized semi. My head weighed twice as much by the time they'd finished. Jewellery was added so that my ear lobes and neckline twinkled like stars in a midnight sky, and my beautifully polished toenails were slipped into the softest, most elegant and most searingly high shoes I've ever seen. I felt about nine feet tall when I stood up, and most unbalanced. 'These are not shoes to walk in,' said Elody with a straight face, when I complained that getting up and walking across the room without falling over would be a feat of quite monumental proportions.

The hairdressers then took over and my hair was coiffed and teased and sprayed and thickened until I looked like I had twice as much of it. It had never looked so glossy and shiny.

Now I'm sitting here and though there's no question that I've never looked more like the girlfriend of an international film star in my life before, on the inside I'm struggling. They're having debates about the cultural role of the media in modern Britain, and assessing the true impact of Shakespeare not just on the theatre but on mankind's very sense of himself (what does that mean?) and I'm feeling like a total idiot.

'It could be argued,' says Isabella boldly, 'that Shakespeare's contribution to the world of literature has had the impact of redefining our very understanding of ourselves as conscious beings.'

Yep, indeed it could, I think to myself, wishing that Sophie and Mandy were here. It's not that I'm stupid – I did really well at school – it's just that this sort of talk makes me want to run screaming from the room shouting, 'Help, help.' Would that be appropriate behaviour? I'm thinking probably not, so I smile and nod and think, Shakespeare? Shakespeare? Now which one was he?

'His plays are certainly the only ones ever written which don't date,' says Rufus, and I feel a rush of pride that he knows which one Shakespeare is. 'You feel that as an actor.'

Oh yeah, watch him go. My money's on Rufus.

'What about Oscar Wilde?' asks Jan James, a small, slim and rather mumsy-looking woman at the end of the table. She's married to Rock James, the huge rock star, but he's not here. He's on some world tour and, if the papers are right (and I happen to know now that they're not always right, so that's why I question it!), he's sleeping with half the girls in the world on the way round. The papers have been incredibly cruel, printing pictures of the young girls he's supposed to have bedded alongside pictures of Jan. She looks two decades and two kids older ... because she is. But what I'm discovering tonight is that she's really sweet. She keeps looking over and mouthing, 'Are you OK?' to me and smiling warmly. Her comment about Oscar Wilde doesn't go down too well though.

'Absurd,' squeals Lord Simpkins, who sounds quite beside himself with frustration – and for a minute I think that his fury may result in an end to the continual stroking up and down my leg. But, no. He's one of the few men I know who can do two things at once.

I push his foot off again, this time quite violently, and though it thumps to the floor, causing Her Ladyship to look up sharply, it still doesn't deter him. It's almost as if he's relishing the sport all the more for my participation in it.

'Why, Oscar Wilde was dated before it even hit the stage. The man and his work can only be defined within the context of the period in which he lived. It's nonsense to understand his work in any other way. Shakespeare deals with much broader, more human issues. Wilde's overrated if you ask me.'

'Agreed, my dear. Agreed,' hoots Lady Simpkins and the couple smile warmly at one another before she turns her attentions back to the rather dashing-looking Edward and His Lordship grabs my knee with the sort of strength that wouldn't disgrace an arm-wrestler.

The debate rages across the table. It turns out that Oscar Wilde is overrated; is underrated; is sometimes overrated; can be overrated, depending on your point of view. I feel like saying, 'Isn't that the point? Isn't the point that everyone has a view and no one's views are wrong because it's art, not science,' but I know that'll be wrong, so I shut up and concentrate on Edward. Now, he's an interesting man because he's fabulously handsome – a combination of Barbie's boyfriend (Ken) and the Kennedys. He's so perfect he looks like he's made of plastic, and I have to say that I fear for him greatly as he bends over a little, moving perilously close to a candle. Will he melt into a small puddle of plastic, Botox and collagen before our eyes?

He has hair that's so thick and glossy it looks almost black against his tanned skin. His eyes are the colour of hazelnuts with an intensity that borders on lunacy. His suit is immaculate, and he wears cufflinks and shoes that are so shiny, someone must have been polishing them for days. There's the perfectly ironed shirt and the thick and well-knotted tie. The man looks as if he's been cut out of a magazine. Really, he's an incredibly handsome man but – this is the thing – desperately unsexy. He's too doll-like, too perfect to be considered a handsome man. I mean, there's nothing manly about him at all. I can imagine him hanging up his shirt and making you shower before he'd touch you. I bet he's got his initials written on every towel, handmade shirt and expensive tie he owns. There's just something mind-numbingly asexual about him even though he's model good-looking and perfect in every way. Isn't that interesting? His good looks are very different from Rufus's which are far more rugged, more masculine and sooooo much more appealing. I look up at Rufus as I compare them and see him take a large gulp of wine.

'This is the point though, isn't it? The very reason that we're here and why art matters so much to us is that it provokes these differences in opinion. We all have different views – this is art, not science.'

Fuck, I should have said that.

Edward's wife Isabella applauds him (she's the one who fell out with Elody – I hope you're keeping up here). She is as good-looking as her husband, but very, very feminine and somehow sexy at the same time. She radiates beauty and I keep feeling myself drawn to look at her. No wonder she winds Elody up so much! She's dressed classically, with none of the flair of Elody, but she looks divine. Her skin is plump and fresh (as well it might be given the various solutions that have undoubtedly been injected into it) and her hair runs down her back in glorious, luscious golden waves. She wears a simple cream shirt and subtle gold jewellery and she reminds me of Grace Kelly. I have to stop myself staring. She must be mid-forties but there's something so luminous and divine about her; she's very thin (I'm finding this is a common theme) and her tiny birdlike frame makes her appear slightly helpless but at the same time so cool and in control. I find myself wishing she wasn't with the rather stiff and pompous-looking Edward, but had someone warm and kind.

Lord Simpkins's foot is jiggling around up by my knee now. I don't know what to do; every time I knock his foot out of my lap, and look at him in a 'stop right now' sort of fashion, he dribbles at me in a rather revolting way and I'm forced to look away again . . . quickly.

'Divine,' he mutters through a mouthful of pheasant jelly. (Yes, you read that right – pheasant jelly – and it's as unpleasant as it sounds. How could it be otherwise? Pheasant and jelly – two words which have no right to be side by side in the same sentence. How I'm yearning for a KFC in front of the telly with the girls right now.) His foot is on my knee; if nothing else, you have to admire the man's flexibility. Once again, I knock it off, and once again he leers at me. Any minute now I'm going to stab him in the ankle. I'll jab straight through his ludicrously expensive woollen socks with my fork.

'Kelly, dear, do tell us how you met our lovely Rufus. Was it through the theatre?' says Lady Simpkins.

'It was; I work there,' I say, quite pleased to be able to talk about work. I do know about theatre administration even though I know nothing about Shakespeare's contribution to man's understanding of his very consciousness.

'Really. I don't recognise you. What are you in?' she asks.

'In the main office,' I say. 'Right by the windows that look out onto Richmond Green.'

'Sorry?'

'That's the office I'm in, the main one.'

'So you're not in a play?'

'Oh no, no, sorry. I thought you asked which ... it doesn't matter.'

'What do you do, Kelly?' asks Isabella kindly. I knew I'd like her.

'I'm head of theatre administration,' I say.

'Oh my,' says Lady Simpkins with a loud hoot and a rather absurd chortle, before she turns to shout over to her daughter Olivia, sitting at the far end, next to Rufus. Her husband's foot is practically in my lap. What then? Is he going to mount me, or have I just got all this wrong and he's just looking for a footstool?

I pull my chair back a little so that his leg tumbles off my lap and goes crashing to the ground rather noisily. I'd normally scream at someone if they treated me like this and threaten to kill them if they didn't remove their foot immediately, but how can I when the guy is the single most important person in the world of theatre and someone my boyfriend admires greatly? His Lordship looks over at his daughter, the Honourable Olivia Simpkins, the aspiring model and actress. ('Aspiring', in this context, means 'failed'. You're never an aspiring model because models start at the age of about three, so you're either a model, or you aren't a model. She isn't.) I've completely taken against her for reasons I can't fully explain. There's something about her that annoys me greatly. She has an hauteur to her, you know; a sense of superiority that is wholly undeserved. She wears her father's title like a war medal. The trouble is, she's never been a soldier and never committed acts of stunning bravery, she just acts like she has.

Now I appreciate that this is quite a conclusion to come to when the woman's sitting on the opposite end of the table, and hasn't spoken a word to me, but I just know. You do sometimes. She's opposite Elody, next to my boyfriend, and she's a vision of Sloaney loveliness – resplendent in the family pearls and taffeta. A vision of wealthy, youthful beauty. She has charm, class and sophistication. She probably knows exactly what knife and fork to use and when to stop drinking. Ahhhhhh . . . I hate this. I've got a mad rampant lord on one side of me, and a big, crazy lady with mad wiry hair on the other. I'm just not used to this sort of company. The food has finished but we're all still sitting there. I'm not sure what to say to anyone. I find myself longing for the life I've left behind. I'm soooo glad I'm going back to work next week, and can chat to my mates, do everything to avoid filing and practise catching Maltesers in my mouth; they'd better not have been practising while I've been away.

'Kelly, can I borrow you for a moment?' Elody taps me gently on the shoulder.

'Sure,' I say, immensely relieved to be given an escape from the conversation I'm not having. 'Excuse me.'

I untangle my legs from the lord's (easier said than done; he's quite strong for a bony old man) and stumble a little as I follow Elody towards the main doors; she reaches out a hand to help me. 'Thanks,' I mutter, as two smartly dressed porters I've never met before swing the door open for us to pass through. I tell you, this never happens at Suga Daddys. You have to open all the doors yourself there. In the corridor there's a cluster of women clutching clipboards and talking intensely. As we approach, they fall silent and nod respectfully as I pass. This is so weird. Such an odd lifestyle when you have a couple of mates over for dinner and suddenly your house, your home, is full of strangers.

'You OK?' asks Elody, when we're out of earshot.

'Sure,' I say.

'You didn't seem very comfortable in there; thought I'd better come and rescue you.'

'Thanks,' I say, amazed at her perceptiveness. 'To be honest, I was struggling a bit.' Once I've made that early confession of weakness, all my feelings come tumbling out in one, big wave of emotion. I feel the tears start to spring from my eyes as I tell her how I feel so out of my depth and how Lord bloody James keeps rubbing his foot up and down my leg.

'Come here,' says Elody, wrapping her bony arms around me. 'Now, stop worrying. Lord Simpkins is a complete shit. This is not your fault. You're not doing anything wrong; you just need to learn the rules of the game. These people may seem incredibly complex but the truth is that they're simple, deluded egomaniacs. All of them. You're worth twenty of that ageing Lothario. You just need to smarten up and embrace this lifestyle of Rufus's if you want him to fall in love with you, and that's going to mean getting tough, girl.'

'He's already in love with me, there's no question of that,' I say.

Elody looks at me as if I'm stark, staring mad.

'He is,' I say rather pathetically. 'He is in love with me.'

'Yep, that's why he's going to Los Angeles without you, but by the time I've finished with you, Rufus will be begging you to marry him, and certainly begging you to go on every foreign trip with him. OK. Is that a deal?'

'It is,' I say, not quite sure what deal I've agreed to, but figuring that any help I can get is worth taking at this juncture given that I'm struggling to get through dinner, let alone the rest of my life.

'OK. When we go back in there, you take my seat and I'll take yours. That way, you'll be out of the clutches of Lord Try-it-on, and you'll be able to keep an eye on Olivia and make sure she doesn't flirt with Rufus too much.'

'Right,' I say. 'Thanks. But, what do you mean – flirt with Rufus?'

'Oh you know what Rufus is like,' she says. 'He's used to having women throw themselves at him. He's used to taking a different woman home every night. He can forget he's got a girlfriend if you're out of sight. Might be better if you're next to him.'

'A different woman every night? What are you talking

about?' That's not Rufus at all. He doesn't have different women every night.'

'Sweetheart, he's a man; a rich man; a rich, famous and incredibly beautiful man. He could have five hundred different women every hour if he wanted to.'

'I know he could,' I try. I can feel my voice rising and ringing with an unhealthy mixture of anger, frustration and confusion. 'All I'm saying is that even though he could, he doesn't.'

'Your devotion is truly touching,' says Elody. 'I think you are extremely kind and patient with him, especially given the history with those two.'

'History? I didn't know ... What history? Are you saying that Olivia likes him, or something?'

'Likes him?' says Elody, her eyes so wide they look as if they're about to burst out of her face. 'Likes him? She's totally obsessed with him. How many times has she slept with him? Christ they're at it all the time those two. Lord Simpkins introduced them in the hope of Rufus helping Olivia to become an actress. He thought that it would assist her modelling career too, if she was seen strutting around the place with Rufus. The two of them just fell into bed together and pretty much that's their history.'

'I find it so hard to believe,' I say. Rufus and I have talked about everything over the months we've been courting. There's never been so much as a mention of the Right Honourable Bimbo over there. He said he's had one girlfriend since he came to England – a girl called Emma, who was a violinist. They were only together for a few weeks. He's never mentioned Olivia. Even in passing.

'Come on, Kelly. There's nothing to worry about.

All you've got to do is make sure you're around him at all times when there are attractive women like Olivia hovering.'

I can't believe this. I never had Rufus down as a womaniser.

'I don't think he's like that, Elody,' I say. 'I don't think he's the sort of man to go off with a whole load of women. I just don't think he's made like that.'

'Trust me, all men are made like that, and men like Rufus who have women hurling themselves at them every day are made more like it than most. You must keep your eyes on him all the time. *All* the time.'

'I can't keep my eyes on him all the time. It's impossible.'

'Then you'll lose him.'

'But what am I going to do when he goes to LA?'

'For the James Bond film?'

'I don't know; he didn't say which film. Something about a press trip.'

'Yeah, that's right. They're promoting *Frozen Lives*, then he has meetings for the new James Bond.'

How does she know so much more about what my boyfriend's up to than I do?

'Look, if you want my advice, get private detectives lined up in LA before he goes,' she insists. 'Go through his case and his pockets, obviously, arrange for bugs to be put in the hotel room and have him followed everywhere. It's the only way. Cindy Kearney's in that film, you know.'

'Is she? Excellent. I think she's great.'

'Yes, and she's also a complete maneater. She used to go out with Rufus, you know. She once joked that she and

Rufus couldn't be in the same room without ending up in bed together. You need to check whether Rufus is doing the Bond movie and check whether Cindy Kearney's definitely in it. If the answer to both questions is "yes", you're fucked . . . to put it mildly. Nice necklace by the way.'

'Oh thanks, it's from Rufus,' I say.

'No, no, no, no, no,' she squeals immediately, leaning over my shoulders and unfastening it.

'I don't want to take it off,' I implore.

'Sweetheart, you're going to have to listen to me. Wearing his necklace is like wearing his ring, with none of the security that goes with ring-wearing. It needs to come off. Christ, you have so much to learn. Thank God you stumbled upon me.'

'But Rufus will be upset if I take it off.'

'Making Rufus upset is good. Don't be a doormat. Anyway, he'll be more upset if you don't look the part and, frankly, the necklace doesn't go with the dress at all. He'll think you don't know how to dress. You don't want that, do you? Not on top of all the other problems you're facing.'

'No,' I say, unconvinced, as she removes the necklace and drops it into my bag. How's everything suddenly gone pear-shaped? This whole dinner party has been a fiasco. I'm being molested by an ancient lord while Rufus sits at the other end of the table making eyes at Olivia and trying to get her into bed, in advance of flying to the other side of the world to screw his ex-girlfriend. Shit. I thought me and Rufus were doing really well.

'Speeches. Three minutes, ladies.' One of the businesslike women with clipboards appears at the bathroom door.

'Speeches? There are only a handful of people here. Why the need for speeches? Anyone would think he was Barack Obama.'

'You go and take my seat. I'll go and sit next to Lord Lusty,' says Elody with a smile, and I feel myself warm to her all over again. It's such a relief to have someone in my corner; someone looking out for me in this world of utter bafflement and confusion.

'Thank you.'

Elody and I walk slowly back into the main ballroom and the door is, once again, swung wide open for us.

'Don't eat pudding,' she whispers as she turns to take her seat. 'You need to lose a stone if you're going to compete with all the young glamour pusses. And keep an eye on Rufus. Watch what he's doing with his hands.'

Fuck.

I slip quietly into the seat next to my boyfriend at the far end of the table, still reeling from Elody's words but hoping that the amazement isn't evident on my face. I need to exude elegance from every pore, not to return to the table with the demeanour of a startled rabbit. I've checked the bottoms of my shoes for stray tendrils of toilet paper and I'm sure that my floaty, aqua designer gown isn't tucked into the back of my corset-style lingerie so I know the basics are OK.

I smile at Rufus as warmly as I can, and see the look of confusion in his eyes. 'Why are you not over there, talking to Lord Simpkins?' he asks. 'Is something the matter?'

'No. Elody wanted to sit next to him,' I say. I can't exactly tell him the truth, can I?

'No, Elody wanted to stay here,' he says. 'But she said you kept signalling over to ask whether you could change seats. I really think you should have stayed over there. James will think he's upset you. Where's your necklace?'

Before I can answer or explain things any more fully, I'm cut off by the sound of a gavel banging impatiently. I look over at Rufus, hoping to catch his eye and to mouth some explanation but he's too absorbed in talking to Olivia. She seems unnecessarily close to him. Why didn't I notice this before? Her nose is practically touching his nose. It's ridiculous. Why's he doing this? Why's he openly flirting with her in front of everyone when we all know that he's slept with her about fifty times before?

I feel like screaming. Shit. Now Rufus thinks I'm an idiot, and on Wednesday he's flying to LA with all these glamorous, beautiful people and I'm stuck here and I can't go out because the press write about me, and ahhh . . . I can feel tears pricking at the backs of my eyes.

'My lords, ladies and gentlemen,' says a tall, crooked man sporting immaculate white gloves. If we were playing Cluedo, he'd be the one that did it. Do you know the look I mean? He was always either going to be a butler, an elderly vicar or an actor in a ghost film. He looks like the sort of guy who's never been young, with shifty, beady eyes and the deepest, most resonant voice I've ever heard. 'May I give you your host, Mr Rufus George.' His voice is deeper than you'd imagine it would be for such a frail man. It reminds me of Barry White.

Rufus smiles, radiating that charm and dignity that he wears so lightly for most of the time but somehow springs from him on these formal occasions, making him irresistible to the eye, impossible not to stare at. I notice that Olivia feels the same way; she's looking up at him with those saucer-like blue eyes, her head tilted to one side. I try desperately to catch her eye but it's no use.

Rufus holds back the tails of his jacket as he rises to his feet and scans the room to make sure everyone's looking at him. He thanks everyone for coming in that way of his that makes you feel like he's talking straight to you, and that everyone else in the room has melted away. 'Thank *you* for coming,' he says. I find myself drifting along on the sound of his voice.

'It's been a most incredible few months for me,' he is saying. 'Because I have met the woman of my dreams; a girl whose very presence makes the world a better place. I'm not given to making grand, romantic statements, as you all know, but that was before Kelly.'

Blimey. How weird is this? He seems to like me after all. It's normally a struggle to get boyfriends to hold my hand in public, let alone sit and watch as they announce in such elegant style, in front of their friends, that they really like me.

'Sweetheart, I love you more than I've ever loved anyone. You mean the world to me. I can't begin to explain to you how much better my life has become since you came galloping into it, knocking everything sideways, making everything better. I love you. Thank you for making me so happy.'

Everyone cheers and claps and smiles lovingly at me. Me? I clap, too, smiling through the confusion, letting the delight of his words wash over me and surround me, protecting me from the fear I felt just a few minutes previously. He loves me; that's all that matters. Elody must be wrong; he's not going to go off with anyone else. Suddenly, the world looks bright again and people are smiling again.

'I love you too,' I mouth over to Rufus, but I can't catch his eye, and the lipstick words float in the air between us, eventually fluttering down and landing somewhere on the table, before reaching him.

Olivia comes over and kisses me on the cheek, introducing herself. 'That was nice, wasn't it?' she says, looking over at Rufus.

I look at her and smile. 'It was wonderful.'

'He's a very good actor, isn't he?'

Chapter 6

Rufus is quiet. He's been quiet since the party last night and, because of the way I'm made, I assume it is I who has upset him. He says not. He hugged me close and made love to me last night when I asked if everything was OK. We even rang his friend Deevers in New York so I could say 'hi' to him in my 'delicious' English accent (what is it with these Yanks and their obsession with the way we speak?). This morning, though, he just climbed out of bed and went to his study which is just off the bedroom. He's been in there ever since - flicking through pages and pages of notes. It's odd; I don't know what to do, and the girls are no bloody help to me. Mandy, Sophie and I have been involved in non-stop 'what's-going-on-in-his-head' texting since around 7 am. They say they aren't experts on the odd behaviours of millionaire, famous film stars and they can't leaf back through their mental catalogue of past problems with men and find one entitled: 'He buys me fabulous jewellery and is wonderful all the time. He gives the most glorious speech about me but now suddenly doesn't seem, deep down, to really care.'

'Are you sure this is not just because of what that woman Elody said?' asks Sophie. 'I mean, perhaps she's trying to put doubts into your mind.'

'Na,' I reply straight away. 'Elody's cool. She's trying to help. I just need to toughen up and stop being so gauche.'

'Gauche? What the fuck is gauche?' asks Sophie.

I decide to wander nonchalantly into Rufus's office in my rather revealing nightdress, unbuttoned at the front. If in doubt resorting to a man's primal urges is usually the best way forward.

'Hi,' he says, barely looking up.

'Hi.' I'm standing here with my breasts practically sticking out of this nightdress, I'm pouting, my hair is falling over my shoulders and the hemline barely covers my modesty. I need more than 'Hi'.

'Is everything all right?' I ask.

He looks up, sees me properly and comes over to me. 'God, you're gorgeous,' he says, slipping his hands into the front of the nightdress and reaching for my breasts. At last – a proper reaction.

It takes him about two minutes to get my nightdress off, as he backs me into the bedroom and onto the bed, grappling with his own clothes as he does so, his hands shaking with anticipation. It's quick, forceful and passionate sex; not like the love-making we usually do; nice though.

I lie in his arms afterwards, and know that I have to say something, or I'll regret it all day. 'I'm sorry about last night,' I mutter, my voice ringing with the fear I'm feeling inside. 'Elody thought it would be better if we swapped places. I didn't realise it would be a problem.'

'Did she?' he asks, looking at me quizzically. 'I thought you wanted to move to be near to me.'

'Well of course I wanted to move to be near you, but I . . .' How can I tell him that the fucking lord was being a sex pest so Elody offered to swap? 'Anyway, sorry if you didn't think it was the right thing to do.'

'Don't worry,' he says, in a way that makes me worry all the more, then he slides out of the sheets and wanders off towards the shower. He's not doing anything out of the ordinary; nothing that he wouldn't do any day of the week, but I find myself reading things into his every move after all I know from talking to Elody. I'm aware that it's my own insecurities screaming in my ears, but it's as if I can hear all these little voices saying, 'He doesn't like you any more ... you've cocked up ... it's all over.' I reach out for my phone; I need more reassurance from the girls. On the phone there are three texts, all from Elody.

'Hi, Kelly; hope you're OK. Just wanted to check you were feeling OK after last night. Lord Simpkins is a shit. Don't worry – he does that to everyone. I'll help you sort these weird people out!!'

Then, 'Hi, do you fancy coffee later? Call me if you do.'

Finally, 'Where are you? Text me back or I'm coming in there to check you're OK.'

Quite nice texts really.

'Would love to have a chat later. Did I upset people by changing seats last night? I hope not. Rufus seems a bit off with me.'

By return, she replies: 'You did NOTHING wrong. Lord Simpkins is an arse and you had to move out of the way. Please don't worry. Rufus is probably nervous about going off to LA on the promo tour. Trust me – everything will be fine.'

I'd kind of pushed the thought of Rufus going off to LA out of my mind. He hasn't mentioned it today.

'You know they were talking about that film last night

– the James Bond movie?' I ask Rufus once he's out of the shower.

'Yep,' he says, rubbing the towel vigorously over his hair.

'When do you have to go to LA for that?'

'On Wednesday I think. I'll be promoting *Frozen Lives* at the same time so will be gone for a couple of weeks. I think it's Wednesday; I'm not sure. It might be worth you checking with Christine or ask Henry; she gives him an itinerary of when he's driving me.'

Why doesn't Christine just give Rufus an itinerary? This is a bloody odd world he lives in, when everything's been out-sourced, including day-to-day information and basic knowledge. Rufus really has no idea when he's going to LA or, indeed, what he's doing later in the day.

Christine, I should explain, is his trusty PA who scares the living daylights out of me. She's the only member of staff whom I haven't managed to form a friendly professional relationship with. I feel like she's looking down at me all the time. She's so bloody efficient and organised, I feel quite chaotic in her wake, as she strides through the house in that 'I know everything, the world is a more organised place for my involvement in it' way. She checks the pictures are hanging straight and that all the books are dusted and facing out, the right way up, in alphabetical order. If they're not, she screeches through the house for one of the cleaners. She told me when I first met her that she thinks her role in life is that every time she walks through the door, the room she's leaving should be tidier and more organised for her having been in it. I live in the fruits of those labours, with everything about me immaculate. It did make me laugh when she said that, though, because I'm completely the opposite. When I walk into a room, any room, I can guarantee it'll be in more of a mess when I leave than when I went into it. Sometimes when I leave for work in the morning, I leave such a mess behind me that the girls text me to ask whether I had a party of monkeys over for breakfast. I don't know how I do it. It seems to me that I walk into a room, sit down, have a cup of tea and walk out again, yet there's bloody carnage left behind.

'Can you ask Christine for me?' I say. I really don't want to have to call Miss Efficient and ask her, and, although Henry is lovely, it does seem bizarre to go outside and find the driver and ask him what your boyfriend, who sleeps next to you every night, is doing.

'Sure,' says Rufus dismissively, and once again I feel as if I've upset him.

It turns out that Rufus needs to fly to LA on Wednesday, leaving Heathrow at 10 pm.

'Will you be travelling alone?' I ask, because I need to know about this bloody Olivia. I have to know whether she's going with him.

'I don't get to travel anywhere on my own, sweetheart,' he says vaguely. 'There's an entourage accompanying me when I go to the toilet on these film trips.'

'Oh.' And that's it. I try several times to get him to run through who'll be there but it's impossible; he's locked in his study, reading and rereading a script, pacing round his room.

'Your name's Bond, James Bond,' I say, on one of the rare occasions when he emerges to get a glass of water, but he's not amused. He just smiles at me indulgently and asks me why I don't go and have a chat to Christine (because Christine is the world's most boring person, and she looks at me as if I'm a pointless little girl who's simply in everyone's way – that's why I don't have a chat to Christine). To be honest, I'm looking forward to getting back to work tomorrow. I just can't wait to see the girls and for things to feel normal again, and for me to feel as if I have some sort of role in life other than being the famous guy's girlfriend. Get me – I'm thinking roll on Monday morning so I can go to work – now that is definitely a first.

For now though, I'll head downstairs and chat to Julie and Pamela; they're always a good laugh.

Chapter 7

EXCLUSIVE: FILM STAR'S NEW GIRLFRIEND IN SHOCKING FOOTSIE SCANDAL WITH LORD SIMPKINS
By Katie Joseph
Daily Post Showbiz Correspondent

Kelly Monsoon, the girl who has stolen the heart of Rufus George, was involved in a huge fight with her new lover on Saturday night, as the world's leading film star found the beautiful brunette playing footsie with theatre impresario Lord James Simpkins.

Guests at George's multi-million pound mansion were shocked as Kelly, who used to live with two girls and is rumoured to have been a lesbian in her past, had to be MOVED away from the ageing theatre owner, and TAKEN to the other side of the table where she continued to eat in silence, under the watchful eye of her handsome boyfriend.

'Rufus was furious,' said a source close to the couple. 'I mean FURIOUS. He felt let down, angry and made a fool of. I don't know whether their relationship will ever be the same again.'

There are fears that Hollywood's most strident bachelor will be splitting from his latest love interest following the incident, which comes just a week after she moved in with him. It certainly does not look good for the couple. George is off to LA on Wednesday to meet the cast and writers of the new James Bond film. It is thought that the handsome, dark-haired actor is destined to be the latest 007, following the surprise retirement of Daniel Craig last year. Meanwhile his new love will be twiddling her thumbs in his mansion, hoping that George is not spending too much time with Cindy Kearney, the slim, blonde former Miss America, who is rumoured to be starring alongside him. Watch this space for more gossip as we bring you the inside track on Hollywood's most unlikely couple. At least Kelly can call on Lord Simpkins if she gets lonely when her boyfriend's away.

Do you know Kelly Monsoon? If you do, call the Showbiz desk now on 020 7765 0064, or email showbiz@daily-post.com. We will pay for information and your identity can be kept secret.

It's Rufus's turn to be angered by the now regular missive from Katie on the *Daily Post*. 'It's one thing making insinuations and getting things wrong, but this is a damn lie,' he shouts, clutching the offending article between his large fingers and pacing across the carpet. 'They're trying to make me look ridiculous.'

'I know!' I say. 'I was never a lesbian . . . not even a bit, not for a night, not ever. Why does she think I'm a lesbian? A few days ago I was going like a train with Greg the barman, now I'm a lesbian. I wish they'd make their minds up.'

'It's the footsie allegation I'm worried about,' he says pompously. 'Lord Simpkins is a very important man.'

'I know,' I say. 'He was being a bit inappropriate though. You know, he kept kind of rubbing his foot against my leg.'

'He what?' says Rufus, looking extremely cross. 'Why didn't you tell me?'

'Because we were in the middle of dinner and I was worried. I just kept pushing his leg off. I moved seats in the end because he wouldn't stop it.'

'So he did it more than once?'

'He did it all bloody evening.'

'Shit, Kell. I wish you'd told me instead of chatting to your mates about it. You must realise that everything you say will at some stage find its way into the papers. *Everything*. Understood?'

The implication is clear; he thinks I told my mates and they told the newspapers. As if Mandy and Sophie have a direct hotline to Fleet Street's leading showbiz reporters. It's bloody ridiculous.

'There's no way that Mandy or Sophie would talk to journalists,' I say. 'No way at all.'

But it seems that no one in the room is listening. Instead, Christine is summoned to hear the briefing on Footsie-gate, and lawyers are called. I go back to my room and lie on the bed. I don't know what to say or do. It's 7 am, and I'm barely awake. Rufus has never looked more furious. It does cross my mind, fleetingly, that he looked nowhere near this angry when they accused me of having a boob job yet, to my mind, that was a much more serious allegation than that I was playing footsie with someone, and actually the current accusation's true whereas the boob job thing is a whole pack of lies.

I hear male voices downstairs, and realise that the requested collection of London's finest lawyers has arrived. They settle down to work out how they are going to clear the precious name of Rufus George.

I decide to get ready for work; at least I've got loads of new clothes to wear. Elody, bless her, gave me lots of little suits and skirts and some fabulous tops that really suit my colouring. I'm just slipping into a fabulous silk kimono-style top when the inevitable call comes. 'Kelly, could Rufus see you in the drawing room,' says Christine. 'It's rather urgent, so do hurry.'

I trudge through the house and knock gently. It may be the house I'm living in but, not for the first time, it doesn't feel like my home. I always imagined that I would love a life in which staff tended to your every move, but I'm finding it really difficult to relax properly when the house is always jammed full of people. It's like I can never be myself in the house, or out of the house because the press are waiting to follow me – in short, being famous is about not being able to be yourself at all.

I have clearly broken some unwritten, unarticulated golden rule by being in the newspaper, even though there doesn't seem to be anything I could have done to prevent it happening. They write about me whatever I do.

'How has this happened?' asks a lawyer with very little hair. I feel quite sorry for him, as he stands next to Rufus. The lawyer's thin strands of ageing hair look all the more limp and hopeless for their proximity to my boyfriend's healthy, thick, dark-brown mop.

'I don't know,' I reply with absolute honesty.

'Which of your friends know that Lord Simpkins was at the party?' asks the portly lawyer.

'Well, my two closest friends – Mandy and Sophie – but you know them, Rufus – they wouldn't have spoken to journalists. No way.'

As I'm being quizzed about something I have no understanding of, and no power to control, Christine pops her head round the door. 'It's Lady Simpkins on the phone,' she says.

'That's all we need,' says Rufus, looking at me like it's my fault that some mad bint with a lecherous husband has decided to call.

I just don't know how this happened. I did nothing wrong and now I appear to have caused a major international scandal, embarrassed my boyfriend and disgraced the film company he's about to link up with. Not bad for a morning's work.

'How did they even know that Lord Simpkins was there?' asks a fat lawyer in a suit that fitted him several pies ago.

'I told them,' I say. 'They're my friends. I tell them everything.'

'Mmm,' comes the reply. 'Without wishing to lecture, Kelly, it may pay you to be more discerning in future. Maybe keep the details of dinner parties you attend with Rufus within his circle. People outside the circle will have a tendency to gossip.'

My friends, who I *know* would not say a word to the press, are being maligned at every turn, and I'm just feeling like the most foolish person on the planet.

'I have to go to work,' I say. I'm finding myself drawn

to that office like a magnet; something I never expected in a million years. Normally the place drives me nuts because the management don't trust us to do anything of significance, so we end up feeling like we're hopeless and never going to progress. Take the proof-reading of the programmes and marketing material for the theatre. Me, Katy and Jenny are more than capable of doing that. In fact, once the programme's been proof-read, we normally spot mistakes in there and get them changed, but Sebastian won't allow any of us to actually do that job. It's driven the three of us mad, but right now none of that matters. I find myself longing to go back to work because it's one of the few things that feel real and part of my life rather than being an extension of his.

This must be how women who have babies feel . . . yes, they love the baby, yes, being a mother is great and I'm sure being a wife has its good points, but you must get to the stage where you long to be yourself, and to return to the world you inhabited before you came to be defined by your relationship to everyone else. I love being Rufus's girlfriend, but right now I'm looking forward to being Kelly Monsoon.

'Henry will drop you,' says Rufus, addressing Christine.

'No can do,' she replies, looking down at a set of notes that have been scribbled all over. You'd think she was preparing the country to go to war and managing the expectations of a nation. I feel like screaming, 'You're managing a diary, lady, not a military campaign.'

'Where's Henry?' asks Rufus, and Christine rummages through her notes.

'Driving Elody.'

'What?'

'Elody called and said that Kelly said it would be fine for her to have Henry for the day.'

'No, I didn't—' I try to say, but I'm cut off by an eager Christine who insists that's what Elody said.

'Well, never mind about that. Who can drive Kelly?'

It turns out that David is the only man up to the task. He's Rufus's male housekeeper. Actually, he's a butler, but that sounds so poncey that I can't bring myself to say it. He does drive sometimes though. He's driven me in the past and he's the slowest driver in the universe.

Christine scuttles from the room and returns followed at some distance by David. He comes staggering into the room like he's on the wrong side of about eighteen glasses of the finest port, like a character straight out of Acorn Antiques – you know, that comedy sketch show in which they stop and start and the furniture collapses on them and no one says their lines on time.

He bows gracefully and asks me whether he can take my bags. Since my bag's really heavy because it's stuffed full of things I want to show the girls and he's about 4000 years old, I think it might be better if I do the carrying myself. 'I'm fine,' I say and off we go towards his car.

Now, I'm the sort of girl who likes the good things in life. I mean, I'm down to earth and all that, but I do like to be treated properly. However this is another world. Being driven to Richmond Theatre in a huge, shiny Bentley by an aged man in a peak cap must rank as one of the most embarrassing things ever to happen to me. It's just torture. I feel like Lady Penelope. Everyone is staring and

I'm sitting there like a complete plonker. I find myself sliding down in the seat so I can't be seen by passers-by. I don't feel grand or special or any of those things that I imagined I would feel. I just feel a bit daft.

OK. I'm here and not before time.

'Thank you, David,' I say.

'Pardon, ma'am.'

'I said thank you.'

'Sorry, ma'am?'

'It doesn't matter.'

I slam the car door and head for the theatre. I am armed with Maltesers and I'm ready for action.

'Morning, Miss Monsoon,' says Fred, the guy on the front desk. He's a bit of an odd-job man is Fred – he opens the place up, checks it's clean, opens the offices and mans the phones until the proper front-of-house woman (Barbara) arrives at midday, then he tends to work back-stage, making sure the lighting and sound people have everything they need. He's never called me 'Miss Monsoon' before.

'You're a right famous celebrity now, aren't you?' he says, in that chippy Cockney accent of his. 'And look at your lovely clothes. My. You've gone all posh on us.'

I should have realised, right then, in that minute, that things had irredeemably changed in my life. But I didn't. I told him not to be so silly. 'I'm Kelly and I'll always be Kelly,' I said, kissing him on the cheek and heading towards the office.

'That's good,' he shouted after me, but I could hear the concern in his voice as keenly as I'd seen it in his eyes. He thought I was a different person now that he linked me with Rufus. Rufus was always treated differently to everyone else at the theatre, of course. From the moment he came into the building to the moment he left, people acted as if the queen were on the premises. Now I've moved in with him, I guess they consider that I'm a bit different too, which is a shame, because I'm not. I've no desire to be different. I liked things the way they were; I like me and the world I've created for myself; I like my friends and I like my life. I've fallen in love with someone. Does that mean the rest of my life has to collapse and reform itself around him?

I've been in the office about two minutes, surveying the two desks where once there were three, when Sebastian comes in. 'Welcome back,' he says rather grandly. I remove my beautiful new cashmere coat and hang it on the coat stand. The brooch on the collar sparkles under the fluorescent lighting. I've been dying to show it to the girls – they're bound to want to try it on and no doubt borrow it for their next date.

'We've missed you,' says Sebastian.

'Thanks,' I say, with genuine relief and gratitude. It's nice to think that people have actually missed me, rather than that they feel obliged to be polite because I'm Rufus's bird and Rufus is very important indeed. 'I've missed this place.'

Christ, you'd think I had been away fighting a war for five years.

'Where will I sit?' I ask, realising that it's my desk that has disappeared!

'Ah yes,' says Sebastian. 'We've been thinking about that, and I spoke to Rufus this morning. We rather thought it might be a little difficult for you to sit with the other girls and be so highly visible to all who come into the theatre. Given the interest in the press, we thought it might suit everyone if you were to be given your own special office.'

Now, I'll admit, just a few months ago, the idea of my own special office, indeed my own office – whether special or not – would have been overwhelmingly exciting to me, but so much has happened, so much in my life has changed – where I live, how I live, how I'm seen, how people speak to me – that the very idea my own self is changing scares me and I really want some things just to stay the same and be part of the old 'me'. It's a small thing, but I want my desk back. I want the messy drawers and the dog-eared books and the Post-it notes everywhere reminding me to do things because I'm always forgetting.

'Can I just have my desk back?' I ask.

'The office we've got earmarked for you is much nicer than the one you were in,' says Sebastian kindly. He can see the way my face has fallen.

'I know, and I appreciate it,' I say, not wanting to offend, 'but I'd like to sit with my friends and go back to working the way I did before.'

One of the things I love about my job is being around the buzz of theatre life, and seeing the various people come and go: the set designers and costume-makers, and the odd actor drifting in and out. It's not going to be anything like the same if I'm stuck upstairs in a tiny office of my own. Sebastian can see how reluctant I am, but he's stuck.

'Do me a favour, go into this new office upstairs

just for now, will you? I'll call Rufus and see what he thinks.'

'Rufus isn't my boss,' I say and I notice the look in Sebastian's eyes. If it weren't for the money that Rufus's presence in the play brought in, we'd all be out of a job. Rufus may not be my boss, but he's providing all of us with a living, so his needs must be met.

'You can look through the marketing leaflets,' he says, by way of compromise. 'Make a note of anything you think needs changing.'

I walk into the office and call Rufus straight away, hanging up like a schoolgirl when Christine answers. I just can't face talking to her right now. I want to talk to Rufus and to explain to him why it's so important for me to have some semblance of normality back. I need him to understand why I need to be within touching distance of the real world.

While I scan through the marketing leaflets, I hear the girls arriving downstairs. The kettle goes on and small talk is exchanged: what they bought at the weekend, what they spent, who they kissed. The yearning to go and join in is almost physical. I feel a need to see them and remind myself that my old life is there, still, waiting for me to reclaim it. I grab the box of Maltesers and tiptoe down the stairs towards the main office; I want to burst in and surprise them with my chocolates. As I creep down the old wooden staircase, excitement rising in me, I start to tear at the plastic covering on the chocolates. I want the box open when I walk in so I can burst in through the door and start pelting them with chocolates. I tear at the cellophane with my teeth, smudging my lipstick in my efforts to get the box open. There, at last, the plastic tears and I begin to remove it. Ha . . . this is going to be fun.

'Where's Kell? Is she back today?' I hear Katy ask. 'I'm dying to hear how it's all going with Rufus. Blimey, she kept that relationship quiet.'

'Did you see the paper today?' says Jenny. 'She's got herself into all sorts of trouble – flirting with some old guy in front of Rufus.'

I hear the rustle of newspaper and the stifling of laughter from the girls.

'Fuck. That guy's like eighty!' says Jenny, and I can hear the distaste in her voice. This is the thing with newspapers: people read them and believe them. Jenny and Katy have known me for bloody years, but they'll believe something written in the newspaper in a heartbeat, without considering whether it might be true or not.

'Why would she do that?' muses Katy. 'It seems odd.'

Thank you, I think to myself. Thank you for thinking that I just might not be capable of this.

'Wow . . . look at this,' says Jenny.

'God, that's beautiful. Must have cost a bloody fortune,' I hear Katy say.

'It's Kelly's,' says Sebastian, and I realise they're talking about the coat that I've left hanging up in the office. The one I only brought in today to show them, because I knew how much they'd like to see it.

'So she's here,' says Jenny.

'Yes. She's going to be working in her own office from now on,' I hear Sebastian say.

'Her own office?' Disgust, amazement and horror combine in Katy's voice to give it a slightly high-pitched edge. She couldn't sound more stunned if Sebastian had told her that I had just become Prime Minister. 'How can she have her own office? She's junior to us.'

'We thought it was for the best,' said Sebastian and the pause that follows is all twisted up with the frustrations of the girls. Shit. I just know what's coming next and I can't blame them one bit; I know how this must seem to them.

'I guess getting your own office isn't something you work for any more. It's something you get if you shag the right person.'

Now if I were a more confident woman I'd storm out there and challenge them. I'd explain that I had been really looking forward to coming back to work and seeing them. I'd show them the box of Maltesers in my bag. Oh yeah – box. Not packet. *Box* of Maltesers. We've never had boxes of Maltesers before.

'Come on now,' says Sebastian. 'What was I supposed to do? The press are following her everywhere. They're outside; look. She'd just be hassled all day. It would have become incredibly distracting to have her here, in full view of people walking past on the streets. She's in the upstairs office and I've just got her going through the marketing brochures, proof-reading them.'

Oh God.

'Proof-reading them? Why is she now qualified to proof-read them?'

I know what they're not saying. I know how the sentence ends. The unsaid words are screaming at me so loudly I can hardly bear it. 'Why's she qualified to proof-read just cos she's shagging Rufus?'

And the thing is – I don't know. I don't understand why people are taking me more seriously and treating me differently. I don't understand why people call me 'Miss Monsoon' and open doors for me. I don't understand why it's assumed that I'm more competent, able and sophisticated because I'm having a relationship with Rufus. It's about the power of celebrity. It's as if the fact that Rufus has given me the seal of approval means I'm better than they ever thought I was.

What's strange to me is that this is all happening now when I've actually been going out with Rufus for ages. It's because people have just been alerted to our relationship, so they're only just seeing me differently. So it's not about who I am or what I'm capable of because I've been Rufus's girlfriend for months, it's very much about how I am perceived now that they know. This is what celebrity is all about, and I'm right in the centre of it all without requesting it, desiring it or wanting it.

Right now I feel like celebrity's most innocent victim. I'm well aware that if my relationship with Rufus were to finish tomorrow and I were to be hurled back down through the layers of pearls and champagne, into the world of the real people, all my privileges would disappear as fast as they arrived. I'd still have the cashmere coats and beautiful silk dresses but they would not suit me quite as well because I would be Kelly rather than Miss Monsoon.

I turn and walk back up the stairs, still holding the box of chocolates and the torn plastic covering in my hands. I don't want to go down to talk to the girls, and though they pop up to say hello later on, there's nothing like the warmth between us that there was before. So much between us has changed. So much between me and people's perception of me has changed.

In the end I proof-read the marketing leaflet with little conviction or enthusiasm. This is the job I always wanted and I guess this is the office I would have dreamed of, but I feel hollow and, above all, bored out of my mind. Googling Cindy Kearney doesn't help in the least because she's truly beautiful. She's stunning in that all-American, blonde Californian way. I think I was born heavier than she is. I can't compete with anything this woman has: her looks, her skills as an actress, her fame and her sophistication. I'm fat Kelly from Hastings. I've never felt so low. There are only two people in the world who I can talk to at a time like this: Mandy and Sophie ... my sisters in arms.

'I'm ugly and fat,' I wail into the phone.

'Kell, it's difficult to talk right now,' says Sophie under her breath. 'My boss is around.'

'Oh,' I say, and it feels like a personal slight.

'Sorry,' whispers Sophie. 'I'll see you on Wednesday night for Mandy's party. And ... for the record, you're neither fat nor ugly. You're going out with the world's most gorgeous man, for God's sake. Doesn't that tell you anything?'

Yep, what it tells me is that no matter who you go out with or what happens to you externally in this world, if you feel crap inside, you feel crap inside – end of story. I'm going to the Rose Garden to sit on a bench with no name and watch the butterflies play.

Chapter 8

Rufus couldn't have been kinder or more understanding. When I got back from work and told him how hard I found it, he apologised madly and said of course he understood and felt bad; it was all his fault that I was going through this.

'I know you're not going to want me to say this, sweetheart,' he said. 'But I think you should give up the job; it's going to be too hard for you to carry on. Have a think about it.'

'But I like my job. It's all I've got,' I said.

'You've got me,' he insisted.

Now it's Wednesday evening and we're in the car on the way to Heathrow Airport for Rufus to catch a flight to LA. The car glides through the traffic, with Henry at the wheel.

'I talked to Sebastian today,' he says. 'I suggested that you take a month off to have a think about things and get settled in. Just say if you'd rather not, but I think there'll be a lot of adjusting for you to do, and it might make things easier all round. What do you think?'

I feel like everything's slipping away from me, that's what I think. My flat, my friends, my old life and now my job. There'll be nothing left of me; I'll just be a female-shaped extension to him.

'I'll try to think of some more sensible solutions to this

conundrum in the long term,' he says. 'But for now, with me going away and everything, wouldn't it be better for you to have a break from the theatre and get settled in and adjusted to your new life?'

All I really want is for Rufus to give me a hug, of course, but he's a man, so he has to come up with some practical answers to pull me back from the emotional pit I'm staggering into. My fears for my own life are all caught up in broader fears for us. Rufus is off to LA. He'll be accompanied by Olivia, if Elody's right, and I see no reason why she wouldn't be. But what the hell is Olivia going for? I don't understand. It seems so odd. To make matters worse, when he gets there, he'll be starring with Cindy Kearney – the world's most beautiful woman, and Rufus's ex. Fuck! I don't think I'd have got through these past couple of days without Elody; she's been absolutely amazing – there whenever I've needed her. She's been quite fun as well, at times. We've had quite a laugh. Well, maybe 'laugh' is overstating it, but I have enjoyed her company. It's been nice to find a new friend, and she does make me giggle.

'I hate having to leave you so soon after you've moved in,' says Rufus. 'This promotional tour has come at the worst time imaginable. Will you be all right? Make yourself at home in the house; invite friends over, redecorate . . . anything. OK?'

He does seem genuinely concerned about whether I'll be OK, which is touching. Not half as touching as it would have been if he'd asked me to go to bloody LA with him, of course, but touching all the same.

'I might do something in the snug,' I warn him. 'I'd love

to fill it with flowers and plants and make it come to life.'

'Be my guest,' he says with a smile. 'I guess the whole place does rather lack a woman's touch.' He gives me the most almighty squeeze then. 'Ahhh . . . I wish you could come,' he says. 'But you'd be bored out of your mind. It's all back-to-back meetings, interviews and press conferences. I won't even get the time to meet up with Courty and Deeves.'

I look over at him; his handsome face is a picture of concentration. I guess he must be in for a busy time if he won't get to see his two oldest mates; he loves those guys.

'You'll be all right, won't you?' he repeats. 'I do worry about you.'

'I'll be OK,' I say, and I will, because I've got loads planned. Tonight is Mandy's thirtieth birthday and she's having a huge party at The Sun – this pub in Richmond that we often go to. We know loads of people in there, and now I'm living in Richmond it's about five minutes away from my house. I'm planning to turn up there to surprise Mandy (Sophie knows I'm coming but we thought it would be fun not to tell Mandy) and to get my relationship with the two of them back on track. I haven't really talked to them properly since I left the flat. We've had odd snatched conversations and loads of texting, but nothing like it used to be. It's funny, but I've never had to try that hard with my friends before. Every morning I'd wake up and Mandy and Sophie would be there. I'd hear about the great things and hear about the bad things. I was there to offer support when the call came through that Mandy's mum had died. I also remember sharing in Sophie's joy when she got a call to say that she'd got a new job.

Then I'd go into the office and sit down next to Katy and Jenny, and we'd chat about life. If Mandy or Sophie were having problems in their love lives, and none of us could work out what to do, I'd solicit the help of Kath and Jenny, and they'd offer their advice, which I'd then feed-back to the girls. Jenny and Katy did the same things with their flatmates and between the load of us we had a kind of network that buzzed and fizzled with advice and feed-back. We've helped each other so much over the years; I'll never forget how brilliant everyone was to me when the drink-driving thing happened. They couldn't have been kinder. They helped by driving me around when I needed a lift and telling me not to worry. They were there for me when I really needed help, all of them.

'Well, could you not have an arrangement to meet the other girls for coffee at regular intervals through the week?' he suggested to me in an entirely reasonable way, but it just misses the point that going to work, for me, was never about pre-arranged outings, it was about the camaraderie of rubbing alongside other people during the day and getting to know them and understand them.

Now it's all about scheduling coffee a week on Friday. I have to be honest; it feels like something very important and worthwhile has just seeped out of my life. I'm also realising for the first time in my life how hard it is to get hold of someone when they don't have a mobile phone. People always complained that they couldn't get hold of Mandy and that she should get a mobile, but I thought they just weren't trying hard enough. It turns out that they're right, and it is actually very tough to get hold of Mand. It doesn't help that the girls can't be contacted at work because they're in jobs where they deal with the public, so are never free to talk. The bloody home phone's touch and go, so I'm relying one hundred per cent on Sophie for all communications, through her mobile phone. I send texts and we do talk a fair bit, but it's just not the same.

Thank God for Elody popping round, calling me up and stepping into my life to replace the friendships that have dwindled so significantly before my eyes.

'I've told Sebastian that you won't be in tomorrow again,' says Rufus. 'Just to give you some time to think this whole thing through and work out what you want to do about the job; whether you want to carry on or not. I do recommend taking a month to yourself to adjust to all this though. I think it would be the best thing.'

What has become clear these past two days is that Rufus never rated my job very highly, and really and truly he doesn't understand why I don't just give it all up. It brings in, annually, less than he earns in a minute for his films, so financially it makes no sense for me to endure a job that no longer pleases or excites me. I can see his point but what the fuck am I going to do all day without it? I suppose I could do an art course. I've always fancied doing jewellery-making or something like that. Perhaps Elody could help me find a course that's really good. And it would be nice to relax and focus on me for a while, especially since there's no shortage of money. I could even do charity work.

'Thanks,' I say to Rufus. 'It'll give me time to think things through. I hadn't quite worked out how different everything would become once we got together.'

'Well, my lovely lady, things are different now, but

different in a good way. You can stop worrying about working so hard and concentrate on enjoying yourself.' He slips his arm around me and I nestle up to his broad chest, feeling his heart beat through the soft cashmere of his jumper. There we remain, silent, warm and happy, while Henry hurls the car through the traffic and out towards the airport.

Mum is on the phone as soon as I walk out of the airport building. The police took me through a secret back door so I didn't have to go anywhere near the loitering paparazzi outside.

'Has he gone?' she asks.

'He has,' I say weakly.

'Shall we come and stay while he's away? You know, to look after you.'

I love my mum to death, but the very thought of her and Dad descending on me is more than I can bear.

'Don't worry. I'll be OK,' I say.

'Well, we'll just come for one night then. I promised Maude.'

Oh God. Not Great-Aunt Maude in the house, hurling herself onto the floor screaming for the air-raid shelter whenever a car backfires or someone slams a door.

'I'll bring her one day next week,' says Mum and I'm too emotionally drained to argue any further so I just say, 'Yes,' in a half-hearted way as I approach the car. Henry gives me a warm, welcoming smile and opens the door. I've slipped on my sunglasses to hide the fact that I've been crying incessantly since Rufus left, but the telltale signs are there: the gentle snivelling as I slide into the back seat and the tracks left in my freshly applied make-up.

'To The Sun, is it?' he asks, smiling warmly at me.

'Yes,' I sniff, in an 'I'm feeling so sorry for myself' sort of way.

'He'll be back in no time, you know,' says Henry. 'Just you wait and see. If you get out and about with your friends, and have some fun, before you can say "boo" he'll be back here, and the two of you will be out partying again.'

I'm silent because I know he's right, but if I speak, I'll burst into tears.

'Use this time to really settle in properly,' he suggests.

I just nod.

'I think Rufus's mum's coming over next week, isn't she?'

'Is she?'

Oh God, not the snotty cow we saw when me and the girls were Googling Rufus.

'She usually comes for the Interior Design Awards. She's a sponsor of them. I'm sure Christine said it was next week.'

'Right. Will she be staying in the house?'

'Sweetheart, she'll be taking over the house.'

The sound of gentle classical music wafts through the car. I'm slowly sinking into the soft leather seats as my phone bleeps and prompts me into action. It's Sophie. 'Am sooo pleased u r cming 2nite. Mandi's been talking bout u all nite; she'll die of happiness wen sees u lol :).'

Now that's just the sort of inspiration I need to get me out of my maudlin, comatose, can't-stop-thinking-about-Rufus state. The idea of Mandy's face lighting up when I arrive fills me with a delirious satisfaction. Off come the sunglasses and out comes the make-up bag. As the car rolls into Richmond, not a trace of my former, tearful condition remains. I want to make this the best night of Mandy's life; I want to burst in there and give her the best birthday ever, with the three of us reunited and drinking all together once again. Bring on the Purple Nasties.

We're just minutes away from the pub when I spritz on a little perfume, check my hair in a small hand mirror and add a dash of lip gloss. I notice that Henry has slowed the car down to such a degree that we're crawling along. 'It's not quite here,' I say. 'Just about a hundred yards further on and we'll be there.'

'Yes, I know. I'm just a bit. Um ... yes, just as I thought ...'

'What is it?' I ask.

'Don't worry,' he says. 'I just want to check something first.'

We arrive outside the pub.

'Don't get out of the car just at the moment,' he says. There's a steeliness to Henry's voice that I've never heard before. 'Just wait here a minute, love.'

While Henry looks in the rear-view mirror and reaches for his mobile phone, I wind down the window and look out at the pub. Gosh, it feels like I haven't been here for ages. There was a time when I'd meet the girls here most nights. We all work in Richmond, you see, so a little drink on the way home was always a nice way to end the working day.

'Right,' says Henry. 'Behind us there are two cars with photographers in. I know the registration plates. If you go into the party, they will follow you and try to get pictures of you and your friends.'

Fuck.

My first thought is: Sod it, I'm going in anyway. Why

should I let some horrible photographers ruin my chance to say happy thirtieth birthday to one of my best mates? I've got a great present for her and can't wait to catch up with all her gossip.

'Rufus wouldn't like it, you know, if there were pictures of you all over the papers,' says Henry. 'Sorry, ma'am, I don't want to speak out of turn, but I know how these photographers can be, and they really will look for the worst photographs possible. They'll end up ruining your friend's party.'

Shit. I feel really torn now. I don't want anything to ruin Mandy's party, but I do want to go in there and have a drink. I feel so bloody lonely sometimes. I've been looking forward to this for ages.

'The photographers are getting out of the car. Can you wind your window up, ma'am. We really should get out of here.'

I think of Mandy's sweet face and of her family all gathered round her and realise Henry's right; I can't plough in there tonight with the world's press on my tail, and ruin her evening. I'll get to make it up to her really soon by taking her somewhere special.

'Yep, you're right. Drive on,' I say to Henry, and he speeds off like Lewis Hamilton, leaving the photographers who are trying to look like normal pub-goers, standing in the street, scratching their heads.

'Sorry, I can't do tonight,' I text Sophie, not revealing why because the truth sounds so absurd. 'But will defo b there for lunch on Sat. Kxx'

Chapter 9

'You'll get used to it, honestly, don't worry,' says Elody.
'You get to the stage when you worry if the papers *don't*
follow you everywhere. I miss the mad press attention that
Jon and I used to get; God it was exciting.'

I look over at her strangely but she doesn't notice.
She's far too busy wandering through my dressing room
and tossing aside some of my favourite items of clothing
with gay abandon. She thinks I need lots of new clothes
('need' you notice, not 'want' – in this new life of mine,
designer clothes are needed, not wanted!). In the process
she's unburdening me of 'old' stuff. (I thought it was new
stuff until she got going, now I realise that anything
that's been on the catwalks is deemed to be already 'old'.
What we're after, I've just learnt, is the designer collec-
tions that are fresh off the sewing machines and unseen
by anyone but the sharpest fashionistas in the world.)
I'm lying on the chaise longue trying not to think about
the stuff she's rejecting. I get quite attached to things;
I'm one of life's hoarders. I don't like this throwing-
things-away business.

More than anything, though, I'm thinking about Rufus.

'Why is Olivia going on this trip?' I ask Elody. 'I don't
understand why she's going.'

'She's an assistant,' says Elody. 'Not sure what she'll be
assisting with, but that's her title.'

'But Rufus already has an assistant. Christine's gone out there with him.'

'Different sort of assistant entirely, sweetheart,' says Elody vaguely, and I realise just how much I don't know about Rufus's life away from me. As soon as he calls, I'll ask him exactly who's out there and what they're doing.

'Did the photographers get pictures of you earlier?' she asks, as she examines the buttons on my cream blouse.

'No, I don't think so. I didn't get out of the car at the pub.'

'Thank the Lord,' she replies with obvious relief, before adding, rather uncharitably, 'you're a few pounds over fighting weight. We could do with keeping them at arm's length until you've shifted a bit of excess baggage.'

'Thanks a lot,' I say. 'I don't know why they're interested in me anyway. I'm not the film star; he is. I'm just Kelly from Twickenham who met this guy and fell in love with him. What's so bloody interesting about that? I'm exactly the same person I was six months ago, and no one wanted pictures of me then.'

'D'er,' says Elody, dropping the shirt and walking over to me. 'That's exactly why they want pictures of you – because you're a normal girl who's going out with a big star; you're living the dream. You're hot stuff right now. Designers are going to want to dress you, stylists will want to advise you, TV producers will want you on their shows and – yes – photographers will want pictures of you. Everyone likes the new big thing and that's you.'

'Oh,' I say, remaining as baffled as ever about the whole thing. I know the papers are interested in me because I've had about twenty-five interviews requested through

Rufus's agents. They want me to do everything from photo shoots to lunch with the editor. I can't think of anything worse, so I just say no. I appreciate that makes them want me all the more, and that's why the house has a cluster of photographers permanently at the gate, but nothing will make me pose in lingerie for men's magazine or have lunch with a journalist who wants to know all about Rufus's home life. I'll keep ignoring them in the hope that they get bored and go away. I'm just not that interesting . . .

'When will they give up?' I ask.

'Never,' she replies.

'But they can't sit outside the house forever.'

'Oh, they can,' she says. 'And they will.'

'Shit. It makes life so hard. I still feel awful about missing Mandy's party. I must phone the girls and apologise,' I say.

'I thought you sent them a text?'

'I did. I told them I'll be there for the birthday lunch we've arranged.'

'Oh, well let it go then. Call them later; you don't want them to worry about you. Let them enjoy their party.'

'Yeah, OK,' I say, because Elody's right. No point in spoiling their fun.

'Try this on.' Elody is clearly tired of trying to find nice things in my wardrobe and has turned, in the manner of a *Blue Peter* presenter, to some she prepared earlier. The garment she's giving me is a black sheath dress. It looks simple and elegant but, if I'm honest, it doesn't feel that different from the sort of thing that I'd pick up in Dorothy Perkins for £15. The only thing with this dress is that it has a price tag of £1500 on it.

'Shit!!!' I exclaim on seeing the ludicrous cost of the thing.
'I didn't pay; don't worry,' she says.

'I know but, my God, who'd pay that for a plain black
dress?'

'Lots of people, my dear,' she says. 'Don't look so surprised.
Rufus will want you to have the best. You're moving into
a new world now. The better dressed you are and the more
sophisticated and polished you look, the quicker you'll ease
your way into it. Let's find the diva in you.'

'Oh, OK,' I mumble unassertively. I fear I'm the most
un-divaish person in the world but I really don't want to
upset this important, sophisticated, glamorous but ever so
slightly mad stylist. I'm loving having someone coming
round at the drop of a hat. When I told her the photographs had prevented me from going to Mandy's party,
she came straight over, she's really a sweet person. I am
also truly grateful for all the new clothes she's adding into
the wardrobe. I'm loving learning from her and developing
myself . . . making myself a better person. Imagine what
Mum and Dad will say when they see me?

I slip into the black dress and Elody pulls a slight face
as she runs her hands over my curves. 'Shame you're quite
so curvy,' she says. 'Dresses just don't look good on lumps
and bumps. Mmmm . . . I'll have to think about that. We
need to disguise a little. Now, what else is in here?'

The phone rings as she rummages through my wardrobe
and I reach over to take it. 'Leave it,' says Elody, but it's
too late, I've picked up the mobile and Jan James is chatting away into my ear.

'Hi. I was just calling to see how you are. I know Rufus
left today, didn't he? Are you all right?' she asks.

'I'm fine,' I say, thrilled that she's taken the trouble to call. With all the stuff about Rock in the paper recently, anyone could have forgiven her for not even remembering that Rufus was going away.

'Look – I won't keep you. I just wondered whether you fancied coming round tomorrow night for a few drinks: a girlie champagne evening.'

'I'd love to,' I say. I feel a renewed confidence about these sorts of things now that I'm friends with Elody. A champagne evening with someone as famous as Rock James's wife would have terrified me just a week ago. I wouldn't have had a clue what to wear, but knowing that Elody will sort all that out for me has given me renewed hope. 'Thanks very much for inviting me.'

Jan tells me to be at her place for around 9 pm. 'You'll meet Zadine at the drinks party,' she promises. 'She's just lovely. You'll adore her.'

'Zadine? As in Joe Collins' girlfriend?'

'Yes, do you know her?'

'No,' I admit. But I feel as if I've known her intimately for years. She's the one who's on every reality TV show; she's the most unbelievable woman – a walking, talking Barbie doll. I feel myself overcome with desire to call Mandy and Sophie and tell them that I'm going to be meeting Zadine.

'Who was that?' asks Elody with unnecessary aggression when I put down the phone.

'Jan,' I say, feeling almost guilty for talking to another woman. Elody has a strangely possessive streak in her.

'What did she want?'

Oh Lord. Why do I feel like I'm in trouble?

'Just to invite me for drinks at hers tomorrow.'

'Oh,' says Elody. 'What time?'

'She said around 9 pm.'

'I'll come here for 9.30 pm, then we'll go,' says Elody. 'Best not to arrive on time, very unsophisticated.'

I don't like to say that it sounded like a very informal get-together or that I'm not entirely sure whether Elody's invited. I'm sure she knows best. 'Good idea,' I say.

'Let's work out what you should wear then, shall we?' says Elody taking my phone off me, switching it off and dropping it into her pocket. 'I'll book you some beauty treatments tomorrow so you're looking your best.'

'It's only going to be women there,' I say. 'I think it's just a casual evening, no pressure.'

'*Exactly*,' says Elody, her palms lifted to the ceiling imploringly. 'That's why looking good is so important. They're trying to catch you out, sartorially. It's a good job I'm here. Now, do you have any wine?'

Rufus has more wine than the average off-licence. He has a cellar, no less, as well as a fabulous wine rack in the kitchen, made out of slate.

'Sure,' I say, leaving the room to get her a drink. I wouldn't mind a glass myself, to be honest.

'Sancerre OK?' I ask, returning with two glasses that Pamela suggested would be just right. I know nothing about wine at all.

'Lovely,' Elody says, taking one of them and enjoying a large gulp. 'Now . . . clothes for tomorrow,' she says, before rooting through my wardrobe again, though she must know exactly what's in there by now. She pulls out a few items then pushes them back in again.

'I'll bring something for you to wear,' she says. 'There's nothing in there that's suitable.'

We walk down to the sitting room and sit opposite one another on the beautiful cream sofas.

'Tell me a bit about Jon,' I say.

'He was perfect. We were perfect,' she says. 'When he died, everything died. I died. I felt guilty. I hated life. I felt it was all my fault.'

'I don't see how it could be your fault. You didn't make him take drugs.'

'No, but I didn't stop him either.'

With that, she throws her wine down her throat and stands up dramatically. 'Elody is going,' she says in a way that could easily sound pompous, but I now recognise as being a persona that she uses to wrap around the pain.

'Ooooo . . . Do you have my phone?' I ask, running after her. 'You took it off me earlier.'

'Yes,' she says, handing me the phone from her bag with a big smile. 'Here it is.' I notice that the phone is back on again, but I was sure she switched it off.

Chapter 10

I am ready for the drinks party; resplendent in the finest red dress that money can buy. The long scarlet gown falls to the floor making me look statuesque and regal. My face glows so much with all the lotions, potions and oils that have been rubbed into it and plastered onto it that I fear I might spontaneously combust. Blimey. I never knew so many beauty treatments existed and all delivered to me in the comfort of my own home. I called Rufus from one treatment and was explaining what they were doing to me. He was in hysterics and told me to make sure I enjoyed myself and that he missed me desperately and couldn't wait to see me again. It's funny, but when I speak to him I feel totally relaxed and happy; it's only when Elody talks about what he might be up to that I start to panic. I even asked him why he needed so many assistants with him.

'Because this is Hollywood, babes,' he said with resignation. 'And they seem to think that your talent is somehow reflected in the size of your entourage. It's nonsense. I miss you, Kelly. I miss you more than I've ever missed anyone or anything in my life before.' He's employing that deep, resonant voice that he normally reserves for the screen and bedtime. I tell him all about my day and he's delighted that I'm getting on so well with Elody. 'I'm glad,' he says, 'but do be careful, she can be quite the dragon sometimes.'

'But her heart's in the right place,' I insist, because I

genuinely do believe that. 'I think she's a good person underneath it all, and she's spent a lot of time with me.'

'I've always liked Elody. You should get to know Isabella as well though,' he says. 'She's wonderful.'

It's 9.45 pm by the time Elody makes her appearance, and I'm starting to feel a bit awkward about this 'turn up there late' theory of hers. If someone invites you to drinks at 9 pm, surely you turn up at 9 pm.

'You are delightful,' says Elody, when I express my concerns. 'But so naïve.'

Elody has arrived with her huge bag of tricks. 'But I don't need it today,' I say confidently. 'Look, I'm wearing the dress you brought round.' I twirl so she can see the full extent of the transformation. It's pathetic how desperate I am for her approval.

'You know,' she says with a smile. 'You're right. You've learnt well. You look beautiful. Let's go.'

As we sit in the car, I can't help but think about how weird all this is. My real friends haven't called at all, and Elody is being so friendly that it's verging on overbearing. I wish I could have got hold of the girls today.

'Elody, I feel so bad about not talking to Mandy and Sophie, but every time I call, I just go through to an answerphone. I don't seem to be able to actually speak to them,' I say.

'Have they not called you?' she asks, incredulous. 'You'd think they'd be worried after you didn't turn up for the birthday drinks. I think they should call you. It's not up to you to call them; don't they know how busy you are?'

I know Elody can be a bit prickly but there's a considerable amount of truth in what she says. If it had been me, and Mandy hadn't turned up for my thirtieth birthday drinks, I like to think I'd have been worried enough to call and check she was OK. I glance at my phone but there are definitely no missed calls. No one since Jan rang to invite me to the party yesterday. Out of sight, out of mind, I guess.

We walk into the James family home, and as soon as Jan answers the door I realise this is all wrong. She takes in my ultra-glamorous appearance and super sexy designer gown and smiles. 'You've been somewhere else first?' she asks. She's wearing jeans and a white shirt. Designer jeans, of course, and the shirt looks like it was made from angels' wings, but she's not wearing a dress that would be better suited to the red carpet, nor does she have the crown jewels hanging from her ear lobes. God I feel a fool. 'I think I'm a little overdressed,' I say, rather unnecessarily, but Jan's not paying too much attention. She's rather distracted by the sight of Elody in the doorway.

'Oh, it's you,' she says, her words twisted with bitterness. 'What made you think you were invited?'

'I'm sorry,' I say, interrupting. 'She came with me. I didn't realise it would be a problem.'

'Of course not,' says Jan through gritted teeth.

'Look ... Elody's come too. How nice,' says Jan, addressing the collection of people gathered in the sitting room. Elody blows an air-kiss out to the guests and the air seems to freeze as she does so.

'I'm sorry we're so late,' I say as Elody glides into the

James's sitting room, whispering, 'Stop apologising, Kelly,' as she passes me. She instructs some poor minion to bring her the very best champagne which, judging by the sour look on her face, angers Jan even more. I'm torn between feeling embarrassed about Elody's domineering nature and incredibly impressed at how confident she is when she's clearly not welcome here at all.

'Meet Zadine,' says Jan, taking my arm and directing me gently towards a small blonde woman with quite alarmingly large breasts (and I speak as one who knows about these things).

Oooohhhh . . . I've always wanted to meet Zadine.

The lady herself steps forward and puts out a small, slim hand. She has sparkling blue eyes, honey-coloured hair streaming across the smallest shoulders and bandages around her head.

'Did you hurt yourself?' I ask, feeling dreadfully sorry for this tiny birdlike creature whom Sophie, Mandy and I have been mocking since time began. 'Was it a car crash?'

She smiles and her entire face lights up. She's nothing like I thought she'd be. She's like a little girl, smiling sweetly and explaining that she had 'some work done'. Jan takes me aside later and, along with Isabella, explains that no one has ever seen Zadine in the flesh without bandages of some sort on.

'It's an addiction,' says Isabella, giving me a big hug when she realises how concerned I look. 'She's the most adorable creature but desperately insecure. When she's not on television on some sort of terrible game show, she's booking up with Edward to have operations to help her look better in time for the next terrible game show. In between all this, she works tirelessly in the hope of impressing her husband who's six years younger than she, and is rumoured to be sleeping with every young model, male and female, in the business.'

'Why does he keep operating on her if it's a mental problem?' I ask, adding quickly: 'Sorry if that sounds rude.'

'No, don't worry. The truth is that it's difficult to turn her away when you know she'll go somewhere else and get it done. Edward did refuse to operate on one occasion and she went abroad. They made a real mess of liposuction and Edward had to do two follow-up operations to get her right again. After that, we thought we'd be better off looking after her ourselves. At least that way we know she's as safe as possible.'

I don't think I've ever felt sorrier for anyone in my life than I feel for Zadine right now.

'Anyway, how are you?' Isabella asks. 'Are you coping OK without Rufus? I called a few times this morning but couldn't get hold of you. I just wondered if you fancied going for a coffee, or having lunch some time?'

'I'd love to,' I say. 'Are you around tomorrow? We could meet up for coffee in the afternoon?'

'That would be great,' says Isabella. 'I'll mention it to Jan, shall I?'

'Yes do,' I say, delighted.

'What's the gossip?' Elody appears and stands unnecessarily close. She has a habit of doing that with me, but after seeing the sadness in her eyes when she told me about Jon and how she feels responsible for his death, I guess I can understand why she likes to keep her friends close by her side.

She's clutching the bottle of Cristal champagne, and tips it to fill my glass to the top, then refills her own. 'This is what life's about,' she is saying in a slurred and affected voice. 'It's all about the quality of the drink. Cheers!'

As she chatters on in her friendly but increasingly drunk fashion, I can't help but be reminded of our motto in the flat: 'It's not the quality of the drink that counts, but the quality of the friendship.' How different this world is from the one I've left behind.

I wish the girls were here right now – we'd have such a scream. You know, even though we've got up to some stupid things together over the years, and are always on the edge of trouble and the edge of bankruptcy, I still feel more embarrassed about Elody's behaviour tonight than I ever have of anything either of my mates has done . . . and that includes pouring red wine all over Luke's head, or climbing out of the toilet window on that double blind date because neither of them could face the guys they were with.

I excuse myself and head off into a corner of the white-walled room where I pull out my phone. Still no missed calls. I don't understand.

'Don't call them,' says Elody, appearing at my side. I should have known she'd follow me; she seems quite determined that I shouldn't be ringing them. 'Leave it for tonight; they're probably out anyway. We'll make a plan tomorrow if you're worried.'

And the thing is, even though she's starting to get on my nerves now, with the way she's always telling me what to do (or 'helping' as she would call it), and the way I seem to have become her special little project, I still put the phone away. She's so extraordinarily persuasive. She also has this aura around her that leads you to assume she's always right.

I smile my way through most of the evening in Zadine's tender company. The woman's so sweet; the hours slip by.

'Can I get you a drink?' she asks, with a smile. 'What sort of wine would you like?'

'Um . . . white?' I suggest.

'French?' she says. 'Or there are some lovely New World wines.'

'Um . . . whatever you're having,' I respond.

'Sure,' she says. She disappears off and comes back with a gin and tonic. Shit, I hate gin. I wish I knew something about wine. I must get Rufus to teach me. I always let him order the wines and I have no idea what we've been drinking.

Zadine and I chat in whispers, so that Elody doesn't hear from her position by the mirror where she's simultaneously checking her hair and quaffing large quantities of Cristal. Elody looks beautiful tonight. She's dressed in black, as always, wearing a ballerina-style dress over leggings and with the highest shoes I've ever seen in my life before. Zadine's dressed all in pink. She looks like a little marshmallow. Her tiny frame is swamped by a pale-pink sweatshirt, and pink denim hot pants worn with cowboy boots.

I tell her about Mandy and Sophie, and how I fear that I let them down. 'They're my best friends in the whole world and we swore that when I moved out and moved into Rufus's house we'd stay the closest of friends but that hasn't happened. It's all been so much harder than I thought it would be, and I just haven't seen them and I can't ring them while they're at work and I can't get through to them on the home phone. I feel awful. Seeing you has really brought back how much fun we used to have together in that flat because we'd always watch the reality programmes that you were in. We always voted for you, you know.'

'Did you?' she asks, and the thing is – we did!

'Then let me call them!' she says. 'I'll tell them that you're really sorry and you love them and can't wait to see them. It'll be funnier if I do it; it'll take the edge off things and save you having to make an embarrassing call. Go on; let me.'

'That would be so cool,' I exclaim. I don't tell Zadine that we mock her relentlessly in the flat and have had more fun at her expense than we've even had at the expense of the worst boyfriends we've encountered.

'Shit. Answerphone!' she declares. 'I'll leave a message, shall I? What are the girls called again? Oh shit . . . Hang on. I'm through . . . Hi, this is Zadine Collins,' she says, her voice rising to the girly squeal her TV fans have come to associate with her. 'Just wanted to say that I'm here drinking with your beautiful friend. We have the finest champagne in the world and she looks gorgeous. Bet you wish you were here!'

She puts down the phone and gives me a little hug. I try to picture the girls in the flat on this cold night, wrapped in duvets on the sofa because they can't afford to keep the heating on and drinking tea in front of the TV. They'll pick up that message and laugh their socks off, squealing with delight. I can't wait to see them. I have so much to tell them about.

'We should go,' says Elody, appearing at my side.

It seems we've only been there five minutes. 'We have some fabulous parties to go to tonight . . . We can't hang around.'

'Oh.' Do we? I thought this was the only place we were going.

'Yep, come on. I'm introducing you to everyone who's glamorous and important in London tonight. Let's go.'

We kiss everyone goodnight and Zadine says, 'I hope your friends like my message,' with such kindness that I could hug her. 'Come to mine next Friday night. Everyone welcome!' she declares. She glances at Elody and glances away. Elody's clearly not welcome but I know in advance that that won't stop her.

Chapter 11

We're back at the wardrobe . . . again. Now I love clothes, like most girls, but this utter obsession with them is something entirely new. I don't mean to sound ungrateful, and I think Elody's amazing when it comes to styling, but I just don't feel that I need a 'glove draw' or someone to come in and organise my jewellery collection. I want to go and sit in the Rose Garden and dream about Rufus but I can't. There's no escape from the dreaded mistress of the wardrobe. She says we have to address the issue of my 'severe clothing deficit' as a matter of absolute urgency, as if we're talking about child poverty or a threat to national security.

'Did you never go out before?' asks Elody, pulling out my lovely little white dress (one of my very best). 'I mean, this is stuff you would not want to be seen wearing in public; let's be honest. Perhaps you were burgled and all your nice clothes were stolen.'

'I do have nice things, and I love that dress,' I say. I can feel tears burning in the backs of my eyes. Why does everything have to be so brutal? She takes clothes so seriously. I guess that's her job, but honestly, they're just clothes. If I happen to like different ones to her, why does that matter?

She's fiddling with that gorgeous necklace of hers as she speaks, clinking the two large diamond-covered stars together. There's always trouble when she's wearing that; it's like her war paint.

'Listen, you wanna sexy white dress, babe, you'll have the sexiest white dress that money can buy, but it'll be one made of the finest materials that will hug you and flatter you. *No* more Topshop shit for you, lady. It's all designer dressing from here on in.'

'There's nothing wrong with Topshop,' I say. I'm slightly reluctant to take on Elody when it comes to matters of a sartorial nature, but some of the best-dressed people wear Topshop clothes and some of their stuff's quite cutting edge. Christ, half of it was designed by Kate Moss, and you don't get much better dressed than her, do you? I just can't imagine going into a designer shop and have snobby sales assistants look me up and down and declare there's nothing in there that's suitable for me.

'All I'm saying is that you can do better, and I will help you do better,' says Elody, sinking onto the chaise longue next to the vast wardrobe. 'There is nothing to fear; I will teach you everything. In fact, I will teach you everything today.' She looks up suddenly and I expect a light bulb to appear above her head. 'Let's go shopping now.'

The prospect of getting out of the house is very appealing, and I would like to learn as much as I can from Elody before Rufus comes back, but I made half a plan to meet Jan and Isabella for coffee. Perhaps if I text them, and suggest meeting later, say 6 pm, at mine, then I can do the shopping trip and an enjoyable girly chat after. Ideal!

'OK,' I say. 'I'll just get my coat.'

'You'll do more than get your coat. You need to dress to shop. If you want the assistants to take you seriously, you need to be properly attired; you need to be better dressed than they could ever be, only then will you be taken seriously.'

Oh Lord. This is hard work. She spends an hour dressing me up and making me look like a film star before I'm allowed to leave home. She slips large black sunglasses onto the end of my nose, in case the paparazzi are out in force, and we're off. 'Head up, shoulders back,' she orders as we march out to the car. She'll be making me salute her next.

I have to say that shopping with Elody is a fantastic experience. When we walk in through the doors of shops that I was scared even to look through the window of before, she is greeted as if she were Princess Diana risen for one last trip to the boutiques of West London.

'My God!!!' they exclaim. 'Wow. It's you. But. Wow. Come in. Come in.'

They treat me like I'm a supermodel, too, telling me how beautiful I am, rushing around to get me a seat and showing me all the latest clothes. Elody is desperately rude to them, but it seems the ruder she is, the more these women dote on her and seem to want to help her. 'Diva rules' as Elody calls it.

'Have you not been shopping at all since you moved in?' asks Elody.

'Yes,' I say. 'I went out and bought loads of plants and flowers to put into the snug to make it beautiful.'

'No, not that – clothes shopping.'

'Oh, no. I haven't had the time yet,' I explain.

'There is always *always* the time for clothes shopping,' she insists, giving me an almighty hug.

I must admit that before this moment, I was really going off Elody. I thought she behaved appallingly at the party last night, and her dismissive departure was awful; she made up some story about us having so many other parties to go to, but we didn't have any other parties at all. I thought it was odd; for all her talk, all her fame and Hollywood connections, Elody does not have people running around desperate to invite her to parties. Instead, we went home, and Elody went onto the internet and looked through the websites, howling with laughter at the catwalk items on sale. 'Look, look, look,' she cried. 'They've chosen the blue shift dress. How funny is that? Blue!!! This season??? Crazy!'

This morning, though, I'm seeing her through different eyes as we wind our way through the streets of Richmond, tearing past the shops I'd normally go into, and heading straight for the ludicrously expensive ones. I buy a terrifying amount of stuff egged on by Elody at every turn, of course, and thus I blame her entirely for my excesses. The clothes are all given to me at half price or less. Despite the hefty reductions bestowed on us, I still manage to spend more money on clothes than I have in my life before. I hand over my credit card sheepishly, convinced that it will be rejected every time.

'What will Rufus say?' I ask Elody. 'Won't he be cross?'

'You can't spend enough to make him cross,' she says. 'He'll make more every time he smiles in this new film than you could spend in a lifetime. Lady, you're going out with one of the richest men in the world; enjoy it, for God's sake.'

She has a point. I decide to enjoy it. When I get home, I'll go through the bags and take back any clothes that are too expensive. I don't want Rufus to think I'm taking advantage of him. I'd hate it so much if he thought that.

'OK, I've got an idea,' says Elody, looking at me quizzically. 'What are you like at gambling?'

'Gambling? I've never been gambling in my life before.'

'Well then, today's your lucky day. I'm going to introduce you to the best sort of fun you can have with your clothes on. Follow me.'

Elody leads me up Richmond Hill a little way, towards a small lane on the left. I've been here before; there's a bar at the end called The Anglers where we went with Sebastian for a drink when he first joined the theatre. I'd never noticed before that, halfway down the lane, there's a discrete black door with a large brass knocker. Elody knocks it twice, and a man in a tuxedo answers and greets her warmly. I'm desperately nervous. What am I doing here? I'm just not the gambling type.

'Elody, I don't think this is my thing,' I say.

'Coat over there,' she responds, indicating the cloakroom.

'I don't want to stay.'

'You'll love it,' she insists. 'I promise you. It's fantastic fun. You're going to totally adore it. No question. Coat over there and follow me.'

To be fair to Elody, we do have a fantastic time, tearing through the place, clutching handfuls of brightly coloured chips as we bet on a random collection of games. I fall hopelessly in love with the roulette wheel, while Elody is far more taken with poker.

'Try it, you'll love it,' she insists, but it seems all too hard-core for me. You have to actually think about it and, if I'm going to have to think about things, I'd rather save myself for work or reading newspapers. Instead, I settle myself in at roulette, avoiding the eyes of the men who circle round me, looking me up and down and trying to engage me in conversation.

'A drink, perhaps, pretty lady?' asks one man. He's twice my age and looks way too much like Jimmy Lapdance for me to take seriously, with that pitted skin that comes from spending too much time indoors clutching a glass of whisky, and not enough time in the fresh air. I hold up my hand in a rather juvenile fashion as if to say 'talk to the hand'. It's a gesture he seems familiar with, as he nods and backs away. I look up and see Elody looking over at me. 'OK?' she mouths, thoughtfully. 'Fine,' I reply, with a smile, feeling an unexpected warmth that she's been paying so much attention to me, and looking out for me. Things happen from time to time to remind me that she's actually a very good person, even though there are occasions when she's mortifyingly embarrassing. I guess everyone's like that. I'm sure I say and do things all the time to cause embarrassment.

I've decided to throw myself wholly behind the number 29 on the roulette wheel, because it's come to represent so much to Rufus and me. The day we met . . . the day we moved in together . . . it means everything. I stuck just one chip on the first time, prompting the croupier to give me a rather patronising smile. I decide that if I am to disabuse him of the notion that I don't have a clue what I'm doing, I'll have to play big-time. I've got £200's worth of chips in my hand. (Elody has £2000 but she's way out of my league; I feel bad enough spending a tenth of that!) I push all the chips along the green carpet-style covering, towards the number 29.

The croupier nods and hurls the ball into the wheel so it clatters around, spinning, ducking and diving its way through the numbers. There are two people gambling alongside me. One is a woman who I would guess to be in her mid-forties. She looks like a housewife who's escaped from the kitchen for the day, but plays like a pro. She's full of confidence, speaking to the croupier in language he understands, chatting about 'the rake' and 'comps'. There's a man the other side of me who's much older, painfully thin and looks as if he doesn't go for too long without a cigarette between his fingers. His hands are stained yellow and they shake and quiver as he leans over to place his bet. No one has bet as much as I have.

'Go on number 29,' I say, as the ball dances across the wheel. 'Go on.'

'It's not horse racing, sweetheart.' Elody has appeared at my side, and is watching in amazement at the fact that I've thrown all my chips on one throw, literally.

'I never had you down as a gambler,' she says, hugging me affectionately. 'Turns out you're a natural.'

The ball slows down. 'Go on, go on.' Eventually it stops, nestling in the number 29 position.

'Yeeeeeessss,' I shriek, throwing my arms up into the air like a goal-scoring footballer, and running around the room in jubilation. Elody is jumping up and down and squealing, while I clap my hands and join her – the two of us bounding on our invisible trampoline while everyone else looks on coldly, emotionless and miserable.

'That was such enormous fun,' I say to Elody, as we emerge from the casino like burrowing creatures coming up for light. 'I don't remember it being this bright outside when we went in,' I say, while Elody smiles to herself.

'Why are you grinning so much?' I ask. The woman lost most of the £2000 she gambled; it seems to me that she has precious little to grin about.

'I'm smiling because I think you're fab,' she says. 'You know that, don't you?'

I look at her and feel filled with delight that she likes me. I hope she tells Rufus that she thinks I'm fab. I'm almost tempted to suggest it to her but fear that might change her view of me entirely.

'Come on,' she says. 'We absolutely have to get you this season's "must have" handbag.'

I'm dragged, screaming and kicking, into Matches (OK, maybe not screaming and kicking, but certainly protesting mildly), where we're treated to the best kind of service that money can buy. I now have the latest handbag from the Chloe range, eight dresses, three pairs of trousers, countless tops and a collection of shoes that would not disgrace Imelda Marcos, but it's clearly not enough.

'Outerwear,' she instructs, as we walk down the concrete steps outside Matches and descend onto the pavement below. 'But first, we need to stop shopping for a while and talk.'

This is a most unusual state of affairs. All morning it's been me stopping her and saying, 'Do I really need another sparkly top? I now have more sparkly tops than the average girl band. Is that not enough?' But now it is she who is calling a temporary halt to the shopping.

'There's something I've been meaning to say,' she utters, ominously.

'What is it?' I ask her, fearing it has something to do with the paparazzi. We had to dive into Caroline Charles, the gorgeous little shop near the hill, when the paparazzi spotted us earlier. The staff in there were great, thank heavens. They helped us through the rows of exquisite garments and bundled us out of the back door before the photographers could work out where we were.

'I'm going to be frank,' she says, adding (alarmingly): 'There's no way to dress this up. It's something I have to tell you for your own good.'

Inside I'm thinking, 'Nooooo . . .' because we all know that when Elody is frank, she might as well just belt you with a really big stick . . . She's brutal!

'Sure. Be frank,' I say confidently, then I feel like putting on a helmet and jumping in an armoured tank.

'When we were at the dinner at Rufus's house, one of the girls said that you had a face like *Baywatch* and a body like *Crimewatch*. Don't take it the wrong way, but that's what they said. I think they're right.'

Don't take it the wrong way? What's the right way to take it?

'It's just that you are really quite fat,' she continues.

'Oh.' The thing is, I thought I'd lost weight. I thought I was looking slimmer and better than ever. 'I'm a size 12,' I say with real pride.

'Size 12!' she exclaims, her eyes wider than any eyes

have a right to go. 'My God, it's so much worse than I thought! Are you really a size 12? I thought we'd been buying you size 10 dresses in the shops; that was embarrassing enough. Size 12! *Zut alors!* That's terrible. You have to let me help you or you'll never win Rufus back.'

Win him back? From where?

'I don't need to win him back,' I protest. 'He's mine, thank you very much.'

'Sweetheart. He's in LA with his ex-girlfriend and a gaggle of *skinny* beauties. He didn't invite you on the trip. I hate to be brutal but it's not looking good. If you were skinnier, I'd rate your chances of keeping him more highly.'

'No. You're wrong,' I protest. 'Rufus likes me curvy. He's always saying how much he loves my breasts and hips and how much he dislikes the Hollywood skinny types.'

'Does he?' says Elody. 'Interesting. He's trying to keep you fat, is he?'

'What? What do you mean "trying to keep me fat"?'

'Well, so that no one else wants you; let's be honest when you're this fat, you're unlikely to run off with anyone else, are you?'

'I'm not fat. Lots of men like me.'

'I know they like you . . . because you are sweet and kind. You are my lovely little fat friend and the men who like you were probably brought up by very severe nannies then sent to boarding school at the age of six. They yearn for someone sweet and matronly. But, hey, don't worry. I can help.'

She can help? What sort of help is she going to be?

'How?' I ask, and I notice that I'm sucking in my stomach and clenching my buttocks so tightly it's starting to hurt. 'Should I start going to the gym or Weight-Watchers or something.'

'Nothing of the kind,' says Elody with a warm though slightly mischievous smile. 'Come on, let's go for coffee.'

We walk down the road, away from the shops and into a small lane leading down to Richmond Green where I order a latte and am reprimanded. My order is corrected immediately to a strong black coffee. 'Decaffeinated,' I request, but – again – I'm wrong, it turns out. Dining out with Elody is a little like being in court with a really pernickety judge. 'Overruled' she shouts in her severe voice.

'The caffeine is good because it gets the heart going and pumps the blood round your body faster,' she explains. It sounds like a state of affairs that any sane person would avoid.

'And that's good?' I question.

'If you're trying to burn as much excess fat as you are,' she says, prodding my fleshy hips rather vigorously, 'every little thing helps.'

Right, that's me told.

'I haven't got that much to lose. I wouldn't want to be too skinny,' I protest.

'There's no such thing as too skinny,' she drawls.

'Some bigger women are really attractive,' I say. 'Take Nigella Lawson. Men love her.'

Elody looks as if she's about to be violently sick all over the table, she's turned a kind of puce colour and has her hand over her mouth to stop her from gagging.

'Don't fall into that trap,' she says sternly. 'Don't start thinking that you can get away with fatness any more than you can get away with large boils on your face. You can't, sweetheart. Men say they like fat women so that the fat women they are married to feel better about themselves and allow them to have sex. They don't really like them; how could they?'

And, you know, even though I'm fairly sure that if you asked 150 million men whether they'd rather spend the night with Nigella Lawson or Elody, they'd all scream, 'Nigella,' I still don't argue back. Elody's terrier-like determination leaves me thrashing in her wake. I'd rather acquiesce than fight.

As she talks, Elody lifts her immaculate black Chanel handbag onto the table between us and fishes inside. The gold chain rattles as she pulls out a small bottle of what look like prescription pills and pushes them towards me. 'Take one a day, every morning, with a large glass of water, keep drinking water all day and you'll find that your appetite dramatically reduces and the weight falls off.'

'Really? That's amazing. Are they legal?'

'Yes, of course they're legal. This is what everyone in Hollywood does. It's dieting the easy way.'

'Thanks,' I say. 'But shouldn't I get them prescribed to me by my own doctor? I can't take your pills.'

'Darling, you can't get them over here yet. Take mine and I'll get some more shipped over.'

'Why can't you get them over here? Are they dangerous?'

'Not at all,' says Elody, with a smile. 'You know America is always way ahead of Europe when it comes to medication. Everyone I know is taking them.' She lowers her voice and whispers a jaw-dropping list of superstar names. 'And Cindy Kearney been taking them for years. How do you think she got that perfume campaign? They're quite safe. The only side effect is that they keep you awake at night sometimes, but that's OK, as long as you're not eating. You burn off more calories when you're awake than when you're asleep so it's best not to sleep too much in any case. Just make sure you don't eat though, that would be fatal.'

'Fatal?'

'To remain fat: it is like some sort of terrible fatality. It is miserable, dark and depressing. I will help to lift you out of this terrible pit of darkness.'

Right. Never felt like a pit of darkness before, to be fair. But if they have such great effects, then why not? It would be good to lose a few pounds. It sounds like this would be a simple way to do it. The thought of going to the gym, and finding pictures of myself in Lycra all over the papers, fills me with horror.

I take one of the tablets out of the bottle and swallow it with a large gulp of coffee. It tastes OK. Well, it tastes of nothing, to be honest, which is all you ask of a pill really, isn't it?

By the time we leave the coffee shop, I'm feeling great, bursting with optimism. We walk past a skinny girl in great, skintight jeans and I think, Yeah! That'll be me in a few weeks. Actually, it would be nice to lose weight. I'm not talking about completely getting rid of my curves or anything, just making the curves I have got a little bit smaller, more in control – that's all. So that I fit in with my new friends; they're all so skinny I look like a barrage balloon next to them.

'Thanks, Elody,' I say giving her an entirely unwelcome hug. She has just been kind to me, in her own way, so I reckon a hug is called for. But as soon as I make contact with her, she recoils; clearly hugging is not something she's comfortable with. I wonder why . . . I don't know all that much about her. She seems to have no friends, certainly no boyfriend, and she never mentions family of any kind. The only hint she ever gives to a softer side is when she talks about Jon. Not for the first time, I find myself wondering who this woman is . . . where did she come from?

'Kelly?' says a familiar voice, breaking through my thoughts.

I disentangle myself from Elody's embrace and find myself face to face with Mandy and Sophie.

'Hi,' I say, jumping with joy; I'm so pleased to see them. They look scruffier than I remember, wearing cheap-looking coats and with Mandy's hair flying in the wind. It's great to see them though, really great. Just odd that they look so different from Elody.

'You look unbelievable,' says Mandy. 'Like a film star.'

I lean over and kiss Mandy on the cheek but notice that Sophie is scowling at me. When I move in her direction, she jerks her head back as if I'm going to hit her. Elody tuts beside me.

'What's the matter?' I ask, thinking that Sophie would be as delighted as me by this unexpected reunion, and would be dying to ask about Zadine. 'Did you get the message last night?'

'Yes, yes, we're very impressed,' says Sophie. 'Although I'd be more impressed if you'd made it for Mandy's birthday drinks.'

'Yes, sorry. There was nothing I could do about that.'

'And why didn't you return my calls. I must have rung about twenty times yesterday!' says Sophie. 'You don't take my calls any more.'

'That's rubbish. Of course I'd take your calls. What are you talking about?'

'I guess you're much too important for us now. I guess you're too busy for us.'

'That's completely untrue,' I say. 'I think about you girls all the time. I'm sorry about the birthday party but Rufus's flight was delayed so I ended up being stuck at the airport all evening,' I say. I don't know why I've just lied to them; I guess it's because the truth sounds so wholly ridiculous.

Mandy starts telling me how much it doesn't matter and that she totally understands. Sophie, on the other hand, has a look on her face that spells absolute anger and fury at me. 'What's the matter?' I ask. 'Why do you look so cross? There wasn't a lot that I could do.'

'Don't worry at all,' chips in Mandy. 'I wasn't expecting you but it's really nice that you tried to come. You look gorgeous by the way, have you lost weight? You look really slim.'

'Really slim?' says Elody under her breath but perfectly audible to everyone within a mile radius. 'As if.' She spits these last words out as if they were rancid mussels.

This is not going too well.

'This is Elody,' I say, as my new friend puts out a small, slim hand wrapped in a black, silk glove. Mandy puts out her hand; it looks twice the size and is all wrapped up in a big, puffy cream mitten in that material they make skiing gloves from. Elody looks like she can't work out whether to shake it or club it to death. Sophie looks Elody up and down, taking in the sheer black maxi dress, black cropped leather jacket and jet-black sunglasses. She keeps her hands stuffed deep into the pockets of her pale-blue anorak.

'I saw you, Kelly. I saw you arrive in that great big, black car, with the flash driver at the wheel. I saw you slow right down and look through the windows at us, then change your mind and drive right off. I saw, Kelly. Don't pretend you were at the airport. I guess we're just not good enough for you now, are we?'

'*No,*' I say, appalled at the conclusion she's leapt to and alarmed at how badly this is all going.

'We're not good enough for you?' says Mandy, clutching her face between her hands. 'Is that what you think?'

'No!' I say. 'No, no, no. Absolutely not. Of course you're good enough for me. You always have been and always will be.'

Elody is mumbling away to herself in French by the side of me, like some terrible comic character from '*Allo 'Allo.* I can only imagine what she's saying.

'Why lie then?' says Sophie.

'Lie about what?' I'm feeling all flustered and worried now . . . which doesn't seem fair considering all I've done is avoid dragging the world's press along to wreck their party. I acted out of concern for them; of course I wanted to go to the party, but to do so would have been unfair on Mandy and rather selfish of me.

'You just said that you were stuck at Heathrow all night but I saw you outside the pub. Why didn't you come in?'

Shit. Why did I lie? I just felt that the truth sounded obscure.

'I thought you wouldn't understand if I told you the

truth, but the reality is that my limo was followed by paparazzi.'

'And the last thing in the world that you needed was to be pictured next to us, I guess. That would do your image amongst your new posh friends no good at all, would it?'

'No, listen . . .' I try, but Sophie is determined to be heard.

'You don't care about us at all. You didn't come to the party; you won't take our calls. Katy and Jenny say you insisted on having your own office then as soon as one was arranged for you, you flounced out and never came back. We talked to them and they were calling you too yesterday and you never returned their calls, then last night we get a message from your new famous friend telling us how wonderful life is for you now. Well, I hope it is wonderful, Kelly. I hope it's wonderful enough to compensate for ruining all your friendships.'

'Let it go, ugly,' Elody screams at Sophie, wading in and placing herself rather alarmingly between me and Sophie and Mandy. She is pouting at them and staring with her heavily made-up catlike eyes. Because she's so thin, though, and Mandy is, er . . . .well, wider, she doesn't provide much of a physical barrier at all. 'One more word from you and the fat girl and you will be history,' she says dramatically, swinging her arms up and almost clobbering me in the face. 'Look at you – in your bad clothes – how dare you speak to Kelly like that when she's dressed in Lanvin.'

Fuck. Now this is *really* not going well at all.

'It's OK, Elody,' I say. 'These are the girls I used to live with. Everything's fine There's just a misunderstanding.'

'My bad clothes,' says Sophie, now fuming alongside a rather shocked-looking Mandy who looks like she's about to burst into tears. 'Is that what Kelly said to you? That we have "bad clothes"? Well, just because I don't have tons and tons of money like Kelly and can't afford to spend all day shopping doesn't mean I have bad taste in clothes. The reason I don't have loads of new clothes is because I spent my money on a lovely present for Mandy, and the reason I'm not clutching dozens of carrier bags like you two is because I've not spent my lunch hour shopping, I've spent it in Pizza Express, waiting for Kelly.'

Oh shit! Lunch. Fuck . . . Why did I forget that we were all supposed to go for lunch today?

'Oh God, I'm really sorry, Sophie,' I say, now feeling about an inch high. 'I completely forgot. We were at this casino and the time just flew by, and I . . .'

'Casino?' says Mandy, looking all worried. 'Why were you in a casino?'

'Too busy gambling with her new friend, then I suppose the two of you went for a nice lunch together,' says Sophie.

'We did *not* have lunch,' says Elody more angered by the accusation that she might have been eating than if Soph had accused her of murdering babies. 'Kelly does not eat lunch any more; she's on a diet.'

Oh God. How much worse can this all get? I am amazed at how much Elody's sticking up for me, and part of me's really flattered, but most of me is thinking, 'Please shut up; you're making this so much worse.'

'God, you've changed,' says Sophie angrily. 'You'd rather ponce around clothes shopping than see us. You'd rather diet yourself to nothing than come for a pizza with the girls. You know, when we didn't hear anything from you, I really thought you were going to turn up for lunch today with balloons and a present for Mandy to make it all right again, but you couldn't even do that, could you?'

'You don't need to diet at all,' says Mandy sweetly. 'You have a lovely figure.'

'Errrrr,' pipes in Elody. 'You are perhaps not exactly the best person to give advice on who needs to lose . . .'

I grab Elody and drag her off before she can finish her insult and compound the problem. When I look back, the two of them are standing there, staring after me. Fuck.

'I feel awful,' I tell Elody.

'I know. I would too if I had friends like that.'

'No, I feel awful because they are my friends.'

'That's what I'm saying,' she says. 'You have fat friends. It's embarrassing. We are agreed. But I know what will make everything perfect again.'

'What?' My heart lifts. I'm hoping she's going to suggest something magical to get my relationship with the girls back on track again. I'm hoping she can think of a great plan for me to sort out this mess that's been caused.

'Shoes,' she says. 'If you feel awful, you have to buy shoes. It's the only way.'

'Yeah, but shoes aren't going to change the fact that I've let down two of my best mates, are they?'

'Best mates? Those two? Darling. Please. No. You are in a different world now, a world full of new, thinner, glossier and much better dressed people. Those two – from your past. Come with me . . . into the future. I need to introduce you to some of my best friends. Here . . .

look . . . these little darlings are called Louboutins . . . they are my very best friends.'

It's all too surreal for words. I'm given a glass of champagne, my feet are massaged and words of flattery are hurled at me while I shop for catastrophically expensive and terrifyingly high-heeled shoes.

'Always buy shoes when you are in distress,' instructs Elody, slipping her feet into shiny black numbers with these odd-looking studs up the heel. 'Shoe shopping is a calming experience. So much better than injecting drugs or drinking a bottle and a half of whisky or eating some bread,' she says, indicating to the assistant that she will take the fancy black numbers which, to be frank, look more like weapons than shoes.

'I usually find that thickly buttered toast, a large mug of tea and a Twix sorts me out,' I say.

'Stop teasing me,' says Elody with lightness to her voice. 'You're being silly now.'

No, I'm not.

It's 5 pm by the time we get back to the house, laden with bags, and feeling exhausted. My head's spinning and my feet hurt. Shopping like this is a bloody stressful experience, let me tell you. I'm desperately worried about the girls, and the horrible meeting I had with them. Bollocks. Those two mean the world to me; I can't believe that happened.

'Wine?' asks Elody. She looks as if she's settling herself in for the night.

'I won't. Thanks,' I say. 'I've got the most terrible headache.'

I've no idea whether Jan and Isabella will be coming round at 6pm, as I suggested in my text, because they didn't reply to it, but just in case they do, I don't want Elody here.

'Listen, I'm exhausted,' I try. 'I think I'm going to have a bath and get an early night. Do you mind?'

'Oh,' says Elody, looking absolutely distraught. 'Is it something I did?'

'No, no. Of course not. I've had a lovely day, but I'm dead on my feet now.'

'OK,' she says, warily. 'I've got like a ton of parties to go to anyway, so I'll leave you to it. Call me if you get lonely and need company, and thanks for being such a great friend today.'

'No problem,' I say with a smile. 'I loved it, Elody. It is I who should be thanking you.'

Elody leaves and I feel instantly guilty. I should have told her that Isabella and Jan might be popping round, and I should have asked her if she wanted to stay. The problem is that she's so unpopular. If they arrive and see that she is here, they'll stay five minutes and leave, and I'm keen to get to know some of the other women, not just Elody.

It's bang on 6 pm when I hear that someone has arrived at the gates.

'Jan and Isabella,' says Pamela enthusiastically. 'They're such lovely people. I'm glad you're getting friendly with them instead of . . . Well, I'm just glad you have new friends.'

The unspoken words, of course, are that Elody's rather bad news.

'Come in,' I say, ushering them into the sitting room,

then quickly changing my mind. While Elody's always keen for us to sit in a rather formal fashion, I'm much happier in the snug at the back of the house.

'Shall we go through to the snug?' I say. The two women look at me blankly. I don't suppose they've even seen the room.

'Come on, I'll show you.'

I lead them to the back of the house and swing open the door to the snug. They both gasp appreciatively. 'It's beautiful,' they say. 'My God. It's a lovely girly oasis.' It does look good now I've finished messing with it. I have filled it with plants and flowers, and put little sparkly fairy lights up around the edge. In the evening it looks almost magical and in the daytime when the winter sun shines through the glass it's like being outdoors. The rest of Rufus's house is so formal and kind of masculine that I wanted somewhere that would be fun for me to hang out with my friends. I imagined bringing Mandy and Sophie here and the three of us lying around, getting drunk and gossiping under the twinkling lights and the soft smell of flowers. After today, that seems incredibly unlikely.

As my new friends settle themselves down, I head into the kitchen to find David and ask him which sort of wine I should offer them. I feel a responsibility to get this right. I know that if I were in either of their houses, they'd uncork the best bottle available, and we'd sip it gently, murmuring in appreciation. The trouble is, they know about wine and I don't. It was embarrassing enough last night. I ended up drinking six gin and tonics because I was too ashamed to admit that I didn't like it.

'Were you thinking of white or red?' asks David.

Bollocks. I don't know. I always drink white but isn't red supposed to be better? I just have no bloody idea about this.

'Hang on,' I say to David and I walk back to the snug.

'I have a confession,' I announce. 'I know nothing about wine. All I ever drink with my friends is the cheapest wine available ... and I usually add lemonade to it. Last night Zadine asked me what wine I wanted and I nearly died. I'd love to bring some nice wine but David asked me whether I wanted red or white and I fell at the first hurdle ... I didn't know what to say. I don't know which is better.'

'You big fool,' says Jan, standing up. 'The best wine is the wine you prefer. It doesn't matter about cost or what's "trendy". You just need to find out what wine you like and that is, officially, the best wine. I think we should do some wine-tasting. Don't you? That way, you can work out what you like.'

'Oh yes,' I say, overcome with delight.

'Lovely idea,' says Isabella, standing up gracefully, and stroking her cream wraparound dress across her knees. The woman is flawless, honestly; I don't think I've ever seen anyone look more effortlessly glamorous. From her gently tanned, slim legs, crossed at the knee, to her high, strappy sandals in a pale-beige colour. Her hair is neatly tied back and her make-up is lovely and understated. She told me when I met her before that she uses fake tanning cream on her legs because the sun is so bad for the skin; I think I need some lessons from her. There are no streaks or strange orange patches like I get, and, when I try to cover the streaks up, I end up going so dark I look like an extra from *Slumdog Millionaire*.

Jan is in the kitchen, telling David what our plans are.

'Brilliant idea,' says Pamela from the other side of the kitchen, heading for the elaborate French-looking dresser in the dining room where Rufus keeps the glasses. 'You can tell me what wine I should be drinking too. I normally serve what I'm told to serve without having a clue what it all tastes like!'

'Then you must come and join us,' I instruct. 'And bring Julie too.'

'No. I couldn't,' says Pamela, wiping her hands on her apron. 'Look at the state of me.'

'Yes you could,' I insist. 'I want you to come. You look lovely. I insist you come.'

So, three becomes five. Julie and Pamela look desperately nervous, as they sit in the corner sipping the wine. 'I feel a bit out of place; are you sure this is OK?' Pamela keeps muttering to me.

'Yes, of course. I want you here.'

'This is a Chablis,' says Jan, sipping gently and allowing the taste to wash around her mouth. 'See what you think.'

'It's a lovely wine,' says Isabella with confidence. They seem to take tiny sips, while Julie, Pamela and I knock the whole lot back every time.

'You're supposed to spit the wine out when you're tasting,' says Jan. 'But that's so inelegant that we've decided against it.'

'And it's more fun zis way,' says Isabella, with a distinctive slur. 'Now . . . what next?'

It's nearly midnight. Five women, about forty glasses, nine half-empty wine bottles and the sound of hysterical laughter permeate the house.

'And finally, the tenth wine. This is Sancerre,' says Jan, passing around glasses. 'I think you might like this one.'

'I ly them all,' I say, with an almighty hiccup. 'All bloody loverly if you ass me.'

Pamela is asleep in the corner and snoring rather loudly, while Julie is trying to cope with a fit of the giggles. I'm just deliriously and hopelessly drunk and loving every minute of it. I now know that my favourite wines are Pouilly Fumé in white and Châteauneuf-du-Pape in red. Will I remember them in the morning? Hell, no. Jan assures me that she'll write it all down for me, and even keep the labels so I remember what I liked.

'Howdyastaysosobernsensible?' asks Isabella, one leg falling off the other as she attempts to recross her legs the other way but fails miserably. 'How do you, Jan? Stay sooo sensible?'

'I don't swallow,' she replies.

'Don't swallow?' says Isabella, almost tumbling off her chair. 'Don't swallow?'

It's too much for the three of us to bear. We practically fall backwards off our seats, laughing hysterically until tears pour down our faces. Then Jan laughs too; more, I suspect, out of amusement at the state we're in than anything else, but once she starts, she can't stop. 'Not that sort of "don't swallow",' she says. 'I meant I'm taking tiny tastes, barely enough to swallow.' But we're laughing so much that we can't hear her.

'Oh sod it,' she says, reaching for one of the half-empty bottles and taking a large slug from it. 'I might as well get pissed too.'

Chapter 12

There are two weeks remaining before Rufus returns from Los Angeles and I have to be honest with you, I'm starting to lose the plot. It doesn't help that I've spent days shaking off the worst hangover known to man or womankind, and that the diet pills are making me feel nauseous and irritable. Added to all that, no one ever phones me. I mean, not ever! I have been ringing Sophie and Mandy like mad, despite the fact that Elody seems to think it's the worst idea in the world. With them making no effort to communicate with me, it means we just don't talk any more. Despite sending texts and leaving messages, nothing comes back. I can't believe they're willing to cast years of friendship aside so easily. God, and I really want to talk to them . . . I hate that Rufus is away, I hate that the papers are full to brimming with pictures of him on various LA beaches with attractive girls swooning around him. And whilst I know I could talk to Jan and Isabella because they're both so lovely, they're Rufus's friends, so I don't feel I can sit there moaning about him.

I talk to Rufus every day and I've taken to calling him in the night because I'm not sleeping properly. I get about four hours sleep, then I'm wide awake and can't sleep any more . . . bloody pills. God, I can't stop moaning about things at the moment – I'm in this terrible vortex of misery that's pulling me further and further into it. So, while we're at it – I hate the fact that the paparazzi are always outside so I'm stuck in here unless I want to be in the news. And I'm . . . 'Oh, hi, Elody. I wasn't expecting you.'

'Kelly darling,' she says. 'I couldn't sleep last night. I kept thinking of your footwear crisis. I think it would be a good idea if we reviewed your shoe situation and ordered some more in from designers as soon as possible. It's just not right at the moment; not right at all.'

Oh God. I can't do this any more. I really want to go to the Rose Garden and talk to Frank the gardener, not look at more bloody shoes. In fact, I'd rather do anything than obsess about clothing and spending money. It's stultifying; all this talk about what goes with what and how 'anyone who's anyone' is wearing boyfriend-style blazers. I don't even know what those are and – you know what? – I don't care.

'Why don't we go out and have fun instead!' I suggest boldly. 'Or we could go and stuff ourselves in Pizza Express and collapse on the sofa and watch a movie afterwards.'

What's the point in being rich and having loads of free time if you spend it all in such a boring fashion? I'd rather have less money and less free time, but at least be having fun with the little I have.

'Telephone,' says David, walking into the sitting room and bowing deeply. He sometimes bows down so far I fear he'll go arse over tit and never get up. 'What do you mean you killed the butler?' Rufus will say, and I'll be stuck there trying to explain.

I have to say I'm pleased with the distraction. I leave Elody standing there in a minor trance, swooning slightly and staggering around at the thought of eating pizza.

'Hello darling,' says mum. I should have known it would be her. She never rings the mobile. Everyone bar Rufus and Mum just calls on the mobile, or should I say everyone used just to call on the mobile, now they don't call at all.

'Hi, Mum. How are you?'

'I'm fine, sweetheart,' she says. 'Are you in?'

'Yes I am,' I say, laughing to myself. 'It's my home phone, Mother.' There's also the fact that I'm always in; the only place I go is shopping and to the Rose Garden. I sit there among the wintry remains of the summer blooms and it's like Rufus is with me; it's pure magic. I love it there. I chat to Frank and feel better about the world. The press haven't managed to discover my secret floral hideaway, so I feel safe. I hope they never, ever find out. I certainly shan't be mentioning it in public, and I know Rufus won't, so hopefully our secret place will remain just that for a while longer. When I'm not talking to an elderly man in gardening gloves, or shopping with Elody, I'm at home because there are paparazzi outside my house. Where else would I be? Where else can I go?

'We're at the end of the driveway,' she says. 'We're coming for two days.'

Whaaaaat? 'Who's "we"?'

'Me and Great-Aunt Maude.'

Oh Lord above. Holy fuck. I glance over at Elody as she whittles her way through my 'shoe wardrobe' (one shelf), casting aside anything unsuitable. Well, this is sure going to be an interesting meeting.

'Why didn't you tell me sooner? There are photographers out there. Be careful.'

'I know there are photographers here. Maude's having

her picture taken with them right now. They've got her pouting and preening and lying down with her legs in the air. She does look a sight.'

Holy fuck. 'Open the gates!!!!' I scream in the direction of David. 'My mum and my batty great-aunt are out there. Get them in here now before they say something ridiculous to the press, or start giving them photographs of me playing with a little duck in the bath aged four.'

David moves with surprising speed considering his advancing years and grabs the entryphone system, telephones security and shouts: 'Code red . . . main gate.' A loud alarm shrieks through the building and David clutches his head in his hand. 'Oh dear, wrong code,' he says, then picks up the phone again and addresses the security guys on the other end. 'Code blue!' he squeals. 'I meant code blue. Sorry.'

Oh God. I hope code red doesn't mean that Mum and Maude have been bundled to the ground and hit with sticks because the security guys think they're trying to break in. The alarm stops wailing immediately and I await the arrival of my hapless female relatives. If I hadn't been feeling so rubbish, I might have found some humour in the fact that Great-Aunty Maude was about to meet Elody Elloissie. On the linear spectrum of sartorial elegance they would be at opposite ends.

I hear Maude before I see her. Her raspy, unforgettable voice carries on the cold winter air and violently assaults my ears. She has the Mike Tyson of voices, does Maude. If I spend too long with her I have headaches for weeks afterwards. I think it's because she wears a hearing aid but has it turned up nowhere near high enough, so she can't hear properly, and in rather the same way as someone with headphones on who resorts to shouting above the sound that only they can hear, so Maude shouts to be heard because her perception of volume is limited by her hearing difficulties.

'Kell,' she howls when she sees me. Elody has walked into the sitting room and is looking at Maude as if my great-aunt had two heads.

'Shall I call security?' she asks quietly, nodding towards Maude.

'No, it's fine . . .' I really don't want to have to say this but . . . here goes: 'Maude's my great-aunt.'

'Oh my God!!!' says Elody. 'You need to keep that very quiet.'

God, that woman can be a bitch sometimes. 'Don't you have any embarrassing relatives Elody? You know, relatives who don't dress head to toe in Prada and sometimes say things in public that have you reeling in embarrassment?'

'Not that I know of,' she says dismissively, and it occurs to me how little I know about Elody. I chat about my friends and family all the time and she tells me about her favourite clothes designers. I once pulled out a picture of Mum and she pulled out a picture of her favourite Louis Vuitton bondage shoes. She doesn't seem to 'do' relatives. She's certain not mentioned any to me.

'Do you have any relatives at all? You never talk about them.'

'Jon is my only relative and he's dead.'

'But he wasn't a relative; he was your boyfriend,' I say. 'Where do your mum and dad live? Are they in Paris?'

'We should work out what we're going to do with these

scruffy old people,' says Elody, blindly and blatantly ignoring my questions. I'm fascinated by her family now she's refusing to talk about them. I guess once people get to a certain age, like beyond twenty-five, you take them for what they are, and what they've made of themselves, without stopping to think too hard about where they've come from. With Elody, though, I find myself wondering all sorts of things – where are her parents now? Does she see them? What are they like? Why has her late boyfriend had more of an impact on her than her own parents?

'What will your relatives do?' she asks me. 'They're going to end up getting in our way if we don't organise something.'

'Mum and Aunt Maude are going to stay here tonight,' I say, and Elody gasps in amazement. You'd think I'd invited a pack of wolves to stay in the house.

'Surely they can stay in a hotel?'

'No. They're staying in the house.' I feel quite protective now. How absurd would it be for my mum to come and pay a visit and for me to stick her in the local B&B? Elody may have a dysfunctional relationship with her parents but I don't.

'I can lend you the money for a hotel if you want,' she offers.

'Elody, it's not about the money.' How could she think it would be about the money when I've spent literally thousands of pounds on clothes over the past few days? 'I'd like Mum to stay here.' (That's not even true but I'm overcome by a wave of overprotectiveness towards my mother.)

'What will they do while we're at the party tonight?' Elody asks brightly, thinking she's caught me out. Clearly the mad old women can't stay here when we've already arranged to go out.

'They can come with us,' I respond, as much to my own surprise as Elody's. The wave of overprotectiveness I'm feeling towards my mother is now out of all control. It's a tsunami.

'To the party?' This last comment, I should point out, is screamed rather than spoken in a voice that has a rather unattractive shrieky element to it.

'Yep.'

So, the decision has been made, and it appears to be entirely my fault so I can't even complain about it; we're going to the party with Maude and Mum in tow. Furthermore, Elody has offered to style them for the occasion. Already I know that this can't end at all well.

'Sure,' I say, bravely and unwisely, and now I'm sitting here, waiting for emergence of the newly styled women.

'Are you ready?' asks Elody. Then, without waiting for a reply, she swings open the doors separating the bedroom from the huge and very grand dressing room. I'm greeted by a sight that almost moves me to tears. Mum looks like a princess, clad in a simple, long cream dress that does wonders for her figure. It sweeps to the floor making her legs look about three times as long as they do normally. As she moves to leave the room, the silk ripples around her feet, shimmering under the light of the candelabras. The sleeves are long and wide at the ends, adding to the lovely floaty look of the dress. At her neckline, there's a simple necklace and matching earrings, and Elody has draped a caramel-coloured shawl over her shoulders.

'Blimey, Mum!' I say when I see her. I have genuinely never seen her look anything like this good. I see the tears of happiness in her eyes, and feel a wave of affection towards Elody.

'Now, it's Maude,' says Elody with a flourish, and my great-aunt walks out of the room with an exaggerated wiggle designed to make her look sexy (but she just looks drunk). She looks much better than she looked but nowhere near as elegant as Mum. She has on a two-piece lilac-coloured suit with a fox-fur stole and a matching fur hat. To be honest, she looks like something out of the forties, which, according to Elody, is exactly the look Aunt Maude was after. She is wearing an alarming amount of Elody's trademark blood-red lipstick and her eyes have so much make-up on them that she looks a little bruised, as if she got into a fight with the fox before draping it over her shoulders.

'You both look wonderful,' I say, feeling a little dull in my simple black shift dress. 'Shall we go?'

'But we'll be on time!' cries Elody with considerable disdain. 'What will people think of us?'

'Come on; these two don't like staying out too late. If we don't go now, it won't be worth us going at all.'

'OK,' she concedes reluctantly, and we troop off to yet another Friday night party with my new friends on the hill, but this time with Mum and Great-Aunt Maude in tow.

Chapter 13

I know about halfway through the car journey that the decision to bring Mum and Maude to the party is not just 'bad' but probably the 'worst decision I've ever made in my life'. I had no idea that Great-Aunt Maude's incontinence is quite such an issue. I had no idea that Elody had insisted on her wearing these skintight control pants that leave no room for her incontinence pads. I had no idea of anything, looking back. It's not until she begins clawing at her head (which Mum says she always does when she feels stressed – I didn't know that either) and rubbing her hands all over her face that I wake up to the fact that problems are afoot.

'What's wrong, love?' Mum keeps asking, as the smell of old lady urine wafts through the car, clashing with the strong musky perfume favoured by Elody to create a truly offensive aroma.

'Everything all right?' Henry asks, winding down the window.

'Everything's fine, love,' replies my mum, gently stroking Maude's arm. 'We just need to get Maude to the party where she can sort herself out and everything will be fine.' She carries on stroking Maude's arm in such a kind and generous way that I feel almost moved to tears. Well, it's either the stroking or the strong ammonia smell floating through the car that's moving me to tears: one or the other.

We get to the house and Maude climbs out; her hair is standing up on end and her lipstick is smudged right across her face. She looks as if she's been in a drunken brawl. The back of her dress is soaking wet, along with the back seat of the car. I look up at Henry apologetically, but he shrugs my fears aside. 'I'll take it and get it cleaned while you're at the party,' he says. 'It'll be as good as new by the time I pick you up.'

'Thanks,' I say. Rufus's staff truly are some of the nicest people in the world.

Elody has not said a word for the entire journey. She just storms up to the door of Zadine's modern house, and rings the doorbell furiously. The Spice Girls song '2 Become 1' bursts out: a rather nasty tinkly-plinkly doorbell version of it, which is more offensive than the real thing. 'Christ,' says Elody under her breath. 'What on earth are we doing in this place? I mean – Zadine Collins? Why would I – Elody Elloissie – come to a party organised by Zadine Collins? Christ, if ever there was a woman untouched by charm and uncluttered by talent or style it was Zadine bloody Collins ... Zadine! Darling! So wonderful to see you. How are you? You look wonderful. Fabulous.'

'My God!' exclaims Zadine, looking past the fawning Elody and staring straight at me. I think she's going to get cross with me for bringing such an entourage, but she seems to have hardly noticed them at all. 'You've lost sooo much weight! How are you doing it? Jan and Issy said you were looking thinner but I wasn't expecting you to look *so* thin. Make sure you don't overdo it; you don't want to lose all those lovely feminine curves of yours.'

Once we're inside, Elody goes storming through the house with her hands in the air, as if to say 'all this is nothing to do with me'. Zadine, meanwhile, is amazing; she's thrilled that I've invited Mum and Maude to the party and even manages not to look too shocked when she catches sight of Maude with her mad hair and crazy lady make-up. She keeps saying things like, 'I'm so glad your mum and Maude could come, especially given who else is here. We should get Maude cleaned up before she meets the special guests though, shouldn't we?'

Maude is having none of it; she's heard the party music and is transported back fifty years to a time when she was the queen of the South London dance floor. Before any of us can stop her, she's waddled into the sitting room and, with make-up that looks as if it were applied by Alice Cooper, and with the bladder control of a two-year-old, she's leaping around to the music with gay abandon. I glance at Elody and she's making that slice across the neck motion that people do when they want something to end as soon as possible. I can assure her that no one wants this to end more than I.

'Ah, look at her; she's having such fun,' says Mum warm-heartedly.

I don't think I ever realised before just how amazing and patient my mum is. In the room there is the usual collection of the rich and well connected, including an older-looking couple, watching from the corner of the room, holding their champagne glasses gingerly by the long stems and glancing with alarm at events taking place before them. I vaguely recognise the woman. She must be an actress; she has that impossibly well-groomed look that so many of these ageing stars have. She looks a little like Jane Fonda; a tiny, little creature with the smallest wrists and the slimmest ankles I've ever seen. Gosh, I bet she was a stunner when she was younger.

Elody walks over to them and they embrace her passionately, kissing her cheek, remarking on her incredibly high shoes, and examining the necklace round her neck. I can imagine the conversation now. 'Oh but, Elody, you always look so perfect. Your jewellery is divine.' People have a habit of noticing, remarking on and admiring Elody without seeming to actually like her that much. You get the feeling that they'd be first in the queue to tell her she looks wonderful, but last in the queue to hold the sick bowl if she was unwell. Not like Mandy and Sophie. I feel so bad about what happened with those two.

Meanwhile, in the middle of the floor, Maude is sitting down with her legs splayed, having overcome the restrictions imposed by the dress by hiking it up to her knees. She's doing that 'rock the boat' song that she says she remembers her children doing at discos when they were younger. She's trying her best to urge the glamorous older couple to join in but, for some inexplicable reason, the prospect of joining an incontinent old lady with mad wiry hair and lipstick all over her face, is not appealing to them in any way. I'm standing there, wondering what to do when Mum walks over to her, helps her to her feet and takes her off towards the door where Zadine is waiting to assist. In front, the two older people are walking towards me. Thank God I've just moved to this area and don't know anyone.

'Hello,' says the lady who's even more glamorous close up. 'You must be Kelly.'

'Yes,' I say, waiting for them to introduce themselves.

'I'm Rufus's mother,' she says with a half-smile. 'It's lovely to meet you at last. Who on earth was the mad woman with the crazy hair?'

Oh God.

Chapter 14

EXCLUSIVE
By Katie Joseph
Daily Post Showbiz Correspondent

Bizarre goings-on in the home of Rufus George! While the actor is away in LA working on his re-incarnation as 007, his new live-in lover appears to have turned his mansion into an old people's home. Look at our exclusive pictures taken last night!

These two ancient women, danced around for our cameras before being whisked inside by burly security men who rushed out while sirens raged through the building. They threatened our photographers who were only doing their jobs, and hurled the old ladies into the back of a black car before driving them through the gates. The ruffians then grabbed the camera off one photographer and ran inside with it so the pictures could not be published. But don't worry! We had not one but two photographers there last night, and the other managed to escape from the thugs to bring you these exclusive shots of the two women who look like mental home escapees. Weird? You betcha! Rufus will be wondering what his lovely young lady has been up to while he has been in LA.

Just one more day before Rufus returns and I CAN'T WAIT. My God, I'm just yearning to hold him and kiss him and . . . well, you know what. More than anything, I'm desperate to have him here; away from that horrible bitch from hell Kearney. If I see another picture in the paper of her smooching up to him with her pretty little heart-shaped face aglow and her blonde hair rippling over the shoulders of her painfully thin body, I think I'll scream. Fucking hell. Why did he have to go out there to promote the film? Couldn't he have done it from here?

I could really have done without the pictures of Mum and Maude being splashed all over the papers, with a follow-up story when the paper realised that the two old women they'd captured on camera were two of my closest relations. Then there was Dodgy Dave. I just knew he'd materialise . . . talking about what a 'goer' I was. Christ! My dad was delighted to read that. The drink-driving story came out too. I knew it would. Well, that's not true. I didn't know it would, but I feared it would and had been warned by Rufus that it might well find its way into the public domain. The hard thing about this life is that people write about you, and you have no real right of reply because things are exacerbated if you add your voice to the debate so, basically, there is no debate. Everyone just says what they want about you and, unless it's truly damaging, it's better to lay low than to strike a blow in your defence.

I think all this press intrusion is having a particularly big effect on me because I'm so bored all the time. I stopped working for a month because I just couldn't do it properly so I'm sitting at home, obsessing about everything and everyone.

I'm losing weight, which is the one good thing in all of this, but the drugs are stopping me from sleeping at all. I mean, really; I don't sleep at night any more, I just pace around and go onto Google and terrify myself half to death as I see pictures of Cindy Kearney. I then get caught up in a horrible cycle of depression about the fact that she must be sleeping with Rufus and that prompts me to dig even deeper and to scour the internet for even more pictures and stories about her; all of which appear to confirm my fears that she's much prettier than me, much slimmer, better dressed and with nicer hair than me, and most damning of all . . . far better suited to being with Rufus than I will ever be.

Rufus is back tomorrow . . . tomorrow!!!! The prospect of it is sending shivers right through me. I've come to terms with the fact that my friends (should I call them 'former friends'?) are no longer interested in me, and my life now revolves around these Friday night drinks parties with my 'new' friends. I have been invited to openings and premieres and things like that, but Elody's been a fantastic buffer, and has told Rufus's agent (because all the invitations etc. do tend to go through him) that when offers come in, he's to send them to her and she'll discuss them with me. So far she's rejected them all, saying that Rufus wouldn't like it if I went to them without him, which I guess is fair enough (even though he is always saying that he's happy for me to go if I want to). When they're important events or going to be full of celebrities, Elody has tended to go in my place – which she loves.

I've also come to the terms with the fact that Rufus and I hail from such colossally different backgrounds that it's like we're almost different species. That was obviously thrown into real stark relief when my mum and Maude and his mum, Daphne, and her new husband, Joey, came to the party together. My mum was almost curtseying at Daphne and I saw Daphne take a distinct step back when she was introduced to my mum. We didn't even bother introducing her to Maude; we decided it was easier all round if we just didn't go there.

I didn't say much more to Daphne that night, other than to enquire whether she wanted to stay at the house, and how long she was staying for. It turns out that no, she didn't want to stay at the house, but she was going to be around for a while – for a week, to be precise, at an interior design show and awards evening. 'I'm the host,' she declared proudly.

'Oh please, do come and stay,' I said, thinking that I ought to, for Rufus's sake, make a point of sounding as if I really wanted her to come, but even as I made the offer, Elody was slashing her hand across her neck as if to suggest that would be a really bad idea.

'Darling, don't stay at the house, Kelly has relatives there,' she said in half-whispered, wholly conspiratorial tones to Daphne.

Rufus's mother smiled knowingly, as if to suggest that she understood.

It was all very rude, if you think about it. But that's what these people are . . . they're all rude; there's no other way to describe them. Anyway, it meant Daphne didn't stay at the house and I can't begin to tell you how utterly relieved I was about that. The thought of two sets of relatives coexisting with the staff running around catering to their different demands would have been too much for me to face on my own.

Daphne spent most of the night talking to Elody about clothes; the two of them speaking the same language of trapeze shapes, bell sleeves, eighties retro and 'darling Vivienne, isn't she a scream!' Also hotly debating the role of pleats on the Paris catwalks, and the surprise news that in New York it was all about ruffles. Who knew? Mainly though, Daphne went on and on and on about how much she loved Elody's necklace. There was a rare moment of lightness and humour between Elody and me afterwards when she said, 'Every time I see that woman she goes on about my necklace; it might be less painful if I just gave her the fucking thing.'

God how I wish Rufus was here.

I've spoken to him loads, of course. We have heaps of phone calls and he says he sends lots of texts but I never get any of them. Perhaps texts don't come through when you text from abroad? Anyway, he ends up reading out the texts on the phone in the evening, which is always quite funny.

I remain entirely paranoid about bloody Cindy Kearney, of course, because Elody does go on and on about how pretty she is and how much they used to adore one another, and how everyone thought he'd end up with her, but the thing is, I've been scouring the newspapers and the TV and the internet and I can't find any mention of the fact that the two of them ever went out together.

'Are you completely and absolutely sure,' I say to Elody,

but she just smiles knowingly in a way that is becoming intensely irritating.

'The reason it's not in the papers is because they fought hard to keep it out of the papers. Theirs wasn't a celebrity relationship; it was the real thing. They adored one another. I think they still do, and that's why they're looking after one another like this.'

Thanks a fucking lot. My feelings towards Elody definitely ebb and flow in direct proportion to her crassness and thoughtlessness. Some days I think she's really sweet and helpful and I don't know how I'd cope in this strange new world without her. On other days, such as when she's really winding me up about Rufus, I could strangle her. She seems so callous, so cruel and hurtful. I know I'm feeling particularly vulnerable because of the diet pills, which have left me feeling depressed and tired, but she's still way out of line sometimes.

'I'm coming off these pills,' I tell her. 'They're turning me into a monster. I can't keep taking them and feeling this horrible.'

'You can,' she insists. 'You just have to get through the difficulty of the first few weeks and you'll get used to them, and they'll get used to you.' Elody insists that if I persevere for another couple of weeks, I'll have dropped a stone in total by Christmas and that way I'll be able to guarantee that Rufus will forget all about the charms of Cindy and return to me.

'What do you mean "return"?' I ask.

'Well, she's attractive. He's away for weeks. He didn't tell you he was going, and he never mentioned that Olivia would be with him or that his ex-girlfriend was in the film. With the best will in the world, it does rather seem as if he's up to no good out there. I mean – what sort of evidence are you after, woman? Would you like a video of them having sex? Is that what you need?'

'No,' I say. 'Of course not. But there isn't any evidence at all.'

'That's because men are very good at hiding evidence, which, in itself, proves that they are having affairs. Have you been through all his things?'

'Been through his things? No. Of course I haven't been through his things,' I say.

'No?' Elody takes a step back in amazement and does nothing to hide her incomprehension. 'What sort of woman doesn't go through her husband's things when he's away with his hot, young and glamorous ex-girlfriend?'

'He's not my husband,' I retort rather pedantically. My heart is racing, my head is throbbing and I feel like shit. Frankly, pedantic is about as good as it's going to get with me at the moment.

'No, my love, and he never will be your husband unless you get a grip.' She illustrates this last point by gripping her tiny hands into tense bundles, squeezing them so tightly that all the sinews in her hands stand out; even the sinews in her scrawny neck have jumped to attention, making it look gnarled and knotted like the trunk of a tree. She looks old, and I feel myself strangely and rather uncharitably pleased by this.

'Get a grip, *ma petite fleur*,' she continues, her eyes narrowing and her eyebrows struggling to raise themselves against the barrage of Botox in her forehead. 'A woman must do due diligence before committing to a man.

Dahling, it is vital. Taking a husband is like buying a house or a business. You have to know what you're buying into. You have to be sure you're getting your money's worth. While he's away you have a perfect opportunity to pry; don't lose this valuable chance. He would be disappointed in you if he didn't think you were taking this relationship seriously. Now, I'm going out for a while to get my skin plumped so it looks its best for Friday night's party. I may be some time.'

Elody disappears, clip-clopping dramatically down the wooden corridor. She probably likes to think she sounds like Marlene Dietrich; a fusion of drama and style wrapped up in arrogance and all personified in those tiny footsteps. The truth, though, is that she sounds more like a show horse. Once the sound of hooves has faded into the distance, I turn immediately to the room in front of me. Is she right? I suppose there would be no harm in looking through his things, if only to reassure myself that, as I suspect, he's not doing anything wrong.

OK, let's try to be logical about this. Logic's not my strongpoint, to be fair, but I do need a little bit of it now. If I were a handsome Hollywood film star with things to hide from my depressed, overweight, unadventurous girlfriend, where would I hide them? With a speed that would impress Linford Christie, I'm straight onto the obvious places: the bedside cabinet, beneath the bed, in his sock drawer, in his cufflink drawer, his handkerchief drawer (yep, I know, a drawer – but he does have a lot of cufflinks and hankies, so he has to keep them somewhere). Nothing. Not even a slight hint that anything untoward has ever been there. In the boxer shorts drawer there are boxer shorts and in the tie drawer there is nothing but neatly rolled-up ties.

In his office, where everything is so organised I'm worried about even standing there for fear of marking the walnut wood floor. I'm worried that my breath will mess up the carefully ordered air. Really, I've never known anything like this. I know he has tons of help, and that there are people racing around after him to tidy up with every step he takes, but still . . . to be this tidy . . . it's kind of weird. Well, to me it is. There's not a thing out of place. It looks like no one's ever been in here. It's like some derelict upper class gentleman's club in Mayfair that is no longer frequented but is still cleaned every day by diligent staff.

To be honest, I don't know where to start when it comes to searching through his stuff. The idea that there'll be anything secreted away is quite absurd. Everything's so perfectly filed and organised. Honestly. How would he have something incriminating in here? The chances of finding a used condom in his scripts drawer, or a pair of lacy knickers in his file of rejected Broadway offers are about as likely as me finding out that my mother is actually Posh Spice. Added to the fact that it's desperately unlikely that I'll ever find anything of interest, is the realisation that I must exercise caution because there are CCTV cameras throughout the house. I'm hoping that Sam, the guy who heads up our security, will just think I've mislaid something and am searching for it, but I hope he doesn't work out that I'm a paranoid girlfriend looking for evidence of infidelity. What if I'm the latest in a long line of girlfriends who have behaved like this? Shit. The thought of Sam and the security guards all sitting around the TV screen saying, 'There she goes . . . just like all the others . . .' makes me feel quite queasy.

I wonder how many girls he's brought back here. He told me he's only had one girlfriend since moving to England, and he saw her for a couple of weeks before they split up, but he could have brought other girls back – one-night stands or brief flings. Let's face it, he could have been lying to me, and actually have had hundreds of girlfriends. That's certainly the view that Elody has adopted.

I'm swaying between a reluctance to behave badly and a determination to uncover the truth. If Rufus is being straight, then he has nothing to fear from my search through his office; if he's not being straight then he deserves everything he gets.

I open the main drawer of his desk (walnut . . . everything in this room is walnut with a green leather desk pad and green leather cushion on the chair). In the drawer there's mainly stationery and a couple of personal notes that are bank related or film related or business related or agent related or blah, blah, blah, blah, blah . . . what's this? There's a small internal drawer at the back of the main drawer which doesn't open . . . that *must* be where he keeps all sorts of incriminating things that he doesn't want me to see. Shit. Where can the key be? I'm going through every drawer in a mad hurry now – not searching for photos or letters as I was previously, but for a key to let myself into this drawer that I'm convinced *must* contain something incriminating, derogatory or downright mean. My conviction that the drawer is full of proof of misbehaviour strengthens with every moment that I can't find the key.

Why would someone have a drawer within a drawer that's locked and no sign of a key anywhere? If that's not dodgy then I don't know what is. Clearly there are things in the drawer that he doesn't want me to see . . . why else would it be all locked up like this? Has he taken the key with him? I *have* to get into that drawer. A hammer? If I could splinter the front of the drawer and stick my fingers inside, at least I'd know what was in there. Then if I could feel something that concerned me unduly, I could take the whole drawer out. If not, it would be easy enough to get someone to repair some splintered wood.

I reach up and open the glass case on the wall, which contains many of Rufus's awards and gifts. Most of the very expensive things are kept in a big vault under the house that no one in the world knows about. (When I moved in, he asked me whether I had anything very expensive that I wanted to put in there for safe-keeping . . . er . . . no! The only valuables in my possession are my lovely jewellery box and the things that Rufus buys me, and there's no way I want those hidden away. I want them with me so I can see them, touch them and enjoy them.) But he keeps some things in the cabinet that he likes to look at. One of those things is a big, chunky dagger, covered in jewels. It's magnificent. Apparently, it was presented to Rufus by the Prime Minister of India and two Bollywood stars, when he went there with the United Nations food programme. They gave it to him to celebrate his Oscar for *The Jewelled Dagger*.

I pick it up, feeling the weight between my fingers, and

begin smashing into the little drawer. I smash some more until the front of the drawer is reduced to splinters of wood. There's nothing in there. Shit. I drop the dagger onto the floor with a dramatic flourish.

'Kelly?'

I spin round like a woman possessed to see Julie standing there. 'What is it?' I spit out. I don't mean to sound so venomous but I'm embarrassed. I had no idea she was there.

'Are you OK?' she asks.

'I'm fine.'

'There's something I wanted to mention. I mean, it's none of my business and I'm guessing now's not a good time but I've been trying to talk to you over the last couple of days, when you've been on your own, away from Elody, but this is the first chance I've had.'

'What is it?' I ask impatiently. It feels like everything's falling apart around me. I'm not really in the mood for guessing games with this woman, however much I like her.

'It's just that a lot of letters have come for you, and Elody takes them all. A letter came this morning marked "URGENT – please, please give this to Kelly Monsoon". I pulled it out of the pile to make sure that it went straight to you, but when Elody left, she took it with her, as she always takes all your letters.'

'Why does she take my letters?'

'I don't know. She told us that all your post was being dealt with by her people.'

'Oh.' The truth is that I didn't know that I'd even had any letters. Why would Elody have taken everything? Unless she does have a secretary somewhere sorting them out for me? Still, she should have checked with me first to make sure that's what I wanted to happen to them. And what happens when they're sorted out? Will she bring them back?

'Thanks,' I say, managing to force out a smile as Julie backs out of the room.

Chapter 15

'Elody. It's me, Kelly. Where are you?'

I need to ask her about these bloody letters and to tell her that there's nothing untoward in the house. There's no sign of any improper behaviour from Rufus at all. In fact, the only improper behaviour is from her – nicking all my post. And from me – breaking into my boyfriend's desk with his treasured dagger.

Elody has only just left the beauticians, but she senses the urgency in my voice and, more likely, is thrilled by the sound of the devastation I've caused in Rufus's office, so promises she'll come over as soon as she possibly can and explain to me where the letters are and why she took them.

'I'll be there before you can say "Gucci",' she says. 'Once I've dealt with some essentials, I'll be with you.' The essentials, it turns out, are waiting for her nails to dry and buying a sparkly clutch bag with matching sequined purse. By the time she arrives, I'm frantic.

'I took your letters so we could check there was nothing rude or offensive in them,' she says. 'You're on the verge of being famous. There are nutters out there. Of course I sent your letters to be opened independently. Rufus would never forgive me if I didn't.'

'So, where are they now?'

'They're being catalogued, but don't worry – I'll drop

them all in tomorrow morning for you to have. They're just letters, Kelly. Don't get so het up. Now, show me the desk.'

I take Elody into Rufus's office.

'You smashed it up with this?' says Elody, quizzically, pointing to the hefty, heavily bejewelled dagger that's lying on Rufus's chair. She notices the blood on the top of the blade.

'Ooooo . . . blood.'

'Yes,' I say. 'I had to give it quite a whack. My hand slipped and I cut my fingers.'

'This is the award he received from India.'

'I know.'

'It's priceless,' she continues.

'I realise that.'

'It shouldn't even be in here. It should be in the safe under the house.'

How the hell does she know there's a safe under the house? Rufus said that no one knew about that.

'I realise that it was given to him and that it's precious.' I'm all too well aware that it's supposed to represent the jewelled dagger from his Oscar-winning film. I know all that. 'I just wasn't thinking and I grabbed it and used it to ram open the drawer,' I try to explain.

'Well, was that wise?'

Der! Wise . . . fucking wise? No of course it wasn't wise.

'It doesn't matter,' she says dismissively. 'Tell me what was in there?' Her limited interest in my welfare is now overruled by her fascination with what secrets I may have uncovered. 'Well . . . what was there?' she demands, starring into my eyes so fiercely that I feel myself shiver. 'Tell me you found something or I'll be furious. You dragged me away from the fucking shops.'

Fuck. I suddenly feel scared. I see her look over at the dagger and it occurs to me that she could kill me. Oh God. There's no one on this floor of the house. Her eyes look as dark as night. For the first time in my life I feel genuinely worried that a woman is going to hurt me.

'There was nothing in there,' I say almost apologetically. 'Sorry, but there wasn't.'

I just want her to go now. I should never have asked her to come back here. She's really scaring me.

'There was nothing in there? Nothing!' she exclaims. 'Why did you make me come here?'

'I wanted to know about the letters. That's why I called you, then I mentioned that I'd found nothing in Rufus's room. I told you about the damage because I was desperate and thought you could help me mend the desk. You know, help me find a carpenter.'

'No,' she says. 'I don't "do" household repairs. Get David to sort it.'

'But I need to keep this quiet from Rufus, I can't involve David.'

'Well, I can't help – I'm still reeling from disappointment that you didn't find anything.'

'Disappointment? I'm glad I didn't find anything. It would have been awful to find that he'd been unfaithful. I have to say that I'm relieved. What were you expecting me to find?'

'Something that allowed you to know for sure. You know . . . just something that would tell you once and for all what he'd been up to.'

'Well, the fact that I've found nothing means I know for sure, as far as I'm concerned. Look, I'm sorry that I dragged you over here. I'll get Henry to drive you back.'

'No. I'm not going anywhere until I've talked some sense into you,' she says, clenching her fists in horror and screwing up her face. This is not a good look for her, but I sense that this would be the wrong time to tell her that. 'Finding nothing means you are a bad hunter ... or it means he's a good hider ... or it means he destroys the evidence as he's going along. It doesn't mean he's got nothing to hide.'

She's all hunched over like Inspector Clouseau as she speaks. I expect her to pull out a magnifying glass. 'Men are always cheating on women,' she says. 'They are ... that's what they are doing ... all of the time. The fact that you can't prove it is your fault. There are things to find, Kelly; why haven't you found them?'

'Elody,' I say, my exasperation showing through. I can be as paranoid as the next woman but, for Christ's sake, this is getting ridiculous. 'Let's just stop this now. I know there's nothing to worry about. Everything's fine. I just need to get on with my life and stop worrying. I need to stop taking these pills and get myself thinking rationally for a change.'

'Stop the diet pills? Are you insane?' she cries. 'Are you?' She grabs me by the shoulders and shakes me. 'You have to keep taking the pills. You have to. Don't let me down. Don't make me look a fool.'

She turns and sits down, examining her eyebrows in a small hand mirror.

What's wrong with her? It's like she's taken leave of her senses.

'Get someone to make me tea,' she instructs. 'Call the staff. I need green tea.'

Her presence in the house is choking me. I want her gone, so I can sort all this mess out.

'It's time for you to go,' I try.

'You called me and I came,' she is sneering at me as she speaks, in the same way as I've seen her sneer at so many people ... people like Mandy and Sophie. How I wish the girls were here now. They'd be encouraging me, reassuring me, helping me and distracting me. They'd have troubles of their own that they wanted to share. I'd help them and our friendship would build on our sharing and helping. God, but life's so different with these women I've met through Rufus, or certainly with Elody it is.

She sees that I do not move to get her green tea, so she stands up, packing away her little hand mirror.

'Fine,' she says. 'I'm going. You are no friend. Stay fat if that's what you want. Look frumpy. I can do nothing else.'

Elody storms out, slamming doors and barging past the staff in the corridors. As the front door shuts behind her I collapse into Rufus's armchair and utter an almighty sigh of relief. Thank God she's gone. I was genuinely scared for a minute there; scared she'd turn on me.

I pick up the phone straight away and call Sophie's mobile. The phone goes to the standard answerphone message that I've heard so many times I know it off by heart. 'Welcome to Tesco mobile ...' Fuck. I feel tears start to run down my face. I'm not normally so pathetic but right now I feel awful. I reach out for the Yellow Pages, and randomly pick out a carpenter, summoning him to this house as soon as possible. It's clearly wholly inappropriate to invite a bloody carpenter whom I know nothing about into the private home of one of the world's richest and most famous actors. But the fact that I have a desk smashed to pieces and in desperate need of fixing before Rufus comes back tomorrow night has assumed a far greater importance in my mind than home security.

It turns out the carpenter can't come till the following morning . . . the day of Rufus's return. Bollocks.

'If I pay you double, can you come first thing?' I ask, plaintively.

'Not till I've finished a job in Putney.'

Double bollocks.

It's midday, after another sleepless night, and the carpenter has just turned up. He's quite handsome actually, in a rugged and dishevelled sort of way – just the type I'd have gone for before Rufus came wafting into my life. I had a lot of boyfriends before Rufus. Well, not boyfriends as such, it might be more realistic to describe them as boys who fancied me. I used to get asked out a lot but never met anyone special, you know. Never met anyone I really wanted to get all dressed up for . . . until Rufus swept me off my feet, some eight months and half a lifetime ago.

I fell in love with Rufus as soon as I saw him. I know that sounds daft but I did. The day I met him something changed in me; the world tilted on its axis and I knew nothing would ever be quite the same again. If that's not love, then what is? It was – boom – heart given away. I just adored him from day one, and whatever happens I know I will until I die. He's perfect. I love being with him, seeing him and talking to him. In fact, the only good thing about these drugs keeping me awake all night is that I get to talk to Rufus in LA in the small hours of the morning.

I spoke to Rufus loads last night; we were chatting away for ages because it was the last time we'd be able to speak before his arrival back at Heathrow.

'I'll try calling you from the plane,' he said, as only a man who flies first class everywhere could. 'But I've got three on-board business meetings booked, so it might be difficult to find the time.'

I told Rufus how much fun I'd been having (lie) but how much I was looking forward to him coming back (oh, so true). I told him I'd lost weight. Nearly a stone! He didn't react with the level of enthusiasm I was hoping for given that Elody has convinced me that it was my excess weight standing between me and a lifetime in paradise with him.

'Don't go dieting for me; I love you just the way you are. As far as I'm concerned, you're absolutely perfect.'

'God I miss you,' I said and, if Rufus were any boyfriend I've ever been out with before, there'd have been a long silence, followed by, 'Listen, I have to go; I'm meeting Darren/Mike/Pete/Dyllis (delete as applicable) in the pub in five minutes, we're going to get shit-faced.' But, no. This is Rufus, so he said: 'Kelly, I've never missed anyone as much as I've missed you. I adore you. I can't wait to see you. To be honest, I've got something important to say.'

I spent a moment in a mild panic about the fact that the 'something' might be his need to address me on the subject of me, randomly and without a shadow of proof, searching through every item of his clothing and paper-work in the search for evidence of infidelity. Or wanting to talk to me about the fact that I smashed up his desk with an unimaginably expensive and unique jewelled dagger handmade on the thighs of virgins in India . . . or something. Or, indeed, that I've organised for a carpenter to come round without knowing anything about the carpentry firm and thus prejudiced our security and safety. But, no, Rufus merely repeated that he loved me more than he'd ever loved anyone and that what he had to say would have to wait until he was back. Then he left to get his flight.

The carpenter is now in the house walking around, taking in the undeniable magnificence of the place while trying to look cool, calm and relaxed, as if he really hasn't noticed its splendour. He's clearly awe-struck by the magnificence of it all. I guess I forget just how lucky I am to live in a place like this. I tend to think of it as a prison these days; what with the paparazzi keeping me locked inside, and my friends no longer wanting to see me, and me not being able to hold down the most basic of jobs (I'm not bitter at all; hell no, not bitter in the least).

'I had a bit of an accident with this . . .' I tell the carpenter. His name's Colin. Colin the Carpenter. That's nice. I always have a particular fondness for people whose names and job titles combine to make them sound like a character from *Noddy*.

I indicate towards the desk drawer and Colin peers inside.

'It looks OK to me,' he says.

'No, inside the drawer,' I explain. 'There's a little drawer in the main one that's all splintered. You'll have to look right inside the drawer to see it.'

He peers in and sees the damage. 'No problem,' he says. 'I'll have it fixed in no time.'

Thank God.

'It needs to look the same,' I plead. 'You know, as if no damage has been done.'

'I'll do my best,' he says, looking up at me. He sees my worried face. 'Is everything OK?' he asks, warmly. 'You seem agitated.'

'No, I'm fine. As long as I can get this drawer mended, everything will be fine.'

'Good,' he says. 'Only I wondered, because of the woman waiting in the car outside. She looked angry.'

'What woman?'

The carpenter has pulled the drawer out and is matching slivers of wood to it as we speak.

'She's outside. Just sitting there. Take a look.'

I peer through the window, and see Elody in the back of the car, with Henry at the wheel. She's staring ahead, motionless, and he's looking down at the steering wheel as if he doesn't know quite what to do. What the hell does she want now?

'It's nothing,' I tell my carpenter friend. He's pulled out the drawer completely and is fashioning a new one out of matching wood.

'I'll call you when I've finished,' he says. 'There's no need for you to sit here if you don't want to.'

I hear the doorbell ringing in the distance and know that it will be Elody. Perhaps she saw me looking at her through the window? Perhaps she's decided to return my letters to me?

The carpenter is sanding, sawing and slicing through wood and looks for all the world like a decent, honourable man – grafting away before us. I'm sure he's perfectly trustworthy, so I leave him to it as I head off to answer the door.

'Just call me if you need me,' I say.

I hear the shuffle of Pamela's sensible working shoes as the housekeeper heads for the door. I know that if she answers, Elody will barge past her and be in the house and getting her latest fix of 'Kelly's wardrobe problems' before I can stop her.

'I'll get it,' I say, skipping down the stairs, past Pam, as if I have not a care in the world. I swing open the door and come face to face with Elody.

'Your outfit's all wrong,' she says. 'Dahling, you look shameful. The sooner that weight falls off the better. Come here let me kiss you. My goodness, you have no make-up on. What? Why would you do that? What were you thinking? Maybe I'll kiss you when you've taken the time to put some make-up on.'

Aaaaahhhhhhhhhhhhhh . . . how have I put up with this for three weeks? I can't do it any more.

'You are still taking the diet pills, aren't you?' she says, looking me up and down once again. The deeply shameful thing is that I *am* still taking them. I'm kind of hell-bent on losing weight because somewhere deep within me I'm convinced that this will make me more attractive to Rufus. I know that this is just nonsense I've absorbed from Elody, and the reality is that Rufus has told me time and again that he likes me curvy, but it's difficult to shift thoughts like that from your mind once they're lodged there, especially when you're in the sort of vulnerable position that I was in when I first came staggering and stumbling into this celebrity world. I also think there's a part of me that wants Elody's approval, which angers me. Why do I want her bloody approval? I don't need her approval.

'You can't come in. I'm busy,' I say. Then I add: 'Sorry,' because I hate having rows like this.

'What do you mean, I can't come in?' she says. 'I have your letters. Your precious letters that you were so desperate for. Anyway, it's not your house. I'll come in if I want to come in. It's Rufus's house and I'm always welcome here.' Elody's voice is laced with a truckload of aggression. 'You're the outsider here, you're the one who doesn't fit in, not me.'

'What? This is my home, Elody.'

'You have let me down. I have devoted weeks of my time to fixing you up and look at you. You are still fat and blubbery, your clothes cannot hang right when you have fat where there should be bones. You are making a fool of me. How can we be friends? How can this work properly? Do you not own a mirror of any kind?'

I say goodbye and shut the door. I don't need any more abuse from anyone, certainly not from Elody. I don't think I've ever done anything quite as bold in my whole life before, as shutting the door in someone's face. I'm standing there in a state of semi shock when there's an almighty clattering on the door: fists banging, a voice shouting and even kicking. I hear the staff behind me rush to see what's going on, and I realise I can't leave her out there. I open the door and Elody reaches in and grabs my hair. My first thought is that she's going to pull out the scrunchie and restyle it, but no ... she drags me outside by my hair, pulling me so fast that I trip over the step and fall to my knees on the gravel.

'You bitch!' she cries, kicking me in the side of my thigh. 'You absolute evil bitch.'

'Get off me, get off me.'

I look up, and Henry is attempting to pull Elody away as she continues to lash out at me and at the ageing driver.

'I wanted you to be my friend. I needed you to be my friend,' she cries.

'I have been your friend,' I say to her, as I hold my hair protectively against any further assaults. 'But you're not treating me like friends treat each other.'

'Oh what? Like these friends?' cries Elody, tipping a pile of letters onto the gravel. All of them are penned in the familiar writing of Sophie and Mandy.

'Where have these come from?' I ask.

'Letters come every day,' she responds dismissively, with a shrug of her skinny, little shoulders. 'Every day these girls are writing or turning up at the gates and demanding to be let in to see you. Always calling, writing and turning up. Do they not realise you've moved on?'

Oh shit. All this time I thought the girls had forgotten about me and weren't bothered about staying in touch, and they were trying to reach me.

As I scramble around on the ground for the letters, Henry bundles Elody into the car. She looks back at me, tears staining her face, her hair flying everywhere. She looks scared and vulnerable and for the first time I notice that she's actually very pretty beneath her armour. 'You've got everything,' she shouts, as Henry starts up the engine. 'I wish I were you; I wish someone loved me. I wish Jon were here. He died two years ago today. Two years . . .' She screams through the open window as the car sets off on its way, 'I wish Jon were here.'

Pamela comes running out across the gravel and helps me to my feet.

'Are you OK?' she asks kindly. 'You aren't hurt are you? Here, let me help you. Gosh after all you've done for that woman she does this to you. You were so kind to her when everyone else refused to talk to her. Honestly.'

She helps me inside as the carpenter comes jogging down the stairs.

'Everything all right?' he asks. 'I heard the fight.'

'Yes, fine,' I say. I've now got Colin the carpenter, Pamela and two of the security guys who have arrived on the scene to check everything's OK standing round me.

'I'm fine, honestly. Just fine,' I keep reiterating.

'Where's she gone now?' the security guards ask, adding: 'Shall we go after her? None of us will have her treating our Kelly like that.'

'Everything's fine,' I reiterate. I don't want to make a big fuss out of this, and sending the security guards after her or phoning the police, as Pamela suggests, won't help at all. In my mind I keep seeing Elody's desperately sad and lonely face, the smudged make-up and the cries for help. I know that I don't want Elody here any more and, once Henry gets back, I'll tell him that he mustn't drive her around from now on. It's not that I wish her any harm but I think she needs more help than I can give her. Professional help, perhaps? Once things have calmed down, and

I get the opportunity to talk to her rationally, I'll try to persuade her to talk to someone who can help.

'Right then, I'm done,' says the carpenter. I've been so busy watching the space from which the car departed five minutes ago that I'd forgotten he was there at all.

'Sorry. I was miles away,' I say.

'I just wanted to say that it's all fixed. No one will ever know it's been touched. Would you like to come and check?'

You know I really can't be arsed. I'm just sick of all this now. I can see Pamela looking at me quizzically.

'Don't worry, I'm sure it's perfect,' I tell him, and I smile at Pamela to tell her that everything's OK.

'Just one thing. This was inside it . . .' he says, and he hands me a small key and a bracelet with two large diamond covered stars on it. The bracelet is made of thick platinum but it's tiny; it would only fit round the smallest of wrists. There's no doubt that this bracelet was made to match Elody's necklace. Fucking hell.

'Shall I invoice you for the work?' says the carpenter.

'Yes,' I mutter, as we shake hands. In my left hand I'm holding the bracelet and the small key.

'It's like paradise here,' says the carpenter as he steps out of the front door.

'Sure is,' I say, but, you know, I'm not so sure.

Chapter 16

I feel like an absolute shit. It's official. The letters from the girls are unbelievably warm and loving. I've spent hours just reading and rereading them, bursting into tears time and again as I'm reminded of what utterly fantastic friends I have. Christ. They say that they understand how busy I must be, but that they really hope we can all stay mates because they miss me so much. Bloody hell. If only they knew how much I'd missed them these past few weeks; I've been craving their company every day.

I desperately want to talk to them, but I still can't get hold of them. Sophie's mobile is never on, the home phone line just rings out, and I know they're both off work this afternoon because it's Thursday, so there's no point in leaving messages there.

As I pace around the sitting room, thinking about what to do next, there's a loud bang outside forcing my knees to buckle beneath me in fear. Fuck. What is it? Please tell me it's not Elody come back to attack me Oh God that woman scares me. What if she's come back clutching a hammer? Or an ice pick? Ah. She might have a gun! I need to get out of here. Fuck. I want to see the girls.

I peer out of the window to see what the sound is. Thank God. It's just Henry, back from dropping Elody off. I smile at him, grinning from ear to ear and forcing him to look at me quizzically.

'Thank God it's you,' I explain. 'I thought it might be Elody, back to beat me up.'

'No, she won't be back,' he reassures me, explaining that he took her to the Royal Institute of Fashion. I know Elody loves that place. It's where she first bumped into Jon many years ago, and where she goes to seek solace and to feel close to him whenever she's feeling low. With a bit of luck, she'll calm down after a few hours in there, and leave me alone.

'She seemed more relaxed when we got there,' confirms Henry. 'It's like she was almost in a trance when she drifted out of the car and into the building. Like a dream. I said goodbye and told her to take care but she didn't hear me. Most odd.'

'Well, thanks for taking her Henry.'

'You might be the only person in the world who ever says thank you to the staff here you know. We've all become very fond of you.'

'Thanks, Henry, that means a lot to me,' I say. Then I give him the news that I notice is very gratefully received; he won't be driving Elody around any more. 'I need you to do me a favour though,' I say, and he smiles and cocks his hat.

'That's what I'm here for, ma'am.'

'I need to go back to my old flat in Twickenham to see the girls. Do you remember where the flat is?'

'Ooooo . . . I'm sure I'll remember it when we get there,' he says. 'Is it in the town centre?'

'Yes. You know that terrible lap-dancing club?'

'Yes,' he says brightly, then changes his mind when he realises how that must sound. 'Well, I don't know it, but I know where it is. Some friends mentioned it once.'

It's funny when we stop outside the old flat. Life's changed so much since I was last here. I'm all dressed up in a gorgeous emerald green dress, fabulous gold earrings and bangles. I need to be dressed up so Henry can take me straight to the airport to meet Rufus afterwards, but I'm worried that the way I'm dressed is almost a barrier, a hurdle between my old life and my new one. I hope the girls don't think I've dressed up on purpose, just to make them look bad by comparison.

Henry pulls up outside and I ask him whether he'll come and collect me around 7.30 pm to take me to the airport.

'So you won't need me before then?' he asks.

'Nope.'

'And Elody can't use me.'

'Nope.'

'And Rufus is abroad.'

'He is,' I say.

'How nice,' says Henry with a grin. 'Then I'll go and spend a few hours on my allotment.'

In the freezing cold? When it's getting dark? Gardeners are mad. I must remember to introduce Henry to Frank from Hampton Court. They'd get on very well ... both loonies when it comes to gardening!

I walk purposefully towards the door, pleased that I've allowed Rufus's faithful driver the time to tend to his cabbages. It's 4 pm. The girls have definitely had enough time to get home from work, and surely it's too early for them to be in the pub. There's every chance that they'll be in. I'm nervous as hell. If they're not here, I'm going to find them. I'll tour the pubs and shops of south-west London until I stumble upon them. I have to see them before going to the airport and there's no way I'm going back to that house before Rufus gets home. I ring the bell.

Henry drives off as I stand at the door, hoping that Jimmy won't come out and engage me in a conversation about lap-dance technique, G-string removal or chicken wings. I ring the bell again. Still no response. Shit, they're not in. What now? I suppose I could get a coffee in Starbucks round the corner and make a plan. Or I could go back to Richmond and see whether they're still at work, or in The Sun.

It's 6 pm before I get into the flat. Happily, it's Mandy who opens the door. And, more happily still, she grins madly when she sees me. I take one look at her and burst into tears. 'I'm sorry, I'm sorry, I'm sorry,' I wail. 'I've been so horrible but I didn't mean to be, I couldn't get hold of you, and life's been so difficult and please, please, Mandy, please tell me we're still friends.'

'Of course,' she says, hugging me and feeling how icy I am.

'Where've you been for the past two hours?' I howl for no good reason. The sight of her has reduced me to a pathetic, needy wreck. 'I've been waiting for you since 4 pm.'

'Come in, come in. Why didn't you call us? We'd have come back sooner.'

'I tried. Like I always try. I ring you all the time on Sophie's mobile but I never get through.'

'How weird. Are you ringing the new number?'

'What new number?'

'Sophie's got a new number,' says Mandy. 'I phoned a few weeks ago to tell you. Elody answered your phone, as she always does, and she said she'd pass on the message. Soph's with Tandem mobile now and she's saved a fortune.'

'Oh good,' I say vaguely, but I wonder why Elody never passed the message on. She knew how eager I was to talk to the girls. She knew I was calling them, yet all the time she must have known that I was calling them on the wrong number. What a horrible thing to do.

'You don't look very happy,' says Mandy, and I suddenly feel more lost and confused than I ever have in my life before. I look at Mandy's warm and tender face and break down into fits of tears all over again. 'Help me, help me,' I find myself sobbing into her large chest. 'I can't cope. I feel like I'm going mad. I don't know what's right and what's wrong and who's decent and who's not. And the bracelet and Elody and I never knew you'd changed your number and I never got any of the letters and I didn't know you'd been round to see me. I feel so scared and so alone.'

'Calm down, calm down,' Mandy is saying, stroking my hair as I let the tears pour down my heavily made-up face and all over the front of her dress.

'Come in the sitting room,' she instructs, and I follow her up the flight of stairs to our little flat on the first floor. I walk into the familiar room with its cheap and tatty furniture, and all the while I'm sobbing my heart out.

'What on earth is the matter?' asks Sophie, jumping up from her cross-legged position on the floor where she's been examining bills and jotting figures onto Post-it notes. It's an activity I remember all too well. The money coming in is never enough to satisfy the demands, so we'd work out how we could shuffle money around and invariably work out that we had about £5 between us to pay the rent, the bills and all food. We'd sit a while and wonder whether there were any part-time jobs that we could get to ease the burden, contemplate the idea of getting jobs behind the bar at Jimmy's place then decide to worry about it some other time. Those times seem so long ago. The problems then seemed insurmountable, but they seem tiny compared the problems I'm facing now.

'I can't cope,' I manage to mumble to Sophie, once she's coaxed me into a sitting position. 'I can't. I don't want to go on leading a life like this. I don't understand the rules; I don't know how to behave. It turns out I don't know anything at all. Nothing that's any use to me, in any case.'

'Leave him and come back here then,' says Sophie in that incredibly down-to-earth, cut-to-the-chase way of hers. 'Just pack your things and come home. You don't have to wear all these posh clothes or have all these absurdly overdressed friends to be happy; they're certainly not making you happy, are they?'

'No, I guess not.'

'Are these new friends of yours making you happy?'

'No.'

'So leave.'

'But I love Rufus.'

'Well, then, carry on being the girl who Rufus fell in

love with but from back here, in your own world. Everything will be OK then. Surely.'

I'm staring at Sophie because what she's saying makes perfect sense, but I'd feel a failure if I moved out, and Rufus would hate it.

'I can't do that,' I say. 'None of this is Rufus's fault; I've just got myself into a total state since he's been away. I feel these astronomical pressures on me because of the lifestyle and the things people say and think. I don't want Rufus to be rich and famous. I want him to be a completely normal bloke from down The Sun so he's not surrounded by weird controlling women, and so we can pop out for a drink like normal people do, without the world's press coming too.'

'Then you need to talk it all through with Rufus.'

'But he can't stop being an actor because I'm insecure about it all.'

'Well, he might be able to reassure you; perhaps in future he'll think about taking you with him when he goes away.'

'I think it's deeper than that. I think I'm just not cut out for this,' I say. 'I need Rufus to stop being a film star and then the two of us can run away together and live in a forest or something where no one will bother us, the papers will leave us alone, and no one will care where I got my clothes from or which parties I want to go to. I love Rufus; I just can't handle all the crap that goes with being with him. It's horrible.'

'What crap is this then?'

Oh God, here we go. I know that if they're going to help me, I have to be honest with them, and tell them how horrible it all feels sometimes . . . so I do. I explain all about the terrible drinks parties where Elody makes me get all dressed up and everyone's bitchy about her. I try to explain the unbelievably obsessive need to be slim and how everyone seems to judge everyone else on the way they look and what they're wearing. I explain again about the paparazzi. 'I know it sounds like I'm being silly, but I promise you until you've been through it, you have no idea how absolutely terrifying it is to have the papers reporting on your every move, especially family and personal stuff from your ex-boyfriends and making digs at you, and writing about things they shouldn't know about, so you've no idea who's spoken to them and you're terrified about what will appear next and who you can talk to and trust and . . . I don't know – it ends up just completely undermining you. I have to be honest there were times when I wondered whether you would end up selling stories. It seemed like everyone else did.'

'Not everyone,' says Sophie miserably. 'We'd never do that to you. You've got lots of friends, Kelly. You know, even Jimmy Lapdance came in here and handed me some photos he'd taken that night we were in there, pictures of us all hugging. He didn't want them to get into the wrong hands. Lots of people think the world of you and would never turn on you. Stop focusing on those that have.'

'Sorry,' I say meekly. She's right, but it's hard to get a perspective on the world when you're bloody cooped up in a massive house looking at the outside world through the eyes of the press. 'It's just that I never go out now unless it's to a pre-arranged night with the people on the Hill,' I try to explain to her. 'I feel I can sort of trust them because they understand what it's like being in this little glass-walled world, but it is hard being at home all the time; it makes me more and more depressed. Especially with the diet pills. It's horrible.'

Sophie and Mandy are staring at me with their eyes so wide open they look like a couple of frogs in the early stages of going through a lawn mower.

'Diet pills?' Sophie eventually asks. 'What bloody diet pills?'

I reach into my bag and pull out the small bottle of Vanitas.

Sophie and Mandy both mutter the name as if it means something to them.

'I've read about those,' says Sophie. 'They're bloody lethal. Bloody hell. There was a big thing in the *Mail* about people getting addicted to them and people have died taking them. You know they're illegal in this country because of the trouble they cause, don't you?'

'Are they?'

'God, Kell, where did you get them from?' asks Mandy, full of concern.

'Elody gave them to me.'

'What a fucking witch,' says Sophie. 'Does she know how dangerous they are?'

'I don't know, but they are helping me to lose weight.'

'You don't need to lose weight,' they both say.

'Kelly, you look worse now than before you started taking them; can't you see that? You look tired and pale and, yes, about a stone lighter and dressed in a load of fancy clothes. That green dress really suits you, but you're not the pretty, vibrant young thing that you were when you left this flat.'

Sophie takes the diet pills and walks out of the room.

'Where are you going?' I call after her. Then I hear the toilet flush and I know what she's done; she's flushed them down the loo.

If I'm honest, I feel a pang of relief. I'm sure I would have just kept taking those pills yet I know this feeling of helplessness brought on by lack of sleep and the depressive qualities of the pills is bringing me down.

'You know you're going to have to talk to Rufus about all this, don't you?'

'Mmm,' I say, without real conviction.

'You are, Kelly. You can't bottle everything up.'

'I don't bottle things up. I told Elody how I feel about things.'

'Great, cos she's really going to help you . . . the crazy lady.'

'She's OK,' I say, not entirely convincingly. 'Well, maybe a little mad, but I'm sure her heart's in the right place.'

'Yeah, in her expensive Gucci wallet,' snorts Sophie.

'To be honest, Kell, she does sounds pretty crazy when she answers the phone, and refuses to allow us to talk to you. She wouldn't let us into the house when we came to visit, you know,' Mandy chips in.

'I didn't know about any of that until today,' I say. 'I didn't know you'd been sending letters or anything. I'm sorry, Mand. I thought the two of you were pissed off with me and weren't answering my calls.'

'I told you she wouldn't know anything about it,' says Mandy, loyally, looking over at Sophie.

'We've been calling non-stop,' says Sophie. 'But, like we said, Elody answers and says you're not available. We assumed you didn't want to talk to us. We thought you were too busy with your flash new friends.'

'Why didn't you just ring the mobile?'

'That's what we were ringing,' says Sophie. 'It's the only number we've got. You said you'd text us your home number but it never came through. We must have rung that mobile about 550 million times. When you missed our lunch then bumped into us in Richmond and we had that horrible argument, I was ringing you constantly the next day.'

'I don't understand. Try it now.'

Sophie dials my number and hands me her mobile. The phone rings and goes to Elody's answerphone. What?

I look up at the girls. They are looking as confused as I feel.

'Elody, it's Kelly here,' I say. 'Can you give me a call back straight away? I'm completely bloody confused about this . . . why are all my calls diverting to your phone? Why are you doing this? These are my friends. You've stopped them from calling me even though you knew I was desperate to talk to them. Fucking hell, Elody, this is just ridiculous. I'm really pissed off.' I hang up dramatically and look over at the girls. 'That'll show her,' I say.

'I thought you were remarkably calm given the circum-stances,' says Sophie. 'I'd have gone and found her and rammed the bloody mobile down her throat.'

'No, I'm too scared of her for that,' I say.

'Why, what's she done?'

'She kicked me and pulled my hair and got really angry with me. We've completely fallen out. It's awful.' I look up at the girls and scream loudly, I feel so bloody fed up with everything.

The doorbell rings in the distance, somewhere beyond the anger releasing itself from its pent-up position in every fibre of my body. Mandy opens the door and I hear galloping up the stairs as Henry comes flying up to see if I'm OK.

Strangely, after that cathartic outburst I feel better than I have for ages.

'Sorry,' I say. 'Henry, nice to see you. It was either scream blue murder or actually commit murder. In the end, I went for screaming. Less bloody.'

'Ah, Elody on the phone was she?' he asks, shaking his head and giving me a sly smile. 'We really should be heading towards the airport in about fifteen minutes. I'll be waiting in the car for you.'

'Thanks.'

Henry walks downstairs and I sit back down on the sofa.

'There's something else,' I say cautiously.

'Oh God,' says Sophie, with prescience. 'What on earth's coming now?'

'Well, I went through all of Rufus's drawers and cupboards and boxes and files and personal stuff to check if there were any signs he was having an affair. You know – doing due diligence.'

'Doing what?'

'Due diligence.'

'Isn't that what you do if you're going to buy a company or something?'

'Yes, but it's essential for a girl to do it if she's about to commit herself to a guy. The truth is that you have to be sure what you're getting yourself into.'

'Fuck me, Kelly. What have you turned into?'

'Elody said that it's . . .'

'Elody? There's a surprise.'

I accept that Elody's name does crop up a great deal in connection to everything bad that's been happening in my life. Too much of a coincidence?

'Anyway, what did you find when you were doing this "due diligence"?'

I pull out the beautiful bracelet.

'Shit! That must have cost a fortune!'

The girls start ahhing and cooing over the chunky chain and dazzling diamond stars.

'Amazing!' they are saying, while stroking it as if it were a fluffy newborn kitten.

'He probably bought it for you,' says Mandy. 'He probably hid it away and was planning to give it to you when he gets back tonight.'

'But it matches a necklace that Elody wears all the time. I can't help it – I'm convinced he's bought it for her.'

'No way!' they both howl. 'Why would he be interested in that harridan?'

'Look,' says Sophie, taking my hands, 'there's one thing I'm absolutely sure of: he loves you. I'm convinced of that.'

'So why's he being so secretive about the fact that he's starring in a new film alongside his glamorous ex-girlfriend? When I ask him on the phone he says that she's not his ex.'

'Who? Elody?'

'No Cindy Kearney, the girl he's starring alongside in the film.'

'She's not his ex-girlfriend. We Googled her straight

away, didn't we, Mand? We wanted to know all about her.'

'Yes, she was. They were madly in love and they just kept it from the press because they didn't want the press to intrude on their love story.'

'Who said this?'

'Elod . . .'

'Fucking hell, Kelly. Elody is a nightmare. Why couldn't you see that? I think she wanted you to feel horrible and vulnerable. She tried to weaken you as much as possible so you'd rely on her, and you could be the friend she wanted, needed.'

'Yep, so I'm starting to realise,' I say, and I am. I kind of wondered about Elody's intentions from the start; instinctively it didn't feel right the way she took me under her wing and insisted on coming everywhere with me, but I overrode those instincts because I thought I could learn from her (because she told me I could) and because I was lonely (she had made sure that I was isolated from all my friends) and because I thought it would please Rufus. Shit. She thought I'd be a tailor-made friend who'd just slot into her life and be there for her, regardless of my needs.

The rain pounds away at the window as my two friends dispense sharp splinters of wit to burst the bubble of gloom and depression settling around me. I know it's time to go to the airport and I know that Henry is too polite to keep knocking, so he'll be sitting downstairs, getting all worried about whether we'll be on time. I reach over for my bag and hug the girls goodbye, promising them that I'll call my phone operator and get my mobile calls and texts sent to the right phone. I take

Sophie's new number and promise I'll text to say that Rufus is safely home.

'Can I leave you some money to help out for a while?' I ask. 'Pleeeaassse. I remember how tough it always was, and I've got loads of money now. Please let me help.'

'No, Kell. We're fine,' says Sophie, but I look down at the Post-it notes, then up into her face. 'This is me you're talking to.'

I leave them £100 plus an extra £20 and ask them whether they'll go out and buy me the beautiful dove-grey dress that they bought me as a leaving present with the £20. I really loved that dress but Elody threw it away. It's time for me to start doing and wearing what I want to instead of pandering to the increasingly bizarre wishes of a mad French fashion stylist with trouble seeping out of every perfect pore.

It's lovely and warm and snug in the car, and Henry's his usual doting self, checking whether the temperature's right, whether I want the radio on or whether I'd prefer a CD. 'Can we talk instead?' I ask him, and I can see the raise of his eyebrows. It might be the most peculiar request ever made of him.

'Do you know Elody very well?' I venture, and I see the eyebrows rise again. I haven't known Henry long, but I think I have the answer to any question I might ever ask about Elody, wrapped up right there in those eyebrows, lifting up towards his hairline.

'I wouldn't say I know her well,' he says.

'Would you say that Rufus knows her well?' I try.

'No,' he says, without hesitation. 'I wouldn't think so.'

Henry's too bloody discreet for words. Perfect quality in a member of staff, of course, but makes him utterly useless for gossiping with. Instead of grilling the old man any further, I suggest some music, and call the phone company to find out how on earth I rejig the phone set-up so that my phone calls come to me instead of drifting off to a phone manned by a crazy fashionista. Turns out it's remarkably easy to do, which is alarming. You just press a series of buttons on someone's phone and all their calls come to you. Bloody hell. Who knew?

'Can I interrupt?' asks Henry, suddenly, cutting through the gentle sound of violins wafting through the car.

'Sure.'

'If you want to know anything about Elody, try Dr Bronks-Harrison. I think she knows her well.'

'Thanks,' I say, and since Henry never says anything without considering the consequences and ramifications, and utters nothing without first debating the appropriateness of speaking out, I realise that Isabella must know plenty about Elody and have a view that I should probably hear. Certainly, it would be worth me calling to find out.

'Hi, Isabella, it's Kelly Monsoon,' I say sheepishly. I'm not very good on the phone and I hate the idea of disturbing her when she's probably just got back from work. 'Are you OK to talk? I mean, I'm not interrupting anything, am I?'

'Don't be silly; it's lovely to hear from you,' says Isabella. 'Isn't Rufus back tonight?'

'Yes. I'm just on my way to the airport now,' I say. 'Can I ask you something?'

'Go ahead.'

'What do you think of Elody?'

'Aaahhhhh,' says Isabella. 'I think it's obvious to everyone what I think of Elody. I think she's bad news. I think she's bitter and twisted and there are times when I want to kill her. What do you think of her?'

'I thought she was a friend, but I'm feeling used,' I say. It's a relief to talk to someone like Isabella about it. 'I've just found out she's been alienating all my friends and making me rely on her more and more. And you know you asked me how I'd lost so much weight so quickly? Well, you were right; I have been taking diet pills. Elody gave them to me and told me they were harmless, but they've been making me feel just awful. Really awful.'

I burst into tears as I'm talking to her; I can't help it. I feel all this emotion come tumbling out again.

'OK. Don't take any more of those pills, and don't see Elody again.'

'I won't,' I say. 'My friends took the pills off me and threw them down the toilet, so I can't take any more of them, and Elody and I had a row and I threw her out of the house, so I won't be seeing her again. Sorry, I shouldn't be saying anything but . . .'

'Of course you should be saying something. I'm very glad you called. I feel terrible that you didn't tell me sooner as perhaps I could have helped. I should have come round to check you were all right, but you seemed to be out and about going to parties all the time with Elody. When I saw you at our little "wine-tasting" you were on great form, and when you didn't return my calls afterwards I assumed that you were busy.'

'No, that was Elody. She had my phone calls diverted

to her phone so I never knew people were calling me. I would definitely have called you back. I always call people back.'

'I can't believe she did that. What an absolute bitch. Have you managed to talk to Rufus about all this while he's been away?'

'I've spoken to Rufus,' I say. 'But I haven't told him about Elody diverting my calls because I've only just found out. Something's just occurred to me. He was texting me every day from LA, but I never received the texts. I thought it was something to do with texts not coming through properly from LA, but that's it, isn't it? It was Elody's fault; that's why they didn't come through. Christ.'

'How have you managed to talk to him at all, if all your calls are diverted to Elody's phone?'

'He always calls on the home phone,' I explain. 'He thinks it's safer not to use mobiles unless it's absolutely urgent. Apparently a tabloid journalist once managed to listen in on his mobile and he's never trusted them all that much since.'

'Sounds like he's right,' says Isabella. 'I wish I'd called you at home.'

'Why would Elody do this?' I ask in dismay. 'Why would she want me to feel so bad?'

'Because she's a very sad woman who's desperate because her career is on the slide and she's got nothing else in her life except for that career and the distorted memory of a boyfriend who died years ago. Her ex made her, and she knows it. She'll never get back the life she had with him, and she takes it out on everyone she meets who's in any way happy.'

'You mean Jon, the fashion designer,' I say.

'Yep . . . I think he's the only person she ever loved. She has no close friends . . . except you and Rufus and I think he just tolerates her because he's too kind not to.'

'Yes,' I say weakly, promising Isabella that I won't worry any more and will call her very soon.

'Text me to say that Rufus is back safely,' she says. 'And make sure you tell him everything, or I'll be round to tell him myself.'

'OK?' asks Henry.

'Fine,' I reply, thinking that everyone seems to have worked out that Elody was a witch except for me. 'I've been a complete bloody fool. I could kill her. Sorry, Henry, but I could.'

'No problem, ma'am,' he says and we roll on through the traffic, heading for Heathrow.

Chapter 17

How my moods seem to swing these days. A few hours ago I was in tears and now I'm wrapped up in Rufus's arms and have never felt happier.

'God, come here now,' he said, when he saw me standing there. We were rushed out of the airport via a series of back doors and escorted to the car away from fans and photographers. 'I've never missed anyone as much as I missed you. But look at you! How did you get so skinny? You're tiny, Kelly. Have you not been eating properly?' He holds me so tightly I fear he might squash me. 'Next time you're coming with me.'

'OK,' I say, delighted by all this affection and attention. Still, I can't quite let myself relax and enjoy it completely.

'Did Olivia enjoy it?' I can't help myself. Elody's horrible little voice is wedged in my head, chipping away at my self-esteem.

'Who's that, sweetheart?' he asks.

'You know – Olivia, Lord and Lady Simpkins's daughter.'

No. It turns out Olivia wasn't there. She never planned to be there. And Cindy? No, she's not an ex-girlfriend; Rufus would never go out with someone like that.

'Kelly, why are you so worried about other women? You're the only one for me. I fell in love with you the first time I met you. I adore you and I'll love you till I die. Please stop worrying. There's nothing to worry about.'

'I'm sorry,' I say. 'It's been horrible while you've been away. Elody kept hinting that you were off with all these other women, and I just became paranoid about it all. I'm sorry, Rufus. I know Elody is a friend of yours, but we really fell out. She gave me these diet pills because she said you wouldn't love me if I didn't lose weight, and even though I know that's not true, I still took them and they made me feel horrible. Anyway, I ended up having a huge row with her and throwing her out of the house. I haven't seen her since, but I worked out that she diverted all my mobile phone calls and texts to her phone. It's been horrible. I mean – she was nice to me sometimes and took me shopping and everything, but then I ended up feeling guilty about spending your money, so I took most of the clothes back and that made her cross.'

'OK,' he says gently, stroking my hair and pulling me close to him. 'Tell me all about it, but promise me you'll never worry about spending money. We have lots of it, and I want you to enjoy it. In fact, I'm going to put some into an account for you tomorrow, for you to spend however you want. Now, tell me everything . . .'

It's 3 am in the morning now and we're wrapped up in bed. Everything is wonderful. I want us to stay like this for ever; all entwined. It's funny; we just seem to fit together so well, as if we were designed to be like this: all snuggled up. Just as I'm starting to drift off to sleep, he strokes my hair gently, then sits up slowly, being careful not to disturb me.

I turn to face him as he stands on the carpet next to the bed in all his naked glory. Even after some eight months of being with him, the sheer bloody beauty of his body drives me nuts sometimes. As I'm staring at his thighs rather unashamedly, he drops onto his knees next to the bed, his eyes not leaving mine.

'It's been a difficult few weeks for you, hasn't it?'

'Yes. It hasn't been too much fun,' I confess. Though, to be honest, the happy combination of Rufus coming back and me being off those bloody horrible diet pills means I feel about 150 times better now.

'I hate the fact that you've been so miserable. I love you,' he says.

'I love you too.'

'How can I prove to you how much I love you?'

'You don't have to prove anything,' I say.

But he seems determined to try. He looks into my eyes. 'Kelly, I love you. I'll always love you. Please will you marry me? I want you to be my wife. I want us to grow old and grey together. I want us to have children and grandchildren. Please say yes.'

'YES!' I squeal. It comes out more loudly than I'd intended, and Rufus jumps a little, if I'm honest. Suddenly my problems have dissolved into nothing. There are no problems. There is no Elody. The press don't matter. There's no worry. I'm no longer a sad unemployed girl whose boyfriend is running around with every other woman in town. Funny how much difference thirty seconds can make. As far as I'm concerned, there are no problems in the world anywhere. Right now – in this moment – everything is more perfect than ever. I've never felt so calm, at peace, happy or sure of anything in my life before.

'I will,' I say once more, just in case there was someone in West London who didn't hear me last time. Then I throw myself into his arms. 'Of course I will.'

'Then you'll need this,' he says, and he opens his hand to reveal the most beautiful and enormous diamond ring I've ever seen. 'I was going to continue the theme and get you a ring with three diamonds in a row on it, but I fell in love with this one, with twenty on it,' he says.

'I've never seen anything so beautiful,' I tell him as I study the ring sitting elegantly on my finger. 'It's amazing.'

'*You* are amazing,' he says. 'You're super-amazing.'

'I have to tell the girls,' I say. 'They'll kill me if I don't tell them straight away. You have to let me call them.'

'But it's 3 am.'

'I'll text them then.'

'Go on then,' says Rufus indulgently. 'But then you switch your phone off. Deal?'

'Deal,' I say. 'As long as you switch yours off.'

Chapter 18

I wake the next morning to the feel and smell of Rufus right beside me. We've been cuddled up together all night . . . me and my husband-to-be. Aaaaahhhh . . . my husband-to-be . . . how mad does that sound? Shit, this is weird. How could I ever have doubted Rufus? After he dropped off to sleep last night I found myself thinking through everything and wondering why on earth I'd spent the time away from him so convinced he was up to no good and out to hurt me. It was Elody of course. Every word spoken, every dark thought in my head – they were all planted there by her. I blame myself for trusting her but I'd felt so awful and isolated and bloody lost. She exploited me.

Rufus stirs next to me but doesn't wake; he just snuggles up a bit closer and pulls me to him until I can feel his chest hair tickling my nose and find myself twitching like a bunny rabbit. God, this is fabulous.

One thing I love about my new home here with Rufus is just how dark and cosy it is in the morning. The soft cream curtains are so thick and luscious that they keep all light out. But the windows are so large, and they face the sun, so when we want to get up, and we swing open the curtains, the sunlight comes flooding in all over us and across the pristine white sheets. What I like most of all, and truly the only thing I'm really enjoying about not working, is that we get up when we are ready to get up, without that horrible alarm clock thing. I also love the fact that it's so warm in the house, not like in my old flat where I'd leap out of bed and run to the bathroom, hoping not to catch pneumonia on the way, then hurl myself into the shower which was always too cold, trying to wash quickly and without breathing in. Somehow the cold lost its awful impact if you held your breath. I sometimes think that the ultimate measure of how much my life has changed, and how far up the social scale I've clambered since meeting Rufus, is illustrated no more dazzlingly than in a comparison of the bathrooms.

'Mmmm,' Rufus sighs as he runs his hands down my back and kisses me on my forehead. 'Come here, Mrs George.'

'Ooooo . . . OK,' I say, kissing him back. 'Mrs George huh? And what if I decide to keep my own name? Will the wedding be off?'

'Keep your own name?' he says in mock horror. 'Well, if you're going to do that, then I guess I'd better change mine. I'll have to be called Rufus Monsoon; how do you think that would go down with the world's greatest film directors?'

He tickles me while he's joking about our names until I can't stand it any more and I'm choking and crying with laughter. 'Stop,' I cry. 'OK, OK, I'll change my name to bloody Kelly George, just please stop the tickling.'

We laugh and joke about the name possibilities. 'Kelly Monsoon George? Kelly George Monsoon? Kelly Rufus George Monsoon?'

'Have you told your mum?' asks Rufus, and I realise I haven't. I didn't want to call at 3 am when I texted the girls, and I didn't text Mum because she's just not into that sort of thing. She's a mum so she has a mobile phone that is never switched on, always needs charging, and certainly won't reduce itself to doing anything as technical as texting. I don't know why she has it.

I reach over and switch on my newly fixed phone to find about twenty missed calls. 'Bloody hell,' I say, turning to Rufus. 'I've got missed calls from just about everyone I've ever met!' There are messages waiting on the phone too, but I decide to leave them until I've spoken to Mum. She answers immediately.

'I knew it would be you,' she says. 'I've heard, I can't believe it. Are you OK?'

'Yes, never better,' I say. 'How on earth did you hear?'

'It's been on the news all morning.'

Oh God. How on earth have the news channels found out already? Is this room being bugged or something? No wonder everyone's been trying to get hold of me. I turn to Rufus and shrug my shoulders, raising my eyebrows somewhere up into my hairline.

'How was my engagement on the news?' I ask Mum.

Rufus looks at me equally quizzically.

'Your engagement?' says Mum. 'What engagement? I didn't know you were engaged. Why does no one tell me anything?'

'That's what I'm ringing to tell you; Rufus proposed last night. So it wasn't on the news?'

'No. Why would it be on the news?'

'Oh, it doesn't matter, Mum. Look, I just wanted to let

you know that I'm getting married . . . to Rufus . . . how cool is that? You're the first person I've phoned.'

'That's brilliant, love,' she says. 'I think we all need a bit of good news at the moment, don't we?'

'Yes,' I say rather vaguely. I'm not sure why particularly at the moment. Good news is worth having any time, isn't it?

'Now then,' Mum says, and I can hear her scrabbling around. 'OK. Things to do . . . shall I book the church or will you? That community centre gets booked up. Marian's daughter was trying to hold her reception there but had no luck at all. I'll get on to them straight away. What date did you want to do, love? Try and avoid the end of April and the beginning of May because your father likes to help out with the gardening down on the seafront then and he'd hate to miss it.'

'Mum, Mum,' I try to interrupt. The idea of the world's press descending on the Hastings Community Centre, and the most famous people on the planet flying in from New York for it, leaves me trembling. Shit. I need to think this through. Kofi Annan and Great-Aunt Maude . . . how's that going to work? And if we leave the cars down by the pier, they'll all get broken into.

'We haven't set a date yet, and I don't know where it's going to be. As soon as I know, I'll let you know.'

'Winter or summer?'

'Sorry?'

'The wedding: winter or summer? I need to get my hats out and work out which one's going to work. I can't wear brown in summer or pale pink in winter can I, silly?'

'Um. Summer,' I say.

'Oh,' says Mum, disappointment pouring down the phone. 'I look much better in autumnal shades. I'm a bit old for pastels.'

'OK, winter,' I say.

'Great. Right. Well I'll go down to the community centre just in case and see what the bookings are like for winter.'

'OK, Mum.'

As I put the phone down to my mother, and begin to regale Rufus with the mad conversation I've just endured, there's a gentle tap on the door.

'What is it?' asks Rufus. 'Mrs George and I are busy.' The staff never, ever knock on the door to Rufus's private rooms.

'Terribly sorry to interrupt, sir.' David's distinctive old voice comes floating under the bedroom door. It has an almost ghostly feel to it. 'There are some people at the door. They've come to see Ms Monsoon.'

'There's no Ms Monsoon here,' says Rufus, laughing as he half smothers me with the pillow. 'She's changed her name. Tell them to go away.'

'I really am sorry to interrupt, sir,' says David, coughing gently as if to illustrate how terribly inconvenient he is finding all of this. 'Only it's the police.'

'Oh God!' I cry. I'm terrified of the police. If there's a police car driving behind me, I go into a blind panic and can hardly drive properly. I don't know why; I guess it relates back to that time I was caught drink-driving. It was awful. Every time I see a policeman now, I'm in pieces. Now there's one in the house! Shit.

'Don't worry,' says Rufus, smiling and giving me a hug. 'You haven't got drugs in your handbag, have you?'

'Of course not.'

'Good. Neither have I, so we have nothing to worry about.'

'Elody gave me those drugs before though, to help me lose weight. It couldn't be those, could it?'

'No. Don't be daft,' he says. 'It'll be something to do with security. We have to deal with the local police a fair bit.'

'Oh,' I say. 'But why would they want to see me?'

'Let's go find out,' says Rufus, kissing me on the forehead and leaping out of bed.

It turns out it isn't someone checking on our security downstairs, but two stern-looking police officers, pacing up and down the sitting room floor as if they were keeping guard outside a prison cell; neither is wearing a uniform. They both look solemn. Thank God Rufus came down with me. He picks up on how serious this appears to be.

'Is there something wrong?' he asks.

'Perhaps you should take a seat, sir,' says the officer.

'I'm fine,' Rufus replies, but I find myself sinking into the sofa all the same. This is about the diet pills, I just know it. What if Mandy and Sophie get in trouble because they were the ones who flushed them down the loo? Harbouring illegal drugs? Shit. I look up and see that one of the men is watching me constantly. He's very tall; a big chap with flinty blue eyes that seem to rip right through me as he stares. He doesn't stop looking at me. There's a smirk playing on his lips. He knows all about the drugs. Perhaps they had sniffer dogs at the drains outside the girls' flat? I knew I shouldn't have taken the slimming drugs out there. Shit.

'We're wondering whether you know anything about Elody Elloissie,' says the smaller man, while the big guy keeps staring straight at me. I don't think he's blinked since I walked into the room.

'I know her,' I say.

'I know you do,' he replies. 'But did you know that she was found dead this morning? We believe she was murdered.'

EXCLUSIVE
By Katie Joseph
Daily Post Showbiz Correspondent

ONE of the world's leading fashion stylists was found dead in the early hours of this morning.

Elody Elloissie, 37, a Parisienne who has lived in London for most of her life is believed to have been stabbed. Her body was found by a cleaner arriving for work at the Royal Institute of Fashion in Richmond, south-west London.

Elloissie's name became synonymous with red-carpet dressing for the rich and famous when she linked up with the late fashion designer, Jon Boycott, ten years ago. They became lovers and together they designed for and styled photo shoots and magazine covers as well as working with a range of wealthy individuals and most of Hollywood's elite over a decade in the public eye.

Yesterday her styling came to an end, though, when

her body was found slumped in the vestibule at the bottom of the white marble steps of the Royal Institute of Fashion. She had been stabbed through the heart. A police spokesman at Scotland Yard said that there would be a further statement today. It is expected that they will announce the launch of a murder inquiry.

The news has left residents of luxurious Richmond Hill reeling. Elody Elloissie was a popular and sociable member of the wealthy clique and worked with some of the world's leading celebrities. Her closest friend, Kelly Monsoon, was unavailable for comment.

Chapter 19

God it's hard to remember everything. The news that Elody has been murdered is still washing over me; nothing's sinking in. It just can't be true. And she was thirty-seven! I can't believe that; I mean, I knew she was older than she claimed to be, but I assumed she was around thirty-two or something like that. She looked bloody good for thirty-seven. Shit, what a nightmare; I know she was a complete bloody pain at times, but she was also someone I got to know; someone I ended up spending a lot of time with. I keep thinking of that sad face looking back at me as Henry drove her away, the previously unseen vulnerability. Little did I know that I'd never see her again; that someone was waiting to stab her and end her life.

It's all so unreal. I'm waiting for one of the officers to say, 'Oh, hang on a minute. Is she called Elody? Sorry, we're supposed to be at the house of Elaine.' The woman was so tough, so confident and competent. It's unbelievable that she's been snatched away. Murdered? Are they sure? I wish they'd go and double-check for me, because I'm not convinced they've got this right at all.

I have so many questions I want to ask them, but the police, in turn, have about 150 million questions that they want to ask me. I know they're only doing their job but they need to know what time it was when she left here and what mood she was in, and why she left. I'm mortified that I threw Elody out, then she came back the next morning and I threw her out again. I can't bear to tell them about the argument and the fight on the gravel driveway. What a horrible thought; I might have been one of the last people to see her and we had a horrible row. Shit. I'm never fighting with anyone ever again. They don't need to know about Elody's behaviour that provoked the argument. It seems disrespectful to Elody's memory to bring it up at all, especially since I know that every word I utter will end up in the newspapers at some stage. I owe it to Elody's memory not to do that.

What time was it when Elody left that morning? 'Midday?' I say, but Christ, it's hard to remember.

'Who do you think did it?' I ask.

'We don't know yet. We're hoping that by talking to her friends and family we'll be able to build up a better picture of her life and particularly her movements yesterday. Hopefully, before too long, we'll be able to work out who had a grudge against her. Do you know of anyone who had a grudge against her?'

Shit. Most of the people on the street had a grudge against the woman, but I can't tell them that. I look up, see the big cop staring and look back down again. 'No,' I mutter.

'Sorry?' says the big guy. 'Didn't quite catch that.'

'No, I don't.'

'Did you have a grudge against her?' he asks.

'No,' I say, looking down at my hands. 'Of course not.'

He scribbles away in his notebook. His name is Detective Inspector Barnes; the other guy is Detective Constable Swann.

'Just a few more questions,' says the constable. It's mainly the Swann guy who questions me. The big guy just seems to stare at me and butt in every so often, wanting more information, more detail and more explanation. I know they're talking to everyone and just trying to find out what Elody's movements were yesterday, but every time I can't answer a question properly or I stutter or stammer, I see the Barnes guy staring right through me and I feel instantly guilty.

'What time did you say she left here?' asks the big guy. I honestly can't remember. 'Around 11 am, at a guess.'

'Around 11 o'clock, or exactly 11 o'clock?' he says.

Didn't I just say I didn't know exactly? 'Around 11 am,' I repeat.

'How sure are you? How do you know it was 11 o'clock? You said 12 o'clock a minute ago. Was it dark or light? Did anyone else see her go? Where was she going? How did she travel there? What was the weather like?'

Once they've started, the questions come raining down on me. They get me to run through everything I did that day – from the moment I got up until I went to bed. As soon as I say something like 'then I had breakfast' they want to know what I had for breakfast and whether I washed up, and was I listening to the radio at the time? Aaaaahhhh . . .

The whole thing is rather complicated by the fact that I can't mention that I found out Elody had been hiding my letters and that's why I called her back from her shopping trip because it seems so incredibly disrespectful to Elody's memory.

Rufus is sitting right next to me so I can't mention the

arrival of the carpenter and the fact that he saw her sitting outside in the car, and how we ended up having an argument. Rufus would go mad if he knew about that. I don't suppose it matters if I don't mention the broken drawer; it's an irrelevance. These guys aren't interested in whether I broke the drawer or not, they just want to know who killed Elody . . . Still, I do feel really bad about lying to them.

'You look worried, sweetheart. Is everything OK?' asks Rufus, sitting down next to me.

'Fine,' I say, rather too quickly. 'Everything's just fine. Honestly. I'm just trying hard to remember everything.'

'I can't remember where she said she was going, but it was Henry who took her so he'll know. You could ask him.'

'We will. You didn't mention the weather.'

'It was cold but it wasn't raining, I don't think.'

'You don't think?' says the big guy – Detective Chief up-your-arse Barnes.

'I don't think it was raining. I don't really remember.'

'Are these questions annoying you?' asks Barnes.

'A little,' I admit. 'I just don't remember exactly what I was doing at specific times. No one looks at the clock all the time, do they?'

'But you understand that we're trying to establish specific time points in order to find Elody's killer? You understand that, don't you? We're here to find out who killed your friend. She was your friend, wasn't she?'

'Yes.'

'Where were you between 4.30 pm and 5.30 pm yesterday?'

'I was at my friends' flat; the place where I used to live. In Twickenham.'

'Where in Twickenham?'

I give them the address, then they want a description of it, and a description of the route we took to get there. Before long they'll want compass bearings and the precise location marked out on an Ordinance Survey map.

'What time did you arrive there?'

'At 4 pm.'

'And you went in then?'

'Yes.'

Well, I didn't go in then but it's too complicated to say otherwise because then they'll ask me fifty million questions about what I was up to, and what I was up to is, frankly, none of their business and doesn't relate in any way to the crime they're supposed to be trying to solve so will only waste their time.

'And what did you do after that?'

'I went to the airport to meet Rufus.'

'What time?'

'At about 7 pm.'

'In a black cab?'

'No, Henry drove me.'

'And Henry drove you to your friends' flat in Twickenham.'

'Yes.'

'Now, is there anything else that you haven't told us, or anything that you think you should add before we take a statement?'

'A statement?' says Rufus. 'Why does she have to make a statement? Is she a suspect?'

'In a case like this, everyone's a suspect,' says the smaller guy. 'We need to take a statement from all witnesses at this stage in the investigation.'

'This is a murder inquiry sir,' says the big guy. 'Do you have a problem with Kelly giving a statement?'

'No,' says Rufus, standing up. 'The problem I have is with your attitude.' Then he turns to me. 'Wait here. Don't say or do anything. I'm calling my lawyers.'

Rufus comes back about five minutes later and says I'm to do nothing until a lawyer arrives. By now I'm feeling quite scared. If Rufus is insisting on his lawyer being involved, then he must think this is serious. Surely they can't think that I did it, can they? I wish the whole bloody carpenter thing hadn't happened on the same day. I just don't want to talk about that in front of Rufus.

We're all sitting there in frosty silence when the doorbell rings and a team of four lawyers walks in. Rufus greets them and takes them off to the snug from where I can hear muffled voices. They walk back in looking quite at ease.

'It's just routine,' says Detective Swann, looking at Rufus and the two lawyers standing next to him. 'But we really do need to take a statement.'

The lawyers both nod, and my boyfriend nods. He then looks at me and I nod. It's like we've all caught this mad nodding disease. I then repeat everything I said previously and sign a form. Shit. I'm sure I should be telling them about the carpenter, but how can I? I'll lose Rufus for ever if I do, and I'll end up having to tell them the carpenter's name and he'll be called in for questioning, and he'll mention the row, and that won't reflect well on

Elody and it'll all become an impossibly complicated mess and I'll have let everyone down and yet it won't contribute in any way, shape or form to the investigation into Elody's murder.

Chapter 20

'Katie Pound is in Richmond for London Today. What's the latest, Katie?'

'Thanks, Bob. You join us live on Richmond Hill where residents this lunchtime are waking up to the news that one of their most glamorous neighbours was murdered yesterday afternoon. That's right murdered. Police announced at a press conference this morning that they were launching a murder investigation after Elody Elloissie, stylist to the stars, was found stabbed to death yesterday.

'Now I should emphasise, for those who do not know this area of south-west London, that nothing like this has ever happened here before. If you look behind me you'll be able to see the amazing houses where the likes of Mick Jagger, Rock James and Rufus George live; in these massive gated homes protected by security guards, fences and alarms. I can't go up the road to show you where Elody lived, but if you look past the police cordon on the left you'll see two officers guarding a door. That was Elody's home until brutal, bloody murder cut her life short.

'Now police estimate the time of death as being around 5.30 pm yesterday. They have CCTV footage of the stylist entering the Royal Institute of Fashion earlier in the day, and it is their belief that someone was lying *in wait for her, clutching a knife and preparing to do the dreaded deed. Then she lay alone and dying before being found by a cleaner arriving for her morning shift some twelve hours later.*

'It's a terrible story and, ironically, a story not unlike the script of a Hollywood movie, the like of which so many of those who live in this part of London have starred in during their careers. If anyone saw anything that could help police, please call Detective Inspector Martyn Barnes from Scotland Yard on 08567898989; he's the man who's heading up this inquiry. I spoke to him a little earlier to find out some more about this incredible breaking news story . . .'

'They're loving this,' Rufus says, as we lie on the sofa, wrapped round each other, neither of us quite able to take in the events of the morning so far. Suddenly the fact that we got engaged last night seems like a lifetime away. 'It's a media dream to have a story like this, isn't it? Glamour and murder. Perfect!'

'I'm sure they think I did it,' I say, quite out of the blue. I don't know whether I do think that, but I'm sure I must be in the frame, and the way that detective guy was looking at me . . .

'No one thinks you did anything,' says Rufus, turning to face me. 'You're not capable of harming a fly, let alone killing another human being. You had a row with her. Everyone falls out with Elody eventually. It doesn't mean you killed her. Christ, if everyone who'd ever fallen out with Elody was in the frame for her murder, most of the women in West London would be banged up by now.'

'Very true,' I say, snuggling up closer to him. Thank God for Rufus and his common sense approach to life.

'I'm joined by Katie Joseph, showbiz correspondent of the Daily Post. *Katie, you've been reporting on the inhabitants of the Hill for the past year. How do you think they'll take this news today?'*

'I think they'll all be wondering who's next. Is this is a serial killer? Is this a guy who's targeting the famous and wealthy?'

'A serial killer? Is there any evidence of that yet?'

'Not publicly, but my sources in the police are suggesting that this is likely to be someone who'll strike again very soon, and the conversations I've had with the Hill's most famous residents indicate that they are very, very scared here right now. The murderer is being dubbed the Hill Murderer. Like the terrible Moors Murderers of twenty years ago.'

'Shit, do you think that's true, Rufus?'

'No way. She'd love nothing more than for there to be a serial killer buzzing around the place. It would keep her in stories for the rest of time. You know who she is, don't you?'

I look back at the screen where the attractive woman, madly overdressed and made-up like a clown, is continuing to talk with apparent knowledge about things she knows nothing about. 'Yep,' I say. 'That's the woman who said I'd had a boob job, wrote that I used to be a lesbian and described my mum and great-aunt as "mental home escapees".'

'So do you think she knows what she's talking about?'

'Nope.'

Chapter 21

It's 3 pm and I'm sitting here alone on the sofa with my knees tucked up under my chin, crying silently. How awful for Elody to have been killed like that. It's unbelievable. There's a light drizzle outside. Freezing cold winds are whipping through the garden as darkness begins its descent. I've switched off the television because I can't bear to hear any more murder speculation. I know she was a pain at times and drove everyone here mad. In the end, she really upset me because of her obsession with clothes and appearances. She should never have given me those drugs and made me feel so paranoid about Rufus but, equally, it was me who took them, and me who allowed myself to become paranoid. She's not responsible for my feelings. I should have told her that I trusted Rufus. I should have told her that I was happy with the way I looked, but I was so bloody insecure that I allowed myself to become enmeshed in her highly complex world with its twisted sense of morality. My fault; not hers!

The truth is that Elody was a person – a real living person, not a fictional character like the one being debated on television. She took me under her wing and looked after me in my early days on the Hill. Now she's become an inanimate object at the centre of fevered speculation. People are building careers and establishing their credibility on the back of her still warm corpse. It's horrible.

It feels like the police aren't looking for a person who committed a murder, but to solve a crime to develop their careers. The journalists who don't know anyone are speculating wildly about what might have happened and why. The world is astonished and involved in something that has nothing to do with them. I really hate it.

I can't escape it though. Rufus has had to go out to a meeting and I'm here on my own. In the kitchen, the radio keeps going back to the 'scene of this fascinating news story'. There are apparently millions of people walking around the place 'intrigued by this story'. Good for them. I hope it's brightening up their dull lives. The trouble is, when someone who spent the previous three weeks popping by to see you is found stabbed to death, it doesn't feel like a 'fascinating' news story, it feels like a complete bloody tragedy.

'We go to the centre of Richmond now, where Sylvia Gilbert is waiting to give us the latest on this incredibly story,' says the man on the radio. 'Sylv, have you got anything new for us?'

'Well, Mike,' says the reporter, almost breathless with excitement. 'We haven't had it officially confirmed, but we believe the police do have a main suspect. The excitement raging now is over who it could be. I went out into Richmond High Street earlier today to talk to some locals to see what they think, then I went into the local betting shop here to see what the odds were for the different characters in this very unusual murder mystery. First, let's see what the locals thought . . .

'I reckon it was Rock James – he looks like real trouble.'

'I think it was Rufus George. I think he tried it on with her and she said no, so he stabbed her.'

'I reckon it was a woman. I think Elody went off with one of the husbands and the wife killed her.'

'So, that's the view of the locals here. Interestingly, when we rang William Hill Bookmakers on Richmond High Street, they said that as far as their odds were concerned, there were just three names in the frame for the murder. One is Kelly Monsoon, Elody's friend, and the girl who is going out with Rufus George. Then there's Henry Alderson, Rufus George's driver, and the last person known to have seen her alive. He's believed to have become increasingly annoyed that he was being asked to drive Elody around as well as act as chauffeur to Rufus and his girlfriend. Finally, there's Dr Isabella Bronks-Harrison who has had a long-term feud with the fashionista and is known to thoroughly dislike her.'

How do they know all this stuff?

When security calls to say there are two men waiting at the gate, I know straight away who it is. I knew they'd want to talk to me again because I was rubbish the first time. I'd just heard about the murder and couldn't think straight.

'Take them to the sitting room,' I say to David, wanting to stay in the warmth of the snug for ever.

'Are you OK?' he asks, looking at me with concern in those clear eyes of his. He may be old and craggy but his eyes remain as bright and alert as ever.

'Yes,' I say, wiping away my tears. 'If you show them in, I'll be there right away.'

I walk quietly to the sitting room, and peer through a gap in the door. The men are in there, ruddy-cheeked and looking even more stern than they did last time, if that's possible. The smaller of the two men wipes a tear from his eye. I'd like to think it's because he feels bad about interrupting me again, but I know it's got more to do with the cold stinging his eyes and nose as he walked from the car to the house.

David offers them seats and warm drinks, but when I walk into the room I notice that neither of them is sitting. They stand in their heavy overcoats, both of them with their hands behind their backs, Prince Charles style, looking round the room. When I walk in, they walk up to me. The smaller of the men looks straight into my eyes.

'You know how serious this is, don't you?' he asks.

'Yes,' I reply.

'You must be aware that we have talked to lots of people about the evening that Elody was murdered. Is there anything you told us in your statement that you would like to change, now you've had time to think about what happened on the day of Elody's murder?'

'No,' I say, feeling myself trembling inside.

'It's our belief that you lied to us, Kelly,' says the detective. 'Do you realise how serious that is?'

'Yes.'

'We do not think that you were in your friends' flat at the time of the murder. We think you went to Richmond and murdered Elody Elloissie after arguing with her publicly earlier in the day, and fighting with her on the gravel outside.'

Shit. Who told them that? It must have been Henry or Pamela. Or the carpenter. Shit, no. Please tell me they don't know anything about the carpenter.

'I didn't kill her,' I say. 'I didn't.'

The bigger of the two men steps forward.

'Kelly Monsoon, I am arresting you for the murder of Elody Elloissie. You do not have to say anything, but it may harm your defence if you do not mention when questioned something you later rely on in court. Anything you do say maybe given in evidence. Is that clear?'

Chapter 22

'Breaking news . . .'

'OK, thanks, Bob. You come back to us as we've just had confirmation from the police that they have arrested someone in connection with the murder yesterday of Elody Elloissie. A police statement issued just minutes ago says they have arrested a 28-year-old female who has been taken to Richmond station for questioning.

'That woman is believed to be Kelly Monsoon, the girlfriend of Hollywood film star Rufus George, and a close friend of Elloissie. I repeat, we believe that Kelly Monsoon, girlfriend of Rufus George has been arrested and taken to Richmond police station to answer questions in connection with the brutal murder yesterday of glamorous fashion designer Elody Elloissie. More on that breaking news story as soon as we have it.'

The dull grey skies hang over us; rain pours down, pelting onto the car as it makes its short journey from Richmond Hill to Richmond police station, bumper to bumper all the way. Flashes burst through the sky as eager photographers try to capture pictures of me: the world-famous murder suspect cowering behind blacked-out windows. Much of the town centre area has been cordoned off since the discovery of Elody's body. No one's allowed through until forensic examinations have been conducted across every inch of the place. It means that traffic is backed up and stationary all the way. Even with the police outriders, it's taking for ever to drive down the hill to the station.

It's silent in the car; the men attempt no small talk, and I'm too thrown and confused by developments to attempt to talk to them. I'm almost light-headed. I don't feel like screaming and shouting and banging my hands against the window like you imagine you'd feel in this situation; I just feel shocked and confused. Genuinely dizzy and amazed at the way things have developed. The small guy drives on through the rain while I sit in the back with Detective Barnes. He has his legs apart and his hands on his knees; confident and happy that he's getting another crime wrapped up. I'm sitting, cowering in the corner, as foetal-like as it's possible to get in the back of a police car. I'm leaning into the door with my eyes closed, hoping, every time I open them, that this horrible nightmare has ended and I'm back in bed with Rufus, planning our wedding . . . a wedding that I now fear will never happen.

God, this is awful. It's unbelievably awful. I can see the dancing, flickering lights from the police motorbikes refracting in the raindrops falling all around us. It seems like there's so much noise and excitement out there. It contrasts staggeringly with the silence and heaviness in the car.

When we left the house they had to throw a coat over my head to protect me from the flashbulbs and the intrusive lenses trained on me at every turn. I felt like a serial killer or Jeffrey Archer or someone.

'OK,' Detective Barnes had said, throwing the blanket

over me. 'This photograph is the most wanted in the world, by anyone, right now. Let's make sure they don't get it, shall we?' He smiled at me then: a drop of tenderness in an ocean of pain and humiliation.

I'm at the centre of a worldwide storm but like everyone who's ever been at the centre of a worldwide storm before me, it's really nothing. There are police outriders, paparazzi chasing us, and non-stop communication on the radio with the custody sergeant but the truth is that I'm just a girl in a car driving through Richmond in the pouring rain with two men beside me. The two men think I murdered someone. I'm telling them I didn't. All the rest of it is just noise.

I'm sitting directly behind the passenger seat. As soon as I was instructed to sit here, I knew why. Oh yes – turns out those nights watching true crime programmes with the girls in the flat late at night weren't a waste of time after all. Who'd have guessed? I happen to know from my extensive viewing that they never sit violent criminals behind the driver in case the person bashes the driver over the head and tries to escape. That's me. I'm the violent criminal. I've been arrested for murder.

Shit. I'm under arrest. They think I'm a murderer. What about Mum and Dad? Great-Aunt Maude? Oh God, she'll wet herself when she finds out. No, really, she will literally wet herself. I hope they're not being pestered by the press. Though the likelihood that they're not being pestered is so tiny that it's not worth considering.

'I'm worried about my mum and dad,' I say to Detective Barnes next to me, and I really hope he doesn't say, 'Well you should have thought of that before committing murder, shouldn't you?' because if he does I might have to whack him which will clearly not do my case any good at all.

'We're keeping the press away from them,' he says.

'Thank you,' I say, and I look at him properly for the first time. The blue eyes aren't quite as steely any more; it's almost like he feels sorry for me. I put my head back against the window, close my eyes and try to stop my heart pounding up into the back of my throat. It's going to be OK; it's going to be OK. David promised to get hold of Rufus immediately and send him straight to Richmond police station with his legal team. It's going to be OK.

The windscreen wipers move quickly as the rain lashes down more heavily. It's dark and dismal in every way possible. The car eases towards the sealed-off area of the high street; the police cordon is lifted by a jovial, pink-cheeked policeman resplendent in his hat and fluorescent waterproof jacket. I feel a sudden pang of fear on seeing the uniformed man. Is that why I'm so relatively calm? Because the men who arrested me were in civilian clothes and thus looked less threatening? It reminds me quite suddenly of having to go into hospital as a young child and being terrified of the doctors. 'This is Dr Bartlett,' Mum said (see, I still remember his name) and I winced in fear and loathing.

When it came to the operation, though, the man conducting it was called simply Mike Harcourt. 'Mr Harcourt' the nurses called him and everything was OK then. Devoid of fancy titles he seemed less threatening; stripped of the symbolism of oppression, people seem less oppressive.

The car swings into the back of the police station,

through throngs of photographers being held back by dozens of uniformed officers. I feel scared then. Yep, for all my philosophising I now feel terrified out of my mind.

'Thanks, Bob, yes – we can confirm that Kelly Monsoon left her home on Richmond Hill in an unmarked police car, heading for Richmond police station around ten minutes ago. She was accompanied by two detectives, and uniformed officers surrounded the entrance to the police station to make sure no photographers could get near. The car had previously foiled the photographers' attempts to get close by picking up Kelly inside the large security gates outside the mansion she shares with movie star Rufus George. There were blacked-out windows on the car and it went through the cordoned-off area, past the Royal Institute of Fashion, scene of the murder for which Monsoon, girlfriend of Rufus George, now finds herself arrested. Back to you, Bob.'

'Thanks, Jennie. But can we confirm; do we know for sure that it is Kelly Monsoon in the car? Have police confirmed that they have arrested her?'

'Well, Bob, no. Police have said simply that it was a 28-year-old woman. We know that a car used by detectives was at Rufus George's fabulous Richmond mansion earlier today, and we know that car headed straight for Richmond police station, going through police cordons on the way. All the rumours here indicate that it is Kelly who's being driven to the station as we speak.'

'Well, what next, then, for the girl who had everything? Kelly Monsoon seemed to be living the dream when she met hunky film star Rufus George and was

swept off to a world of money and fame. Today though, her dream lies in tatters as she stands accused of brutal murder. I'm joined by former Detective Chief Superintendent Mike Dover. Morning to you, sir. Could you tell us a little bit about what Kelly will be going through, and what awaits her when she gets to the police station?'

'Of course. Good afternoon, Bob. Well, when she gets to the police station, the first thing that will happen will be fingerprints, photographs and DNA samples will be taken, then there'll be a full body search. It's unusual for someone who's committed a murder not to have some marks on their body. In particular, they'll check her hands, looking for hilt wounds. If the victim was stabbed, as has been widely reported, then it's likely the perpetrator of the crime would have cut him or herself between the thumb and index finger — the area we call 'the hilt' during the attack. Unless, of course . . .'

'Sorry, I'll have to stop you there, former Detective Chief Superintendent, because we're now going back over to Jennie in Richmond where I believe the car containing Miss Monsoon has arrived at Richmond police station. Is that right, Jennie?'

'Yes, Bob. That's right. The car, which we believe contains Kelly Monsoon, has now arrived at Richmond police station. Back to you, Bob.'

'Thanks, Jennie. Well, amazing breaking news there, brought to you live as it happens, twenty-four hours a day, here on Sky. So, former Detective Chief Superintendent, anything else you can tell us about what the future holds for Kelly?'

'Well, she'll be interviewed in detail and will be asked

to run through everything she's said previously. The initial interviews are likely to be conducted by specialist police interviewing unit Tier Three. She'll be videoed, and then she's likely to be put in a cell overnight and interviewed again in the morning when police will challenge her on aspects on the story that they do not believe.'

'So, you're saying that Kelly Monsoon's story is not believed? Has she been deliberately lying to police?'

'We don't know that, Bob, but clearly they have reason to be suspicious or they wouldn't have arrested her. It's my view that they'll tackle these issues once she's spent a night in the cell.'

'And will she be locked up with other murderers?'

'She'll be in her own cell, at the police station. They may well transfer her to Scotland Yard in the morning. Can I just remind viewers that Kelly is not a "murderer". She's innocent until proven guilty.'

'Yeah, yeah. Will there be rats in the cell?'

'Er . . . no.'

'Are we becoming too soft on criminals? After all, this woman has committed a serious offence.'

'We don't know that yet, Bob, she's innocent until proven guilty.'

'We'll be back, after these adverts.'

A shock wave of exhaustion and displacement hits me like a thunderclap. What am I doing here? How has this happened?

'Let's just run through the whole day again shall we?' asks the policeman. 'Everything you say is being taped and videoed.'

Arriving at the cells was the most terrifying experience of my life. We drove through a large, dark-blue, prison-like gate of metal bars, and into a small courtyard where I was taken out of the car and led into the building.

'This is the custody suite, and this is the custody officer,' they said, introducing me to a small, round blonde woman who took my details and said she needed to take fingerprints, a photo and DNA samples. Next, they strip-searched me. The lady who did it was very gentle and respectful but a strip-search is a strip-search. It was humiliating, embarrassing and horrid.

The lawyers came and kept demanding to know what evidence the police have. They asked whether the police have a warrant for my arrest and talked about 'pace' and my rights, and all these other things I've only ever heard about on the news. They wanted know whether the police found any marks on me. The only mark I have is a bruise on my right thigh. Since I got that in a fight with Elody, that hasn't helped my case too much.

The worst thing about all this is that Rufus isn't here. He hasn't called or made contact at all.

'Will Rufus come?' I kept asking.

'No,' they kept saying.

I know I've let him down, and I know I've embarrassed him, but surely he can see that I need him now more than I've ever needed anyone in my life before.

'Your parents are desperately worried about you,' my solicitor told me. She meant well. She wanted to remind me that there are lots of people out there who care about me deeply, but all her kind words did was ram another stab of guilt straight into my heart.

'Why have they arrested me?' I asked. 'I mean – I know they've arrested me because they think I killed Elody, but why do they think that?'

'They think you lied to them, Kelly. The police check and double-check every statement made and if you tell them things that later turn out not to be true, it does alert all their suspicions. They want to talk to you about your alibi for the time of the murder, what happened between you and Elody on the day of the murder, and some things that they allege you said to other people, about wanting to kill Elody.'

Now, I'm in a heavily lit interview room with fluorescent lighting that could brighten Wembley. The room's completely plain, and decorated in a cream colour. There's nothing here to distract me or provoke me. I guess that's the point of it.

I tell the police everything I can remember. Rufus isn't here, so I tell them all about the carpenter and I explain that I didn't want to mention what I did in front of my boyfriend, in case he got really cross. They shake their heads as if I'm the most stupid person ever to walk the earth . . . which I guess I might be, all things considered.

'This is a different story to the one you told us yesterday,' says Detective Inspector Barnes.

The lawyer in the room with me is called Sue Lawrence and apparently she's the best criminal lawyer in the world. She's also gorgeous. I don't think the detectives could quite believe their luck when she walked in. She sat down and crossed her legs over and I thought poor Detective Barnes might go tumbling off his chair. It's not so much that her skirt's short as her legs are incredibly long, slim, and shapely. I'm so glad she's on my side.

'I'd like a word with my client, please,' she says, with a batting of her eyelashes and a smile playing on her glossy lips.

Away from the guys she asks me why I didn't tell them about the carpenter yesterday.

'I was just so embarrassed in front of Rufus,' I repeat. 'I'm not normally the jealous type but I went all through his stuff while he was in LA, checking to see whether there were any clues that he was having an affair or anything and, when I couldn't get into one drawer, I smashed my way in. I had to get a carpenter to repair it. I never told Rufus. It's got nothing to do with Elody's murder or anything.'

'You don't know that. Your job is just to tell the truth and they'll work out what's relevant. If you don't tell them the complete truth at all times, you'll get yourself in more trouble,' she says with great pomposity. I don't feel like I'm in any position to complain though. This woman, right now, appears to be the only person in my corner. To be frank, the only person who gives a shit.

'Was there anything in the drawer?' she asks.

'A bracelet which matches the necklace that Elody always wears.'

'Say that again.'

'In the drawer that I broke into there was a bracelet which I think belongs to Elody. It was hidden right at the back. I don't know why and I haven't had chance to discuss it with Rufus. It's pretty fucking scary though, and I'd rather not be discussing it with the police.'

'So you think that Elody was having an affair with Rufus?'

My lawyer looks absolutely horrified. Really, she looks quite scared.

'Yes,' I say, which just compounds everything. Her pretty petal-like face looks as if it's about to completely crumble away. 'I mean no. I mean I don't know. It's just all weird. Why would her bracelet be in there if they weren't? But then he came back from LA and proposed to me and he seems to love me. I don't know.'

'You know it was her bracelet, do you?'

'No, I don't know anything. It matched her necklace exactly, though. What are the chances of it not being her bracelet, really?'

'Who have you mentioned this to?' she asks.

'My flatmates,' I say. 'Mandy and Sophie.'

'Fuck.'

'So, well done to Chelsea. Now, back to our main story of the day. Police have confirmed that the woman arrested in connection with the murder of Elody Elloissie is Kelly Monsoon, the girlfriend of film star Rufus George. More on that story as and when we get it and in a change to the TV listings, tonight's Panorama *programme will now feature famous female killers.* Newsnight *also has a change of subject. Jeremy Paxman will be hosting a panel discussion called: "Why do women kill?" and will be talking to friends and colleagues of Kelly Monsoon, including Lord and Lady Simpkins, the theatre impresarios who became close friends with the woman now accused of brutal murder. For now, though, it's over to*

> *the regional news teams to find out what's happening in your area.'*

I'm back in with the police, and the questioning is relentless.

'So what time did the carpenter arrive?' they ask ... again ...

'It was around midday.'

'And Elody was outside at the time.'

'Yes.'

'How did you know she was outside?'

'The carpenter told me someone was there so I went to the window and looked out.'

'Did she see you looking?'

'No. I don't think so.'

'How did Elody get through the security gates to be sitting within sight of the window?'

'She's known to security and Henry was driving her. He's Rufus's driver. He would have been allowed straight through.'

'Why was Henry driving her? How often does Henry drive her? Did you not say earlier that you asked Henry not to drive her? Do she and Henry get on? Have you ever seen them arguing? Does Henry seem like a man who is capable of murder?'

The questions keep coming; some things I'm asked to repeat and other things I'm asked for the first time. Now I've decided to just tell them everything that happened, I'm much happier. I'm not very good at lying. I was only doing it to protect Rufus. There are some little secrets we have that I just don't like to reveal, and some things I did (like smashing up the desk) that I don't want to have written about in the papers when they're nothing to do with Elody's murder, and will just be embarrassing for Rufus.

'And you're sure that you went from your home in Richmond to visit your friends in Twickenham at 4 pm?'

'Yes.'

'And Henry drove you all the way there?'

'Yes.'

'What happened then?'

'I knocked on the door but no one was in so I hung around until they got back.'

'You told us yesterday that you went straight in.'

'Yes, I know. I got confused by everything.'

'We came back and asked you again, and you still insisted on the same story.'

'Yes, as I said – I was very confused by everything.'

'You lied to us. You told us you had an alibi and you don't.'

I sit there silently, not knowing what to say.

'Where did you "hang around"?'

'Just in Twickenham.'

'Where in Twickenham?'

'I don't know, just around the coffee shops and stuff.'

'Which coffee shop?'

'Starbucks.'

'So you're saying that between the hours of 4 pm and 6 pm you were sitting in Starbucks in Twickenham.'

'Yes.'

'On your own?'

'Yes.'

'So you have no alibi for the time when Elody was murdered?'

'No. I just sat and had coffee.'

'What sort of coffee?'

'Skinny cappuccino.'

'Where is the coffee shop?'

'It's on the High Street.'

'Where on the High Street? Describe how you got there from the flat.'

'I walked to the traffic lights and turned right into the High Street and there it was, on the right.'

'And you walked in and sat down.'

'Yes I did.'

For God's sake, what does he think I did – disco-danced across the tables?

'Welcome to London Tonight *where we are asking the question: what happens when best friends turn on one another? Everyone's seen the wall-to-wall coverage of the Elody Elloissie murder case this week, and the fact that Kelly Monsoon, Elody's best friend, has been arrested for her murder. Could you murder your best friend? Do you ever feel like murdering her? What happens when best friends turn on one another? Can best friends get so close that love turns to hate? Why do women have best friends and what happens when it all goes wrong?'*

Chapter 23

The cell is not as horrific as I feared it might be; not that I spend a lot of time thinking about police cells, you understand, but when I was done for drink-driving I thought they'd throw me into a cell and I imagined it being cold and dark and packed full of brightly painted, vulgar hookers and terrifying drug dealers waiting to corrupt me. I always had this vision, based entirely on my experiences of watching bad cop shows on TV, that the cells were where you really suffered for your crime, at the hands of faceless thugs who'd committed offences so much worse than anything you could ever dream of doing.

This cell's not bad though. It's got pale-pink walls because the colour is supposed to make people feel calmer and I'm in an all-female section. Apparently there are ten cells for women and forty-two for men. I haven't seen anyone else though. There's a plastic mattress in the far corner of the room in the kind of royal blue favoured by the makers of school uniforms. The colour reminds me of gym knickers.

The bed lies beneath a long, thin window too high for me to look through, but big enough to cast natural light into what is otherwise a rather inhospitable and unnatural place. There's fluorescent lighting everywhere. That's the thing I noticed most when I walked in here. Light floods the long cream corridor, forcing brightness into every hidden corner of the cell. The place has the feel of a hospital ward. It reminds me of where Dad went for an operation years ago. All very clean and sterile, but characterless. Desperately soulless.

There's a stainless-steel toilet in the corner of my room and the door is the same deep blue as the barred gate that we came in through on our way in to the courtyard. The huge, metal cell door is the worst thing about the place; it's big and sturdy and when it clanks shut with that horrible metal slam, I feel myself shiver all over. It has a kind of heavy metal cat flap in it through which they look in every hour to make sure I'm OK.

The police come to the cell in the morning to wake me and feed me, but I'm already wide awake, as I guess they knew I would be. I don't suppose that many people locked up for murder sleep soundly on their first night behind bars. I'm not hungry either; strangely I seem to have lost my appetite. It's like Elody's controlling me from beyond the grave.

It's 7 am when I'm taken to wash and prepare myself for the rather gruelling day ahead. The grimy sinks and plastic mirrors mark a bitter contrast between my life before the death of Elody and life afterwards. Funny how I always thought the sumptuous bathrooms in Rufus's magnificent house acted as a symbol of how far I'd come in life when compared to the tiny brown and rotten bathroom that I'd endured while living in the flat. What I'd give for a brown bathroom now.

How peculiar life's waves are, lifting me out of the bright blue sea on a foam-topped crest before dumping me aggressively against the cold, grey rocks.

I'm taken back up to the interview room when I've finished washing, and instructed to sit face to face with my detective friends. This time there's a real frostiness in the air. If I thought the guys were miserable yesterday, I was mistaken. Today there's real grade-one freeze going on. The two detectives are pacing the room when I walk in. My solicitor sits quietly in the corner.

'Would you like to tell us again what you did on the afternoon of Thursday 3 December?'

Again, I explain about the visit to Starbucks.

'We have been through CCTV footage taken at Starbucks on that day and you were not seen going in or out of the building in the time period. Don't you think that's a bit strange?'

My solicitor touches my knee and tells me not to say anything.

'So you don't think it's strange then?'

'Well, it might have been a different coffee shop,' I say, despite Sue Lawrence's request for me to remain silent.

'You described to us in some detail yesterday the precise situation of the coffee shop you went into. Are you now saying that you didn't go into that coffee shop after all?'

'I just get confused.'

'Let me help you,' says Detective Barnes, leaning in so close to me that I think his nose is going to touch mine. 'I think you're lying to us. I don't think you went to a coffee shop at all but went to Richmond to confront Elody about the fact that you had found jewellery that you think belonged to her in your fiancé's drawer. We know you're capable of aggression because of the way you smashed up that desk and fought with Elody on the driveway to your home, resulting in the large bruises now present on your right thigh.

'We know very well that you're capable of lying because you've been doing that to us since we first came to talk to you about the crime. We know you and Elody had a huge fight and we know that you told several people that you were having real problems with Elody. Henry, Mr George's driver, admits that during a conversation you told him you hated Elody and "I could kill her". We have a message on Elody's phone in which you are hurling accusations at her and express deep dislike for her.

'We know that you did not stay in Twickenham because we have CCTV from outside Suga Daddys nightclub of you getting into a black cab. Your flatmates describe you as being "freezing cold" when they met you. You weren't in a coffee shop, Kelly. You took that cab to Richmond didn't you, Kelly? When you were in Richmond you murdered Elody Elloissie. Come on, Kelly. We know. You murdered her.'

'I'd like a word with my client NOW,' screams Sue Lawrence.

'I bet you would,' says Barnes. 'I bet you fucking would.'

Sue Lawrence is looking at me as one might look at a naughty child who has just spray-painted the *Mona Lisa* orange. She's annunciating every word as if talking to a three-year-old. 'You *must* tell the absolute truth,' she says. 'The *absolute* truth. *No* lies. Do. You. Understand? Do you?'

'Yes, I understand, and of course I know I have to tell the truth,' I say, rather too dismissively.

'No. No, Kelly you don't seem to "know" anything of the sort.' She's raising her voice again now. 'You don't seem to understand that if you tell one more little lie for whatever reason, you will be charged with murder and there is every chance that you will go to prison for a very long time. Now, I don't believe you murdered Elody, and I suspect that these policemen don't think you murdered Elody, but, if you keep lying, you will end up in jail. I don't know how to make this clear for you, Kelly.'

'It is clear,' I say. 'I understand. It's just that there are things that I don't think should be said.'

'You need to stop deciding what should and shouldn't be said, and start answering the questions honestly.'

'But Rufus always said that anything I say will, at some stage, find its way into the papers.'

'Kelly, you need to forget about all that. If you don't stop lying to the police, the fact that you are in the papers will be the very least of your concerns. I don't care how petty some of the questions seem, answer them honestly. If you're worried, don't say anything at all, just don't lie. Whatever you do, don't lie.'

'OK,' I say, suitably chastised. It's not like I'm lying to cover up anything terrible. I just don't see why the public has to hear how awful Elody could be when the woman's body is lying on a slab, and I don't want to ruin our favourite place by telling everyone that's where I was.

'Hello, welcome to Breakfast Chat *with me, Lucy Love-shaw. Well, there's only one thing being talked about at the moment and that's the shock news that Kelly Monsoon, the pretty young girl who stole the heart of film star*

Rufus George, has been arrested for the murder of top fashion stylist and her best friend, Elody Elloissie. The story is causing excitement across the nation because it's so unusual . . . most killers are men. So today we ask: Why do women kill?

'I'm joined in the studio by a panel of experts including our very own Breakfast Chat *agony aunt Gillian O'Connor. Next to Gill is Mandy Mitchell, whose mother was jailed for murder, Lady Helen Simpkins, one of the few people who spotted Kelly's potential as a murderer before the gruesome act, and Petra Moon from Women Against Violence. Gillian, let's start with you. This was a particularly brutal murder, wasn't it? Has it surprised you to hear that a woman would murder another woman in this way, and what do you believe is the motivation behind it?'*

'So now you're saying that you didn't go to a coffee shop in Twickenham? Sorry if we're being a bit slow keeping up with all of this, but your story is changing a lot.'

'Yes,' I say, sobbing uncontrollably.

'Yes what?' asks the detective with the mad, staring blue eyes.

'Yes, I'm saying that I didn't go to a coffee shop in Twickenham.'

'Where did you go then?'

'I went to Hampton Court Palace.'

'Very nice. Why did you go there?'

'Rufus and I have a special place we like; it's called the Rose Garden. It's beautiful. We love it; it's so quiet. We can be ourselves and no one hassles us or annoys us. There's this gardener there called Frank. You can ask him. I talk to him every time I go there. He saw me. We always have a cup of tea and a chat. He's lovely. The place is lovely and I promised Rufus that I would never, ever mention to anyone where our special place was, so I didn't want to say.'

'OK.' The detective runs his hands through his short, thinning hair. He looks exasperated. I hate the fact that I'm being such a pain but if it gets out that Rufus and I love it in the Rose Garden, the place will be full of his fans and we'll never be able to go there again. 'So, tell me what really happened, from the moment you got into Henry's car to go to your friends' flat until you met your boyfriend at Heathrow airport later that night. The truth, Kelly. I need you to tell me the truth.'

'Excuse me. Can I have a word please, sir?' A tall, incredibly slim man has entered the room and stands just inside the door.

'DC Paul Campell has just entered the room,' says Detective Swann. When the police first started doing that – mentioning everyone coming in and out for the benefit of the tape – I thought they were saying it for my benefit. I even went to stand up and introduced myself back on one occasion, but Sue urged me to sit down and suggested that introductions weren't really necessary. 'They all know who you are,' she said.

Detective Barnes stands up and walks towards DC Campbell. They exchange a couple of words and both men leave the room.

'Are you OK?' asks my lawyer.

I nod and look down at my hands. Sue starts to talk

to me about breathing deeply and turning to her for help if I feel worried when the door opens and a different detective comes in, accompanied by the tall thin guy. The only good news so far today is that the terrible Barnes guy has disappeared for a while.

'I am showing Kelly Monsoon exhibit A,' says the detective, pushing a plastic bag towards me containing Rufus's dagger, the jewel-covered one that he was given after winning the Oscar.

'Do you recognise this?' asks the detective.

'Yes!' I say. 'It belongs to Rufus.'

'You are saying that this dagger belongs to your boyfriend?'

'Yes,' I repeat. 'Where did you find it?'

'In Elody Elloissie's body,' replies the detective with a sanctimonious sneer. 'It had gone through her ribcage and into her heart. Furthermore, the DNA left on the dagger has been analysed and it's your DNA. Your blood, Kelly.'

'You couldn't have checked her DNA out so quickly,' says my lawyer, standing up confrontationally. 'It takes weeks.'

'Yes we could,' says the new detective. 'She's on the National DNA Register. It took us an hour to get a precise match.'

Sue looks at me with coldness. 'Why are you on the DNA register?' she asks.

'I got done for drink-driving years ago,' I say.

She sits back in her seat and scribbles some notes. I'm sure I know what she's writing 'This woman is fucked.'

'Police have been seen coming in and out of Rufus George's fabulous home all morning after the astonishing arrest yesterday of his girlfriend, Kelly Monsoon. Monsoon is being questioned at Richmond police station by police from the Scotland Yard murder squad in connection with the murder of leading fashion stylist Elody Elloissie. She's been in custody overnight but it's believed that her boyfriend has not been to visit her.

'We are joined again by Ex– Detective Chief Superintendent Mike Dover. Mike, what are the police doing?'

'Well, Felicity, they'll be taking everything away that they think will help with their inquiries ... computers, discs, tapes, security footage, clothing ... anything that will help pin down whether it was Kelly Monsoon who killed Elody Elloissie.'

'And they'll be able to tell that by looking at her clothing, will they?'

'Well, if they find the clothes she was wearing on the day that Elody was killed, they will.'

'OK, thanks, Mike. Back to you in the studio, Bob. Remember, there's a four-hour special on tonight with Lord and Lady Simpkins, former friends of Kelly Monsoon, describing the woman they got to know, and how they always believed she was capable of murder.'

I've gone over and over and over the situation with the dagger, and how I used it to smash open the drawer. I know that for every word I say, they'll have 526,000 questions about what time it was, what angle the clouds were sitting at and how many stones there were on the gravel driveway at the time. The questions come fast, thick and furious. They barely give me time to answer one question before another one's fired at me. They don't so much do that good cop/bad cop thing, as bad cop/bad cop/bad cop. It's the new, slim detective who does most of the questioning. The others chip in whenever they feel he hasn't asked quite enough questions in quite enough detail for their liking.

'So, tell us again where the dagger was when you last saw it.'

'It was on the chair,' I say.

'Which chair? Where? What colour was the chair? How was it lying? What time was it when you saw it?'

Chapter 24

Again, there's a knock at the door. Hell, what is it now? Oh great – the big guy's back again. Barnes. Shit. I don't like this man at all. He's convinced I'm guilty; I can see it in his eyes and in the way he stares at me constantly and asks all these nit-picky questions that I can't remember the answers to.

'DI Barnes has just entered the interview room,' says Detective Swann. Fuck, fuck, fuck.

'Hello, Kelly,' says Detective Barnes, pulling his chair forward and leaning right across the table. My palms have gone all sweaty and my heart's racing. Perhaps I did kill Elody? I don't know anything any more. 'Now, where were we?' he says.

Flippin' heck. I know exactly where we bloody were. We were with him going on and on about how I have no alibi for the time of Elody's murder, I had a reason to kill Elody, and the murder weapon belongs to me and has my DNA on it. Even I can see that this is not looking good.

'Let's go through this once again, shall we?' he says, looking at me like I'm some piece of dirt he's just kicked off the end of his shoe. 'Start right at the beginning . . .'

There's a knock at the door before we can begin. Bloody hell, it's like Piccadilly Circus. My solicitor looks as if she's about to have a nervous breakdown. She glares at me as if it's my fault that there's a knocking sound, and

I instinctively bring my hands above the table to show that it's not me.

'Can I have a moment, sir?' says a woman I haven't seen before.

'DI Barnes is leaving the interview room,' says the other detective.

I drop my head into my hands. I'm relieved not to have to go back through this whole horrible bloody story again and again, but terrified of what new information is going to 'come to light'. Every time there's a knock on that door there's some other piece of evidence that indicates that I must have done the murder after all. All we need now is for someone to appear with a photograph of me stabbing her. I just can't believe it's come to this. We sit there, with me wringing my hands together and trying to understand what's going on. My solicitor stands every so often and paces around the room in frustration.

We sit there for another ten minutes. It feels like about forty-seven hours then, suddenly, the door swings open and Barnes comes back in with another man. They tell the policeman who's sitting there that he's no longer needed and the two of them sit down next to Detective Swann. Barnes can barely look me in the eye. Oh Lord, what now?

'My name's DI Smith,' says the new officer, talking to me as if I were about six years old.

'Hi,' I say.

'We've just had the final pathologist's report back which gives more precise detail on the estimated time of death and more detail on the manner of the death,' he says, slowly and patiently. 'The official time of death has come in and it is different from the estimated time of death.

This can happen from time to time. The pathologist makes an estimate of time of death in the first instance while more detailed investigations take place.'

'Oh.'

'There's a discrepancy between the original estimated time of death, thought to be between 5.30 pm and 6 pm, and the more accurate prediction. We've been told that the time of death is now considered to be 9 pm.'

'How did you get the estimated time of death so wrong?' asks Sue, standing up and leaning over the table aggressively. 'We were explicitly told that the time of death was estimated at 5.30 pm. It is a gross miscalculation to now suggest that the time of death is wrong by some three and a half hours.'

'It happens,' says the detective. 'The first estimated time of death is rarely more than half an hour out but, in this case, officers discovered that the heating was switched off at night, meaning that the body decomposed at a slower rate, thus forcing us to conclude that the time of death was actually much later in the day than we originally predicted.'

I have to admit that I'm hardly listening to the exchange. They've changed their minds about what time Elody died. Until they change their minds about whether I killed her or not, there's not too much interest in all of this for me.

The same cannot be said for my glamorous lawyer who is up and bouncing around like Tigger, all animated and excited and demanding to know precise details about what the official time of death is to be recorded as.

There's a conversation about the moisture levels in the

vestibule where Elody's body was found, and temperature variations through the evening.

'My client has an alibi for 9 pm,' says Sue.

Oh. Now I get it.

'She couldn't have killed Elody. She was at the airport.'

'I know,' says the policeman, looking at me. 'Can you tell us exactly what you were doing between the hours of 9 pm and 10 pm on the evening of Thursday 3 December?'

'That's easy,' I say. 'I was meeting my boyfriend at the airport.'

'Did anyone see you?'

'Yes. There were security officers helping me through, and there was Henry the driver and Rufus's assistant.'

'What's her name?'

'It's Christine,' I say, but Sue interrupts.

'You've spoken to her about this. She's talked at length about what she was doing at this time. There's footage from the airport. I think it's time to accept that my client couldn't possibly have committed this crime.'

The policemen both nod. 'We also have video footage of you at Hampton Court Palace, sitting in the Rose Garden talking to the elderly gentleman. We spoke to him too. Frank Gower. He confirms your time of arrival and time of departure. Why did you lie to us?'

'Rufus always told me not to tell people about our special place or everyone would want to go there. He has so many fans and they follow us everywhere. I just wanted the Rose Garden to be special – you know – for it to be our special place. It never would be if I mentioned it. It would end up in the newspapers and that would be it . . . my favourite place in the whole world ruined for ever.'

'Yes, thanks, Bob. That's right; you come to us live outside Richmond police station where we have just been told that Kelly Monsoon is to be released without charge. You'll remember that the girlfriend of Hollywood star Rufus George was arrested yesterday and held in police custody overnight. Well, today, in a shocking twist to this story, we hear that she is to be released later today without charge. Police have not said whether they have another suspect in mind but sources close to the police reveal that they are questioning Dr Isabella Bronks-Harrison inside the station at the moment. She's a former friend of Elody Elloissie, but fell out with the fashionista several years ago. Police are insisting that she is just helping with inquiries but we believe that she is now the main suspect in this most incredible of murder investigations. Back to you, Bob.'

'Thanks, Bindy. Now, in a change to tonight's scheduled programme Evil Women Murderers there will instead be a panel discussion on the difficulties of being accused of a crime that you did not commit. What does it feel when the world turns against you? That's tonight at 10 pm, here on Sky One and features a discussion with Lord and Lady Simpkins, the couple who have known Kelly all her life, and say they knew from the moment she was arrested that this was a huge miscarriage of justice.'

Mum stands there, clinging on to her handbag in front of her with both hands, the strain showing in her fiercely knotted knuckles. She has her heavy dark-blue coat pulled tightly around her. She looks nervous, understandably, and much older than last time I saw her. When she sees me, her eyes light up, she smiles, and loosens that fearful grip on the worn leather straps of the only handbag I've ever seen her with. Dad's there too, trying to look relaxed and in control, but looking utterly deflated and unable to make sense of the events that have forced him to bring his wife to a police station in south-west London.

He relaxes too, when he sees me walking towards them and I force myself to smile and greet them warmly, pretending that nothing's wrong.

'A simple misunderstanding,' I say. 'Please don't worry. Everything's going to be OK.'

I might be more assured that everything is going to be OK if Rufus were here to meet me too, but there's no sign of him. I'm led out through a heavily guarded, dark-blue back door and moved through ranks of police officers positioned so as to hide me from the waiting paparazzi. No Rufus anywhere. Shit. I know it would be mad for a huge celebrity film star to be here. I know it would make the whole thing much harder to manage but, but ... I kind of just really wish he was here anyway.

I wish he'd sat at home and thought, I know it's mad for me to go to the police station but, sod it, I'm going anyway, I want to see Kelly.

Why isn't he here? Why didn't he visit me at the police station?

They put a blanket over my head as they lead me the final half-metre to the car; my lawyer was very insistent on this before we left the station. Sue said that pictures of me today would keep resurfacing for the rest of my life, long after the details of this case had drifted to the backs of people's minds, and though I was released without charge and thus had nothing to hide my head in shame from, it was still better that no pictures were taken of me. Did I agree? I didn't care. I was just looking out for Rufus, vainly peering through the gaps in the blanket at the scores of people assembled to witness my release from custody in the hope that I'd see him standing there.

A car driven by a specialist police driver will take me home. It turns out that Henry came to the police station to collect me but was sent away by police when they realised how many people were gathered at the big metal gates. It was considered to be safer for a specialist police driver to make the short journey up the Hill to my 'home'.

I sit in the back of the car, still beneath the blanket but peering out through small holes at the world as it passes. It feels as if I've been locked away for years. Time's a strange enough concept anyway – sometimes days fly past, other days drag, the minutes moving so slowly into hours that you begin to think the clock's taken leave of its senses – but when you're locked away from the signs of normal life, your sense of place and time, and your sense of yourself within that place and time disappear completely. I might as well have been locked away for a thousand years because, though it's only been two days and one night, I've come out a different person. I didn't kill Elody and I can prove I didn't kill Elody, but it's as if my innocence is an entirely meaningless concept. I'm still at the centre of everyone's story.

The Hill remains closed off to traffic while police analyse and interrogate to find out who killed Elody. Their main suspect is innocent and out of custody, so I guess they start again, combing through her possessions and reading every note she ever wrote.

Mum looks round at me and smiles warmly. 'You all right, love,' she says with a smile.

'I'm fine,' I say but I'm not. I want Rufus to be here.

'I'm sorry we're in a police car, love. We were going to bring your father's car but Aunt Maude weed in the back and it smelt dreadful so Henry offered to drive, then the police said no to that.'

I smile briefly, but behind the gesture is a whole bloody world of pain. *Where is Rufus?*

'We knew this was all a terrible mistake and you could never have killed anyone. Everyone knows. I don't know what the police were thinking of,' says Mum kindly. 'We've had so many letters of support for you from people all round the world, and the staff in the house have been amazing to us. They've been telling us how much you mean to them and how kind you are. Love, we're so proud of you.'

I was arrested for murder. She's still proud of me. Thank God for mums.

I walk into the house flanked by Mum and Dad, and Dad gasps when he sees just how amazing the place is. I forget that he's not been to visit yet. When Mum came with Aunt Maude a few weeks ago Dad didn't come. (Was it really just a few weeks ago? It feels like it happened about forty years ago.) He looks around the place, trying to look nonchalant but I can tell he's thinking, Bloody hell! This place is amazing!

I give him a little hug. 'Nice house,' he says, gravely. 'Very nice. Better than that bloody awful flat you lived in before. Do you remember when I painted the door and the nightclub man from next door came across. God he was awful. You've done well here, love.'

I notice straight away that things have been moved around and that the computer is missing. It must have sent poor Rufus up the wall to have all these police crawling over the house. Shit. I really messed this up, didn't I? Everyone's been through so much because of me, and I still can't work out exactly what I did that was so wrong.

I mean – I can, I'm not stupid. It's just that I can't believe the way it's all panned out.

'You'll be able to carry on with organising the wedding now, won't you?' says Mum. 'You won't change your mind and go for summer, will you? I've bought a beautiful chocolate-brown coat that will really only work for an autumn or winter wedding.'

'Leave it, Jayne,' says Dad. 'I think the poor girl's been through enough this past week without you hassling her to organise a wedding.'

'Oh a wedding will be a lovely thing for us all,' says

Mum. 'Imagine! We'll be able to show the world that the problems are all behind us and we're setting off on a new road to a bright future.'

I'm thinking that it'll take more than a bright and gorgeous wedding for the British population to forget about what's just happened. I can just see the headlines now. Instead of PRETTY BRUNETTE TO MARRY HOLLY-WOOD STAR they'll be saying MURDER SUSPECT IN SHOCK MARRIAGE TO HOLLYWOOD'S FINEST. Shit.

My fears about the future, and particularly about our proposed wedding, are not allayed by the sight of Rufus. He comes through the door from the sitting room looking twenty years older than he did when I last saw him. He practically pushes past my parents, kisses Sue Lawrence lightly on the cheek and stands in front of me. 'Welcome home,' he says, with not an ounce of conviction. I feel my heart fall through the floor and I want to scream. I feel like shouting, 'I know I did badly. I know I shouldn't have hidden things from the police, but everything I did was to protect your friend Elody's memory and to protect our relationship from public scrutiny and public interference.' But I don't of course. What's the point? Rufus has clearly made up his mind about me.

'Can we talk?' he says, just standing there, making no effort to touch or comfort me.

'Sure,' I say, looking back at my parents as I follow him into the den at the back of the house. Mum is smiling from ear to ear while Dad's face reflects the concern that I feel.

'Why did this happen, Kelly?' he asks. His manner and the way he is looking at me are so grave. It's like I'm back at the police station again, being grilled by those aggressive detectives.

'Because I didn't tell the police the truth. I didn't want to mention the Rose Garden to them so I said I was at the flat. They thought I was covering something up.'

'I can't believe you lied to the fucking police,' he says with such fury, that I find myself stepping back away from him.

'You told me never to mention that we go there,' I try.

'Yes I did, Kelly. But when I said that I had no idea that you were going to be arrested for murder, did I?'

'No.'

'I'm finding all this very difficult to come to terms with. My mother's furious,' he says.

I just look at him then. He's worried about what people think. He's worried about his reputation. He couldn't give a toss about me.

'Did you think I killed her?' I say.

'Of course not. Of course not. How could you even ask that? Of course I didn't. But don't you realise how bad this looks? Do you have no idea of the impact this will have on me . . . and on you.'

'Really? I had no idea there'd be any impact,' I say, loading my words with as much sarcasm as they'll carry.

'And what about going through all my things when I was in LA? What about the fact that you don't trust me?'

'I can't defend the way I behaved,' I say. 'I don't know what was wrong with me. I was awful. I shouldn't have done that.'

'The bottom line is that you didn't trust me, isn't it? All this nonsense about the carpenter coming to mend the drawer. That was because you thought I was hiding something from you.'

'Because Elody persuaded me to . . .'

'Forget about Elody,' he yells. 'I'm not interested in fucking Elody. I'm interested in you. I'm interested in the fact that you simply didn't trust me and tried to hide that from me, and in the process lied to the police so much that you got yourself arrested for murder. You were so bloody keen to squirm your way out of things that you lied. Shit, Kelly. You lied to the police when one of our friends had been murdered. And you know what really hurts?'

Go on tell me. I've gone so beyond pain these past few days that we need a whole new word for hurt. Nothing he can do can wound me when I feel as if my heart's been blown apart.

'I spent every minute of every day in LA missing you like crazy.'

'I'm sorry,' I say, trying to catch his eye but being met by nothing but coldness and contempt, which make me suddenly feel very defensive. 'What do you expect when I find a bracelet exactly like Elody's in the drawer?'

'It was for Mum. She's always loved Elody's necklace – you know – the one Elody always wears, because it was given to her by Jon. I saw the matching bracelet so bought it for Mum, for Christmas.

'When I was living in New York, Mum would always come to my house to visit before Christmas and be like a schoolgirl, trying to find presents. I thought she'd come to the house to visit when she was over for the Interior Design Awards and I thought she'd start hunting for presents, so I hid them. I taped the jewellery to the inside of the drawer; it was the only place I could think where Mum wouldn't look. I didn't realise that she wouldn't be here because you wouldn't invite her to stay. Anything else you need to know so you can start trusting me again?'

'I did ask your Mum to stay,' I retort. 'But Elody warned her not to come.'

'Oh yes,' he says. 'I remember now. Everything is Elody's fault, isn't it? Shit, Kelly. This is insane. I rushed back and proposed to you because I wanted to spend the rest of my life with you, but all you were doing was going through my things. You didn't trust me. I don't understand why.'

He carries on after that, musing vocally about the way things have panned out between us, but I'm still stuck back in the beginning of his soliloquy. The bit where he says, 'I wanted to spend the rest of my life with you . . .' 'Wanted' . . . past tense. It's over. He says he's organised for money to be transferred into my savings account, and practically throws my passbook over to me. He's put more money in there than I'd need in ten years. Everything he does seems to confirm my worst fears . . . this relationship is over. He's making sure that I'm looked after. Or, if I'm being cynical, he's making sure I have no reason to go to the press. Either way, he wants to make sure that I don't go without, but he no longer wants to be with me.

Rufus sleeps while I sit here, staring up at the oh so beautiful walls, covered in the most expensive wallpaper that money can buy, chosen by his wonderful mother with her immaculate taste and her team of perfect interior designers. And as I'm looking at all this wealth and luxury, all I can think is: God this is shit. I mean, I love Rufus so much it terrifies me sometimes, but I can't do this now. I've messed it all up. These few months here have changed me beyond recognition. No, that's not true; they've shown me who I am for the first time in my life and made me realise that what I want and what I'm getting are two very different things.

Elody was the most stylish person I ever met, and where did it get her? She's dead now. She was dressed beautifully when she slipped down those steps and the dagger that murdered her was beautiful and priceless, like the woman herself. But she was never happy. Are any of these people happy?

Elody had everything in abundance but in the end it amounted to nothing at all. I want so much more than this . . . I don't want fluffy carpets and expensive heating systems to keep me warm, I want someone's love. I want someone with me who loves me and understands me. I want someone who forgives me when I get things wrong. This is just crap.

Chapter 26

'Thanks, Henry.'

'No problem,' he says. 'Let me give you a hand with your bags.'

He climbs slowly out of his seat, walks round to the boot and lifts out my luggage. I've left half of my stuff at Rufus's house. Henry says he'll bring it over later.

'Can I say something?' Henry says, looking at me nervously.

'Of course.'

'I feel bad about what happened to you. I feel bad that the police told me to recall everything you said in the car. I told them that you said you could kill Elody. I regret that. I shouldn't have said it. Everyone knows you couldn't have killed Elody. I just answered their questions. I wanted you to know, none of us thought for one second that you killed Elody.'

'I think Rufus may have had his doubts.'

'No,' says Henry. 'No, that's not true.'

'Why didn't he come to the police station to see me then? Why did he hide away and pretend none of this was anything to do with him?'

'He tried to come to the police station but the police said he couldn't. They said you had no right to visits as the prime suspect in a murder investigation. They wouldn't let him phone or visit. Christ, he was trying everything.

His legal team all told him to keep away or he'd be arrested. At one point I thought he might go and get himself arrested just to be there with you and support you through it all.'

I'm looking down at the road.

'Kelly, are you OK?' he asks.

'Yes.'

'Have you thought this through? Do you really want to go?' As he speaks, he lays the second of my three bags down onto the freezing cold pavement.

'Yes,' I say. 'I have no choice.'

'You do,' he counters, but I shake my head. I really don't think I have any choice but to stay away from Rufus and all his life represents, until I can work out what I, Kelly Monsoon, want out of life. I have so much to think about. I can't go back there. Not now, probably not ever.

It's 4 am. I had no desire to alert the world's press to my decision to leave the house, so asked Henry if he'd mind driving me. He'd taken Mum and Dad back to Hastings at midnight, so I knew he'd be around once the world had gone to bed. When I called Sophie and Mandy they couldn't have been more supportive.

'Of course you can come back here,' they say. 'We'd love to have you back. Any time.' They even cancelled the new flatmate, due to move in on Monday.

It's odd to think that when I moved to Richmond, I thought it was the beginning of a vastly different life. Ha! Well, that was true. But it wasn't a life that I wanted.

I can't believe now that I caught the bus because I didn't have any money and was too scared to ask Rufus. What a wimp. I remember dragging those bags along, thinking my fingers were about to break under the pressure of all those handles. Christ. Well, if I've learnt one thing from Elody, and particularly from my experiences with the police, it's to have more confidence, speak my mind and really think about myself a bit more rather than everyone else. I was so obsessed with not letting Rufus down, and not letting Elody down, that I told half-truths and almost got myself bloody locked away. Never again!

'Henry, thank you; that's so kind of you.'

'No problem,' he says, climbing back into his car. 'We're gonna miss you, you know.'

'I'll miss you too,' I tell him and we look at each other for a brief second through the open window, a look full of sadness and understanding. It's like he acknowledges that so much has happened this week that the only way I can cope with it all is to get away.

'Come back soon,' he says and I just smile because I can't imagine how I can possibly go back after all that's happened. I can't imagine anything in the future at all, to be honest. All I know is that it's 4 am on Sunday 6 December and I'm standing outside the flat where I once lived, hoping that I don't make things too awful for Mandy and Sophie by being here. The press are bound to track me down eventually, of course, but if I can just stay here for a while until I've sorted myself out, got my head straight and worked out what to do with my life, that would be the greatest treat of all.

I might go abroad, or just get another job here. I don't think I could go back to the old one. My days in Richmond Theatre are definitely over. But how will I get another job? Who'd want want to employ me? Perhaps I should 'sell my story' as I'm being urged to by so many tabloid editors and publishers. 'You'll make a million,' they insist. 'Get yourself an agent.' Christ, I can't think of anything worse. Having experienced first-hand what it's like to have people talking about you all the time, I'd never do that.

There's much to think about but I'll do that tomorrow. I knock on the door gently. The best sound I've heard in ages is of footsteps thundering down the stairs. Mandy hurls herself through the door and hugs me tightly. Sophie's there too, pulling me close to her and letting me cry my eyes out on her big, soft, towelling dressing gown.

We all walk into the small entrance hall leading to the stairs up to our little pad. I feel so safe here. I know that's ridiculous because I was a million times 'safer', whatever that word means, in the big house in Richmond surrounded by guards and state-of-the-art security systems, but this place is safe because it's full of people like me. It's got Mandy and Sophie in it and they understand me. There are no fabulous Parisienne stylists and no women walking round with clipboards and shouting instructions as if they were trying to take over the moon. There's no Christine to consult before I can work out whether my boyfriend wants coffee and no elderly butler always just a second away from us, awaiting instructions. I guess you get used to that way of living; Rufus certainly doesn't seem to think it's odd, but then he grew up with it. It's part of his heritage; part of who he is. No one asked him to make any changes. I'm not criticising because it would have been daft for him to come and live in my flat, but I suppose I mean that Rufus made a mistake by expecting me to slot in and quietly get on with my new life while he travelled off to the other side of the world. I lost my job, my friends and my independence and every value I've ever known went out of the window. Nope, I love Rufus more than I've ever loved anyone in my life before, and I can't imagine life without him, but I can't do what he needs me to do. It turns out that I have more sense of myself, and sense of individuality, than I ever realised and that's got to be a good thing. Hasn't it? Has it?

We drag the bags up the stairs and I take in the dreadful peeling paint and scuff marks traced across the walls. Never noticed them before. I can get them fixed now. One of the advantages of having some money – in the short term at least – will be the ability to make this flat nice.

'Let's leave them here for now,' says Soph, letting go of the heavier of the bags that she had gallantly offered to bring up for me. I think she regretted it the minute she attempted to lift it but, kindly, she didn't say anything, just grimaced as she bobbed it up the stairs.

'The guys'll bring them in for us.'

'What g—?'

We walk into the sitting room and I see straight away what guys she's referring to. There, sitting on our madly dilapidated sofa, are Jimmy Lapdance and three of his biggest bouncers, all of them done up to the nines in their gold jewellery, impossibly shiny black shoes and, in one case, a matching impossibly shiny black head. Jimmy jumps up and swaggers over to me.

''Ello, doll-face,' he says. 'This is Morgan, Mather and Prentice.'

I smile at the three bouncers while Jimmy surveys them

proudly. His little hairy hands rest on his fleshy hips while he taps his foot in time to an imaginary drumbeat. 'You got yourself into a bit of a trouble, didn't you?'

'Er . . . yep,' I say. 'A leetle bit of trouble.'

'Jimmy's come to help us,' says Sophie. Now this is odd, because there's nothing about Jimmy that would move you to think he could help. He certainly doesn't look like an angel of mercy, with his tub-shaped torso and ungainly swagger. He has more product in his hair than the Twickenham branch of Boots sells on the average Saturday afternoon. He drips in jewellery, clanking and banging like a badly oiled machine with every move. But still, he's a real heart-of-gold sort of guy, and I can see why the girls brought him round in this time of great need.

'Right, this is the thing,' he says, his little eyes twinkling in a way that is more pretty than menacing. 'You're gonna need protecting from the paps, ain't ya?'

I love the way he calls them 'paps' like he's used to dealing with the world's media every day.

'Yes, I guess I will,' I reply, touched by the way in which these guys have come to our assistance, the most unlikely of knights in shining armour, but very welcome ones!

'We're gonna have a shift system outside the flat. There'll always be a bouncer there so the paps can't get too close.'

'OK. Thanks. That would be great,' I say, but I have to confess that I'm not filled with confidence. Surely it'll take more than Jimmy and his mates to hold back the media enough to make my life worth living.

'I know what you're thinking,' says Jimmy. 'You're thinking, how can that dodgy old bloke and his mates keep me safe? Well, I'll tell you, doll-face, we can and we will. No one will get past my guys.'

'It's very kind of you,' I say, but grateful as I am, I'm wondering what Jimmy is getting out of this; he's making quite a commitment to me.

'We might be handing out leaflets and trying to get some of me Suga Daddys girls into the picture from time to time . . . that OK?' he says.

I say yes because it is. I don't care what Jimmy does with the photographers if it's legal and it results in them being kept away from me.

'They won't get near you when you're in the flat,' says Jimmy.

'So now we just need to work out what places you're going to want to go to out of the flat, and how we make sure you're safe there,' says Mandy.

'The Rose Garden,' I reply, before I've even thought about the question. 'I'd really love to be able to go to the Rose Garden.'

The bouncers look from one to the other. Jimmy looks like a man who's never heard anything quite so ridiculous in his entire life. 'What d'ya wanna go there for?' he asks.

'It's beautiful and tranquil and I'm just kind of in love with it,' I say. This is all above and beyond the remit of the bouncers who shuffle in their seats. I can almost read their minds: We came 'ere to make sure no geezer got no pictures of her, we never expected to be hearing all about the bleeding Rose Garden.

'There's a guy there called Frank who Rufus knows well. I'll get him to look out for me,' I say.

'OK, why don't the three of us go down there tomorrow

and take two bouncers and case the joint,' says Mandy, opting to take a rare and quite alarming foray into the language of the all-American cop movie.

'Yes,' says Sophie with a smile. 'Tomorrow will be case-the-joint day.'

Oh good.

Chapter 27

EXCLUSIVE
By Katie Joseph
Daily Post Showbiz Editor

As the story of Elody Elloissie and the mystery over who murdered her once again dominates the headlines, Katie Joseph takes a look behind the stylish woman and reveals what life was really like for the one-time golden girl of fashion.

Elody Elloissie was a lonely woman with few friends. She never knew her own parents, never knew the love and devotion of a family around her. He story is desperately sad. The woman who would go on to become the queen of the red carpet dressing had humble beginnings when she was found left outside a hospital like a waif and stray from a Dickens novel. The hospital named her Elody after the nurse who looked after her and the young girl began a life of moving from foster home to foster home until a permanent carer could be found.

Elody's childhood was miserable, fractious and painful. She was eventually adopted when she was six years old but still she couldn't settle down to a normal life because her new adoptive parents brought her to England where young Elody had a terrible time adjusting to the new language, new friends and new surroundings. She was isolated and alone and struggled to make any meaningful friendships.

By the time she was seventeen, she was a rebel without a cause. She had left home and moved in with a succession of disreputable men until she came across Jon Boycott, the fashion designer who died two years ago, from a drugs overdose. Elody never recovered from the death of her great love.

It was through this boyfriend that she met and fell in love with the world of fashion. She was a natural when she went along with her boyfriend to fashion shoots and helped to style the models. She went to work on a magazine and became an instant hit. Verda Petron, former editor of French *Vogue* recalls, 'She was a quiet girl who just got on with the job. She was always first in the office, always last to leave. When Jon died, though, she changed. She became brittle and determined. I never saw her cry over Jon's death but she was a changed person as a result of it. She worked harder and became determined to be successful at any cost. It was almost as if she blamed herself for his death.'

Elody was at her most successful in the 1990s when she and Jon became the golden couple of fashion. Celebrities and stars wanted her to work with them and magazine designers wanted to feature her. She was a star. The trouble with being a star in the fickle world of fashion is that it is bound to come to a sudden end. Elody was always seen as being part of the Jon and Elody brand, known as 'Jelody'. When Jon died and it all ended, it stung her badly.

'It was as if all the anger from the rejection she'd faced

as a child re-emerged with Jon's death,' said leading psychologist Dr Matthew Stevenson. 'Elody became a liability; lashing out at models she'd once worked with and turning up drunk at catwalk shows. She was desperate to win her place back in society and for people to look up to her again, but she was *persona non grata* which sent her more deeply into the cycle of depression.'

By the time she sought help, and managed to get control over her drinking, the world of fashion had left her behind. She was never again the star she once had been, and that haunted her to her dying moments, at the hands of an unknown murderer in the exclusive Royal Institute of Fashion. The most haunting thing of all is that the murder happened on the second anniversary of the death of Jon Boycott.

'I see that Katie woman has been made editor now,' I say to Mandy and Sophie who just look at me blankly. I guess they haven't become quite as obsessed with the machinations of the national press as I have.

'It's just this woman who's been writing about me in the *Daily Post* since she first got wind of the fact that I was seeing Rufus. It was she who "broke the story" as they say in the media. Now I've become such a huge story she's got herself a promotion on the back of it all. Well done, love: showbiz editor. Wow, won't Mum and Dad be happy! She's written today about Elody's background. It's awful. I never knew what a tough life she had.'

I lay down the paper, trying to fold it beneath the blanket thrown across my head. The girls are silent. They hate it when the subject of Elody comes up because they really don't know what to say. We're in the car on the way to Hampton Court and it's a complete bloody farce. It's ridiculous. I need an entourage of six just to get to the Rose Garden and sit on a bench with no name. They bundled me out of the house with more aggression than the police ever used, and hurled me into the back of Jimmy's terribly discreet (not) pink Mercedes and we went off, hurtling through the streets of Twickenham pursued by half the world's media with Jimmy shouting 'Awright, darling,' to every woman he passed. Oh God.

'You're like Princess Diana,' says Mandy when she sees how many photographers there are alongside us. There's a silence in the car and I peek out at her from beneath my woollen roof. It's not a helpful comparison to make since the Princess died in circumstances not unlike this . . . except she wasn't in the back of Jimmy's candyfloss-pink stripper mobile with its garish leopard-skin interior.

We phoned ahead to the palace where I spoke to Frank who has closed off the Rose Garden for an hour for 'essential pruning'. Quite why such basic garden mainte-nance should involve the closure of an entire garden is something I won't worry myself about. I'm sure there are few people in the world who'll question lovely Frank's gardening strategies so we might just about get away with this.

He's waiting for us when we arrive. I'm about as flus-tered as it's possible for a woman to be and he's sitting there, entirely at ease, saying he enjoys the quietness when the garden's closed and thinks he might work this pruning rouse more often.

'Tea?' he offers, handing me a little plastic cup that he's

removed from the top of his flask. He gives it to me with hands that seem so much larger than they ought for such a slight and wiry man. They're wrinkly and mud-covered. I wonder why he doesn't wear gloves.

I take a gentle sip and feel my teeth retreating from the sugar attack. He must have about eight spoons in there. Jeez. It's nice though.

'My grandson Lawrence made the tea today,' he says proudly, and I feel myself smile. Lawrence is such a lovely guy. He works in the gardens too and is sweet and desperately shy. He's also huge; a great big lumbering hulk of a man. Every time I see him I think of Mandy – he's just her type.

'Is it OK for me to come here?' I ask. 'Or is it going to make things difficult for you?'

'It's fine,' he says. 'In fact, if you don't continue to come here you'll make an old man very sad. Just call up beforehand and speak to me, or Lawrence, and we'll shut it for an hour. No one will mind. Call Lawrence's mobile telephone; you've got the number, haven't you? He'll pass the message on to me.'

'Are you sure?'

'Of course I'm sure, love. And what'll they do if they do mind? Sack me? I'm nearly eighty and haven't been on the payroll for fifteen years so there's not a lot they can do.'

'Thanks,' I say, taking another sip of the tea.

'Kelly. Someone to see you,' Mandy shouts through the flat before running into my bedroom where I'm lying on my bed wearing nothing but my underwear.

'Shit. You look really thin. You have to start eating,' she

says. There's a look of pure horror on her face. I know she's right; I haven't really eaten since I got back here ten days ago and I realise that's silly, but I can't bring myself to think about putting anything in my mouth.

I'm surviving on a diet of sweet tea and HobNobs from Frank in the Rose Garden every day. 'The thought of food makes me feel queasy,' I say.

'I know, but if you don't eat you're going to get ill. You know that *Heat* magazine had a picture of you this week. You were in the "too skinny by far" section.'

I smile when she says that. It puts things in perspective really. When I was deliriously happy I was in the 'too fat by far' section of the magazine.

I can't believe what's happened. I can't believe anything. I can't believe how much I miss Rufus. Every minute of every day crawls past; every one of them tortured by the thought of him. I feel all twisted up and ruined inside. I miss him so much it's insane. I'd give anything to go back in time. Anything.

'I don't want to see anyone,' I say to Mandy, as I've been saying to both the girls since I got here. I don't want to see anyone, talk to anyone or think about anyone. All I want to do is make my daily visit to the Rose Garden to drink tea with Frank and listen to him talking about the roses. I've spoken to him about Rufus, of course, and he's told me how wonderful Rufus is.

'You're not helping, Frank,' I say, but he just smiles and looks out towards the palace.

'Give him a chance,' he's always saying. 'Just let him talk to you.'

I can't do that though. I can't have him anywhere near

me. I won't be able to cope. I'm barely coping at the moment. Just existing and hoping this nightmare comes to an end while knowing all the time that it can't. It's a nightmare without an ending.

'Come on. Clothes on,' Mandy insists. She's really cheered up over the past week ... ever since Frank's grandson Lawrence took a shine to her. They've been out once or twice and I think they really like each other. I'm pleased; Lawrence is a lovely guy.

'Get dressed quickly; it's important,' she says again.

'It's not Rufus is it?' I ask, a wave of terror running through me at the thought of him sitting out there in the flat, drinking tea from chipped mugs with Sophie.

'Of course it's not Rufus,' she says.

The bouncers won't let him anywhere near the flat. He comes round several times a day, and calls constantly, but the girls know that if they let him in, or hand the phone to me just once, I'll leave the flat for ever. Since they're terrified about what I'll do, I know they want to keep me here where they can keep an eye on me and make sure I'm as safe as possible, so they continue to send Rufus packing without giving him any explanation whatsoever.

'It's the police,' she says. 'That guy Detective Inspector Barnes – the good-looking one. He wants to talk to you.'

Oh joy.

'Hi,' I say, walking into the sitting room, and I see his eyebrows rise.

'Have you not been well?' he asks and he sounds genuinely concerned. 'You look so pale and thin. You must eat.'

'Yeah, thanks. I've had that lecture once today,' I say, flopping onto the sofa next to him. 'What information do you need now?'

The police have been back a couple of times since I was released without charge; they've been nice actually. Popping in to check I'm OK and moving the photographers away from outside. They've been keeping me briefed on things as they search the land for the killer, but have got no closer to finding the guy who did it. It's always Barnes who comes round, and at first I thought he was just being diligent. Then I noticed the way he looked at Sophie. I think he fancies her.

'We've had some interesting information come to light,' he says in his police-officery way.

'Oh,' I say, sitting up and immediately paying closer attention because, despite my fragile physical and mental state, I'm as keen as anyone for them to find the person who callously murdered Elody and bring him or her to justice. I notice that the girls are sitting right forward too, looking at the detective with rather too much attention. Sophie is dressed up in the tightest of jeans, a rather low-cut top and the highest shoes she owns. She has an astonishing amount of make-up on: bright red lips and so much blusher that it looks like she's been slapped. She is smiling at him like an affectionate drunk. I think she needs to work on her approach a little; I don't know whether Detective Barnes is likely to fall for an alcoholic clown. I look over at him. I suppose he's attractive, really. If you go for the big and hairy look. Mandy and Sophie clearly do.

'We've cleaned up the CCTV footage,' he says which is a rather baffling introduction to any sort of conversation, so we all just stare at him. 'You know, the CCTV footage from the door at the back of the building. I think we might have mentioned last time we were here that the only logical point of entry for the assailant was that rear door, but the footage from it was very patchy. Well, it was sent off to be cleaned up and it's come back. Clean.'

'And . . .'

'And,' he goes on, 'that means no one entered through the back door.'

'Oh. So what does that mean?'

'It means the assailant must have entered through the front door.'

Gosh, these policemen are bright.

'But,' he continues, 'everyone who entered through the front door had a watertight alibi for the time of the murder.'

He's got us now. We're all looking from one to the other in total confusion, wondering whether an 'assailant' was beamed down from the ceiling, or climbed out of a desk drawer.

'So where did this "assailant" come from?'

'We're not ruling out suicide at this stage.'

'Suicide?'

'Suicide,' he repeats gravely. 'I say we're not ruling it out because we haven't established it yet, but we have established that it is possible for her to have stabbed herself. Scientists have looked at the angle at which the dagger entered the victim's body and the way in which it had been pushed. It's clear that she could have done it. A pathologist called Michael James is looking at the body again; he's the best in the business. He has biomechanics and doctors with him. We'll know more when they finish.

One thing that is odd is that there's no suicide note. It's unusual to say the least for a suicide victim not to leave a note of some kind so we're going back through her possessions and final movements in the hope of finding one.'

'Oh.'

The detective looks across at us, lingering a little longer than is strictly necessary when he comes to Sophie's cleavage, then stands up to leave.

'Well, I won't keep you ladies any longer. Just wanted to keep you fully briefed. I'll call back if there are any more developments,' he says.

'Oh please do,' says Sophie. 'Let me show you out.'

'Thanks Bob. Yes, you join us live at Richmond police station where we have just heard from the team investigating the death of Elody Elloissie that they now believe she committed suicide. That's right; despite conducting a massive murder investigation, arresting one of Elody's closest friends — Kelly Monsoon — and interrogating another — Isabella Bronks-Harrison — they now think the stylist took her own life. I'm joined by Katie Joseph, the senior showbiz editor of the Daily Post *newspaper.*

'Katie, you revealed last week that Elody died on the anniversary of her former lover's death. Do you think that's why she committed suicide?'

'Yes, I think that's probably why. She was very cut up when he died. I don't think she ever properly got over it.'

'Thanks, Katie. For more of our exclusive interview with Katie Joseph, see www.sky.com. Now over to Brett for the weather.'

THE MYSTERY OF ELODY'S SUICIDE BID
EXCLUSIVE
By Katie Joseph
Daily Post Showbiz Editor

Our woman in the know gives you the full behind-the-scenes story on what happened at the heart of the police operation to convince them that Elody Elloissie had committed suicide. EXCLUSIVELY in the *Daily Post*, your top newspaper for showbiz news.

It was Michael James, a pathologist working with Scotland Yard's murder squad, who found the crucial mark that would convince police detectives that Elody Elloissie had committed suicide. A 'hilt' wound found between her thumb and index finger confirmed to them after a two and a half week operation to find a murderer, that she had taken her own life.

They investigated the shape, depth and direction of the mark, and became clear in their minds that this was not a murder after all, but the actions of a woman feeling so miserable that she wished to take her own life.

But what continued to baffle police was why there was no suicide note left. Was this a spur of the moment decision? Then, yesterday morning, while searching through files on her computer, they found a video message explaining that she planned to take her own life on the anniversary of the death of her great love, the fashion designer Jon Boycott. *Daily Post* believes that the video reveals that Elloissie felt she was personally responsible for the death of her boyfriend because when she found her boyfriend's body – half-dead after a night of drug-taking – she fled the flat in panic, rather than calling an ambulance. Even though she returned to the flat and rang for help, over an hour had passed – a period of time in which critical care could have been given to her boyfriend.

'I killed him as surely as if I'd plunged a knife into him myself, and that's what I plan to do today, to myself, to say sorry for what I did to Jon, and to be with him once more.'

Elloissie goes on to explain that the reason she didn't call for assistance straight away was because she worried about what the revelation might do to Jon's career. 'As soon as I calmed down, I rushed back and called an ambulance, but it was too late. I killed him.'

Police will outline their discoveries at the inquest, which is scheduled for the end of next week. It marks a tragic end to the story that has captivated millions in this lead up to Christmas. It is believed that Hollywood producers have been in discussions about making a movie about the doomed affair, which led to the death of Elloissie who was, at one time, the world's most influential stylist.

Chapter 28

'I can't hear it,' says Mandy, walking round the flat and straining so much she looks as if she's about to go to the toilet. Her eyes are all screwed up and she has an intense concentration about her. 'Oh no, hang on. I can hear something. What's that? Yes, stop. I can hear it now. Nope. It's gone. You need to ring the phone again.'

'This is bloody insane,' says Sophie dialling my mobile from her phone. We all fall silent, listening for the sound of ringing.

'Yes,' they both say, leaning over slightly with their heads tilted. We all wander through the flat in this bizarre, hunched over, straining with concentration manner, listening intently in the hope of hearing it ring.

'I can definitely hear something,' I say, hoping that we'll find my bloody phone after a morning of searching for it. I know I had it last night because we had a little impromptu pre-Christmas Eve drinks party, and Mum called to check I was OK. But what did I do with it then? No one knows.

The phone goes to answerphone so I hang up. 'We're never going to find this thing are we?' I say, as the two girls peer at me through eyes that are still suffering the after-effects of last night's alcohol. 'Come on, let's have a cup of tea.'

I head in the direction of the kettle while Mandy swings

open the fridge door to pull out the milk. 'Aha!!' she cries making the two of us jump into the air. 'Guess what's in the fridge?'

'Oh God. If it was once living, please just throw it away and don't tell us about it,' I plead, fearing that she's found a dead mouse or toad or bat or something stuck in the ice at the back where we really should have defrosted.

'Nope. Nothing terrible . . . Da . . . da . . . da . . .' She holds out my phone, freezing cold, but all intact. 'Happy Christmas Eve,' she says.

'What the hell was it doing in the fridge?' I ask. She shrugs, Sophie shrugs and we all burst out laughing. 'I think that must be the end to the perfect party,' I say, because we did have a load of fun last night.

It's been over two weeks now since I left Richmond and, though not a day goes by when I don't feel my insides turning themselves inside out with the pain of not being able to see Rufus, I know I've done the right thing. I know he needs to be free to find someone who's like him and can live in that odd world of his.

Mandy and Sophie have been brilliant. We've had so many nights lying on the sofa chatting over huge pizzas (I've got money now so we have one each and we eat them with Châteauneuf-du-Pape as I explain how I developed my newfound love for wine after our wine-tasting night). I also tell them about Rufus and what it was like living with a screen god.

'The paparazzi surrounded the house, constantly,' I say. 'It was awful.'

'They surround the flat too,' counters Sophie. 'They're outside 24/7 now, afraid to leave the place unmanned since you upped and escaped at 4 am last time they took a coffee break.

Last night at the drinks get-together, we invited Katy and Jenny who I used to work with because the girls were desperate for me to put them straight on the situation with me being given my own office. Once I ran through it all from my point of view, they got it completely. We even had a game of Malteser-throwing to celebrate the fact that everything was great with us now, but it turned out I'd lost the knack a little and hurled the Maltesters with such force and with no regard at all for direction that it's taken me half the morning to clear the chocolate-shaped dabs off the wall.

'Good fun last night, wasn't it?' asks Mandy, tipping boiling water into the mugs and watching me as I cradle my freezing cold phone.

'Yes,' I say.

'Messages from Rufus?' she asks.

'Forty-three,' I reply.

The two girls look from one to the other.

'You should talk to him you know,' says Sophie. 'You've spent eighteen days ignoring his calls, not accepting the flowers, refusing to allow him to come into the flat and not reading his letters.'

'No, I read the letters,' I tell them.

Not only do I read them, but I memorise them. Every word, every pause, every comma on the page. They are handwritten, which I love more than anything because I know he never handwrites anything. I'm still praying that's because he wants to make them as personal as possible and that's why he puts pen to paper. Half of me wonders though whether he has to handwrite them because the police haven't returned his computer yet. Let's hope not . . . first option is so much more romantic.

I tell the girls that I'm over him and have moved on, but the truth is that there's not a second in the day when I don't yearn to be with him. Every night I lie there thinking of him; I go to sleep crying and I wake up crying, then I wipe my eyes and pretend everything's OK.

'Why don't you see him?' asks Mandy. 'Just go and meet him somewhere and talk to him. Do it today . . . on Christmas Eve. Go on . . . it has a nice romantic ring to it.'

'No I can't,' I say, looking down at my hands and fiddling with my fingers and trying desperately not to cry. I feel like a part of me was lost when I walked away from that house. I watched a programme about a cow being separated from her newborn calf and the cry she gave made me want to weep because that's what I want to do. I feel like lying down in the street and howling like a wild animal whose newborn's just been torn away. I think of Elody sometimes and I feel so jealous that she doesn't have to live with this pain I feel every minute of every day.

'I don't know why you can't see him,' Sophie says and Mandy nods in agreement. 'Look at you; you're a wreck. You're not eating, you can't think straight. You need to talk to him.'

'If I see him, it'll kill me.'

Rufus has been calling at the flat almost hourly, shouting up to my bedroom at the back from the alleyway off the street. I know the bouncers from Jimmy's help him through and make sure no one sees him but they won't let him

get too close. They know the rules; I watch them sometimes through a crack in my bedroom curtains. They see
him coming and smuggle him through so he can call up
to me, telling me how much he loves and adores me, and
saying how sorry he is that he didn't support me.

'I didn't know what to do, Kelly. This was as new to
me as it was to you. I was terrified. Absolutely terrified.
Please talk to me.'

Then I see Jimmy appear, pat him on the back, and
lead him away.

I wander out of the kitchen and into the bedroom to
get dressed.

'Where are you going?' asks Sophie, coming and sitting
on the bed while I slip on a big woolly jumper and brush
my hair. I stick on a hat and my big coat and some
sunglasses and tell her I'll be back later. She knows where
I go every day. Lawrence was at our little party last night
and he, Mandy and Sophie were tucked away in a huddle
for most of it, looking over to me occasionally as I stood
with Katy and Jenny explaining how difficult it was at
work after I'd moved in with Rufus, and telling them about
the coat incident which had upset me so much. I'm sure
that in the little Lawrence huddle there was talk about
me sitting with Frank in the gardens every day.

'I'm off,' I say.

'One second,' says Sophie, taking my hand in hers, and
preparing to give me yet another of her talks. She's become
quite the old romantic since she started seeing Detective
Barnes. She denies it, of course, but I know she's been
sneaking out when I've been lying in my bed. I've heard
the giggles as she and Mandy get ready to go on their

respective dates, and I've seen the happiness in their eyes. I'm pleased for them both, honestly I am. They deserve to be happy. I just hope she never crosses that Barnes guy because he's a bloody nightmare when you're on the wrong side of him.

'Most people spend a lifetime looking for what you've found in Rufus,' says Sophie. 'I never thought I'd say this, Kells, but you and Rufus . . . well, it works. It does. You need each other. I can't bear to see his gaunt and pale face again, begging me to let him in just so he can see you. I can't bear to see you, getting thinner and thinner and teetering on the edge of illness constantly. And what for? No one's asking you to go back there or start the relationship again. Just talk to him, Kell. You have to.'

I smile and hug her but I know I can't do that. Every time I see a picture of him I want to howl and scream, every time I glimpse his name or a reference to a film he once starred in, I feel this wave of unbelievable sickness rush through me. I feel light-headed and ill just being alive. I can't see him in the flesh. There's no way. I can't see him. It'll kill me.

Chapter 29

The Rose Garden's pretty this time of year. Odd, because there are no flowers around, of course, just the bare thorny sticks sitting all frost-covered and jagged in the hard ground, but it's still gorgeous. There's something lovely about being in a garden all year round, seeing it change through the seasons. I'm finding myself loving every aspect of this place: not just the blooms themselves, but the whole thing about nature – working its way through its natural cycle, year after year. I love the way the hedges sit around the outside, as if placing a protective arm around the garden, and I like the way the benches lounge around the edge as if having their own imaginary conversation with one another. This place has got a life of its own; that's why I like it – because it's vibrant and real and alive.

The other great thing about this place in winter, obviously, is that hardly anyone comes here. I mean that. Most times there's me and Frank, who seems to do little more than wander around smiling at people. I guess that's quite enough of a job, really. It would be nice if more people were employed in such a capacity. Lawrence pops over when I'm here now, which is lovely. He was shy at first, but since he's met Mandy and knows a little more about me, he's relaxed in my company. I guess that now he realises I'm not a raving loony who's about to attack everyone and murder them, he feels he can breathe more easily. He tells me all about the area of the grounds that is his responsibility. He took me over there once. It's magnificent with great sprawling lawns running down to the river, beautiful statues and plants. But it's not like my Rose Garden. This place is still my favourite.

My phone rings in my pocket; I should say 'vibrates' in my pocket. I switch the ring off when I'm here; it seems disrespectful to have it tinkling away when there might be people around desperately searching for a slice of solitude; time for silence to wash over them . . . time to think.

I know who it will be on the phone, of course. It will be the man I'm helplessly and hopelessly in love with . . . a man I'm desperate to talk to, but am terrified of coming into contact with because I know that seeing him will make me feel worse than I do now and, when that happens, I honestly don't think I'll be able to go on. I just need to forget him. I know I can do that, but I also know that it'll take time.

'OK, love?' It's Frank, dispensing his greetings and brightening up the place. 'How are you doing there, beautiful?'

'I'm fine, Frank, how are you?'

'All the better for seeing you, my dear. Mind if I join you?'

'Of course not. I even have biscuits!'

It's become quite a habit, this. He has his flask of sweet tea and I bring biscuits and we sit on the little bench with no dedication and chat about nothing in particular.

'How was the party last night?' he asks. 'Lawrence had a great time.'

'It was fun,' I say, unconvincingly.

'Sounds like you had a wild time. Lawrence says you were in bed by nine.'

'I was tired.'

Frank knows all about what's happened to me, of course. He knows about Rufus and me because it was through Rufus that I met him. I sometimes wonder whether he still sees Rufus. I doubt it. Rufus is busy. The idea of him coming down to the Rose Garden to drink heavily over-sugared tea with an octogenarian is slightly unlikely to say the least.

Frank's craggy features have settled into a smile. 'What a pickle you're in,' he says eventually. 'More tea?'

'I'm not in a pickle,' I say, thinking that 'pickle' is about as wrong a word as you could summon to describe the hash I've made of things.

'You are,' he says. 'You're madly in love with a man who's madly in love with you but you're too proud to do anything about it.'

'That's not true!' I say. 'I'm not in love with anyone.'

'OK. Fine. We'll change the subject. What are you doing for Christmas?'

'I'm going back to my parents' place in Hastings. I get the train this evening.'

'That'll be nice. Do you get on well with your parents?'

'Yeah. They're pretty cool. You'd love my dad – he's mad about gardening.'

'How about your mum?'

'She spends most of her time looking after my mad relatives.'

'She sounds kind.'

'Yeah. She is.'

'Like you.'

'Yeah . . . hardly! I don't look after anyone.'

'You looked after Elody pretty well. I'd say that you made a very sad, lonely and complicated girl very happy during her last weeks. You should be proud of yourself.'

'I have to say Frank that pride is not something I feel when I think of Elody. I was arrested for her murder, you know. I wrecked everything. I don't feel proud.'

'What if I said to you that you haven't wrecked anything? What if I say to you that the video the police found on her computer was recorded before she even met you? You're not responsible, Kelly. You never were. You messed up enough for the police to suspect you but that's all – it's over now. Tea?'

'Er . . . yes please. Do you not think I'm completely useless for getting myself into that mess?'

'When you get to my age, dear, nothing really surprises you or horrifies you. I lost two close friends in the war – I saw them die and couldn't do anything about it. Most of my relations are dead. My wife died two years ago and my son and daughter-in-law five years before that in a horrific accident. Lawrence was thrown from the wreckage. He was in intensive care for ten months. You soon realise that the only point in life is people. Without them there is no life. If you find a special person who matters – don't let them go.'

The tears are rolling down my face as Frank talks but, to his credit, he pretends he hasn't noticed. We both look out across the thorns and branches.

'Why didn't Rufus come to the drinks party last night?' he asks suddenly.

'I didn't want him to.'

'Why not?'

I just shrug, because if I talk any more on the subject of Rufus with this kindly old man in this beautiful garden, I know I'll just drown in tears.

'Gosh you're a lady of few words this morning, aren't you?'

'I find it hard,' I say, choking on tears. 'This is a difficult day . . . Christmas Eve. This is a day I always thought we'd spend together. This is a difficult place in which to sit and talk about him.'

'It seems to me that every day's a difficult day when two people are hopelessly in love but don't see one another. Even the staff at his house miss you,' he says.

'Do they?'

'Yep.'

'How on earth do you know?'

'Henry comes down here quite a lot. He's a keen gardener you know. He wanted to say "hello" because you'd mentioned me to him. He also wanted to know whether I'd seen you, and to find out whether you were OK.'

'Tell him I am.'

'You want me to lie to him?' says Frank. 'I could do that. Or I could tell him the truth – which is that you're fading away before me because you miss Rufus so much.'

'I'm not.'

'You are, sweetheart. Did it never occur to you that you might have thrown the baby out with the bathwater?'

'What does that mean? People are always using that phrase but I don't have a baby and I take showers rather than baths. What on earth does it mean?'

'What it means is that you met someone you love dearly and have thrown him away with the lifestyle and his ridiculous friends because you didn't like the nonsense that surrounded going out with someone famous. Couldn't you just have said, "I can't live with all this nonsense"?'

'He wouldn't have listened.'

'Bet he would.'

'You don't know him.'

'I don't know him well, but he listens to me when I talk.'

'He what?'

'He listens.'

'When?'

'He comes most days.'

'What do you mean "he comes most days"?'

'He comes in the afternoons. Always asks whether you've been here and I always say no because that's what you want me to say. He knows I'm lying though. Yesterday he actually said as much to me.'

'You never told me he came.'

'He told me not to tell you.'

'Why are you telling me now then?'

'Because I'm sick of all of this. I'm eighty years old. I know how short life is, and I know how precious life is. The two of you need to sort this out and get back together or it'll be the biggest mistake since Hitler invaded Poland, and we don't want that, do we?'

'No,' I say.

'So you won't mind too much if I tell you that he's here then?'

'Here?'

'Yes, he's here; I told him to wait by the maze until I'd spoken to you. Don't let an old man down, Kelly. Tell me you'll go and talk to him. It's Christmas for goodness sake.'

Fuck. I don't want to let an old man down any more than anyone else wants to let an old man down, but Jeez, I don't want to see Rufus. Really, I don't want to see him so much that the thought of doing so makes me want to weep.

'Come with me.'

'No,' I say, remaining in my seat on the bench. 'You can't do this, Frank. I don't want to see him.'

'See him. Just see him. Not date him, marry him or live with him for the rest of time. See him. Let him talk to you. If you don't, you're not being fair. I'm serious, Kelly. This is silly. There are two people whose lives are being ruined by this. It's not just about you – it's about him too. Imagine how he felt when he woke up to find you'd disappeared and wouldn't talk to him?'

My legs are like jelly when I stand up and follow the old man through the gardens and out towards the maze.

'Hello, Malcolm.'

'Morning, Ethel.'

'Hello there, Deirdre; how did Howard's operation go? Everything all right, was it?'

He seems to know everyone here.

'None of us will be here for ever,' he says, turning to me. 'You either take the chances while they're there or regret not taking them once the opportunity has passed; that's the only real choice any of us has. Don't think you're being big or clever by turning down a chance of happiness, Kelly, you're not. I watched my family almost wiped out in a car crash; I watched my wife die of cancer. If I had my time again, I'd take every opportunity in the world to be with the person I loved. If you won't listen to anyone else – listen to me, Kelly. I mean it. Here we are – he's in the maze.'

At the entrance to the maze stand Morgan, Mather and Prentice. They've been joined by Lawrence, and by his side is Mandy, looking all sweet and lovely in a big duffle coat and those enormous cream mittens of hers. She taps my shoulder affectionately as I pass her. I can't believe this. The whole clan are involved. This must be what they were planning last night. The entrance to the maze is in front of me but suddenly I'm hit by a colossal fear.

'I can't go into the maze,' I say to Mandy, turning round to face her, and seeing the smile slide off her face. 'I can't see him.'

'Oh, you can,' she says, with uncharacteristic firmness. 'Do you know how much bloody trouble we went to to set this up? Get your skinny arse in there now.'

'OK.'

Left with no choice, I walk in and turn left, immediately seeing a choice of pathways to take. How is this ever going to work? I'll never find the man.

'Rufus, where are you?' I'm trembling as I speak. I can't bear this.

There's no sound. Christ, if he's expecting me to find my way into the middle he's in for a shock. I have the sense of direction of a leafy green vegetable. It's sometimes a struggle for me to find the kitchen in the mornings.

'Rufus, please. I'll never be able to find you.'

I continue walking round, praying this isn't some terrible practical joke by the girls. Hoping Rufus will be there when I find my way into the middle. 'Ruf . . . are you there?'

'I'm here. Is that you? Kelly, is that you?'

'Yes, but where are you?'

'They told me to come and wait in the maze for you. Perhaps we should both head for the middle, and meet there.'

'I guess so,' I say, unconvinced of my ability to find the middle of the maze.

Suddenly the pressure of seeing him has been lifted by the silliness of us both being in a maze, trying to find one another. Finding my way to the middle has become a bigger challenge than the fear of coming face to face with Rufus.

'You could stand still,' he suggests. 'I'll come and find you. You'll have to keep talking though, so I can follow your voice.'

'OK,' I say, then I can't think what to say.

'Talk,' he insists. 'I can't work out where on earth you are if you don't talk.'

'Well, I'm here. Near the bushes, in the maze.'

'Yeah, thanks for that,' he says, and I can hear in his voice that he's smiling as he speaks. 'Near the bushes, huh? Well that's really helpful.'

'Your voice sounds like it's getting closer,' I say, and I'm suddenly filled with an overwhelming urge to see him. Where did this come from? I've spent weeks avoiding him and now I've heard his voice and can sense his presence, I'm just desperate to see him.

'Say something,' he says. 'It's impossible to know where you are if you don't say something.'

'I love you,' I say.

'Say it again.'

'I love you, Rufus. I miss you. Where are you? Come and find me, please.'

There's an almighty rustling of the bushes and clambering, pushing and a considerable amount of swearing before Rufus appears through the hedge, covered in twigs, with a small rip in his jacket and a streak of blood across his face.

'I came as quickly as I could,' he says, grabbing me and lifting me up into his arms. 'I love you, Kelly. I want to marry you. Please say you'll marry me.'

And then I don't know what happens. I don't know whether it's because it's Christmas, because I've hardly eaten for nearly three weeks and am feeling very vulnerable, or because all my best friends in the world have arranged this in order to make me happy again but I say, 'Yes.'

'I'm sorry?' he says.

'YES!' I shout back feeling weak with pleasure. 'Yes, yes, yes, yes, yes.'

All that remains now is for us to find our way out of this damn thing. We can hear the voices outside, but it's so incredibly difficult to work out how on earth to get to them. Then, a sighting through the twigs. Thank God it's winter so you can see a little through the branches. Not like the summer when the densely leaved trees would have trapped us for hours. We step through the gap and suddenly we're surrounded by people – all of them cheering and clapping, as they form a tunnel for us to pass through.

'I love you,' says Rufus, taking my face in his hands, but I'm beyond replying. The drama of the last few weeks has caught up with me and I collapse backwards and the whole world disappears.

Chapter 30

'Kelly, Kelly. Are you OK?'

I look up and see the shimmering, vague and drifting faces of Frank, Lawrence, Mandy and Sophie, and is that Detective Barnes? Holy fuck, I hope not. There's Rufus. Oh my God, oh my . . .

'Come on, Kelly, sit up. Come on.'

I look up this time and it's just the girls, trying to manoeuvre me from lying to sitting for no good reason.

'What are you doing?' I ask.

'We're trying to give you water,' they say. Oh, OK. Perhaps they had a reason then.

'I don't want water, I want the sweet tea that Lawrence made,' I say. 'It's in Frank's flask.'

'OK,' says Mandy. 'I'll go and get some.'

'I'm so pleased,' says Sophie when we're left on our own for a minute. 'I'm so happy for you. You and Rufus are getting married after all. Yey! It's gonna be the best Christmas ever.'

'Where's Rufus now?' I ask, as Mandy comes back with the flask.

'The guys all went to wait in the Rose Garden until you were OK. We didn't want you to faint again. He didn't want to go but we made him. Shall I get him?'

'Thanks,' I say, and watch how she scampers off, leaving me sitting on the floor sipping sweet tea with Mandy.

It seems like seconds later that Rufus is there, striding towards me and beaming with joy.

'I'll leave you two alone,' says Mandy, standing up and backing off towards the roses.

Rufus and I walk back into the Rose Garden hand in hand, me still feeling a little queasy and leaning heavily into him at every step, him walking slowly so as to balance my weight on his hip as he moves. Both of us are so shot through with happiness that we can barely speak.

'Let's get married soon,' I whisper.

'Straight away,' he agrees.

We arrive in the garden and everyone stares. I think they're too worried about making a fuss – forming a tunnel or cheering madly – in case I collapse again. They just look and smile warmly. Frank is sitting on the bench with no inscription, looking at me with such incredible warmth and pride that I feel like bursting into tears. *No*, I mustn't, not now. *No* more drama, Kelly. Control yourself.

'I'd like to make an announcement,' says Rufus, coughing a little and turning on that actorlike voice of his. 'Kelly and I are getting married. She's moving straight back into the house and we're going to get married as soon as possible.'

There are cheers all round then. Sophie even treats us to that quite unbelievably loud wolf whistle of hers that has us all wincing in pain.

'Now we're sorry to have to run out on you like this, but we've got a little bit of catching up to do,' he says, taking my hand and pulling me off in the direction of the exit. 'I also need to feed this girl before she fades away completely. But we look forward to seeing you all very soon and Frank . . .'

Frank looks up from his seat on his favourite bench.

'Thank you,' says Rufus. 'From both of us. We're more grateful than words can ever say.'

'Bye and thanks so much to all of you,' I add, as I'm practically dragged through the gardens in the direction of Rufus's car.

'Home, Henry,' he instructs and Henry gives me the biggest broadest smile ever.

'Nice to have you back, Kelly,' he says.

Then it's my turn to smile. 'I can't tell you how nice it is to be back.'

Chapter 31

It's funny going back into the house again. This time it feels far less stressful than last time. You know, this time it feels like I should be here rather than I'm here on a temporary basis until he finds someone better suited to his needs. I'm not fresh off the bus and feeling embarrassed about every part of me. This time I'm thinking: I'm fine. If you don't like me, the problem is yours.

I've had a takeaway sandwich, a packet of crisps and a chocolate bar in the car – the most I've had to eat since I met Elody all those weeks ago. I ate the whole thing and you know what? I don't feel guilty at all. I really don't. This is me; I am who I am. Take me or leave me.

This time I'm convinced that Rufus needs me, wants me here and will do anything to make sure I don't leave. It gives me a confidence that I've never had before. It's also lovely to see the staff and how happy they seem. While Rufus is always friendly with them, it feels like I've reached a whole new level of rapport; we're high-fiving and smiling and I'm asking after Pamela's mum, David's sister and whether Julie ever managed to get it together with Mike, the guy from the record shop. 'Yes,' she says, excitement squeezing out of her despite her efforts to keep it in and look as smooth and unruffled as possible in front of Rufus.

'Brilliant,' I say, genuinely delighted, and we give each other a little hug. You see, I'm like these people. Before I met Rufus, so less than a year ago, I would have been out socially with the likes of Julie. I'd probably have fancied Mike from the record shop; he sounds nice. Just because I happened to meet Rufus doesn't change the fundamental constituents of my being. These are my people and the fact that they work for me and not me for them is a matter of luck, timing and circumstance, and I hope I always remember that. I think it's what most of Rufus's friends have forgotten. They're more successful than most people because they happened to have been born in a particular place to particular parents with particular views. Their schooling and upbringing gave them the push up the ladder that most people don't get, but it doesn't make them better than anyone else.

Rufus is looking at me in amazement as I hug Pamela and tell her how pretty her hair is.

'He's been miserable without you, love,' she says, and I hug her again.

'Why do the staff adore you so much?' asks Rufus as he leads me upstairs with rather more haste than is appropriate given that the staff are all watching us so closely.

'Because I talk to them,' I reply, as he swings open the bedroom door and pushes me inside. 'I talk to them as individuals and not as staff.'

He's awake when I open my eyes. It's around 3 pm.

'You've been fast asleep,' he says.

'Haven't you been sleeping?' I ask.

'Nope. I don't sleep much any more.' He leans up on his elbow and begins stroking my hair as he speaks. 'To be honest, I'm afraid to sleep because once, while I was asleep, the most wonderful girl I've ever met disappeared. I don't want to take that risk again.'

'Ha, ha,' I say. 'I'm not going anywhere this time.'

'So you'll stay here for Christmas Day?'

'Oh shit! Christmas! No, I can't. I promised Mum that I'd go back home. She'll be devastated if I don't go.'

I pick up my phone to call and explain that I'm going to be later than expected.

'Grrrrrr . . .' he says, kissing me on the forehead. 'Promise me you'll come straight back then. And promise me you'll let Henry drive you. I don't want you getting onto trains in the dark.'

'Thanks,' I say, because having Henry drive me there would be just amazing.

'So, before then there are a couple of things we have to do, aren't there?'

'Are there?'

'Yes. We need to book the Plaza in New York – the most famous wedding venue in the world. Nothing, my love, *nothing* is going to go wrong now. We'll have the best dress, the best guest list and the best venue. We'll have the time of our lives. Now, I thought, to save you having to organise the whole thing yourself, what we'd do is get Jamelia Walker to help organise it. She runs a company called Celebrity Bride. They're the best wedding planners in the universe and . . . while you were fast asleep . . . I called them. She can come round at 4.30 pm on the twenty-seventh. What do you think?'

Silence.

'Well, what do you think?' he asks again, all excited now.

I just snuggle up next to Rufus and breathe in his scent, soaking in the familiarity of it, and delighting in the return of it. I want to absorb the man as much as I possibly can, just in case what I'm about to say sends him running for the hills.

'Did I do good?'

'No,' I say and I see him flinch and look at me with concern and confusion.

'You haven't changed your mind. Please tell me you haven't changed your mind.'

'I haven't,' I say with honesty. 'I want to marry you more than anything. But I want this to be a marriage about us, not about the brilliance of Jamelia Walker or Celebrity Bride. How did we get back together? Was it Jamelia who set that up? Was it any of these fantastically proper and sophisticated friends that you dinner party with every night? Was it? Was it Lord and Lady Simpkins – the guys who were talking to the press about how evil I am throughout my time with the police? Do you want them to come?'

'No of course not,' he says, looking quizzical. 'I went round to see Simpkins after what he did and told him I wanted nothing to do with any theatres he was involved with. I made it very clear that if he said a word in public about you again, I'd be round there to discuss it with him personally, and it wouldn't be pleasant. Of course I don't want someone like that hovering around anywhere near our wedding day.'

'Good, because I want this wedding to be about you and me and our parents. I want it to be about Frank and Lawrence, about Mandy and Sophie. I want Katy and

Jenny to come and to show everyone how good they are at Malteser-throwing now, because they are good, Rufus. They've left us way behind. I want my friends there and I want your friends Deevers and Courty to be there, and I want them to be having fun, not worrying about how they're going to look in *Hello!* magazine. I want them to be able to get drunk and party all night. I want this wedding to reflect who we are, not who people think you are and who I once wanted to be. Am I making sense?'

'Yes,' he says. 'But I'm not sure what sort of wedding you're after. I mean – we could have all those things you've just described at the Plaza.'

'I know,' I say. 'But I've never been to the Plaza. Why would I want to spend the most important day of my life there?'

'Because it's lovely.'

'No. People who've never been to the Plaza before do not suddenly decide to go there on their wedding day because "it's lovely". They do so because they think it makes them look good. I'm past caring how I look, Rufus. I want to marry you but I'd like us to get married my way. Will you do that?'

'I'll do anything you want,' he says. 'As long as I get to marry you at the end of it all, nothing else matters.'

'Good. Because the thing is – we're different. That doesn't need to matter at all, but you need to realise it. I have normal parents who worked hard to put a roof over my head and food in my mouth; they struggled a lot and this is my chance to say thank you and to give them a day out that's as special to them as it is to me. I have a mad Great-Aunt Maude who's just thrilled to wake up alive every morning because she's convinced the war's still going on. When you leave the room to make tea she cries because she thinks you're never coming back. This is where I come from, Rufus. We don't have private jets and pairs of shoes for every social occasion. We eat tea not dinner, and we have one knife and one fork. If there's a starter, and to be honest I don't think there ever has been, but if there were a starter then we'd have to lick the same knife and fork clean and use them for the main course.

'We have a tiny garden and no security guards. It's been hell for Mum and Dad since I came to live with you because the photographers can get right up to the house. And before you say it – yes, they could have asked you to sort out their security for them and help them keep the papers at arm's length but they're proud people, Rufus. You don't have to have drivers, cars and multi-million pound film contracts to be proud of who you are and what you've achieved in life. They're proud people and I love them, so – no – I won't be getting married on the other side of the world in a room full of people I don't know but who look good in the pictures. The wedding planners can come if they want but I won't be here to meet them. I won't be a Celebrity Bride so Jamelia can go and boil her head, as beautiful as it no doubt is. This is our wedding, it's my wedding, and it'll be me and Mum who decide what happens. For starters, everything at the wedding must match her chocolate-brown hat or the wedding doesn't happen. Do you hear me?'

'I hear you, sweets,' he says. 'Not sure whether I understand you in any way though. Did you say your mum wants to wear a hat made out of chocolate?'

'And what if she does? What if she wants all the bridesmaids' dresses made out of chocolate?'

'Then we'll have all the bridesmaids' dresses made out of chocolate. If you're happy, I'm happy. That's all I've ever wanted: for you to be happy.'

'Good. Then what are you doing for Christmas?'

'No plans,' he says. 'I tend to think I'm a bit past celebrating Christmas. I've got no desire to sit in a paper hat, reading bad jokes and eating turkey.'

'Well, that's bad news, because that's exactly what you're going to be doing. Pack your bag, sunshine. You're coming to Hastings for Christmas.'

'Right,' he says. 'But can I just ask: what's this got to do with us getting married?'

'Our wedding planner lives there,' I say. 'Her name's Jayne Monsoon, but she likes to be known as "Mum". Now come on, stop dawdling. Let's hit the road.'

To say Mum looks surprised to see us would be to totally underrepresent the look of utter shock and amazement on her face.

'My word,' she says, with that starry, mad-eyed expression that has unveiled itself to me so many times over the years – usually when she's had too much sherry or ginger wine, but sometimes when I flunked an exam or got into trouble. The look says, 'Well, there's something I wasn't expecting, now give me a few minutes and I'll work out exactly how to deal with it.'

Her first mission on seeing us is to insist that Henry comes in. 'I won't have you driving back in the dark with no food inside you,' she announces, as Dad comes out into the hallway to greet us and nearly trips over the end of his own slippers when he sees Rufus standing there, looking bashful, clutching a box of champagne.

'Nice to see you son,' he says, patting Rufus on the back in such a friendly way that I can see Rufus relaxing instantly as he slips out of his coat and hands over the box of booze. The champagne inside it is worth more per bottle than my parents have spent on alcohol for the entire Christmas period. They wouldn't know good champagne from bad, but I'm glad Rufus has taken the trouble to bring the best for them.

'Do you mind if I come in?' Henry asks Rufus.

'Of course not,' he says. 'No, please do. You'll make Kelly's night if you come in and have something to eat.'

We're all sitting at the dining room table with mum's famous Christmas Eve pork joint sitting in the centre, taking pride of place.

'Help yourself to any more, Rufus. Shall I cut you another slice? More potatoes?'

Rufus pats his stomach appreciatively but declines the offer of a fourth serving.

'Yes, leave a little room for pudding. Good idea,' says Mum.

Rufus looks quite terrified by this thought. I don't think he's ever seen anything quite like this feast being laid before him.

'I saw the news about Elody,' says Mum. 'Is it OK to mention?'

'Of course,' we both say. It's perfectly fine to mention it; in fact it would be weird if it weren't mentioned. I think I'd be more worried if everyone skated around the subject and was scared to address it. The truth is that she killed herself. We should be able to talk about it.

'Did it surprise you, love?' asks Mum. 'I mean, was she the depressed sort?'

'I don't think I really knew her at all,' I say. 'She was obviously more troubled than any of us realised. I tried to find out about her and I'd ask her questions all the time – about her family and friends and home life, but she never seemed to want to talk about them.

'I used to think that maybe she was like Jimmy – you know the guy who runs the nightclub cum strip club near my flat? He always acted really hard and cool and as if he'd had a tough background on the streets but his parents showed up and were as nice as anything, proper, decent middle-class folk; nothing could have embarrassed him more. I always thought that Elody's parents were probably middle-class business people from Harrow, or something. I imagined the mum in a cardigan typing away wearing horn-rimmed spectacles and the dad taking his homemade sandwiches in a plastic Tupperware box. Nothing would have embarrassed her more than that. I guess I stopped prying because she didn't want to talk about it and I figured that was her prerogative. Sorry – I'm waffling.'

It's a bright, clear and dry day when we wake up; in different rooms, of course, because this is Mum and Dad's family home and even if they allowed us to sleep in the same bed, I'd refuse on the grounds that it would be too embarrassing for words. Imagine coming down and sitting opposite Mum and Dad at the small dining table in the little kitchen, with them knowing what Rufus and I had been up to overnight . . . No, no, no, it's all wrong. I can't imagine sleeping with him under Mum and Dad's roof when we're married, let alone now.

I can hear voices downstairs so I wander down and find Mum and Rufus standing by the patio window looking out into the garden. 'No, they're not hyacinths; those are the gladis,' she's saying, and he's pretending that he gives a toss. 'It's hard to tell them apart in winter, isn't it?'

'Morning,' I say brightly, and they spin round.

'Oh, Merry Christmas, love,' says Mum, giving me a hug. 'Let me get you a cup of tea.'

'I've just been talking to Jayne about the wedding,' says Rufus. 'I told her that you've put her in charge of it.'

'That's very thoughtful of you, dear,' says Mum, walking over with my tea in a lovely big mug. 'But I don't think I'm really the best person to ask. I mean – I know I was very keen to organise everything for you last time, but I don't think I realised just how famous you both are when I was talking about the community centre. I mean, I don't know any famous people or posh dress designers or anything like that.'

'That's why I want you to do this, Mum.'

'Well, I'd love to help,' she says warily. 'But I'd better not do it on my own. I'll need you to help me.'

'Of course I'll help you,' I say. 'We can organise the whole thing together. Mandy and Sophie will help too.'

'OK. When are you thinking of getting married?'

'Twenty-ninth of April,' Rufus and I both chorus.

'It's the day we met. Our one year anniversary,' I explain.

'Oh dear.' Mum looks quite distraught.

'What is it?'

'Well, that's a very difficult time of year for brown,' she says. 'I've bought brown now. There's no going back.'

'Let me buy you a brand-new outfit that's perfect for April,' Rufus offers, gallantly. 'As a Christmas present.'

'OK, well maybe just a summery scarf to brighten it up,' she says. 'I don't want you spending all your money on me when you've got so much to plan and pay for. We'd like to help with the wedding though, wouldn't we, Tony?'

Mum looks over at my dad who's sitting in his favourite

armchair, pushed out of the way, into the corner of the room, to make way for the Christmas tree.

'Of course,' he says. 'It's only right.'

Rufus doesn't know quite what to say. The idea of my parents digging into their measly pensions to pay for a wedding that Rufus could afford to cover entirely out of his small change clearly appals him, but he also recognises that Mum and Dad are proud and to deny them the chance to pay for their daughter's wedding would be plain rude.

'Right,' says Mum. 'Well, where are we going to hold it then?'

'The Hastings Community Centre,' I say with confidence. 'I thought we could get married at that pretty little church in Battle village and all go over to the community centre afterwards.'

I'm expecting her to jump up and clap her hands together in joy . . . but no. She looks at me as if I'm stark, staring mad.

'Sweetheart, some of the most important people in the world will be flying in for this wedding,' she says. 'It would be much better if you got married somewhere near the airport to make it easier for them. Somewhere bigger and a bit nicer than the community centre, love. Anyway, to be honest, I don't think you'd get it now. It gets booked up months in advance, and I don't care who you are, you won't get the centre unless you're on the shortlist. Did I tell you about Marian? She's been running kids clubs down there all year so that she can get it booked for her daughter but it's no good – the place is booked out.'

Oh God.

'Rufus, I don't want to get married in New York,' I say, just in case my husband-to-be is mentally planning the sophisticated, star-struck wedding of his mother's dreams.

'No, not New York!' cries Mum. 'No, we need somewhere lovely. Let's get our thinking caps on. Tony, are you listening over there? We need everyone with thinking caps on. We need to plan a beautiful wedding for these two and we need to do it sharpish.'

Chapter 33

'Oh God, Kelly, you look amazing.' Sophie is standing in front of me with beautiful pale-pink tea roses weaved into a crown on her head. I've got them dotted through my hair, which is down, cascading over my bare shoulders as I stand here in this beautiful white sheath dress. We almost did it. We almost held the wedding on 29 April but then Frank was ill and we knew he really wanted to come, so we put it off. He's much better now and the benefit of waiting until the beginning of July is that it's infinitely warmer and the roses are all in bloom. Yep, you guessed: Rufus and I are holding our wedding ceremony in the Rose Garden at Hampton Court Palace. I couldn't be happier. He couldn't be happier. Mum and Dad couldn't be happier, and Frank? Frank looks like he just won the jackpot. He had to retire 'unofficially' as well as officially after his illness, so he's not here so much now. Neither is Lawrence, actually – we've employed him as head gardener at the house, and Frank comes once a week to check on him, and to drink sweet tea with me.

'Ready for the veil?' asks Mandy, and they place the soft, long flowing veil over my head.

'God, sweetheart you look lovely,' says Dad, taking my arm and leading me towards the path that will lead us into the garden and to my future husband. I have four bridesmaids: Sophie and Mandy are the main two, then there's Katy and Jenny in the second tier, threatening to start throwing Maltesers at me when I'm about to say 'I do'.

The band strikes up 'Here Comes the Bride' and I look towards the end of the garden where Rufus is waiting with Courty and Deeves – his two great mates who've flown over for the ceremony with their wives. They're lovely guys – such fun – and their wives will become great friends of mine, I know they will. I've made them honorary flower girls and they're standing by the exit, ready to sprinkle the ground with petals when everyone leaves. Henry, David and Lawrence are right next to them – all looking so incredibly smart. Next to them are Rufus's staff. Sorry, my staff! They're also my friends. There's Pamela all dressed up in pale blue, and the lovely Julie looking gorgeous in a pink dress that I helped her to pick out. She, Mandy, Sophie and I went shopping together and had a ball picking out clothes. She's invited Mike from the record shop to come as her guest. I see him standing next to her. She's right; he's very good-looking. Christine's next to them, in a shimmering coffee-coloured dress. She looks lovely. I've managed to strike up more of a friendship with her than I ever thought possible. It's amazing what being in love can do for you!

Frank's sitting down on the bench with no inscription, on a velvet throw, watching patiently with a smile etched across his face.

There are four ushers here: Morgan, Mather, Prentice and Jimmy. They stand with their sunglasses on looking more like bouncers than they've ever looked before.

'Don't worry about security. We hired security separately,' I say, but they can't. They've spent so long watching my back that on the most important day of my life they want to be sure that nothing bad happens. The only way to guarantee that is to stay watching.

We had to have a separate service this morning to make the wedding vows official. Ruf and I jumped into the car and zoomed off to Richmond Register Office, hoping to keep the whole thing low key and go for a great big breakfast afterwards, but it wasn't to be. The press caught up with us so we had to rush back home early. Now, we're here. The press have been held right back. Despite an unwanted bidding war breaking out between *OK* and *Hello!*, we have no magazine deal, no journalists in attendance and no desire for any publicity.

Sophie was a little bit annoyed at the decision. '*Heat* called?' she said, alarmed. 'Surely we can make an exception for them. It's *Heat*. I mean *Heat*. Surely it's OK for you to be in *Heat*?'

'Not today,' I said, and she let it drop. She looked confused but said she understood. I don't think she'll ever really understand why I wouldn't want to be in *Heat*, but that's OK. A year ago I wouldn't have understood either.

I'm right next to Rufus now and he takes my hand as the service begins. We keep it short because the last thing we want is for everyone to be bored out of their minds. There are poems about us and poems about love. Mandy reads about roses while Lawrence looks on adoringly.

'Roses are ancient symbols of love and beauty,' she says. 'The rose was sacred to a number of goddesses, including Isis and Aphrodite, and is often used as a symbol of the Virgin Mary.'

As she talks I just look around at all these wonderful people. Mostly though, I look at the wonderful person next to me – Rufus. I think of the sacrifices he's made. His mother was furious when he said that the ceremony wouldn't be in New York, and at one point she refused to come to the wedding, until he persuaded her that he loved her and needed her to be there on his special day. She seems relaxed as she sits there, talking to my mum. Perhaps I'll get to like her, over time.

Rufus says he's planning to dance with Great-Aunt Maude later, when we have a huge party in the grounds of the palace, with fireworks over the river, food, drink, wine and fun. Then, we have to somehow work out a life together. I have to work out what my role in that life will be. I didn't want to be a Celebrity Bride and I don't want to be a Celebrity Wife. I want to be more than that. I'm not sure quite what yet though. Will we have kids? I hope so. I'd love that. But there's a whole lifetime before that happens. Rufus has to go to LA for the filming of the Bond movie and I've promised I'll go with him. What on earth will they make of me there? I've put the weight back on and, you know, I don't care. If they don't like me as a size 12, it's their problem. I won't diet to please them and I certainly won't lie to please them. I won't pretend to be someone that I'm not.

I look over at the bench with no name and see Frank, wearing his best suit, and smiling for all he's worth. He stands up when we approach and pulls the velvet throw aside. A shiny gold plaque gleams in the sunshine. 'A bench for lovers like Kelly and Rufus, and for all who are entranced and delighted by the magic of roses,' it reads.

'Thank you,' I say, staring deep into his soft warm eyes. 'It's absolutely perfect.'

Ebury Press Fiction Footnotes

An exclusive interview with Alison Kervin:

What was the inspiration for *Celebrity Bride?*

I am quite fascinated by the issue of 'celebrity' and the change that becoming a celebrity imposes on a personality. But I thought . . . what if a sweet, normal girl found herself hoisted into the world of celebrity, and carried on being her usual, bright and normal self? I also wanted it to be an out and out romance and a tale about real people in a make believe world.

Dream-casting time: who would play Rufus and Kelly in the movie of *Celebrity Bride?*

Oooo . . . I love this game. My friends and I spend a lot of time working out who will play each role. The debates get quite heated and I end up listening to them arguing about why Julia Roberts is wrong and Catherine Zeta-Jones in her younger days would have been perfect (I think they're right there, but in the absence of a time machine, that's not going to work). I'm thinking of Hugh Jackman for Rufus, Obviously George Clooney's a contender but I wonder whether he might be a bit old for it by the time they make the film (Sorry George. I know you'll be devastated!) Maybe Brad Pitt? Might be nice to have Brad Pitt and Angelina Jolie acting together as Rufus and Kelly, but she'd have to put on a bit (a lot!) of weight first, and I'm not sure she's much of a pie and chips eater. For Kelly (assuming Angelina doesn't want to go down the pie route and assuming we go for Hugh Jackman as Rufus), I'm thinking Anna Friel? She's a good comic actress, isn't she? Again, she's very slim, but I bet she'd be more likely to fill up on jam donuts than Angelina.

Which celebrity wedding would you have liked to have gone to and why?

I suppose it would have been good to have gone to Charles and Diana's wedding because Diana ended up becoming such an incredibly influential woman, and their wedding and her entry into the royal family became such a hugely significant moment.

Who are your favourite authors?

This isn't the sort of question you can give a one-word answer to, so here's a selection. Graham Greene is a genius (read the first few pages of *End of The Affair* and look at the beauty of the language, the rhythms and simplicity of the images he creates). I'm slightly obsessed with GK Chesterton at the moment (more his journalism than his fiction). Margaret Attwood is blindingly good.

Confession time: which classic novel have you always meant to read and never got round to it?

Ulysses. I'm ashamed to admit it, and I recognise that it's a work of sheer genius but I can't 'do' it. I'm quite good at reading highly dense, plot-thick novels, and have a huge crush on Russian literature, but *Ulysses* - sorry but I've tried and failed and I'd rather sit and eat my hair than try again.

Which fictional character would you most like to have met?

I'd quite like to meet Rufus George, to be honest . . . I think he sounds lovely. I like writing female characters. In terms of women who would I like to meet? Maybe Cathy in *Wuthering Heights* because she's such an incredibly forceful and clever character.

Who, in your opinion, is the greatest writer of all time?

It's very hard not to pick Shakespeare here. He has such a dominating influence over literature that it's almost as if you have to mount a defence for not picking him! But it's easy to over-write and over-embellish and over-tell stories as a writer, and then you read: 'To be or not to be . . .' and realise that the most famous statement in the whole of literature is just six words that are so basic they'd be known to the average three-year-old. It's extraordinarily clever, and difficult, to take a vastly complicated subject and reduce it to six simple little words like that.

Other than writing, what other jobs have you undertaken or considered?

I was a journalist for a long time, before writing books, and I did a brief stint at the Rugby Football Union as match-day PR officer for the England team (a lot of the time I was 'looking after' the wives and girlfriends of the players who were a great bunch of women and many of them have become great friends), but it's pretty much been writing all the way since I left college.

What are you working on at the moment?

The follow-up book to *Celebrity Bride*, in which we follow Kelly on her adventures with Rufus as his wife. I'm drafting out loads of ideas for that at the moment, and it should be a fun book.

What question have you never been asked in an interview, but think you should have been?

I've never been asked why I write . . . yet I think 'why?' is at the centre of most good literature. Understanding character's motivations and why they behave the way they do, and building into all the stories you write a sensible assessment of 'why' is crucial. So, odd that people never ask why . . .